MISDEEDS OF A BILLIONAIRE

Billionaire King Series

EVA WINNERS

Visit www.evawinners.com and subscribe to my newsletter.

FB group: https://bit.ly/3gHEeoe
FB page: https://bit.ly/30DzP8Q
Insta: http://Instagram.com/evawinners
BookBub: https://www.bookbub.com/authors/eva-winners
Amazon: http://amazon.com/author/evawinners
Goodreads: http://goodreads.com/evawinners
TikTok: https://vm.tiktok.com/ZMeETK7pq/

EVA WINNERS
· EVERLASTING ROMANCE FOR EVERY CENTURY ·

AUTHOR'S NOTE

This book touches on some sensitive subjects and some readers might find it disturbing.

There is trigger content related to - family loss, suicide, violence.

Resemblance to actual persons and things living or dead, locations, or events is entirely coincidental.

This one is for all those that love their alpha billionaire with a touch of gray.

Billionaire King Series Collection

The series covers each Ashford brother separately. While each book in the series can be read as a standalone, events and references to the other books are present in each one of these. So for best enjoyment consider giving each Ashford brother a chance. 😊

Enjoy!

PLAYLIST

https://open.spotify.com/playlist/6agXiSGPBsrQQFJMgcjlvx?si=
fuYaIsi9S6Kmh7OO7Lvt1A

Blurb

My one-night stand.

A ruthless bastard.

A heartless billionaire.

The man who ruled his empire with a cold head and an even colder heart. And most importantly, my son's father. Except, he wasn't aware of that little fact. To the media, Byron Ashford is a Billionaire King. To me, he's a reminder of the hottest, most forbidden, night of my life. And my biggest mistake.

I hadn't seen him in years and hoped we'd never cross paths again.

But then, my best-laid plans always seem to go awry. Now, I need his help to bail me out of trouble. He's a billionaire and I'm just a broke, debt-riddled surgeon.

Against my better judgment, I sought him out. It should have been easy, in and out. Except, nothing with Byron Ashford is ever easy. He refuses to hand out free favors. And the price for his help?

My freedom. Literally.

He wants to shackle me to him with a marriage I don't want, then throw away the key.

His demands are scandalous. His rules are dangerous for my heart.

It was supposed to be a mutually beneficial deal, but nothing about Byron is ever that simple. Once he slips the ring onto my finger, the rules change.

His demands grow. He no longer just wants to own my body. He also wants my heart and soul. But I'm not that young, naive woman anymore.

Too bad this billionaire forgot one thing. Nobody can own your heart unless you give it freely.

And this time, I'm not blinded by his smile and especially not by his lies.

Love is a puzzle.
When you're in love, all the pieces fit.
But when your heart gets broken,
It takes a long time to piece it back together.
And sometimes the pieces never quite fit right.

Prologue
Byron

My father and Nicki greeted me the moment I stepped out of my office.

There'd been a pressure in my chest for months. Ever since I walked away from her. Or maybe it was she who walked away from me.

"Byron, your father and I—" I stopped listening. Nicki's voice grated on my nerves. I didn't have it in me to deal with her nor my father right now. I was just about to return to my office when the scent caught my attention.

Fresh apples.

It was like a jab straight to the groin. Even worse, my heart.

Ignoring my father and Nicki, I rushed past them to where my executive assistant sat. I paused by her desk, my fingers clutching the edge of the dark mahogany.

"Mrs. George, has someone been here to see me?" My heart thundered wildly, each beat echoing her name.

No. No. No.

It couldn't be *her*. She made it clear she wanted nothing to do with me.

"Yes, Mr. Ashford, a young lady came up." She glanced behind me to where my father stood and trepidation entered her expression. But that wasn't unusual. Most people felt uncomfortable around him, apprehension and fear surrounding them. "She wanted to see you but she didn't have an appointment. She left the same time your father arrived." Nobody ever came to see me. "She just took the elevator down."

I had no idea how long it took me to get downstairs. I followed the scent of apples like a damn bloodhound. I had just stepped out of my building when the humidity of the July air and the commotion of the city slammed into me—honking, smog, chatter, laughter... and screams.

An accident must have just happened, two cars smashed against each other. A fire hydrant soaking the street. Something pulled me toward it, like a magnet. A dark foreboding filled every cell of my body. Morbid and so fucking wrong.

My lungs burned as I turned the corner. I couldn't breathe. Each step felt like an eternity. Until I saw it—the worst possible scenario I could have ever imagined.

A long red mane of hair sprawled across the dirty pavement, golden and strawberry highlights glowing too bright amidst the blood and debris.

Blood. Too much. I hoped not enough to make this more awful than it already was.

I ran, cursing and pushing everyone out of the way until I fell to the ground beside her. A drunk bastard sobbed, babbling a slurred apology, while roaming his hands over her, jerking her limp body. Fear, unlike any I'd experienced before, shot through me and I pushed him away.

"Get the fuck away from her," I growled, clenching my fists and fighting the urge to beat him to a bloody pulp.

I cradled her head and tried to will those hazel eyes to open for me. Pushing her hair out of the way, I placed two fingers against her pulse. Seconds felt like days, centuries, as I tried to find proof that she was still alive.

My heart twisted, jerking out of my chest and throbbing painfully. I ignored it, praying for a pulse. *Just give me a pulse.*

A faint thump under my fingers brought a wave of relief. It slammed into me like a tsunami, washing me away.

Shouting like a lunatic, I demanded doctors, nurses, and ambulances. "Get someone here now!"

My hands shook so badly, it took me several tries to brush the wet strands off her face.

"Don't you dare die." My voice was hoarse, pent-up emotions of the last few months swirling inside me. "Please, do this last thing for me. Don't go, baby."

Something glinted in her hand, bunched in her bloodied palm.

A sonogram picture.

It almost broke me. Three decades of this fucked-up life, and nothing had ever broken me. But this cracked my heart and shattered it into a thousand pieces.

"Ambulance!" I roared, feeling like my heart was failing. "Someone call an ambulance!"

Chapter 1
Odette

Three Months Ago

Holy guacamole.

Exam room number five held the most gorgeous male specimen I had ever seen.

My heart skipped a beat as I stared at the man sitting on the gurney. My eyes roamed over him, and I convinced myself it was strictly a clinical appraisal. Besides, attractive men had come and gone over the years, and I'd cared for them without any hiccups. Yet, it didn't explain the very *nonclinical* butterflies that were taking flight in my stomach.

Dark hair. Sharp jaw. Deep aquamarine eyes that reminded me of catching rays on the beach and feeling the salt in the air and across my skin. It sucked the oxygen out of my lungs and drained the tank of my brain's generator without so much as a blink.

"Are you coming in or are you planning to stand at the door to examine me?" he snapped, annoyance clear in his voice.

And like dust in the wind, the attraction was gone.

I shook my head, clearing it from my initial fascination. No amount of good looks could ever excuse an asshole.

With the patient chart firmly in my hand, I walked into the room with the confidence my father had instilled in me—chin tipped up, spine straight, and with a professional focus that rivaled my father's. He owned this private little hospital on the French Riviera, and with the usual barrage of patients that came through these doors, his focus was unrivaled.

"Mr.—" I glanced at the chart in my hand and read the name. "Mr. Ashford. What brings you in today?"

There was only one downfall to the location of Father's hospital. It brought in all kinds of snobs and pricks. The trust-fund kids of the rich and famous were the worst. Although there was nothing young about this guy. He wasn't exactly old, but at the not so tender age of—I read his date of birth—thirty-four, there was nothing young about him.

"Obviously, I need to see a doctor." *Well, duh, asshole.* I pressed my lips together to ensure those words didn't come out. Yes, I was cranky. Father had me tending to his patients late into the night, and then today, he'd given me the morning shift.

"I'm just going to take your blood pressure and check your heart rate." Fuck it, he could whine to my father about whatever his problem was. I'd gather his vitals and Dad could take it from there.

Those dark aquamarine eyes found mine and he cocked his eyebrow. "Aren't you a little young to be playing doctor?"

Annoyance flared within me. If there was even a flicker of attraction left, he'd just dumped gallons of ice water over it and extinguished it forever with his arrogant tone.

"Aren't you a little old to be so cranky?" I spat back, knowing full well my father would send me packing if he heard me speak to a patient like this.

But I couldn't help it. Yes, I was twenty-two and much younger than this old—and way too gorgeous—prick, but there was no need to discount my qualifications. And I never said I was a doctor. Nurses usually took patient vitals, if he wanted to get specific. I was still in my first year of medical school and only helping Dad over my spring break.

"Touché"—his eyes roamed over my nurse's coat, searching for a name badge he wouldn't find—"Nurse Betty."

I shook my head. It was better not to get into it with this guy, I knew the type. "I'm not a nurse. I'm a med student. Please take off your shirt."

He didn't move and I raised my eyebrow. I almost expected a smart-ass comeback. When he didn't say another word, disappointment washed over me. I didn't have to like the guy to enjoy good banter, but obviously he couldn't keep up.

Or maybe he's in pain. Well, there was that.

I stood, watching his long fingers unbutton his expensive shirt, one by one, before reaching for the diamond cuff link on his right wrist. The bronze skin of his chest indicated he spent a lot of time out in the sun. And what a chest it was.

The butterflies in my stomach took flight again—despite my objections—and the small peek at his abs had my heart skipping a beat. I averted my eyes before he could call me out on my lack of professionalism—*again*. This man was all strength and power, oozing sex appeal.

Like a magnet, my eyes returned to him. I was simply unable to keep my gaze from him.

Maybe I needed a checkup too? Either that, or I needed to get laid. Stat!

"Are you going to watch me strip?" His voice startled me out of my gawking and my cheeks heated. I was burning up. This goddamn prick. I didn't know whose trust-fund baby he was but there was no doubt that he was somebody's. Nobody who worked their ass off from the ground up was this arrogant and blunt—or tanned.

I turned around and busied myself with reading through the

notes in the chart. Last name Ashford. First name Byron. *Byron Ashford.* I shook my head again. Definitely a rich prick's name.

He was here because of a *sunburn.* I frowned. Was this guy for real? *Scratching strength from his attributes.*

The sound of soft material moving against flesh seemed to echo through the small room. I kept double-checking what the nurse recorded until the sound of rustling ceased behind me. I put his chart down and pulled my stethoscope from my pocket. Then I reached for the blood pressure monitor, ripping open the cuff as I turned around.

My steps faltered.

Holy... mother... of... God. I'd never been a huge fan of large, muscular men, but for this guy, I'd make an exception. *Holy shit.* I couldn't help but ogle him. Grudgingly, I had to admit he had a fantastic body—at least the upper part—which left me curious about the rest of his body.

Dear Lord, let me sin with this man naked.

The warmth intensified and I was fairly certain my mouth was somewhere on the floor. There might have even been some drool there too. This man—jackass or not—had an objectively magnificent chest. Skin golden brown, his muscles were defined even in his relaxed pose. And those abs! The sudden and quite uncharacteristic urge to pour alcohol, water, juice—any-fucking-thing—all over him and then lick him clean was overwhelming.

I didn't even want to get started on those thick biceps. They'd be the envy of any athlete. He was clear of tattoos with the exception of ink on his right bicep.

I frowned. It looked like periodic elements; I recognized the methyl group bonding between the carbon and its atoms. Bizarre as it was, it didn't keep me from studying every single inch of him.

Fever licked at my skin, a current of liquid heat rushed down my body and pooled between my thighs. I squeezed them tight, trying to ignore the throbbing.

I couldn't believe this was happening. Getting horny at the mere sight of a man. *A patient, at that!*

"Are you going to examine me?" The heavy bass of his voice felt like a lover's caress.

I had to get my shit together. Check his blood pressure and then get the hell away from him before I did something stupid. Like tackle him. Right here, on this examination table. I'd straddle him and—

He cleared his throat, pulling me from my dirty thoughts.

I need to get laid, I thought again.

"Okay," I said, shaking my head and trying to sound professional. "Let's do this. Examine you, I mean. Obviously."

The shadow of a smirk appeared at the corner of his mouth. "Obviously."

Shit, why did I say that? This couldn't be what an education at Stanford got me. Drooling and gawking at patients? Though in my defense, one didn't just happen across such a hot specimen on a regular basis.

I slipped the cuff around his bicep and took his blood pressure. *Piff. Piff. Piff.* The little sounds of the balloon inflating filled the space between us. I released the valve and the cuff let out a long, slow hiss of relief. Next, I plugged my stethoscope into my ears and placed the diaphragm against his chest, ignoring his slight flinch under my fingertips.

"One seventy-eight over ninety-five. It's high." I ripped the cuff's lip free with a quick jerk. "Your chart says you're here for sunburn. Where is it exactly?"

He flicked me a look. Exasperated. Annoyed. "On my back."

God, why was he so damn cranky? So damn insufferable.

I shifted around the table, all businesslike, when my eyes locked on his back. My hand paused mid-air at the sight of his burned, scarred skin. His strong, beautiful back was covered in angry, red and near-white scars, the surface epidermis—skin—disfigured. My guess it was an old chemical burn with the sunburn on top of it.

"How long since the initial injury that caused the scarring?" I asked, getting straight to work. Blistering and swelling over his entire back had to be painful, even without the underlying tissue damage. No fucking wonder he needed to see a doctor.

His shoulders tensed. "Years."

His answer was clipped. Flat. Yet I couldn't help but think that it bothered him. He was so beautiful and strong in every single way, and although he didn't strike me as vain, something told me he didn't like to reveal his back to strangers.

I swallowed the lump in my throat and reached for his chart, coming to stand in front of his sitting form and doing my best to avert my eyes. "The doctor will have to check you to approve, but I'll recommend an injection of corticosteroids to ease the symptoms of itchiness and pain. We can do one application of silicone gel here today, and you can continue its application over the next seven days."

"Aren't you a doctor?" I couldn't quite decide whether he was mocking me or not, but I decided to give him a break, considering his obviously uncomfortable state.

"Not yet, I'm only in my first year of medical school."

He looked at me and grinned. "A newbie, huh?"

I smiled. "I wouldn't exactly say a newbie." Desperate to force some distance between us, I walked back around to assess the degree of his burn, jotting down notes in his chart. "Didn't your doctor warn you against the dangers of sunbathing? The scar tissue will be sensitive to any kind of sun exposure."

He shrugged. "I fell asleep on the deck."

I shook my head. "Let's check your temperature."

"It's high," he stated flatly. My brows furrowed as I met his aquamarine gaze. "Higher than usual," he added. The intensity in his eyes was wrong—on so many levels—but my body didn't care. It demanded *him*. Jesus, I'd lose my medical license before I even got it.

"Does your temperature usually run higher than normal?" I asked curiously.

"No, not unless I'm angry or—" He paused and I raised my eyebrow, waiting. "Or having sex."

My mouth parted in shock as I imagined this specimen having sex. Good Lord. My imagination took hold and hot images played in my mind. The way his muscles would bulge as he thrust—

I shook my head, scolding my promiscuous thoughts, and brought the thermometer to his mouth.

"Open." I leaned in, willing my hands to steady, and placed the thermometer under his tongue. "Close."

He clamped his teeth together. *Beep. Beep.* There was a beep, an interval, and one last beep.

"One oh three," I stated. "It's high. Let me get you a glass of water and some Motrin. The doctor should be with you soon."

I headed to the little storage drawer where Father kept water bottles. Then I turned to the cabinet and pulled out a mini-package of Motrin. I made my way to him, his legs in all their manspreading glory. I stopped a foot away from him, fighting the urge to step between them.

"What's your name?" he asked as I extended my palm out, handing him the two little pills.

"Nurse Betty," I answered with a touch of snark.

He frowned and shook his head as if he didn't care. He took the pills, put them on his tongue, and reached for the bottled water I'd forgotten to offer him.

Our fingers brushed. A fleeting touch, but it burned like the fires of hell. I yanked my hand back, meeting his puzzled look. Didn't he feel this? It literally charged the air with so much electricity I was certain the entire room buzzed with it.

He unscrewed the top to the bottle and then downed the water while I watched his Adam's apple move with each swallow, mesmerized. Even the seemingly innocent movement was sexy as hell on this man.

My eyes found his, and again like a fool, I let myself drown in them. The air around me buzzed, sending a tingling sensation over my arms and across my chest. I shook my head, attempting to clear the fog.

The door swung open, and both of us glanced over to find the doctor. My gaze flicked to the patient to find his eyes already on me. A shadow of what looked like disappointment crossed his face before it disappeared as quickly as it came. We tore our eyes away from each other and regret washed over me. The tension was just starting to build between us and there was something intoxicating about it.

Unlike this enigma of a man, I wasn't as good at hiding my emotions, but I forced myself to switch into professional mode.

After all, the doctor was my father.

Chapter 2
Byron

The girl was barely legal.

But there was something about her that was appealing. I just couldn't put my finger on it. Her hair was red—strawberry blonde with more red than blonde. Her eyes were a mixture of green, brown, and gold—the most unique shade of hazel I'd ever seen. They were fascinating. The kind you could get lost in.

She seemed the type of woman who would be sweet and innocent, but wouldn't take anyone's shit. My weakness. I liked them with a backbone. Add in a mouth and brain on them, and I was sold. A doormat made my dick limp within a millisecond of attempting conversation.

Each time she met my gaze in wonderment, her mouth would part and her cheeks flushed. The bad part was... I felt it too. And it was the last thing I needed right now.

Especially with the screaming theatrics I just got from my last mistake. It was the reason I was snappy when I first came in. That fucking woman slipped a sleeping pill into my scotch and caused me to pass out on the deck. I should have known that telling her the two of us would never marry despite what our fathers wanted wouldn't go over well. Nicki was a spoiled brat that wanted what-ever she couldn't have. I still remembered the fit she threw when her father gifted her the wrong color car for her sixteenth birthday.

Needless to say, Nicki didn't take my honesty well. Although I'd never understand what she thought she'd accomplish by drug-ging me. It didn't matter. She was history.

I didn't need more drama in my life.

Women were a headache I really didn't need. Even when the rules were clearly stated upfront. They always seemed to forget them. After a week or two, they'd begin to think I'd get down on one knee and propose.

Would it be the same with this one? Somehow, I didn't think so.

Our gazes locked, those golden specks shimmering yellow. She closed her eyes and shook her head. This forceful attraction between us, drawing us to each other, was so strong I could almost taste it. Except, it made no fucking sense. She was way too young—at least a decade younger than me.

Once the doctor strode in, her entire focus was on him. My gut told me it wasn't for pretense either. She was serious about her job.

"Odette." *Odette.* It suited her.

The doctor gave "Nurse Betty" a nod and extended his hand for me to shake. The man's silver hair was evidence of his many years in the field.

"Hello, Mr. Ashford." His voice was heavily accented. A Frenchman. "I'm Doctor Swan. How are you?"

It only registered at that moment that Odette had no accent. She was an American.

"Could be better," I answered, my eyes flickering back to her.

"We'll get you fixed up and on your way in no time," he assured. He turned his attention away from me. "Odette, do you have the vitals?"

"Of course."

"And the patient's chart?"

"All here," she answered, smiling. She handed the doctor my

chart, and as he read the notes, he asked, "Your recommendation?" His eyes breezed over the pages. He must be her mentor, maybe she would be completing her residency here?

"Injection of corticosteroids and a weeklong application of silicone gel."

He raised his head and met her eyes, his smile warm and affectionate. A love affair maybe?

"Excellent, and the right choice. Good job, Odette."

The woman nodded and met his gaze, but she didn't gush. No blush. She must have been accustomed to praise. Then the doctor turned to me and I realized my assumption of a love affair was all wrong. This had to be her father or a family member. They had the exact same eyes.

"I agree with the treatment," he said. "Odette helps me. She's in school and I take advantage of her skills when she's home." I nodded, feigning disinterest. "If you're going to be in town in seven days, we can do an extra injection before you depart, but no lying out in the sun. If you must, a UV-protection long-sleeve shirt should do the trick."

"That won't be a problem," I assured him. However, I might have to think of an excuse to see this young woman one more time.

"Good." The doctor slid his glasses up his nose, then turned to Odette, switching to French. "Go ahead home. I will finish here. Will I see you later?"

"Yes. I'm meeting some friends at Le Bar Américain for drinks. But I'll have dinner with you beforehand," she answered in fluent French. *Fuck.* I immediately found myself wondering if she moaned and whimpered words in French when she was getting fucked.

Wrong time to get a hard-on. Especially in the state of pain I was in with this fucking burn.

"Bien. Go get some rest, then," he said, switching back to English

With a last look my way, she nodded, kissing his cheek on her way out. "See you later."

And it wasn't until she was leaving the room that her eyes found me one more time.

Dr. Swan prepared the injection while my thoughts drifted to that fucking day my back burned the first time, leaving me with my scars. My second deployment with my SEAL team could have killed me. If my commander hadn't come back when he did, I probably would have been burned alive. But he did, and we'd been best friends ever since.

As I sat on the hospital bed, I let the doctor inject me with that fucking needle. I didn't feel the stick, but I felt the cool sensation that followed right after. Leaving me with a promise that someone would be right back to attend to me and apply lotion on my back, he wished me well and left the room.

The door opened shortly after. I didn't look up, expecting a nurse.

"I'm just going to apply this to your back and you can be on your way." The same voice. Husky. Warm. So fucking warm. I liked it. Scratch that. I loved her voice.

"Thanks."

"Don't mention it."

Silence followed. I heard her soft footsteps against the tile floor of the room as she worked efficiently, preparing whatever it was she was about to do.

"Odette, huh?"

She didn't answer as I watched her pull a container down from a shelf in my periphery, the lid clanking against the countertop filling the silence soon after. The sexy med student gloved up her hands as the fresh scent of crisp apples seeped into my lungs. Somehow, I knew she would smell fucking delectable.

Next, her fingers came softly to my back, sending a shudder through me that had nothing to do with the cool gel. I hated anyone touching my back and couldn't remember the last time anyone had even come close to it.

"Weren't you leaving for the day?" I attempted again. For some stupid reason, I wanted to hear her husky, soothing voice. *If my brothers could see me now.* Usually, I complained about people that constantly yapped, yet here I was chitchatting like some neglected grandma.

"Mhmm. I'm just going to finish you off," she stated calmly, her movements never ceasing. "Then I'm out of here."

I glanced over my shoulder, catching her expression when our gazes met. Her mouth parted. Her cheeks turned crimson, the meaning of her own words sinking in.

"Nothing would make me happier than you finishing me off."

Her cheeks flushed. The golden hue in her eyes glimmered, but she scoffed, choosing not to answer.

However, the look she gave me told me she had plenty to say.

I sat in my office on the main deck of my yacht, all the windows and doors opened. I came to the French Riviera to chase a lead on a potential acquisition with Winston.

The Ashford businesses expanded into many branches, but our weakness was in luxury brands, and jewelry designing had sounded promising. My brother entertained the idea of buying small jewelry stores in prime locations and turning them into Ashford Diamonds. After this weekend, though, I'd ensure we never ventured into it, no matter how intriguing the prospect of it was. Dealing with the designers was like speaking in an alien tongue. When inquiring about their portfolios and financials, the answers seemed to change. All the damn time. I had no patience for their bullshit.

Winston disagreed. Not vocally, but I knew my brother well enough to understand his body language. In fact, I wouldn't be surprised if I learned he ventured into the business after all.

The loud buzz of an alarm cut through the silence, immediately followed by a string of curses.

"Turn that fucking thing off." Winston's booming voice competed with the shrill alarm.

I shook my head. He really had to get his shit in order. He was barely two years younger than me, yet he whored himself around like every woman was the last piece of pussy he'd ever get.

"Byron, turn the alarm off!" he bellowed, loudly enough for the entire French Riviera to hear him. I ignored him. He'd eventually figure out it was his own alarm clock.

The afternoon sun slanted across the Riviera, the scent of the sea wafting through the air. The sound of the waves crashing against the boat should've been soothing, yet I couldn't find peace.

It was fucking ironic. I was one of the richest men in the world, yet I couldn't even enjoy the fruits of my labor, nor my billionaire status. Like the fact that I had a yacht but I couldn't lie out on the deck for fear of sun exposure on my scarred back.

I still remembered that nurse who treated my war wounds after my skin had pretty much melted. She had red hair—ironically kind of like the young med student I met today—and she cringed whenever she had to change my bandages. Nothing fucked with your self-esteem like that. No amount of money, wealth, or power could erase shitty feelings like those.

My mind drifted to the past. That near-fatal day.

Sweat trickled down my forehead as bullets flew all around. We were out in the open, exposed and vulnerable to the enemy. It was a fucking trap, and we were getting attacked from all sides.

Death surrounded me. Flames burned the compound. The stench of chemicals, gunpowder, and blood filled the air, invading my lungs.

River, Astor, and Darius, who weren't part of the Navy and usually flew Black Hawks, shouted a warning. I bet they regretted their decision to take patrol duty today.

I saw it too late. A loud explosion shook the earth while blinding pain burst through me. My knees gave out. My ears buzzed and I shook my head, trying to clear the loud ringing in my ears.

Sharp pain shot through me. The stench of burning flesh filled my nostrils and took me way too many heartbeats to realize it was my own flesh that burned.

Three men surrounded me. I stared death in the eyes, but I was going to go down fighting. Ignoring the blinding pain that tore through me, I reached for the gun that lay next to me. I aimed to kill. Bang. Bang.

Kristoff, my commander and good friend, killed one guy. I killed the second. We both shot the third.

Kristoff reached for me, and I knew by the look in his eyes that it was bad.

"Fuck," he grunted, lowering himself onto his knees.

"I don't think I'll get out of this one," I gritted. Even talking hurt like a motherfucker.

He shifted me around so the sand wouldn't rub against my back. I was honest-to-God scared to ask how bad my injuries were. My whole body ached, but the initial pain on my back numbed.

"You will." Determination was etched in his voice and expression. "We're going to get the fuck out of here. So you can take care of your sister and your brothers."

"Royce and Winston will take care of Aurora," I grunted, my consciousness slowly slipping away. His form blurred until I couldn't see him anymore.

Focus. Breathe. Live. Survive.

Breathe. Live. Survive.

Those words kept repeating in my mind. The last thing I remembered was Kristoff throwing me over his shoulder and barking something to the rest of the men.

When I woke up, the skin on my back was gone. Fourth-degree burns affected my muscles and flesh. Nerve endings were severely damaged—although not destroyed—leaving me with little feeling on my back. Unless, that is, I got a sunburn.

Needless to say, my back wasn't a pretty sight and women cringed at it. *All of them but one*, my mind whispered.

I felt the itch of the young med student on my back like the ghost of my sunburn. It had to be the reason for my lack of manners when she'd first strolled into the hospital room. I couldn't even remember a single fucking word in French. *Me.* A man who finished college two years ahead of his class, including several French classes. *Me.* A man who served as a United States Navy SEAL.

Those hazel eyes seemed to shoot straight into my soul.

The way she'd stayed strong despite my sour attitude taking up space on the exam table worked miracles for my libido, even under the excruciating pain on my back.

I glanced back at the file that had been waiting for me when I'd returned to my yacht. *Twelve years.* For Christ's sake, I was twelve years older than her, and for some idiotic reason, I couldn't stop thinking about her.

Odette Madeleine Swan.

Finishing up her first year at Stanford. Her father was a French doctor, her mother a fashion model who died twelve years ago. She had an older sister, and they'd both been raised in the States until her mother's untimely death. Their father brought them back to France and they completed high school in France. As complicated as my family was, hers was the exact opposite.

Simple. Clean. Loving.

Winston appeared at the all-glass door of my office, wearing nothing but swim shorts.

"Will you put some goddamn clothes on?" I grumbled.

He waved his hand. "What for? We're on the French Riviera. We might as well act French and lounge around all day naked."

"Except nobody is lounging around but you."

An idea popped in my head then. It was a bad idea, I knew it. I had honed and perfected every last idea and turned them into smart decisions over the years. This wasn't one of those.

"Shower and get ready, Winston. I'm taking you out for dinner." My brother shot me a suspicious look. "I hear Le Bar Américain is all the rage," I clarified.

At the mention of a bar, his eyes lit up, and for once he listened. I picked up the phone and dialed up my old friend River who'd served with me in Afghanistan. He had a security company in Portugal but happened to be on the French Riviera as well.

He answered on the first ring. "Don't worry. Your psycho ex is tucked away at The Ritz Carlton. I gave her enough money to make it around the world five times over."

Fucking Nicki. The worst thing I could have ever done was have a casual relationship with her. And then a shit-faced Winston —on Father's nudging—had her fly out and meet us in Italy where we were docked for a few days. He'd said it was for me. Bullshit. I knew it was so I'd be too busy to ride his ass.

"Thanks for handling that, River," I said dryly.

When I woke up with my back burned like a fucking roasted potato, I was in so much pain I'd been fully prepared to murder her. Nicki didn't even have the smarts to hide it, the sedatives sitting in plain sight. I should have set that whole fucking "friendly" relationship on fire. But I was a fair man, so I gave her a chance to explain herself. Except the dumb bitch took the route of denial, swearing she only gave me a vitamin.

I'd recognize the aftertaste in any fucking lifetime. I'd gotten used to them enough during those first few weeks of recovery. The doctors pumped me full of sedatives to numb the pain and minimize my movements.

Lucky for her, River was there and got her out of my sight before I could actually follow through with my plan.

"Yeah. How's your back?" River, much like myself, served in the military and had scars. His scars were invisible. Mine... very much in your face.

Those hazel eyes flashed in my mind. "Good."

"What possessed you to bring Nicki along on your spring vacation?"

River and I went way back. To our early Navy days. To our shared deployments when we barely got out alive. To some fucked-up nights when we shared weapons, alcohol, and women because we didn't know how to deal with our issues. Whether it was PTSD or something else.

"I didn't," I hissed. "Winston let her on board because he's an idiot and my father had her flown over so she'd parade in front of me in hopes I'd fall for her charm."

"And onto her ass," River snickered. "She does have a sweet ass, but God the moment she opens her mouth, you realize her ass isn't worth the hassle."

Wasn't that the fucking truth.

"Are you up for meeting Winston and me tonight?" I changed subjects. "Or are you on your way back to Portugal?"

"No, I'm still here. Probably for a week or so. Where do you want to meet?"

"Le Bar Américain."

"Seriously?" The surprise in his voice was evident. "Isn't that more of a hookup scene?"

I chuckled. "Are you in a committed relationship I don't know about?"

"Relationships are not my thing," he noted in a tone drier than gin.

"Ditto," I retorted, knowing he'd understand exactly who I was referring to. It would take an extraordinary circumstance for me to commit to a relationship. Especially with someone as greedy, self-ish, and tactless as Nicki.

Shifting away from the topic of the opposite sex, we discussed an acquisition I was working on, aside from the jewelry business. It was a security company with an established presence in Europe, and River was an expert in the area since he owned one himself alongside our buddies from the service. Just like me, River, Astor, and Darius had built their own empire. Kian... well, he came from an empire. A Brazilian cartel empire.

As far as my empire, my mother's inheritance from her mafia princess background gave me a leg up when starting up my businesses. Father was only good at spending money and schmoozing with questionable characters. He always relied on me to clean up his messes, and if I wasn't available, he moved down to the next son in the hierarchy, like we were his personal PR cleanup crew.

At least my war buddies—Astor, Darius, and River—didn't have to contend with bullshit like that. I wasn't sure about Kian whom I'd only met a few years ago. He kept his familial relations to himself.

We concluded the conversation by agreeing on a time to meet at Le Bar Américain and hung up.

Standing from my desk, I headed to the master bedroom at the front of my yacht. Once inside, I stripped out of my clothes and stepped into the shower. The water was cool and felt good against my skin. The injection had soothed the pain, and I couldn't help wanting those hands on my back again.

That soothing, soft touch.

My cock instantly grew hard. *Fuck!* If only thinking about her had my shaft stirring to life, I didn't want to imagine what touching her would do.

I should pretend I never met her and carry on. Common sense urged me to do this. I just didn't think I had the self-control.

I finished showering and dressed in something casual. *Maybe it'll make me look younger,* I thought wryly.

I put on tailored chinos and a lightweight linen shirt by Vitale Barberis Cononico so I'd fit in with the visitors of the Riviera who tended to just lounge around their pools—or their yachts—wasting the day away. My brother was already standing in the main salon, wearing his white Bermuda shorts and a black T-shirt, finishing the look off with a blazer and straw fedora. He had no issues fitting into the leisurely life of the French Riviera. It was his sole purpose in life—sex, beach, alcohol, food—and not necessarily in that order.

He yawned, probably still fighting his hangover. The sun had started to dip below the horizon, yet my brother acted like it was morning.

I shook my head. "You ready?"

"Born ready," Winston muttered. "Let's go."

It didn't take us long to get there. As we pulled up in front of the all-glass building, a line snaking around the bar came into view. It was connected to the Riviera Hotel in the back. The place attracted the most exclusive guests from around the world.

I jumped out of my red Ferrari, River not far behind in his black Porsche. It was what I loved about my superyacht. It stored my car.

I handed the valet the keys to my car. "Have it parked up front," I instructed in French, handing the guy five hundred euros. By the looks of it, River was doing the same thing.

"Man, are you sure this is a good idea?" River grumbled. He'd opted for deep green chinos and a black T-shirt with combat boots. "This is like a hotspot for the screamers."

Music pumped. Girls screamed. Some men did too. Or maybe they were just boys. Trust-fund pricks that hadn't earned a cent in their entire life. Their whole purpose was to live it up and spend their family money.

"I seem to recall you like screamers," I taunted. In fact, I saw it firsthand. It might sound fucked up to some, but sometimes River and I shared women. It worked in my favor. In and out. Keeping my scars out of sight. "I'm willing to bet that hasn't changed."

River flipped me the bird as we strolled toward the entrance. Between our expensive cars and tipping generously, we were given the VIP treatment, as the bouncer instantly unclipped the belt and let us walk on by.

A hostess appeared, probably alerted to our presence, and

showed us to a table in the VIP lounge set off to the side. The bar was crowded, bodies pressed against each other with little room to move. I was certain it was well past capacity, but no one seemed to mind.

My eyes wandered over the crowd as we took our seats in the plush chairs. A table just outside our area was packed with young tourists doing shots.

"Bang!" one of them shouted. "You can't beat the champion."

"What can I get you?" the hostess offered, sparing us the hassle of a trip to the bar.

"Cognac," I answered. River nodded for the same.

"Any particular brand?" she asked.

"Anything top shelf," I said, letting my eyes roam the crowd in search of a certain redhead.

When it was Winston's turn, he responded, "Johnny Walker Red Label."

The hostess gave him a blank look as I shook my head. He knew full well they wouldn't have that shit here. He picked up the drink menu, muttering some shit under his breath. Probably about savage places that didn't carry the labels he loved so much.

"Just get something else, Winston," I said, my patience running thin.

"Fine, vodka." She scurried away while my eyes traveled over the crowd. "This is like a cattle bar," Winston grumbled.

River chuckled. "This is being young. You're just an old grouch."

It was then that I spotted her. She strode in, past the line, wearing a simple white summer dress and Hermès silk scarf tied around her hair, holding it up off her shoulders. Her sun-kissed skin glowed even from here, and I wondered if she'd still smell like apples.

She twisted to the right, toward the bar. From this angle, I had the perfect view. Two thin straps lowered to an open back that dipped low, exposing her elegant, toned muscles. My hands itched, and deep down, I knew her curves would fit perfectly in my palms. Almost as if she were tailored for me.

My fists clenched at my sides as I remembered she'd seen my scars, and she sure as shit didn't act repulsed. Maybe—just fucking maybe—she was the one I had been looking for.

Mine.

Why in the fuck did that word enter my mind as I stared at her? Maybe because she looked even better than I imagined out of her scrubs.

Her smile widened and she jumped excitedly, waving her hand.

"Ah, I see why we're here now," Winston deadpanned, following my gaze. "Who in the fuck is she?"

I never looked away from her. "My nurse." The smile that crept across my face as I said it hid a wealth of meaning.

Chapter 3
Odette

Le Bar Américain was packed by the time I strolled in. The beautiful view over the French Riviera attracted everyone to this place. The breeze swept through the terrace, warm and soothing. Lights glimmered from pergolas with rays of sapphire and ruby skating across the whole terrace, illuminating it every few seconds.

The music reverberated throughout the large area, alternating between hip-hop, dance, and R&B. Some watched while others danced, and many drank. Accents of gold and marble statues were everywhere. Lushness covered every corner of this place.

My favorite time to come was when it was less packed, but spring break was a busy season here. And this was the preferred hangout spot for our friends. No amount of crowd would keep us away. It helped that we didn't have to wait in the long lines.

Marco looked up from his place behind the bar, his dark eyes meeting mine and instantly he grinned. Ignoring the line of customers, he hopped over the bartop and approached me, his air of confidence obvious to those around us. Women gawked, staring at his ass shamelessly. Not that I could blame them. Marco was a part-time model, part-time bartender, waiting for his big break.

"Hey, Maddy!" He wrapped his arms around me and pecked me on the cheek. "How is Doctor Swan doing today?"

I chuckled. "Not a doctor yet."

I'd known him for a decade and he'd always been incredibly nice. Billie didn't particularly care for him, but Marco always went out of his way to be kind. It was a running joke during our high school years that we'd end up dating. We never did though. Neither one of us had any romantic notions. We were just good friends.

"But you have it in the bag." He smacked my butt playfully. "Your sister is over there."

I followed his gaze and found my sister, Billie, at the table with all our friends, laughing and drinking like it was their last day on this earth. I shook my head. We were like two opposites, but we got along great. She always had my back, and I always had hers.

"I hear you and Pierre broke up." Of course the news had traveled fast. Men gossiped as much as women.

"Yeah." It was best not to elaborate on it.

"Need me to kick his ass?" I shook my head and he smiled. "I told you the two of us were meant for each other."

I threw my head back and laughed. He'd been joking about this since we were kids. He still tended to use it as a way to make me feel better. I couldn't see him as anything else but a brotherly figure.

"Are you working all night?" I asked instead of answering. I never wanted to lead a man on—intentionally or not—that I was looking for a relationship with him. Our friendship was more important. When we first moved here after Mom died, he was one of the first people Billie and I met. I was ten, Billie a bit older. Marco was my age. He helped me transition during that time, and we built a lasting friendship.

"Yes. I couldn't pass it up. Tips are good this week."

I nodded in understanding. "Of course."

Marco financially supported his mother and his sister. I didn't know how he succeeded in not going bankrupt. It wasn't like our own father was wealthy—certainly not by local standards—but we didn't have to work two jobs to get by. Billie was able to attend college without needing a job, and I'd gotten into Stanford with a scholarship, Father's financial help, and a casual job at a coffee shop.

He walked me to the table where our friends were already en route to getting drunk.

"Maddy, you're here!" my sister screamed at the top of her lungs, jumping to her feet and putting both her arms up in the air. "Our future surgeon who will save the world."

I shook my head in disbelief. She was halfway to hammered. The two of us loved each other and had each other's back, but we couldn't be more different. Billie was the more creative one—all her focus on diamond and fashion designing. I, on the other hand, was into science and medicine. Billie was like our mother; I was like our father.

Turning my attention back to Marco, I leaned over and pecked his cheek. "I'll see you later."

The usual gang was already seated around the table and I grinned.

"The life of the party is here," I announced as I joined the table. "Miss me?"

"Woman, where were you?" My sister's voice came out a bit slurred, and I made a mental note to order her some water or else she'd feel like shit tomorrow.

"Having dinner with Papa. You were supposed to be there too. Remember?"

She waved her hand, her movements slightly off. "I'll eat tomorrow. I'm watching my weight for the summer."

Reaching over, I took her glass and downed it. "If you want to give up calories, give up the alcohol. Not food."

She pouted her lips. "But—"

"No buts." I turned my attention to our friends. "How long have you guys been here?"

"Before it opened." The answer came from Desiré, my sister's best friend. Although I had a feeling once Billie learned of her role in my breakup, the two wouldn't remain such good friends. She and Desiré had been close for many years. The latter had just been dumb enough to fall for Pierre's cheating ass and his charm. She seduced him and got what she wanted, but so did Pierre. But I wouldn't be the one to tell my sister that. I had no doubt that Desiré would eventually slip and tell Billie herself. I just hoped it'd be once I was back at Stanford.

Billie and Desiré were the same age and went to the same college for fashion. Heck, they even had the same hair color. Desiré's long legs and stunning complexion made her the perfect candidate for modeling. Yet, the only thing she managed to accomplish was snatching other women's boyfriends.

Like Pierre, my ex, for example. Not that I was bitter or anything. We broke up three months ago, after giving long-distance dating a try. It didn't work out. Of course, it would have been better if we'd broken up before she jumped his bones, but no, Desiré took advantage of the slightly open window and slithered her way right in.

"We are lit," Tristan drawled. "Best spring break ever. I loooove France."

"France seems to love you too," I remarked, smiling. He had his arms around two women wearing nothing but swimsuits. And here I was worried about being underdressed for the club.

Tristan and I were in our first year at Stanford and had become good friends. He was my study buddy. We pushed each other when we were too tired or tempted to skip a night of studies.

His sister—more than several years older than him—sat at the table very much proper and serious. She was a doctor at George Washington back in the States. It would seem being a doctor was a requirement in their family. Her eyes traveled around the terrace—

a slightly bored expression on her face—until they landed on the bar. She was watching Marco.

Hmmm, interesting.

Marco needed a serious woman in his life. "That's Marco," I remarked casually. "He's our friend." Tristan's sister turned her attention to me, raising her eyebrow. "We can introduce you," I offered.

She shook her head just as her phone buzzed and she turned her attention to it. Tristan was overly friendly; his sister not so much.

My eyes roamed the terrace, looking for familiar faces, until they landed on the one person I'd hoped not to see during my break back home. My ex. With a new woman on his arm. From what I heard, he'd been cycling through women like they were going out of style.

I stiffened and my jaw clenched. He was my ex, but it still irked me that he was getting laid while I had been on the long stretch of a dry season.

"Okay, that's it." My sister's voice pulled my attention away from the cheating bastard. Her fingers wrapped around my upper arm as she tugged me to the back of the open terrace, away from our table. "I demand to know what happened."

I blinked. "What are you talking about?"

My sister's subject changes could be jarring and disorienting. One minute she was talking about the weather and the next about a trip to the moon.

"You and Pierre," she hissed under her breath. "Every time someone mentions him, you get all moody."

I rolled my eyes. "I'm not moody."

"Yes, you are."

I let out a heavy sigh, too tired to argue with her. "Fine. It's pissing me off that every time I turn around, I hear he has a new woman. And I'm here in the fucking desert."

My sister's brows scrunched. "Huh? What desert?"

My sister's airheadedness grated on my nerves tonight. Usually, I didn't mind it, but I could feel my temper flaring. I needed to get laid as soon as possible.

I turned to my left, meeting my sister's brown eyes. She had our mother's eyes and her gorgeous blonde hair.

"I just meant I want a ménage à trois," I sighed wistfully. It was random, but I knew it'd get my sister going. She was going through a sexual revolution. Or was it exploration? Either way, she claimed by the time she was married, she'll have tried everything and anything so she knew what she was giving up when she finally said "I do" to some poor schmuck.

"Oh my gosh," she gushed. "That's on your bucket list?"

That was one department that Billie never lacked in. Sex was her expertise. She had only one rule in life: try everything once. If she didn't like it, she'd just never do it again. I, on the other hand, needed to evaluate the pros and cons of any situation.

Ménage à trois included.

My eyes traveled back to Pierre. "It is now," I muttered.

Pierre wanted to explore a ménage à trois, except it wasn't for me. He wanted two women. I refused, and I was certain it was the reason for his cheating. Desiré jumped right into that boat and gave him exactly what he wanted. But then he was done with her too.

"What happened with Pierre?" Billie was relentless in her hunt for information. I truly wished she'd become a reporter. Her nosiness would come in handy there. Instead, it left me subject to all her investigations.

I flicked a glance her way. "He cheated."

Fury flashed in my sister's brown eyes. "That motherfucker." She lunged forward, probably to stride over to him and punch him in the face.

"It's been months. I'm over it, and he's not worth it."

"Damn straight he's not worth it." She tried to pull free but my grip was too tight. "But my sister is and—"

"Billie, let it go," I ordered.

The best adjective to describe my older sister was *firecracker*. She was five foot four, yet she wouldn't hesitate to take on anyone. Sometimes it worried me for her safety. I'd seen her punch an MMA dude once because he called her a little kitty. Thank all the stars he was a gentleman and didn't punch back.

At the end of it all, it turned out to be a translation issue and he didn't mean to call her a kitty, but tigress. Anyway, that was neither here nor there.

"Who did he do it with?" She turned to face me and put her hands on her waist. "I should at least punch her."

I shook my head. "It doesn't matter."

"Yes, it does," she hissed.

"No, it doesn't. He's history and so is she."

Silence followed, stretching like a rubber band. I didn't want to ruin their friendship.

I shrugged. "It doesn't matter."

Billie met my gaze and somehow I knew... I just fucking knew she already had the answer.

"It's Desiré, isn't it?"

"Come on, Billie." I sighed heavily. "The night is too nice to ruin it with all this crap."

"She's a friend," she said, her voice rumbling. "You're my sister. No comparison." Her eyes darted to Desiré, narrowing to slits. "I'm going to beat her ass."

Before I could say anything, Billie marched to her best friend with indignation and raised her hand. My ears buzzed and my eyes widened. Jesus, she wouldn't hit her. Would she? Just as I opened my mouth, Billie yanked a bracelet off Desiré's wrist.

A round of gasps tore around the table, but she didn't pay attention to anyone and kept her glare on her best friend.

"Skank," she shouted. "How dare you! Backstabbing bitch. I hope Pierre gave you herpes."

I winced. That was going a bit too far, but I wouldn't reprimand my own sister. After all, she was doing it for me.

My chest warmed. I loved Billie because no matter what, she *always* had my back. She whirled around—like a queen with an entourage—and came back to me.

"I love you." I pulled her into a hug. "That was a bit harsh," I whispered in her ear.

"Nobody fucks with my sister," she muttered. "Should I have said gonorrhea?"

A strangled laugh escaped me. "No, herpes was probably better." I squeezed her harder, taking a deep breath. I didn't expect her to take my side so passionately, although I should have known. "I'm so lucky to have you."

She grinned. "Want me to go back and punch her?"

I shook my head. "Please don't," I said, smiling. "I promise, I'm fine. So no punching anyone and let's forget Desiré and Pierre."

She shifted slightly and met my gaze. "Only if you get back at those two assholes."

A laugh vibrated in my chest. Leave it to my sister to think of revenge at a time like this. I wasn't a doormat in a relationship, but I wasn't revenge thirsty like Billie either. I'd witnessed my sister make her ex-boyfriends regret leaving her by spraying her perfume on their pillows so they'd miss her. And sure as shit, they came crawling back. Of course, she never took them back. Right-fully so.

"Sure. I'm sure it'll be easy enough to find two hot men available for a night of sex. I'll show Pierre what he missed out on," I mused, unable to hide a self-satisfied grin.

It would definitely be a win for me, not to mention double the pleasure with two men. Pierre, that selfish bastard, had just wanted to watch two women making out.

Her eyes traveled around the terrace until she looked over my shoulder. Her eyes widened and her mouth parted.

"Oh my panties," she murmured, her cheeks turning crimson.

Curious to see what had her so flustered, I followed her gaze and froze. Three gorgeous men sitting at the VIP table—one of them I'd already met. What were the odds of running into *him* again?

"Hello again, Odette."

I blinked as the voice rumbled, sending a shiver down my bare back.

Byron Ashford stared back at me, greeting me with a smile and those gorgeous blue eyes. He leaned back in his chair. His white shirt clung to his stomach from the humidity, highlighting his enticing abs. My eyes lingered on them for a second too long.

What could I say? I loved abs on a man. And those biceps. *Jesus.* I studied that tattoo that intrigued me for some reason. You didn't see too many people with chemical elements tattooed on their bodies.

God's gift to women, except I was certain this guy was even hotter than God himself. His five-o'clock shadow didn't take away from his face. If anything, it gave him more appeal. Those full lips that I was certain did many sinful things. I wanted to seduce him, have him do sinful things to my body.

Glancing down at myself, I frowned. Now I wished I had spent a bit more time getting dressed. I went for comfort and casual, not hot and demure. It'd never crossed my mind that I'd see him again.

"Nice to see you out of scrubs," he said, his voice raspy. Something about that growly tone sent a fresh flurry of tingles down my chest. My nipples hardened just from the way he looked at me, and suddenly, I knew. I had to sleep with this man. It'd be an out-of-this-world experience, that I was sure of.

I took two steps closer to their table, Billie right next to me.

"Mr. Ashford," I greeted him, offering a smile as I smoothed a hand down my short dress. "I'm surprised to see you in a place like this. Stalking me?"

I heard the words come out of my mouth, low and breathy, and had to give myself credit. It had been a while, but I could still flirt. Our gazes met and something in his blue depths hit me right in the chest. *Loneliness.*

He leaned over, putting his elbow on the table, his tone dark and decadent as he said, "Do you want me to stalk you?"

I licked my lips, my heart fluttering like the wings of a captured butterfly. His gaze locked on my mouth, burning with something hot. Promising.

I caught the hint of vulnerability in his eyes that I was certain he hid from the world. I didn't know how I knew it, but I felt it as if it were my own. Byron Ashford wore a mask, but underneath it all, I had a feeling there was more to this man than met the eye.

"I'm not much for stalkers," I commented nonchalantly. "But I might make an exception." I gave a playful lift of my shoulder as my gaze darted to the other two men at his table. Geez, talk about gorgeous friends. Nodding at them, I added, "Just this once."

Ménage à trois, here I come!

"But only if you introduce us to your friends," Billie chimed in, her eyes locking on the one with a scruffy beard and slightly bored expression on his face. But his other friend... ooh la la.

My eyes returned to Byron, something about him pulling me.

"This is my sister," I introduced her. "Billie."

His eyebrow arched, barely acknowledging her. It wasn't that I wanted him to ignore her, but the fact he seemed more focused on me had my insides jittery.

"This is my brother, Winston." He tilted his head to the man directly to his right, and now that I studied his features, I could see the resemblance. Same eyes. Same chin. Dark hair. "And this is my friend River."

I sighed dreamily. River had every woman's dream hair. I never cared for longer hair on men, but something about the way he wore it. Clean. Off his face. So damn sexy. The wavy locks that fell just below his chin. Just enough to run my fingers through.

Although he isn't as sexy as my Mr. Ashford, I thought silently.

I nodded my head in acknowledgement. "Nice to meet you."

"Likewise," River answered, smiling and revealing a set of perfect teeth. "What brings you to France?"

"We live here," my sister answered before I had a chance to even open my mouth. "Well, I do. Maddy is usually back in the States, attending college for her medical degree."

I noted Byron's brows scrunch, likely at Billie calling me Maddy when he knew me only as Odette. Only close friends called me Maddy. It was short for Madeline, which was my middle name.

"And you?" I asked curiously. "You couldn't have come just for the sun and the sea," I jabbed mildly.

The joke was missed on River and Winston, but Byron's lips curved into a smile. Butterflies took off again. Why had I never felt these butterflies before?

"Work," Byron answered vaguely.

I raised my eyebrow. "And what is work?" I questioned. "Something boring, I presume."

River chuckled. "You can say that again."

Byron never answered.

Chapter 4
Byron

My brother had a smug grin on his face that he tried to hide.

I wanted to wipe it off his face with my fist. He thought he had it all figured out in his buzzed state. He didn't know jack shit.

"Not all of us can have exciting medical careers," I said dryly. I wouldn't say my career was boring, exactly. After all, we did run an empire, but if she hadn't heard of the Ashford family, I'd rather leave her in the dark. It was really refreshing running into a woman who had no fucking idea who I was.

Odette snickered softly. "So you're telling me you're boring, huh?"

"I never said that," I drawled. "Don't jump to conclusions."

She rolled her eyes, clearly unimpressed. "Well, whatever boring thing you do for a living must be a secret since you're refusing to share it."

"I'm a businessman," I told her, keeping it vague.

Her lips curved into a grimace. "Wow, it's even worse than boring."

Winston and River laughed and it took all my restraint not to smash their skulls and knock them out. The audience was really unwelcome right now.

"Well, I hear France is a free country, so you are entitled to feel any way you want." My tone came out sharper than I intended. For fuck's sake, this woman had me losing the even temper I was known for.

Thrown off by my harsh tone, she shot me a curious look. Almost as if she were trying to figure me out like I was her next puzzle. Then she shrugged, and I couldn't help but wonder what was going on in her head.

"Well, I guess it was nice seeing you again," Odette said—or was it Maddy—her eyes darting between me and River. If it were any other woman, I wouldn't have minded. But her... I didn't want to share her. I didn't fucking want anyone even looking her way.

Except, this woman wanted a ménage à trois, based on the conversation I'd overheard between her and her sister.

I cracked my knuckles under the table as I watched her bare back saunter from me, keeping my expression blank all the while. One hint of weakness and Winston would be on me like a dog with a bone. Fucker!

"She seems like marriage material," Winston remarked.

I shot him a glare. Someday I might really murder him. Marriage was never on my to-do list. Of course, our father had gotten it up his ass lately that one of his sons should get married. All eyes were now turned to me, since I was the oldest.

I'd rather cut my dick off with a butter knife than marry someone to appease my father.

He already had his sights set on who it should be too. As if. Nicki Popova was the last person on earth I'd marry. I'd rather shut my dick in a door than connect my family with theirs. The Popova family had a long history in politics and a list of connections even longer. Our family had only been in politics for two generations. My grandfather ventured into it, and his son—my father—followed.

Grandfather had morals and standards; my father didn't. He'd sell his soul to the devil in order to get what he wanted.

The presidency.

"Adorable, smart, young. If you don't want her, I'll take her." Winston loved to get on my nerves. It was his specialty. "Unless you'd rather marry Nicki."

"Would you shut up, Winston?" I downed my cognac in one go. Something about the shackles of marriage with Nicki had me breaking out in hives.

"What?" My brother raised his glass. "To love, marriage, and kids."

I could see right through him. He pushed for me to get hitched so there was no danger of Father putting any kind of pressure on him. I wasn't even sure why he worried. None of us ever listened to the crap Father said. Senator Ashford was not someone to look up to nor did any of us heed his advice. He had been more than content to spread his seed, abandon Alessio and Davina—two children he had out of wedlock—and he never lost any sleep over it. Even before Mother died, he was never around much, leaving my siblings in my care. I could have forgiven all that, but not what it cost us. Our baby brother, Kingston, and almost our baby sister.

Our father lost his head-of-the-family status when Kingston went missing, although it wasn't until recently that we knew for certain it was due to his "dealings" with the mob. Our family was glued together only for appearances' sake and to ensure our empire remained intact.

"So are we thinking about marriage?" River asked.

"I'm not," Winston deadpanned. "Byron is. Nicki would have married him, but he kicked her off the boat before she tried to kill him with sleeping pills. So she's out of the question."

Breathe, Byron. Breathe.

"You already know my thoughts on that woman."

Nicki wasn't marriage material. At. All. I suspected Father hoped for Popova support so it'd help his campaign for reelection.

He just refused to give up his dream of becoming the next U.S. President. There was no chance in hell I'd ever allow any children or wife of mine to be put through that. Gold digger or not.

"Marriage is bliss... I hear," Winston offered, grinning widely.

"Then get married, Winston," I said tonelessly.

There were so many fucking days lately that I could barely tolerate him. But he was my brother, so I had an obligation.

"I'd marry *her*," my brother egged on, tilting his chin in Odette's direction. "Those eyes with flecks of gold. That smile. *And* a future doctor? Fuck, I could stop working and she'd support me."

Winston had enough money to last him ten lifetimes.

Not that I'd ever let him get within two feet of Odette Swan. That woman ticked all the boxes for me. Sharp mind. A petite frame. Eyes that I could get lost in. There was something idealistic and angelic about her, even when she was being snarky.

Yes, I was attracted to her. I knew from the first words she'd spoken that I was a goner, but could I be blamed? She was beautiful, smart, and had a spine of steel.

My gaze strayed back to the woman. Something about her tugged at me. I couldn't pinpoint what. Maybe it was the vulnerability in her gaze. Or maybe it was the loneliness I could see her trying to hide behind her big smile—something I knew about intimately.

I watched her dance with her sister, throwing her hands up in the air, her face glowing with laughter and mischief. And her hips, the way they swayed, it was hard to tear my eyes from her.

My gaze traveled over her smooth, bare legs. Blood heated in my veins, my cock hardened, and my fingers itched to touch her skin. I wondered if her waist-length hair was as soft as it looked. Fuck, lusting after a woman. I couldn't remember ever feeling this way before.

The responsible professional from the hospital was nowhere to be found. In its place was a sensual young woman who knew exactly what she was doing.

She looked good. Beautiful. She was dressed down compared to other women in this place, but it only made her stand out more. Maybe it was exactly that which I liked about her. I might as well admit it.

I liked her. The years between us be damned.

A guy next to her shouted, "Nice ass. Move faster, I don't have all night."

She didn't even spare him a glance, flipping him off over her shoulder. I strode over to him casually, then smacked the fucker upside the head. I turned my attention back to her. Our eyes met, but she continued moving. Slower. More sensual.

Mischief danced in her eyes. Time stood still. I waited. For what, I didn't know. But then someone bumped into her and the moment was lost. Shrugging her shoulder, as if dismissing me, she headed for the bar. I watched her speak to the bartender just as a frat-looking Frenchman grabbed her ass.

Couldn't this woman go a single minute without men falling all over themselves for her?

My shoulders tensed and I prowled through the crowd the next second. Something dark coiled in my stomach. I watched him lean into her—completely ignoring her personal space—and then whisper something in her ear. She reached for his hand and removed it off her ass, but the fucker obviously wasn't getting the hint.

He reached for her, his face twisting into a scowl, but before he could touch her, I lunged for his wrist and twisted it.

"I believe the lady said no." I stared down at him through my rage.

This fucker had one of those model-perfect faces, but the arrogance in his expression ruined it completely.

"She's my girlfriend."

I stilled, but before I could say anything and turn this relationship to ash, Odette hissed icily, "*Ex*-girlfriend."

Thank fuck.

I'd have hated to be in my thirties resorting to filthy methods to break up a couple. From the conversation with her sister I'd overheard, I knew plenty. This guy wasn't good enough for her.

Odette stared him down. "I told you before, I don't do do-overs. For anything or anyone. Don't fucking bother me anymore."

Iciness radiated from her every word and every pore. This woman was impressive. No fucking wonder I liked her.

"You heard the lady," I said, my tone rivaling Odette's arctic one. "Get fucking lost."

He scoffed. "She's just playing hard to get," he muttered. "Fucking cunt."

My expression went from agitated to homicidal. I grabbed him by his cheap T-shirt and tossed him onto the ground. Then, my hand wrapped around his throat, and I tightened my hold. A whimper squeezed past his lips. So I squeezed a bit more. I was just about to throw in a punch and ruin that pretty model face when soft, cool fingers wrapped around my bicep.

"He's not worth it," she said softly, shaking her head. We were attracting an audience.

I turned my attention back to her ex.

"Apologize," I said. He mumbled something unintelligible. "We didn't hear you. Apologize to the lady." His face reddened, but he wanted to appear tougher than he was. I could see from the expression in his eyes he was thinking of saying something stupid, so I offered him one more chance. "Last warning. Then I'm throwing a punch and scarring that pretty face."

That got him reconsidering his words.

"Désolé," he muttered in French, his eyes flashing with hate.

"We didn't *hear* you," I said, squeezing his throat just a bit tighter. This guy would never fucking model again. I'd ensure it. My smile contained a dark threat, and I let him see all of it.

"Désolé!" This time, he screamed the word. I eased my grip. "I'm sorry, okay," he whimpered. He shot a fearful look in my direction, his face reddening with panic.

"Is his apology sufficient?" I asked Odette. I needed her to understand that this would be the last time he'd ever come near her, if I had any say in the matter.

"Yes, it's sufficient." Odette's fingers tightened around my bicep. "Come on, Mr. Ashford. Dance with me."

Jesus Christ. Did she just call me Mr. Ashford?

I let go of the creep and took a step back, running a hand over my jaw. Fuck, when was the last time I lost my head like this?

The guy disappeared before I could say "beat it." I turned my attention back to Odette. She gave me a wide smile and something in my gut kicked at the sight of it. She was beautiful, but when she smiled she was stunning.

"Well, Mr. Ashford." She beamed, taking my hand into hers. My other hand came around her and rested on the small of her back, pulling her closer to me. "Don't tell me you can't stand rude and cranky people."

"Touché," I acknowledged. "I should apologize for that."

Her glimmering eyes found mine and her grin grew wider. "You should, Mr. Ashford."

"Please, call me Byron."

She smiled. "Only after you apologize."

"Dr. Swan—"

"Nope." She cut me off, rolling her eyes. "Dr. Swan is my father. I'm Odette. Friends call me Maddy."

"Why do they call you Maddy?"

"It's short for Madeline. My middle name."

I huffed. "Then I'll call you Madeline."

Her brows scrunched. "Why not Maddy?"

I leaned closer to her, the scent of apples filling my lungs. "Because I'm not your friend. I'm going to be the man to fuck your brains out and make you forget all about your ex and this ménage à trois you think you want."

Her sharp inhale filled the space between us. Her body was flush with mine, pressing into me. I could tell by the color rising in her cheeks and the way she swallowed deeply that she felt this attraction too. Her shimmering eyes found mine, the gold in them more pronounced.

"Are you sure you're up to the task, Mr. Ashford?" The challenge shone in her eyes and in the way she tipped her kissable chin. I bet she did the same when she was being stubborn.

Our gazes locked. Attraction danced. I couldn't have been the first man to fall so spectacularly at her feet. She was gorgeous, with a face and body that could tempt the devil himself. No woman had ever succeeded in spiking my heart rate so completely, let alone so quickly. Until this med student walked through the door, that was.

"Byron," I corrected her. "I don't want to hear you screaming Mr. Ashford later on. That's my father."

Her cheeks turned crimson and her mouth parted. I had to exercise all my self-control not to smash my mouth against hers. I was already tempted to just drag her out of here and have her to myself for the rest of the night.

"I heard your conversation with your sister," I drawled. "If you want to tick a ménage à trois off your bucket list, I'll deliver it. But on one condition only."

She blinked and her blush spread down her décolletage, disappearing into her dress. But she didn't look away.

"What's the condition?" she breathed softly.

"Afterward, I get you all to myself, and you let me show you that you only need one man to satisfy your every desire."

Amusement flashed in her expression and she arched an eyebrow. "And who might that man be?"

"Me, Madeline," I said. "You'll only ever need me."

Chapter 5
Odette

I felt my cheeks flush and found myself smiling broadly as I watched him, letting my eyes roam freely over his face.

"Byron, then," I deadpanned, while my heart threatened to beat out of my chest. His strong body was so close to me. His scent overwhelmed all my other senses. He smelled nice, like citrus and sandalwood—all wrapped in sex. It was all man. "And I won't forget to scream the right name."

I faked the confidence that I didn't really have at that very moment. My sister had tons to spare, but I was usually the reserved one. But not tonight. Maybe not ever again. This man brought it all out of me. To hell with caution and smarts—I didn't want to miss out.

"Good," he said, his eyes lingering on my lips as we continued swaying to the beat of the music. "I can't wait to hear your hoarse voice as you scream it for the hundredth time."

He was confident enough for both of us. I actually liked that quality in him. Maybe not in all men, but something told me he was good for it.

"Did it ever occur to you that maybe you'll scream *my* name?" I asked, feigning innocence and plastering an exaggerated frown on my face.

To his credit, he played along. He tilted his head, considering my question. "You're right, Madeline, that hadn't occurred to me. What I can guarantee, though, is that you'll be screaming first. Always first."

I felt my jaw drop open. This man was not at all what I expected. I shook my head, barely containing my smile. At this rate, we'd end up in the corner before this song was over. The throbbing between my thighs intensified with those images. I wouldn't mind that at all. And if his friend River joined us, it would be the full package.

My eyes darted over to his friend whose gaze was already fixed on us, but something about Byron pulled me back to him. It was as if every cell of my body needed him. It was thrilling and slightly terrifying.

Byron's gaze was on River as he gave him a terse nod, which moved River into motion.

"What's that about?" I asked curiously.

He smiled darkly. Sinfully. "I told him we're doing this."

My heart leapt, pulse drumming in my ears. It almost stopped my breath. I gulped, trying to get a grip on myself and not act like a silly, giddy girl.

"So did you really doze off while sunbathing?" It was safer to change subjects. My whole body buzzed with anticipation, and I really hoped he'd deliver. I hadn't gotten laid in over nine months.

"That's what I said," he answered. I scoffed softly and he frowned. "Why does it seem like you don't believe me?"

I leaned in so my lips grazed his ear and said, "I don't believe you. You're not the kind to just doze off."

"I'm not?" Interest laced his voice as he pulled me tighter against him. The music around us blared, but I could feel his every word as it trailed down my neck.

"No, you're not." There wasn't an ounce of doubt in my voice. "You're not relaxed enough."

He frowned. "Meaning?"

"You're too—" I searched for the right word. "Too intense. You would never just doze off in a chair. On a plane. On a beach. Anywhere, in fact."

I smiled as he twirled me around and brought me back to him, the bodies crowding around us virtually nonexistent.

"Am I right?" I couldn't resist asking.

He paused for a moment. "Maybe," he answered cryptically.

I couldn't resist an eyeroll.

"I'm so right," I claimed. "I read you like an open book."

That seemed to amuse him. "Okay," he caved. "Since you read me like an open book. What was my first impression of you?"

I snickered. "Considering your welcoming greeting, it must have been fabulous."

"Maybe I was just blinded by your beauty and hated the fact that someone so gorgeous would be taking my blood pressure?"

I snorted. "Somehow I doubt that. But humor me." Our bodies moved as one on the dance floor. You'd never guess we hadn't danced together before. "Tell me, what was your first impression?"

"The first thing I thought was how much I'd like to strip that crisp, white uniform right off you. And then I noticed the dimples in your cheeks. When you smiled, it brought me to my knees."

I chuckled, shaking my head and feeling my cheeks flush. I was sure I was beet red, but I refused to be flustered by his compliments. This guy must have rows of beautiful women at his disposal daily. I could hardly imagine anyone impressing him.

I kept my voice light, hiding the effect he had on me. "Or you've been in isolation without a woman in sight for quite some time."

He chuckled. Honestly, it was jarring to see him so relaxed. "Your turn." I raised an eyebrow, wondering what he meant. "Your first impression of me."

I snickered. I certainly hoped he wasn't fishing for a compliment.

"I thought you were a dick," I semi-teased. "A cranky, old dick."

He gave me a lopsided smile, making him appear younger. I grinned, giddy from the flirting. "I have a dick, if that's what you mean. And it is neither cranky nor old."

I burst out laughing. That was the last thing I expected to hear come out of his mouth.

"Mr. Ashford," I spluttered as if shocked by his comment. "That's not how you speak to your dance partner."

He looked at me, all our earlier playfulness wiped clear off his face. "But you're not just my dance partner, are you?"

"Oh, really. What am I?"

"Baby, you're a woman that I intend to have sprawled across my bed, screaming my name."

It felt like all the air had been sucked out of the room. My heart beating out of my chest, I whispered, barely loud enough for him to hear, "That's awfully presumptuous."

His eyes danced with mischief. "Just stating the facts."

He pulled me closer to him. God, he felt good. Warm. Hard. Big.

My pulse kicked into high gear. He radiated heat, every inch of his big, muscled frame brushing against my soft body, and I had to fight the urge to press myself against him.

"I can't decide whether you're a good idea or bad one," I murmured into his chest, my eyelids heavy. I was falling under his spell.

I felt his smirk more than I saw it. "I'm definitely a good idea." He bent his head, his mouth brushing over my temple. "The best one you'll ever make."

I smiled softly as the air swirled between us, surprised at how charming I was finding him. Normally, I'd scoff at a man so cocky. But then, normally I wouldn't flirt with a perfect stranger, nor would I be bold enough to ask for a threesome.

My cheeks had to be burning by now.

I had always been a good girl. The responsible one. My ex even called me vanilla. That was going a bit too far, but I certainly wasn't my sister. Either way, a ménage à trois had never crossed my mind. Not until Pierre dumped me, and now, I wanted it more than anything.

As revenge. As payback. But most of all, for me. My pleasure.

The chance to have one had been dropped into my lap, and I wasn't about to pass on it. Somehow, deep down, I knew I was safe with him. Knew he'd ensure I loved every single minute of it. Feed me my pleasure before his own. I didn't know how I knew that; I just did.

"Are you ready to relinquish control, Madeline?" A shiver danced down my spine at his words. The man hadn't even kissed me yet, and pleasure zipped through my body. I drowned in his deep blue eyes. They were dark, reminding me of the deepest part of the ocean.

Byron's words made me feel alive. It felt like a live wire buzzing through me, and the electricity wouldn't stop until I had him. Both of them.

Tonight, I was a different woman. Kinky and naughty—a far cry from *vanilla*.

He stepped closer, running his arm up my back. My body shuddered from his electric touch, and my breath caught in my throat.

"You can say no," he whispered hotly. His voice was gruff. Raspy. Seductive. And it was working.

"I'm not saying no." There was no chance in hell. This type of man came around once in a lifetime. I didn't care if he gave me one night or one month; I'd seize this chance and enjoy every damn second of it. "Do you want me?"

Despite my growing confidence, I felt my old insecurities sprout up. All night I felt like I'd been playing a part, and I had no idea where the bravery came from. Or this flirty side of me. Maybe it was just waiting for this man to kick in. But still, I needed to hear him say the words.

Byron brushed a strand of hair off my shoulder. The touch sent my pulse into overdrive. At this rate, my heart would freaking stop when he finally had me naked.

"You have no idea how much," he rasped. His cologne was intoxicating. His stubble brushed over my cheek like sandpaper, and my mind immediately created images of him between my legs, eating me out while his stubble ground against my soft skin. "But fair warning, I'm not keen on sharing you with another man."

I tilted my head. "You haven't done this before?"

"I have."

Surprise coasted over me. "Then why—"

He lowered his head until his mouth hovered next to my ear. My heart skipped a frantic beat, and I clutched his shoulders as if needing him to ground me. "Because with you, I feel far too possessive to watch another man touch you. Even if it's River, who I trust with my life." A gasp tore from my lips at his admission. Somehow I didn't think this man was usually open and upfront like this. "But for you, I'll give it a go. Just don't be surprised if I give him a concussion afterward. I have to make sure he doesn't remember you, how you feel, the sounds you make."

His voice was deep and gruff. A long beat passed before he turned his head and sought out my gaze, his eyes burning. My skin was too hot for comfort and my breaths came out shallow.

"Okay."

"Are you ready?"

I swallowed a gulp as excitement shot through me.

"I'm ready," I breathed while my heart drummed against my ribs. I stared at his full lips, wondering—no, wishing for them on my skin. "So fucking ready."

"Then let's go." We stopped dancing and those lips spread into a dark smile. Full of secrets. Full of promises.

"Let me tell my sister not to wait for me." Gosh, was this really happening? My cheeks burned at the insinuation that I'd be spending the night with him. I licked my lips nervously, and his eyes traced the movement. "Unless it won't last all night."

Wonderful, now I sounded like an inexperienced virgin.

"It will last as long as you want it to." His voice glided over my skin. "I hope a lot longer than a night."

Holy. Shit. Yes. Please.

"I have an afternoon shift tomorrow," I tossed back saucily, insinuating I was all for extended sexcapades.

"Your sister is sitting with my brother," he said, his eyes flickering over my shoulder. "Let's go tell them not to wait up. Shall we?"

He extended his hand and I took it, like this was the most natural thing in the world. Like I'd done this a million times before. I hadn't. Pierre was my first boyfriend. While Billie liked to experiment, I liked stability. But tonight, I'd be a woman of the world.

Okay, maybe that was going too far.

We reached the table, Winston and Billie in some lively discussion.

"Hey, I'm going," I told my sister in French, my cheeks burning.

"I'm out too," Byron announced. "River too."

Heat rushed through my body, and I squeezed my thighs together. Was he waiting for us? Was he ready for us? Oh. My. Gosh. I was so ready for them—both of them. It felt so forbidden. Risqué.

"Okay." My sister's answer was clipped. Winston didn't even bother acknowledging his brother.

Billie's eyes met mine, those freckles on her nose and on her cheeks more pronounced. Byron's brother must have pissed her off. It was the only time her freckles stood out like this.

"You okay?"

She blinked, took a deep breath, and then exhaled. She repeated the motion and only then did she answer. "Yes, everything is *parfait*."

53

Yeah, nothing was perfect. My eyes flickered to Winston. He seemed aloof, almost grouchy. What the fuck was his deal? Earlier, he reminded me of Byron when I first entered the patient's room, but now I wasn't so sure.

Billie and Winston shared a fleeting gaze, but both quickly looked away. *Hmm.* I decided to file that thought away for a later day.

"Want me to stay with you?" I offered, despite the fact that it'd be difficult to give up my opportunity at a ménage à trois. For the first time in my life, I *wanted* to be selfish.

"Absolutely not." She stood up from her spot. "I'm going back to my table." She came up to me and pecked my cheek. "See you later. Be safe."

And with that, she scurried back to where all our friends sat. I let out a relieved breath. This was easier than I thought.

"Let's go."

Byron's words turned my skin hotter. My heart raced faster. I nodded, and without another word to his brother, we made our way to the back of the bar. I frowned. I certainly hoped he didn't think I'd be taking my clothes off in a corner.

"We have a room upstairs," he explained as if reading my thoughts. I knew the bar was connected to a hotel, but it was so fancy; I'd never stayed here before. "We thought getting a room would be faster than going back to my yacht."

He drew me closer, never letting go of my hand and using his big, muscular body as a plow. We made our way through the crowded bar and toward the elevators connecting to the back of the hotel. River waited there, leaning against the elevator door. As we approached, it felt like nearing a domain of sin. Metaphorically, of course.

"Hello, Odette."

"Hello, River," I breathed.

Holy shit! *I'm doing this. I'm really doing this.* I swallowed hard. Adrenaline pumped. My heart raced.

Byron's fingers stroked my knuckles and my skin sang under such a simple touch. I couldn't wait to see what happened when he touched me elsewhere. Tingles burst through me with anticipation.

His confidence screamed from him. Not loudly, but in just the right way. He didn't need to broadcast it, and he knew it. Maybe it was that which was my aphrodisiac.

My body buzzed and my lips parted, waiting.

He let go of my hand as we entered the elevator and gripped my waist firmly.

Ding. The elevator door closed behind us.

I swallowed roughly, lifting my face to Byron. I studied his chiseled jaw. His face. His lips. His eyes.

But he didn't even blink. He was waiting for me.

So I made the first move, closing the distance between us eagerly.

Chapter 6
Byron

River leaned casually against the wall, his eyes sharp against our petite woman. No, not *ours*. She was fucking mine.

I inhaled a deep breath, then exhaled. River's eyes flicked to me, and I nodded.

He pushed a button and stopped the elevator, keeping his eyes on her. There was heat in his gaze, and fuck it, I didn't like it. In the past, I never minded sharing a woman with him. We'd take bets, and with a bit of cunning and strategy, we'd seduce a woman. It was win-win. The woman would get the greatest pleasure of her life, and we got to keep our scars out of sight.

Except this time, the plan to go along with Odette's threesome might have backfired. She had seen my scars, and I didn't think she minded them. She saw them all, and still, desire filled her expression. She still wanted me, but not only me.

Fuck, jealousy ate at me.

I guess there was a first time for everything.

This is for Odette, I reminded myself.

She had never done this. It was only natural that she was curious. She closed the distance, her soft body pressing against mine. There was strength in her. Bravery. But also something vulnerable that tugged at me. It made me want to protect her, made me want this to feel good for her.

River came up behind her, gently brushing her red strands from her neck. A visible shudder rolled down her tiny body, but her eyes never strayed from me. Did she want me as much as I wanted her?

I cupped her cheeks, closing the rest of the distance between us. My lips hovered closer to her, barely a breath away.

"Ready, my temptress?"

She lifted her chin, desire hazing her beautiful eyes.

"Yes." Her voice was barely a whisper. A needy plea wove through it.

My lips barely brushed against hers when a soft moan vibrated in her graceful neck. *Jesus*. It was the sweetest sound I'd ever heard. Moving my hands down her body, I felt her twisting herself into my touch.

River's mouth was on her neck. She dropped her head back to rest on his shoulder, allowing him better access. And still, her eyes were on me. Exquisite. Hungry.

My left hand traveled south from her waist, until I found the hem of her skirt. River's hands traveled down her back before stopping on her gorgeous ass, squeezing it. A gasp fell from her lips and she arched, pushing her breasts into me.

Her head fell forward, resting her forehead on my chest. There was barely any distance between this woman and my ex-military buddy. Between her and me. The two of us knew how to bring earth-shattering, mind-blowing pleasure to a curious woman. River's gaze flicked to me as he trailed his mouth along her neck. There was a question in his eyes, asking me if I was all right.

But this wasn't about me. It was about Odette, no matter how badly I wanted to kick him out and keep her for myself. I nodded wordlessly as River's hand pushed her red mane to the side, brushing kisses along the edge of her shoulders.

My fingers traveled up her inner thighs until they reached her folds. I cupped her pussy and her breath caught.

She wanted me there. *Needed* me there.

She lifted her head, searching my face and parting her mouth slightly. She looked like pure lust. And her eyes—the flecks of gold in them shone brighter still.

"P-please," she begged, all breathy and needy. Her hips arched into my touch, grinding and needing friction. I brushed my fingers along her soaked folds, the thin material of her thong the only thing separating me from her pussy.

As River trailed his mouth along the back of her neck, and lower, she clutched my shoulders, her fingers curling into my biceps.

I brought my mouth to her chest, my fingers still teasing her entrance. Her moans filled the space.

Her delicate fingers pushed into my hair and gripped it as I dropped kisses along her décolleté. I savored the taste of her, the scent of apples swirling in my nose and making my cock throb. She was intoxicating.

I pushed her panties aside and my fingers brushed along her folds, finding her clit.

"Byron, ohhh—"

I roamed my lips over her neck, kissing the hollow of her throat. Licking her. Nipping her. Out of the corner of my eye, I saw River's hand wrapped around her red strands and his mouth kissing the edge of her bare shoulders, his hand grazing her arm slowly, up and down.

She writhed. She moaned. She panted.

In previous times, River was always the one to make sure the women we brought into our bed felt cherished, heightening their pleasure with his touch, his whispered words. I was always a fuck-them-and-leave-them kind of man.

With Odette, I wanted to give her pleasure, whisper sweet nothings, and give her my all. Fuck her, but never leave her. She was that addictive to me. I couldn't even pinpoint what it was about her that pulled me in so quickly. I had thought it could be her beauty, but it was also the fact that she didn't cringe away from my scarred back, and the fact she had a backbone and told me off without a second thought. I wasn't sure, but I knew I wanted her unlike any other woman before.

My fingers circled her clit. She shivered, her little whimpers telling me she liked it. Her body writhed back and forth between River and me, but she kept her eyes on me. Always on me. As if it was just the two of us.

The palm of my hand ground against her pubic bone until her breathing hardened.

"More," she demanded, and that one word just about had me exploding in my pants.

I thrust my fingers inside her pussy at the same time I took her mouth, my tongue exploring, swallowing her gasp. I wanted to devour every sound she made and keep them as mine.

It was the first hint of my addiction.

Chapter 7
Odette

Sensations collided inside of me. Like a tornado.

I wanted more. Bring. It. On.

I never knew that pleasure could feel this way. No wonder my sister was up for anything. This was exhilarating. Exquisite. Intoxicating.

Their hands were all over me. River's mouth on the back of my neck had my body trembling. His hands roaming my back and my ass made me feel alive and sensual. I felt ravenous, greedy, needing more of their touch and lips everywhere. Every kiss felt like the strike of a match, sparking every cell in me to life. A tremble rocked me as two men touched me. Kissed me. Consumed me.

And Byron. Holy fucking hell. There was no chance I'd ever forget his name now.

His gaze met mine. Blue. Like a darkening sky. A flicker of possession—possibly obsessive madness—flared in his gaze. And God help me, I liked it. The deep, rough noise thrummed between my legs, and my eyes grew half-lidded as Byron's grip on me tightened.

This man was *addictive*.

He pressed his front to mine, all hard muscle and strength. My breasts burned under the heat of his body. My nipples hardened. Sparks lit beneath my skin, sizzling from the hyperstimulation of two men. Byron's heart beat hard against my chest—in perfect rhythm with mine—and my foolish heart found it so romantic.

My lips sought his, craving the taste of him. I craved his hands all over me. On every inch of my skin. I was ravenous for everything and anything he'd give me.

He broke the kiss.

"Everything you want," Byron said, his voice making my blood hotter.

"Anything you want," River murmured.

Both of them pressed harder against me—one behind me, one in front of me—crowding me. Adrenaline pumped through my veins. I was getting drunk from this feeling.

My dress rucked up around my waist, River's hands were on my bare ass, gripping and squeezing. Byron's fingers worked inside me, my walls clenching around them. I was close. Months of no sex finally catching up.

Byron's hard cock ground against me, and by the feel of it, he was huge. With a capital H. He consumed my mouth, hungry and demanding. Possessive. Everywhere he touched me made me burn.

As Byron claimed my lips, crushing his mouth against mine, River skimmed his lips along my neck, kissing me sensually and sliding his nose along my skin, inhaling deeply.

Byron stroked my clit faster and harder. His fingers plunged deeper into my pussy. My knees quaked. I was trembling, the only thing keeping me upright was the support from River's roaming hands. My sex ached for more. More of Byron. More of this sensation. More of this pleasure.

My desire burned hotter. Pleasure coiled tighter. Byron fucked me with his fingers, relentlessly as he devoured my mouth. Then he crooked his digits, hitting that spot inside me.

Ecstasy slammed into me, washing my mind of any reason or

thought. White-hot pleasure crashed through me. River's mouth never stopped trailing kisses, nipping and licking, over the back of my neck and down my bare back, while Byron swallowed my moans, owning them greedily.

It was just me and the two men, alone in the world. It was the best orgasm of my life.

Then I rocked against Byron's hand, eager for another round. "Not so fast," he grunted, pulling out his fingers and bringing them to his lips, sucking them clean.

Jesus Christ.

The ache between my legs came back full force. Throbbing. I felt empty. I needed him. Maybe both of them, together.

"You smell like apples," River whispered behind me. I looked at him over my shoulder, meeting his lustful eyes for the first time since we entered the elevator. Fuck, he was hot. Byron was sex on legs, but this guy could make you melt. "I bet your pussy tastes like apples too." He grinned mischievously. His eyes darted to Byron for barely a second, before a smug expression passed his face. "I want to lick every inch of you, kiss you, eat you."

Byron growled. He *actually* growled, and my eyes snapped back to him.

A soft chuckle came from behind me, but I kept my focus on Byron.

Was he—

No, it couldn't be. We didn't even know each other.

I raised my eyebrow as Byron's mouth came crashing down against mine in a bruising kiss, consuming me hard. "Nobody is taking your pussy but me," he grunted against my lips. His hand found its way back underneath my dress, thrusting his fingers inside my drenched pussy.

"Mine."

Oh. My. God. Byron *was* jealous! And if River's chuckle was any indication, he knew it.

Except, I kind of liked it. His jealousy. His possessiveness.

Byron's fingers still inside me, thrusting in and out, I rocked against him while watching him under my lashes.

"I thought you've done this before," I breathed, my heart hammering against my ribs. I could feel another orgasm creeping up my spine.

"I have." I raised my eyebrow. "I just don't want to share *you*."

His admission sent a coil of satisfaction through me. Hot and heavy.

"What will River do while *you* eat my pussy?" I didn't think I had it in me. Filthy words. Even filthier, sinful deeds. And I fucking liked it. I suspected it had everything to do with this man in front of me.

Byron Ashford could deliver. And without an ounce of doubt, I knew he *would* deliver the ultimate pleasure.

He spun me around, away from River, and pushed my back against the wall. Then, he fell down to his knees.

"He can watch." Byron's voice was dark. Possessive. So fucking threatening that I feared if River even tried to kiss me now, there'd be hell to pay.

This ménage à trois had barely gotten started, and as fun as it was—while it lasted—I fully anticipated a night with Byron would supersede my wildest fantasies, without another man in the picture.

So. Goddamn. Delicious. And thrilling.

As riveting as it was to have two men, I'd prefer only Byron. I couldn't pinpoint why. I felt this unspeakable connection to him. Maybe it was the hint of loneliness I'd detected in his eyes. Or maybe it was that possessive look in his blue electric gaze that had me intrigued. For some reason, I wanted to explore it and see where it took us. Just the two of us.

Albeit, they worked well in sync and pleasure from both their mouths and hands was hotter than I knew what to do with. Byron was more than enough for me, and I wanted all my attention on him. I'd never let Byron know that I preferred only him, though. He was cocky enough already.

So I looked at River. Maybe it would be better for him to watch. It hit me in a rush. The idea thrilled me, making me all hot and bothered. It would seem I was into way more than just vanilla sex.

"Do you want—" My voice was breathless, the idea of asking him doubled the pace of my heart, making me feel hot and edgy.

I never got to finish my question because Byron yanked down my panties, the sound of material shredding filling the space. His strong fingers wrapped around my ankle, hooking my thigh over his shoulder until his head was between my legs.

He growled against my folds, like he'd found his personal heaven. My head fell back against the wall and my eyes fluttered shut, River forgotten.

His tongue flicked against my wet center. He ate my pussy with abandon, my hips grinding against his head. He was relentless.

Licking me. Devouring me. Consuming me.

My eyelids peeled open to find River watching—leaning against the elevator door with his arms folded casually—as his inflamed gaze roamed my body. For a fraction of a second, our gazes connected, something in his eyes telling me I was already his friend's. Yes, River wanted me, but there wasn't that same obsessive madness in River's gaze like there was in Byron's.

My eyes lowered to the magnificent man on his knees. This would forever be ingrained in my memory as the hottest night of my life. With Byron Ashford—the man who was hotter than Satan himself.

The way he already knew how to make my body unravel. He nipped at my clit, and I brought my hands to his head, my fingers entangling through his hair. I held on to his hair as I fucked his face, moaning and panting.

"Byron," I screamed. "O-oh—"

I pushed on his head, needing some space. My pussy was too sensitive from the last orgasm. It was too much. Not enough. He refused any space between us. He laved and licked, relentless and eager. So fucking eager.

My hips bucked against his mouth. Pleasure coiled. It twisted like the most exquisite agony, until a wave slammed into me.

Byron thrust his tongue inside my entrance, his thumb rubbing my clit as white-hot pleasure spiraled in me. Knowing River was standing by, watching, heightened everything. My heart drummed in my ears, racing so hard that I couldn't catch my breath. River's heavy gaze caressed my skin, but all my attention was on the man on his knees.

Pleasure overwhelmed every fiber of my body, blazing through my veins. It flooded every cell. It sent shudders through me.

"Should have known you'd taste perfect," Byron murmured and my heart warmed. His hands came around to my ass, caressing it and grabbing a handful. A shiver shot up my spine, ready for anything else he would dish my way.

My entire body was so attuned to him, I could feel his gaze on me. I peeled my eyelids open, watching him through heavy eyelids. He looked like a king even down on his knees.

"I guess I lost," I murmured, smiling softly. When he gave me a questioning look, I added, "I screamed your name first."

He rose to his feet. It didn't escape me how he blocked the view of my pussy and legs from his friend. Jesus, it felt selfish to have had so much pleasure while all River could do was watch, although by the looks of it, he didn't mind.

I met his eyes again when he shot me a devilish grin. "I'm out of here," he said, pushing the button that got the elevator moving again.

Ding.

"Night, lovebirds." And like a phantom, River was gone.

Probably with a serious case of blue balls.

Chapter 8
Odette

We barely made it out of the elevator when Byron's hands cupped my ass and his mouth took mine. My legs wrapped around his waist before he slammed us both against the wall. His mouth ravaged my neck hungrily, almost as if he wanted to erase all traces of River.

I had just orgasmed—twice—and the way he touched me, kissed me, had me trembling for another one.

This chemistry was mind-blowing. Unbelievable. Yet, there it was. Swirling between us. Consuming us. If someone had told me earlier today this was how my night would go, I wouldn't have believed them.

It felt so damn right. So natural.

In my opinion—which, in truth, could be totally skewed from my extended abstinence—he was worth every sin. Every dark pleasure.

I knew I'd never get the opportunity to be with a man like him again. Right after spring break, I'd be back at Stanford. Medical school was intense. I wanted to become a surgeon, then do a few years with the UN in Africa. These goals were as real to me as my own name, but for the moment, nothing existed but this man.

He nipped my collarbone, sucking on the sensitive flesh where my neck and shoulder met.

"Door," I panted, tilting my head to the side. His mouth on me was heaven. His hands felt even better.

Byron produced a key out of somewhere and swept it over the fob. We stumbled into the room, and he threw me onto the bed, a dark, possessive look raking over my body. I was still wearing my dress, but I might as well have been naked.

We stared at each other, both of us panting, while the air between us crackled with so much electricity I feared an explosion.

"Second thoughts?" I whispered.

He raised his eyebrows, his chest rising and falling in sync with mine.

"Fuck no."

He pulled his shirt over his shoulders, and my breath caught. Just like it had when he took his shirt off in the exam room. He had such a gorgeous chest—broad, muscular—with olive skin. And those abs.

I trailed my eyes over a smattering of hair that ran from his navel and disappeared into his jeans. It had my pussy screaming for him. So achy with need.

I licked my lips, my eyes soaking him in. "Are you going to take your jeans off?"

His dark hair made his eyes appear a brilliant blue—the power behind them commanding me. Something about this man brought out a side of me I didn't know existed. Or maybe I was just waiting for him all along.

In one swift move—his eyes locked on mine—he unzipped his pants, discarding the jeans. Of *course* he went commando. His cock sprung free. Hard. Smooth. And so big that it had my eyes widening and my pussy throbbing.

This chemistry between us was raw and all-consuming. There

was no mistaking who was in charge here. He was all male and pure dominance. Possessive and dangerous.

I allowed it. In fact, I needed it.

He began to stroke himself, slowly, his gaze never wavering. My mouth fell open. My heart raced in my chest, beating in overdrive.

Oh. My. God.

Seeing him touch himself was so fucking hot. Pleasure rippled down my spine. Arousal trickled between my thighs, and shamelessly, I let my legs fall open, letting him see what he did to me.

His blue eyes darkened to almost black pools. The muscles in his shoulders and arms flexed as he jerked himself—hard and fast. My chest rose and fell, the buzzing in my ears increasing. Fuck, I wanted him inside me. This man was what fantasies were made of. Porn had nothing on the vision of this man jacking off. It was hot... erotic.

His eyes locked on mine, and his jaw clenched. "Lose the dress," he murmured darkly. "I need you naked."

My sex clenched. My blood hummed with lust. He didn't have to ask twice. Kicking off my sandals, I reached for the hem of my dress and pulled it over my head. It had a built-in bra, and since he'd ripped my panties off earlier, I was completely bare in seconds.

Naked and kneeling on the large bed, I waited for his next command. This was his territory, and I was desperate to please him.

"Get over here and suck my cock, Madeline." His voice was pure sin. Dark. Raspy. Demanding.

I scurried off the bed and down to my knees, desperate to taste him.

I took him in my mouth, my hand fisting him up and down. He tasted so freaking good. Salty. Musky.

"Look at me when I'm fucking your mouth," he growled.

Lifting my chin slightly, I could see him watching me through hooded eyes. I could feel the heat of it on every inch of my skin.

He thrust in and out of my mouth, hitting the back of my throat.

"Fuck... your mouth is heaven," he grunted.

My orgasm inched closer, tasting his precum. He tipped his head back to the ceiling and closed his eyes for a moment, before he pulled out of my mouth with a soft pop.

I wiped my mouth with the back of my hand. "What happened?" I asked frowning. Maybe my blowjob skills were lacking. The familiar self-consciousness returned, crawling up my spine.

"First time I come, it will be in your pussy," he growled with urgency. "Get on the bed."

Oh.

He didn't wait for my answer. Instead, he pulled me off the floor, leaving me standing naked in front of him. His eyes dropped down my body—slowly and lazily—drinking me in as he skimmed over my skin.

"You're so fucking beautiful."

His eyes met mine again, blazing with desire. An undercurrent of darkness and passion ran between us, and my earlier worries about being enough flew out the window. His mouth took mine, his tongue sliding between my open lips, sucking on my tongue.

My knees buckled and his hands came to my waist, holding me up.

"Are you afraid?"

I shook my head. I was so turned on, I feared another orgasm would slam into me before he was even inside me.

"Then what is it, Odette?" The expression on his face told me he was used to getting what he wanted. Whether that be answers. Or business deals. Or me.

"I thought you were going to call me Madeline," I noted saucily.

"When you're a bad girl, I'll call you Odette." I shook my head, but my lips curved into a smile. "Now tell me what's the matter."

My cheeks heated and I squirmed, wrapping my arms around his body and burying my face into his hard chest. "It's been a while since I've had sex, and I've only been with one man. You've probably had many women. I might embarrass myself."

He cupped my cheek and made me look at him. "I'll make you feel good. That's all I want. No embarrassment. No shame. Understood?"

A choked laugh escaped me. "Far cry from a ménage à trois, huh?"

He scooped me up and laid me down on the bed. "Fuck your ménage à trois. You're mine. Understood?"

"Yes," I breathed.

He spread my legs and smiled darkly as he kissed my ankle, then skimmed his way up my inner thighs. My knees fell open, widening, leaving me completely open for him. His face lingered over my pussy, inhaling deeply. His eyes closed, bliss crossing his face.

"You taste just the way you smell," he murmured darkly. "Like apples. All mine."

The air crackled between us. My erratic breathing filled the space and my body quivered from the sound of his voice and the look in his eyes. This man was a god, but with the way he watched me, you'd think I was a goddess.

He leaned in and kissed me, his tongue stroking every corner of my mouth. My legs parted wider, and I felt his hard cock pressing against my hot entrance. The head of his cock dipped into me, barely the tip. My hips arched, my pussy clenching to feel him inside me.

My head fell against the pillows and my eyes rolled into the back of my head.

"God, that feels so good," I rasped, opening my eyes to find his gaze locked to where our bodies almost joined. The fire in his gaze was enough to turn us both to ash. He slid in deeper and deeper, and we both groaned at the sensation.

"You're so tight."

"You're so big," I whimpered. He brought his hand to my breast and cupped it before pulling almost completely out, only to thrust back in. "Ohhh—" He thrust again. This time, he plunged deeper and harder, filling me.

Both of our mouths fell open. I could feel his throbbing shaft so deep inside me, making my insides tremble.

"So fucking good," he ground out, thrusting in again. In and out. In and out. My eyes rolled back in my head, my spine arching off the bed.

I froze. "Byron," I said, panic lacing my voice. He stilled, his eyes finding mine, worry in his blue gaze. "Condom."

He blinked, then blinked again. "Fuck." He shook his head as if to clear the fog in his brain. The very same one that filled every part of me. "I never forget," he muttered, almost as if he were speaking to himself. Then his gaze found mine—filled with something soft and dark—followed by his lips. The kiss was soft, without any reservations. Lazy and sweet. Like I was already his. He pulled away, barely an inch, with a long, deep lick. "I'm sorry, baby. I'm clean."

I swallowed, my heart warming up in an unusual way for a man I'd just met. Yet, it felt right. Like he was the one. It felt like just the way Dad described his love for Mom.

"I forgot myself too," I murmured. No sense in beating ourselves up. He hadn't finished inside me. "I'm clean too. I got checked after—"

He cut me off with a kiss. "I trust you."

Funny thing was... I trusted him too. "Please tell me you have a condom," I choked out, my voice a needy whimper.

He slid out of me, cum—or maybe my juices—smeared all over his cock. I ached for him to be inside me already. He got up and grabbed his wallet, pulled a condom out, then threw it back on the nightstand. He handed it to me.

"Put it on me."

I licked my lips, my heart beating so hard I feared it'd crack my ribs. The crackle of the foil filled the room as I opened the package.

I sat up, leaning over kissing him softly as I rolled the condom on. Then I pushed him onto his back and straddled his large body.

He pulled me closer, dragging my face to his. His blues captivated me, tempting me. Just a look into his eyes and I could get lost forever.

"You want to fuck me?" His mouth brushed against mine.

"You have no idea how much," I repeated, his earlier words echoing around us.

"Then fuck me." He smirked, giving me a slow, sexy smile. "I'll fuck you when you're warmed up."

I smiled against his mouth. "Promise?"

"On my honor." He slapped my ass lightly. "Now ride my cock, Madeline."

It'd seem I was back to being a good girl since he called me Madeline. He took my mouth in a desperate kiss. His big hands grabbed my hips, and I could feel his cock at my entrance. He guided me down, his thick cock filling me up, then without a warning slammed me the rest of the way.

"Ohhhh." My eyes rolled back in my head, my pulse throbbing.

Our eyes locked as he moved me up and down, and I could feel every single inch of him. His thick shaft swelling inside me. His eyes hooded as he looked up at me like I was the most beautiful woman he had ever seen.

"You feel so good inside me," I whispered, leaning forward to kiss him. Kissing him was enough to get me off. Better than the sex I'd experienced with my ex.

My hips rolled. Our tongues danced, swirling against each other. A light moan traveled up my throat. Desperation ate away at me, burning and clawing at my insides. I needed all of him.

My breathing grew ragged, my breasts bouncing as he picked me up by the hip bones and slammed me back down on his cock. Hot pleasure built inside me as his pelvis ground against my sensitive flesh. My movements grew more frantic with every thrust. I rode him hard.

He hissed, his eyes fixed on where we were connected. With heavy breaths, both of us watched him fuck me. Something about watching his cock slide in and out of me had my pleasure twisting tighter and tighter, overwhelming my senses.

His strong fingers dug into my hips, lifting me off him and then slamming me back down onto his thick, long cock. He fucked me deep and hard, and I fucked him just as hard in return. I wasn't sure where he ended and I began.

His hand came to my throat, pulling me down to take my mouth for a consuming kiss. My breasts rubbed against his hard chest. Everywhere our bodies touched, friction sizzled. My skin burned.

"Harder," I moaned. "Fuck, I need it harder."

His grip tightened as he pumped into me at a piston pace. I might have been on top, but he held all the control.

"Come for me, baby."

The orgasm hit me hard, shooting stars behind my eyes and stealing the breath from my lungs. My nails dug into his biceps, and I bit down where his shoulder met his neck. I convulsed around his thick shaft, my insides clenching around him like he was my lifeline.

I felt his cock jerk as he came with a rough noise. We panted as we clung to each other, my body on top of his, slick with sweat while our hearts raced wildly in tandem.

"Holy shit," I breathed, my mind mush. We lay there, our breaths heavy in the sudden quiet that followed. Oh my gosh, what had I done? I was the good sister—the reliable one. The lust-fueled fog slowly cleared and reality swarmed my thoughts.

I'd had a naughty moment in the elevator with two men and then sex with a complete—drop-dead gorgeous, but still—stranger. But it was a toe-curling, *amazing* experience. Was it wrong though?

"Are you all right?" Byron's muscles turned rigid. "Did I hurt you?"

I shook my head. "No, no. I just..." I buried my face in his neck. "Might be a bit embarrassed."

"You have nothing to be embarrassed about," he grumbled. "You were—are—perfect."

Even with me on top of him, he held all the control. I liked that, more than willing to give him control for my pleasure.

Heat instantly flared in my body, blooming low in my stomach at his hard, sculpted body molding against my soft one. He radiated heat from every single inch of his body and his comment rushed to the front of my mind. *He runs hotter than normal.*

Then I remembered. *His back.* "Is your back okay?" I asked, concerned and ready to shift away so it wasn't rubbing against the sheets. He turned us over so we were side by side, facing each other.

"My back and my dick have never been better," he said casually, discarding his condom.

A choked laugh escaped me, and I let myself relax and enjoy the moment. Inhaling deeply, I soaked in the masculine scent of him—citrus and sandalwood. Finally... I finally understood the expression *la petite mort.* The little death. It had never been like this. Never. Until tonight.

I pushed a lock of hair behind my ear, feeling self-conscious. Silence hummed between us and Byron stared at me with an intensity that burrowed beneath my skin.

"You are beautiful." The gentleness of his voice surprised me, but I loved it. It settled over my skin like a warm breeze. But I loved his hands rubbing over me even more.

I met his heavy-lidded eyes filled with desire. My hands rested against his chest, my fingers tapping lightly against his muscles. "So are you," I murmured.

His mouth twitched. "Compared to you, I'm a scarred old man."

"Well, old man," I teased, roaming my hands down his chest

and over his sculpted abs. "I respectfully disagree. I think all of you —including your scars—are perfect and beautiful."

He continued rubbing me with soft strokes, our breathing returning to normal. "This old man is ready to show you round two. Do you think you can handle it?"

Suddenly, Pierre was a distant memory. His words diminishing me, calling me vanilla, no longer mattered because I just had the most exuberant experience with this man. And we weren't done.

"Bring it on," I rasped, feeling excitement bubble inside me as my thighs throbbed with anticipation.

"This man will keep you up all night," he rasped, his mouth skimming over my skin. "Because you're mine."

He followed through with his promise.

But he lied. I wasn't his, and he'd never be mine.

Because when morning came, I woke up to a cold reality and a matching set of cold blue eyes.

Chapter 9
Odette

I sat up abruptly, covering my naked body with the sheet.

A man who looked like an older version of Byron sat casually in the chair, smoking a cigar at... my eyes darted to the clock... freaking ten in the morning.

"Who are you?" My hair whipped back and forth as I searched for Byron. I fought the urge to bring the sheet up to my chin, hiding myself. Why was this guy here?

His gaze evaluated me from top to bottom. I did the same.

His gray five-piece suit molded to the man perfectly. An air of ruthlessness swirled around him, his top lip curled in disgust. Along with a patriarchal nose and high cheekbones, the guy looked to be in good shape. And attractive, for his age. But it was the look in his eyes that set me on edge. His hair didn't contain a single thread of silver, but it was clear he had to be at least in his sixties. It was perfectly styled, not a strand out of place.

"Again, who the fuck are you?" I hissed. "And what are you doing in my room?"

"This is my room." The tone of his voice clearly portrayed I didn't deserve a sliver of his attention. "I'm Senator Ashford and you are in *my* room."

My brows furrowed, and I shook my head. "No, it's not."

His cobalt eyes flashed with irritation. "Yes, it is. Look at the bill on your nightstand and tell me what the name reads."

The anxiety shot through me. I scooted over, careful not to expose my naked body. A glimpse on the receipt stated *Ashford*.

I narrowed my eyes. "This doesn't mean anything. Byron's last name is Ashford too."

"And who do you think finances him?" he spat out.

My brows furrowed. That made no sense. There wasn't an ounce of Byron that screamed pampered. Arrogant, yes. Ruthless even. But not pampered.

Senator Ashford cleared his throat, narrowing his exacting gaze on me. His displeasure drifted through the air, permeating the room. Then, without warning, he stood up and I scooted backward, my back hitting the headboard of the hotel bed.

He reached into his pockets, pulling out a stack of bills and throwing them onto the bed.

"I'll pay for your services since clearly my son hasn't."

Oh, he did not— "I'm not a whore," I spat. "Who in the fuck do you think you are?"

He took three steps toward the bed and the air shifted. Tension was placid on my tongue.

"I'm Senator George Ashford, you insolent little girl." Splotches of red crawled up my neck, my cheeks burning hot. "You will get dressed and get lost. In case your puny little brain"—what the actual *fuck*—"gets any ideas about going to the press. If you give my eldest a hard time, I will squash your family. Understood?"

Maybe this guy was high. I mean, everyone knew that a lot of those American politicians used and abused drugs. *And power.*

"You might be a senator back in the States," I retorted coolly, feeling my anger simmering deep down in the pit of my stomach. "But you're nobody here."

He stared at me, devoid of any emotion. Except for the smile. Cruel. Vicious. Knowing.

"Did you expect him to propose?" *Huh?* I frowned. I was twenty-two. Marriage was hardly on my mind. It was one night—one incredible, amazing, fucking special night—and I knew better than to have any expectations. Maybe that we'd see each other for the next few days, but I hadn't let my imagination run beyond that. "My sons have higher aspirations than to connect with the likes of you. Our kind doesn't mix with yours."

No fucking idea what *that* meant.

My chest flared with anger. "What do you mean your 'kind' doesn't mix? You don't even know me."

His nostrils flared, annoyance clear. "You have nothing. No connections. No achievements. We are the Kennedys of our time."

Jesus, he really had a pompous attitude and way too high an opinion of himself.

"Listen, I don't give a shit what you think," I snapped. "Your son and I are adults, and we can do whatever we want."

Red washed his complexion while our gazes burned into each other's.

"Let me make this short and sweet. Byron doesn't exist for you and neither does his money." I frowned. Money? Then realization settled in. The bastard thought me a gold digger.

"I don't want nor need his money."

His jaw tightened. "But you want him."

Man, what was with this guy. "I'll be damned if I let you mess up my... our... plans."

I hesitated. "Plans?"

He took a single step and brushed off his sleeves. "My family is none of your business. You don't really think I'd give you ammunition to use against us." His eyes narrowed into slits. "Now, be a good little whore and give me a show. Let's see your tits and ass."

This man was out of his goddamn mind.

"Get the fuck out or I'm calling the police." My voice trembled slightly, but I held his eyes. "Try getting a glimpse of my ass or tits and it will be the last thing you see because I'll claw out your eyes."

He snickered, his eyes slithering over me. "You really are a spiteful little thing. I bet you are something else in bed. All fire."

My eyebrows shot to my hairline. "Excuse me?"

"You'll excuse yourself in a minute," he snarled. "But first, we're going to clear some things up."

My shoulders hardened and I sat up straight. "You need to learn some manners. I have nothing to say to you, and I don't want to hear what you have to say. So, pardon my French. But... Get. The. Fuck. Out."

His jaw was tight, but he only arched a brow.

"Are you sure you don't want to hear what I can do to your father?" Hyperawareness inched over my skin, coupled with a terrible feeling of dread. When I remained silent, he continued, "Yeah, I've looked you up, Odette Madeline Swan. I know all about your sister and your father's hospital. I can have the hospital shut down in two days." Tiny spiders crawled all over me as I registered his words. This man wasn't right. "I can have your father's legacy destroyed within the next twenty-four hours."

An incredulous laugh burst from my mouth, but I willed myself to stay calm. "Don't you dare threaten me."

Senator Ashford's eyes turned to frozen blue Arctic lakes. I shivered.

"You won't be getting in my way." There had to be a meaning behind his words, except I couldn't grasp it. "I have squashed greater obstacles than you. And you, my dear, I can make you disappear and your body never found."

I wanted to show backbone and fight him, I really did. But something about the menacing grimace on his face shot an alert through me. Suddenly, I wanted to fold up inside myself until I turned invisible. Or simply run.

Trying to appear brave, I let out a weak laugh and responded, "You're delusional."

"Then I'll have to prove it to you and make your father's hospital history," he decreed. "If you so much as try anything with my son and his fiancée—" I couldn't hear the rest of his words because my ears rang with fury. *Fiancée!* That motherfucker. Shame and rage filled me instantly, and had that fucker been here, I'd have strangled him and not lost any sleep over it. I hated cheaters, and I definitely never wanted to be the other woman. "She's from an accomplished family. And you, little whore, are just a side piece."

My jaw fell open, and the only reason it didn't audibly thump against the floor was because I was still on the bed.

"You're mad," I rasped. "Crazy." Why would he do all this just because I hooked up with his son? His thirty-four-year-old son, at that. Something was just plain wrong here, or maybe this family was just fucked up.

He pulled out a phone, and I watched as his fingers darted across the screen. "One wrong move and I'll have your father in the unemployment line. Piss me off more and I'll make your father and sister pay."

A void opened in my chest. Last night, I had magic. A dream. This morning, I was in a nightmare.

"Good, I finally made my point." He bent forward, grabbing a handful of clothes—uncaring if they were mine or not—and threw them at my chest. "Get dressed, then get out. If you ever come near my family again, your father will be the first one to pay."

He didn't bother turning his back, nor did he leave the room. His eyes pierced through me, challenging me to say something else. I knew he wouldn't give me the respect of privacy, so I knew there was no sense in asking.

God, this had to be what a walk of shame felt like. I never thought I'd experience it. And that fucker Byron let his daddy do his dirty work. He hadn't seemed like the type at all.

Jesus fucking Christ. I certainly picked winners.

"Trust me, you have nothing I haven't seen before." There was no warmth in his tone, but his leering eyes didn't ease me. Pervert.

Keeping the covers tightly around me, I shifted off the bed and padded to the bathroom, the long sheet trailing behind me. The moment I shut the door, I locked it. Without wasting any time, I dressed.

I thought last night was amazing. Incredible. Unique.

To wake up to something like this was a slap in the face. Flames bloomed in my chest. Anger buzzed in my ears.

The moment I was dressed, I yanked the door open. Senator Ashford was still in the same spot.

I stomped through the room toward the exit door. "Fuck you and your son, Senator Ashford," I snarled.

Then slammed the door behind me so hard the entire floor shook.

Chapter 10
Byron

Carrying two cups of coffee from the coffee shop locals craved about, I strode back to the hotel. The day started fucking amazing. I hadn't felt so relaxed in a very long time. My cell phone was switched off, and I wouldn't mind leaving it off. Permanently.

Fuck it, maybe I'd even entertain an early retirement. We had plenty of money, enough to last us several lifetimes.

Grinning like a young fool, I opened the door of the hotel room and my steps faltered as my eyes traveled over the space. The bed was empty, sheets crumpled, and the scent of crisp apples lingered in the air. But there was also a strong air-freshener scent.

"Odette?" My voice bounced off the walls, but no reply came.

I prowled through the room and made my way into the bathroom. Empty. But her scent was everywhere in the room and the bathroom, drowning my senses. I wanted her again. I wanted to kiss her, fuck her, laugh with her. And she was nowhere to be found. Almost as if she was never here. Except for her Hermès scarf that lay discarded on the carpet.

Why did she leave? My eyes darted to the clock. She told me

she had an afternoon shift today, but maybe there was an emergency and she had to cover for someone.

Just as I was about to resolve to go to the hospital and see her, a knock on the door sounded. My heart made a weird flip. I strode out of the bathroom expecting to see Odette and instead came face-to-face with my father.

"Byron." There was a smugness about him and my annoyance flared.

"What are you doing here?" The words flew out of my mouth. I didn't want to see him right now. I could go without seeing him for a century and not miss him.

He shot me that familiar cold glare that I grew up with. He excelled at making everyone around him—especially my mother, when she was alive—feel worthless. Except, the tables had turned. My mother bested him. All her fortune was tied to her children, and now, it was us who were his superiors. Without us, he'd be easily bankrupt.

He made his way to the love-seat, which only hours ago, I had fucked Odette bent over it. He flopped his ass on it, and I wanted to bark at him to get the fuck away from it.

Crossing his legs, he said, "I want to know why you sent Nicki away."

I made my way to the desk and leaned against it, watching my father. He seemed nervous, sweating like a pig.

"I didn't invite her," I deadpanned. "So I sent her packing."

He waved like it was nothing. "You two are going to get married and—"

I narrowed my eyes on my father. "I will *never* marry her."

"She's from good stock," he started, like he was talking about a cow. Although when it came to Nicki, the comparison wasn't far off. "Her family has connections and wealth."

I cocked my eyebrow. "Then why don't you marry her."

He chuckled like I had just uttered the funniest joke. I was dead serious. "It crossed my mind, but she wants you."

A grim smirk slashed my face. "Well, she won't have me. So you can tell her you're the next best thing."

Despair entered Father's expression. "Byron, you have to listen to me. I—"

"Let me cut you off right there, Father." His spine stiffened. He hated being interrupted. "I don't have to listen to anything you have to say. I'm a grown-ass man. I make my own money. Run my own company. Have my own fortune. So why don't you cut the bullshit and tell me why you're really here."

Our wills battled. Our gazes locked, anger and so many unspoken words sizzling through the air. It didn't matter. He'd lose; I'd win. I'd been winning for the better part of the last two decades.

He spoke first. "I owe her father two and a half million dollars."

I let out a sardonic breath, shaking my head in disgust. I wished it was in disbelief, but we had been here way too many times before. He didn't see family when he looked at me. He only saw dollar signs.

"Is that all, huh?" I asked, sarcastically.

"It's pocket change to you," he sputtered angrily. I'd disagree with that assumption. Yes, I had plenty of money, but none of it was pocket change. I worked for it. My brothers worked for it. So did my baby sister. Regardless of our mother's inheritance. My father, on the other hand, just liked to grease palms and pretend to be a hardworking man of the people.

"And dare I ask why you owe him so much money?"

He shrugged. "There was a charity gambling event."

My brows shot up. Father didn't believe in charity. He only believed in self-serving causes. "And what might that charity cause be?"

He cackled like some old woman. "A few whores can retire early."

"One day, all this shit will catch up to you," I hissed. Father was a spoiled, entitled prick. That was all it boiled down to. "And who was there?"

"Nobody." He answered so quickly, I had no doubt he was lying.

"This is the last time I'll ask, Father. Who was there? I want names, ages. Fucking everything."

I got the low-down. All the dirty, fucked-up details.

My jaw clenched as I listened to him tell me about the rendezvous these old men had had with high-end escorts-slash-hookers for the past month. And how my father's tab was settled by his "prestigious" fellow friend—Nicki's father.

Twenty minutes later, I sent my father packing with a promise to settle his debt, if only to keep my name out of the mud alongside his.

Now, I'd settle my own affairs, go back to the yacht, then go after the woman that had me feeling things I never felt before.

Chapter 11
Odette

By the time I arrived at the hospital—three hours later—the tension was so strong, it overwhelmed all my senses. In a daze, I went home, took a shower, forced myself to down a cup of coffee, and finally went to the hospital for my shift.

As I rushed toward my father's office, I caught glances of the other doctors and nurses. I couldn't decide if it was all in my head. I hated to admit it, but Senator Ashford—the fucker—managed to unsettle me.

There was no chance in hell he could do the things he threatened me with. He probably just wanted to get his way, and just like the rest of the world's stuck-up and entitled pricks, he exercised his connections and power to make me feel small and insignificant.

I finally arrived at my father's office just as three men in dark suits were making their way out. They didn't spare me a glance. In my Lululemon leggings and plain white top, I looked like a nobody. I preferred to wear minimal but comfortable clothes under my white uniform.

Pushing the door open, I froze halfway through. My father held his head in his hands, hunched over his desk, looking just the way he did the day we learned Maman died.

Billie! Oh my gosh, Billie.

"Dad?" I whispered softly. He raised his head and glanced at me. He looked like he'd been choked half to death. "What happened?"

My father watched me, desperation in his eyes spreading like spilled red wine. Unease slithered through me, the words of Senator Ashford echoing in my brain.

"Sit down, Odette."

My feet moved independent of my mind. I felt like I was in a fog as I sat down in the chair across from him, heart in my throat.

Did I bring disaster to my family?

"What's going on?"

"We have to let the hospital go," he said. I watched his mouth move. I heard the words. Yet for some reason, my brain refused to process them.

"I—I don't understand."

My father's parents left him this building and the hospital when they died. It belonged to him—to us. There was no way he was saying what I thought he was saying.

"The bank's taking the building," he said. "The hospital. Everything." Shock inched over my skin, coupled with a terrible feeling of dread. It drummed to the rhythm of my heart, preparing me—our entire family—for the impending doom of a guillotine.

He pushed his hand through his thick hair. "When your mother was alive, I made some bad business decisions. I had to mortgage off the hospital for capital to push the business forward. Your mom's modeling income helped to pay interest on the loans, but then she—"

But then she died. More than a decade, and my father still choked up talking about her.

"What about our house?" My heart raced as I attempted to

come up with options and save us. Senator Ashford threatened this exact thing only hours ago. How could it be happening already?

Father shook his head. "That house is not worth enough to pull us through. I don't want to touch that. It's for you and Billie. Your security."

I swallowed. My father's eyes locked with mine. Utter silence enveloped us, and each breath I pulled in crippled me another notch. The panic swam through my veins, drowning in my eyes. No amount of practice would allow me to hide it.

We didn't have much, but we were comfortable. Always. It was our father who'd made it possible, yet now, I wondered how many sacrifices he made.

"What if I quit med school?" I suggested. "I could work here with you for free until we get the hospital back on its feet."

Dad shook his head. "It's too late, ma fille." He let out a heavy sigh. "The debt has already been bought by developers. The bank didn't want to risk not getting paid and was more than happy to sell the property and the building."

"W-what do you mean?" We never had to worry about money before.

"I missed the last four months' worth of payments, ma chérie. I've always struggled with running the business side of the hospital."

His admission was laced with shame and regret. I closed the distance to my dad and fell down to my knees, wrapping my hands around his knees.

"I'm sorry, Daddy." His hand came to rest on my head, his touch soft and comforting.

"No, no, no," he murmured, his voice tired. "I'm sorry. It's my job to take care of you girls."

He had given us everything, and I couldn't help him, couldn't save him. The broken look he gave me tore my heart right down the middle. Our entire world was crumbling.

And it was all my fault.

Chapter 12
Byron

Seeing my father put me in a sour mood. I'd be okay going years without seeing my old man.

No such luck for me.

Talk about a mood and erection buster. And the morning started off magnificently. If only he didn't show up. Talk about bad luck—that was all he brought to all of his children. Misery and bad luck. The sick fucker had actually booked a room on the same floor as me. Needless to say, I vacated the fucking hotel and went back to my yacht. He couldn't follow me there.

I should have known he was here for money. He always needed more funds, mainly to support his habit of high-end whores. He wanted to grease more palms. Well, the fucker would have to do it on his own going forward. I was done with it.

He received a monthly allowance. He might even have to take lessons in budgeting 101. He was in the habit of spending money too quickly.

I had a business relationship with my father. All my mother's funds were left to her children. It was the best way the mafia princess could guarantee her children inherited her wealth. Father didn't even know about it until she was dead. I still remembered how green he turned when the will was read.

But that was neither here nor there. I had more important things to do. I'd taken a cab back to my yacht, since Winston must have helped himself to my car last night. After I settled some phone calls, I jumped into the red Ferrari and drove to the clinic where I knew Odette had the afternoon shift.

I pulled up expecting the same serene and welcoming feeling of The Swan Clinic from yesterday. Instead, I was met with chaos.

The long path along the shoreline that led to the hill where the hospital sat—a luxury castello once upon a time—was lined with vehicles. Ambulances. Private transportation. Buses.

Parking in front of the clinic, I exited the car and pulled the first person I found to the side.

"What's going on here?"

She shrugged. "Moving patients around."

Well, no shit. Clearly this woman wasn't as smart as my woman.

Deciding she wasn't worth questioning, I let her go and went in search of Odette. I focused on the best thing that happened to me. Aside from my siblings. *Odette Madeline Swan.* I couldn't help a smile that curved my lips. I smiled more with her than I had in a long time.

Turning the corner, I spotted her. Same crisp white uniform. Her hair pulled up in a ponytail. No makeup. She directed orders in French to nurses and some boys, speaking in a firm but soft voice. Her confidence was such a turn-on. It pulled everyone's attention to her. Including those boys who pretty much drooled, staring at her.

It was too bad the scrubs didn't resemble a nun's habit. They should.

"Monsieur?" A voice demanded my attention and I turned to find Dr. Swan next to me. "Ashford. Monsieur Ashford. What are you doing here? Is your back okay?"

The old doctor didn't seem as calm and put together as yesterday. His hair was ruffled, like he had pushed his hand through it way too many times. His glasses were crooked and the look in his eyes was off.

"Yes, all better," I assured him, my gaze flicking back to his daughter who now spotted me. "I was just hoping to have a word with your daughter."

Surprise washed over his expression. "With my Odette?"

No, she's my Odette. The protest was on the tip of my tongue, but I didn't think her father would take it well. I studied the doctor and something definitely seemed off about him. His hands trembled and his complexion was pale, almost yellowish.

I was just about to ask him if he was all right when I heard Odette's voice and the old Dr. Swan was forgotten.

"Monsieur Ashford, why are you here?" Okay, not exactly the greeting I was going for. I thought she'd throw herself into my arms, wrap her legs around me, and shove me into the broom closet so we could take advantage of each other. Buuuut... she probably wanted to appear professional. After all, her father was here. "Is it your back?"

I gave her a knowing smirk. Her nails had dug into my back, and fuck if the way she had clung to me didn't make me get a full-on erection right here. Goddamn it!

"Non," her father answered while I shifted to hide the bulge in my pants. I should have worn jeans. "He said he came to have a word with you."

"Oh."

Her eyes widened innocently in question and her expression clearly stated she was confused about what I could be here to talk to her about. So it was going to be like this, huh? Feigning ignorance.

"Can we talk in private?"

Odette stiffened and her lips thinned. I got the distinct feeling that she would rather chop her hand off than talk to me. Instead, her eyes darted to her father, then around us, and back to her father, until they finally came back to me. Jesus, what was it with her? We had the most incredible night of sex, and now she was acting like a cold stranger.

I had every intention of keeping her. We'd follow this through and see where it took us. For the first time, I wanted a serious relationship.

"Today's not a good day," she ended up answering in a clipped tone.

"It's important," I gritted, slightly annoyed. I wasn't accustomed to being denied. "I'm sure your father can spare you for a few minutes."

She opened her mouth, clearly ready to argue, when her father stopped her.

"You go ahead, Odette," he encouraged. "I'll handle this for a bit. You've been going nonstop for hours. You need a break."

"But—"

"Go on. Boss's order."

I grinned. It was clear Odette didn't like orders. Her eyes flashed golden before her shoulders slumped. It had to be a way Doctor Swan ensured his daughter understood he was in charge.

"Thank you, Doctor Swan." He nodded and left us. The moment he was out of earshot, I demanded, "Take us into your office."

Odette glared my way. Apparently, she didn't like it when I bossed her around either. "Or I could do what I intend here with an audience." Her spine stiffened. Something felt off about her, I just couldn't place it. "Lead the way."

She stomped—yes, stomped—her way toward the long hallway, opposite from where her father stood with other nurses speaking in urgent French. She stopped before jerking open the door of a room and my lips curled.

Exam room number 5.

It was where I met her yesterday.

The moment the door behind us shut with a soft click, she whirled around, letting me see the full wrath in her eyes. There was judgment and something else in them. Disgust.

It caused me to rear back. What the fuck happened? I'd been inside her only this morning. She moaned and writhed under me, demanding more and now... this?

My heart twisted in an unfamiliar way.

"What's your problem?" I demanded to know. It came out harsh, and I instantly regretted it. I meant to ask what was wrong and offer help, instead it sounded like an accusation.

Her lips thinned and she refused to meet my eyes. I wouldn't have it. I closed the distance between us, cornering her body. I cupped her face, forcing her eyes to meet mine.

"What's the matter?" I asked again.

"What can I do for you, Mr. Ashford?" The offer was cold—the question formal—but my dick didn't care. Not at all. Instead, it jumped at the opportunity to feel her pussy strangling my cock and to feel her soft lips on mine.

"Well, now that you mention it—" I skimmed my mouth over her jaw, the scent of apples like a bubble around us. It'd be impossible to ever see an apple again and not think of this woman. The moment my lips brushed against hers, a moan filled the room and sent heat to my groin.

"That's right, baby," I murmured against her lips. "Give me your all."

In the next second, her fists came to my chest and she pushed me away.

"What do you want, Byron?" she panted, her eyes hazy.

"I thought it was clear." I grabbed her by her nape. "I want you."

She turned her head to the side just as I readied to kiss her again. "You had me last night and this morning. Now be on your way."

I straightened, pulling away to look at her face. "What in the fuck is the matter with you?"

She snickered. "Un-fucking-believable." Odette could curse magnificently in English. In French, too, but she seemed to prefer to do it in English. Other than mixing in random French words here and there—like whipped cream—her English was impeccable.

I groaned inwardly. Why was I thinking about whipped cream? Oh yeah, the little minx smoothed it over my dick last night and then insisted on sucking it clean off me. Jesus H. Christ.

"You and me, baby, are un-fucking-believable. Now, tell me what your problem is so we can resolve it and move on to fucking."

She pushed me away—hard—but she barely managed to put another inch between us.

"What the fuck is wrong with you? Haven't you destroyed enough?" The raw, angry words sliced through the air. The hate in her eyes had me reeling and doing a double take. "Get lost, before you bring more shit to my door."

I frowned. What in the fuck was she talking about? She took advantage of the space between us and, to my surprise, was storming for the door.

I plowed after her and grabbed her wrist. "What the fuck, Odette?"

She yanked away her arm and hissed, "Let go of me."

"Did somebody bother you?" Idiots sometimes became obsessed with the Ashford name. They could have seen her with me and decided to harass her.

She shot me an icy glare, then let out a sardonic breath. "Yes, somebody bothered me. Just like you're bothering me now. Last night was fun." Ouch. I sensed a but coming. "But today's a new day, and I have realized my mistake. Now, if you'll excuse me, I have a shit ton of work to do."

"Then I'll wait and take you to dinner later." She blinked, and I thought maybe my English didn't come through well. "Like on a date," I added in French.

"I'm not dating you." She practically snarled the words.

"Why not?"

"Because touching you is a plague I can't survive." Another wave of anger crashed over me at her words.

Fuck, why did my hand shake? It never shook. I never lost my cool. Worry swarmed through me, building and building.

"Fine, then be my whore," I lashed out, my words calmer than my body. She fixed her eyes—full of fury like she was a woman scorned—on me, and I didn't like what lingered in them. "So I can get you out of my system."

"Hard pass. I have better men to whore myself to." Jealousy slithered through me. I never cared whether a woman stayed or went. Yet with her, I did. I wanted her to stay. I wanted her to want me with the same intensity as I felt. "Now get out." Her words were calm, detached, but her eyes drowned with anger. "Or I'll have you escorted out."

"I dare you," I hissed, pulling her back so we were nose to nose. "Have them escort me out and the entire hospital will know we slept together."

She was petite, barely pushing five foot four, but her personality made her my equal. It gave her another foot at least, letting her stand as tall as I was. The same attraction from yesterday sizzled, leaving me confused. Why was she fighting it?

Her eyes dropped to my lips, then flicked up, locking with my gaze.

"Goodbye, Mr. Ashford. Let's never cross paths again." Then, without a warning, she yanked her hand out of my grip and rushed through the door.

Touching you is a plague I can't survive.

The words pounded against my skull as she walked away from me, leaving me to stand with my heart in my throat. My chest twisted.

I stared at the door she disappeared through—for seconds, minutes, maybe hours—confused as fuck at what just happened.

Did I just get dumped by a woman for the first time in my life?

My pulse beat, hard and fast. Angry. So full of emotions that it suffocated me.

Rather than heading straight back to my yacht, I detoured to the liquor store and bought out the store, even though I had a fully stocked bar on my yacht. I got drunk on the second floor of my yacht, staring at the fish overboard. The ugly fish heads stared up at me, mocking my pitiful love affair, which also had to be the shortest love affair in history.

Sitting under the warm sun, I took a swig from the bottle of vodka, and for some dumb reason, I could almost hear her voice. *Stay out of the sun.*

So I took another gulp. And another. Until I could no longer hear her voice. The responsible older brother was gone. The head of the Ashford family had fallen so far, he might even supersede his father's shame.

Be my whore.

Fuck, did I really say that?

I deserved to go down in flames for being such a dick to her. She didn't deserve it. Except, I couldn't understand what happened for her to change so much? To be so cold and impersonal. So fucking angry.

Maybe someone hurt her? Fuck, was it me?

A violent shudder ran through me. *No, no, no.*

I tilted my head and downed the rest of the strong, insipid alcohol that was sure to give me a hell of a headache tomorrow. I didn't give a fuck. I wanted to wipe my mind clear. Forget everything. Last night. That damn hospital. Her. Everything. My whole fucking life.

Touching you is a plague I can't survive. I wanted to forget her words. I needed to forget *her*.

Pushing my hand through my hair, I tugged on the short strands.

"Fuck," I mumbled. Even that reminded me of her. The way

her delicate fingers clutched my hair as I ate her out. The way she moaned my name. Screamed it, even. I closed my eyes and let oblivion take over. Unfortunately, it only made matters worse. Images of Odette bending over the sofa and giving me a perfect view of her ass. The way she spread her thighs for me, moaning my name as I fucked her so hard that fucking sofa skidded over the floor.

Inhaling deeply, I craved her scent. Fuck, it was so addictive. Crisp apples and her. It would be impossible to mistake it for anyone else. Why couldn't I smell her anymore?

My eyes shot open and I rubbed them. The sun was setting. I must have passed out. My skin tingled. My muscles ached. Fucking great.

At this rate, I'd have to go back to the hospital for another shot. It wasn't a bad idea. At least I'd see her again. One more time.

My fucking God. When did I turn into such a wimp? I needed to get my shit together. My family depended on it.

"Byron?" Winston's baritone voice sent a piercing pain through my temples.

"I'm working," I growled, despite the fact it was obvious I wasn't. I didn't even have my phone on me. I pretty much hung off the edge of my boat.

"Clearly."

Today would surely rain pigs—or whatever the fuck the phrase was—because my brother was the sober one while I drowned my sorrows in poison. I felt nothing but emptiness inside me.

"What do you want, Winston?" I said monotonously. "I've had my fill of taking care of others. Now, let me be."

He lowered himself and sat down next to me. "At least you kept your shirt on so your back didn't burn again."

I reached for another bottle and unscrewed it. I attempted to read the label but ultimately gave up. It didn't matter. Tonight, I wanted to kill my liver. Damage it so it'd hurt more than this fucking thing in my chest.

I took a swig, then wiped my mouth with the back of my hand. "Nothing beats a French brand of vodka." I offered the bottle to my brother. He shook his head. "I'm good. I'll keep an eye on you tonight."

"No need. I'm perfectly fine," I said blandly. *Touching you is a plague I can't survive.* Her voice whipped in my skull. Over and over again.

"Is this about Father?"

I squinted. "Why would this be about Father?"

Winston shrugged. "He was here on the yacht at the crack of dawn. Looking for you."

"Well, he found me," I drawled. "All he needed was two and a half million." I took another drink. "I gave it to him. Good riddance, asshole."

At that moment, I didn't give a fuck. Not about the money. Not about my father. Nothing, apart from one thing. I wanted to know what happened to make Odette so angry.

My brother grabbed the bottle out of my hands. "How about we have something to eat?"

"I'm not hungry." I reached for the bottle, but Winston threw it into the water. "Fuck, Winston. Stop polluting. Try and save the planet for the next generation."

He sighed. "I'll dive for it and get it out." When I rolled my eyes—or attempted to—he added, "I promise. As soon as you get something to eat and hit the sheets."

I opened my mouth to say something, even though I didn't know what, when he raised his palm. "Either you hit the sheets or I'll dump all the bottles I find on this boat into the sea and pollute your precious planet."

"Asshole."

A smile broke across his face and he cackled. Actually cackled.

"I learned from the best, Byron." He punched me in the shoulder, laughing. "That's what we Ashfords are. Assholes. Except for Father, he's just a wannabe."

Chapter 13
Odette

It was impossible to breathe.

It had been two days since I'd woken up after an amazing night with Byron, only to come face-to-face with his father. Two days since Senator Ashford delivered on his promise. Two days since my father dropped the news of us being broke.

I shook my head. I couldn't think about the senator. I didn't have enough strength nor energy to go down memory lane. When Byron came to the hospital, I couldn't look at him. I was so mad I wanted to murder him. Both Byron and his fucking father.

They were the perfect example of the rich thriving on the sufferings of the poor. We weren't exactly poor, but their misdeeds certainly cost us a lot. I'd bet their motto was use and abuse. Shaking my head, I chased the bitter memories away.

Sitting on the balcony that hung over the sea—literally—my sister and I stared out into the darkness. It mirrored our mood. The moon glimmered, but I couldn't find beauty in it. Not even the smell of the sea could comfort me. The gentle sounds of the waves washing onto the shore usually soothed, but tonight, it felt like a countdown.

"I still don't understand." Billie's voice was a ghost, kind of like her complexion. Neither one of us could comprehend this. My sister was struggling to comprehend how her life in Paris—among elite fashion and diamond designers—wouldn't be happening. At least not yet. She had finished fashion school, but in order for her to thrive, she needed to live in Paris. Or Milan. Not here on the French Riviera. "Usually there are warning letters. Time frames given," she muttered.

Images of Byron and his father flashed through my mind. It was all their fault. It was my fault. It turned out I played reckless with the wrong man. Instead of being responsible, I took a risk and hooked up with a billionaire who had power. Who was ruthless. The Ashfords ruined us. The moment I slept with Byron Ashford, I signed our family's destruction. All my father's hard work went up in flames.

And it was all my fault.

I finally found the courage to look him up yesterday.

The Ashford family was pretty much royalty in the States. And the fucking world. They were one of the richest families on the whole goddamn planet. Byron's mother was shot dead in the street two decades ago. There was a lot of speculation about Senator Ashford's shady deals with criminals and his affairs with women half his age. If not younger. I also found news stories on Kingston Ashford, the youngest brother, who was kidnapped at the age of ten.

Jesus Christ, that family was a trainwreck.

And Byron... fucking liar. There were photos of him with a woman taken only a few weeks ago and the world was taking bets on their union. The merging of the Popova and Ashford lines would make their families untouchable. Both were richer than King Midas.

How did I not know any of this? If only I'd have paid more attention to tabloids and business papers. But that was never my forte.

Turmoil churned in my stomach. I couldn't tell my sister any of this. All I could do now was protect her. Protect our family. We could always open another hospital on the French Riviera, one day.

It won't be the same, my heart whispered.

Ever since the fiasco in the hotel room, numbness took up residence in my heart. Although, I couldn't decide whether it was due to the loss of my father's hospital or the man I'd spent a few short-lived hours with.

Definitely the former. The latter was a prick. A mistake.

"I should drop out of med school," I muttered to myself. I sat wearily, unable to get myself together or figure out what the right thing to do was.

Horror splashed across Billie's face. "No, Maddy. No, no. That would break Dad's heart. You know how proud he is. He said so himself. Dropping out of med school is out of the question."

Inhaling a deep breath, I slowly let it out. How could one event enact so much change? Now, it seemed our whole fucking world was falling apart.

"Dad shouldn't have to worry about my tuition at Stanford." My voice was detached. Dull. Tired. I had barely gotten any sleep over the last two days. "My scholarship is good, but it doesn't cover all of it."

My sister leaned across the small table and took my hand in a comforting grip. "We'll figure something out. It's spring. You can still apply for more scholarships. Your grades are good and your professors love you."

"Maybe." Shame poured onto my shoulders with the knowledge I brought this to our door. God, how could one innocent night wreak so much havoc? I had single-handedly squandered away our life.

A small rock flew through the air and bounced against the table. A whistle followed.

"Man, why does Marco still do that?" Billie grumbled annoyed.

"We're adults now. He knows he can just call us or knock on the door, right?"

I could barely force a smile on. "I guess he likes this method better."

"Maddy, you there?"

My sister rolled her eyes. "So fucking annoying," she mouthed.

I shrugged.

"Kind of romantic." I stood up and leaned over the railing. Marco stood on the corner of the alley that connected our house and the neighboring one.

"It would be romantic if he had a yacht and docked it in front of our house rather than leer from a dark alley."

Okay, she might have a point there. But this was what he'd always done.

"Hey, Marco." My sister mimicked gagging behind me, shoving her finger into her mouth. I reached behind me and smacked her hand gently. "What's going on?" I returned my attention to Marco who for some reason loved to play Romeo.

"I heard the Ashford royalty is in town."

Seriously, that was the reason he'd come?

"Okay..." I didn't know what else to say. "I didn't know America had royalty," I remarked sarcastically. "And why in the heck are you tracking their movements?"

I hadn't told anyone what happened with Byron. As far as I knew, nobody recognized Byron when we were in the bar that night. I certainly had no clue who or what he was.

"I heard from a buddy that the Ashfords are celebrating something. Merging of the families or some shit like that."

Irrational jealousy knifed through me. Air halted painfully in my body as everything constricted. I shut my eyes, squeezing out the images that kept haunting me. His mouth on mine. His words in my ear. The way he felt inside me.

I shivered. I guess I was indeed his last fuck before he settled down. His kind and my kind didn't mix. Wasn't that what his father said? I didn't know whether to laugh about it, or cry. In this day and age, you'd think none of it would matter. Rich or poor; old or young; French or American... I thought we were way past those sorts of judgments.

Turned out, not. At least not for people like Senator Ashford.

"A fact check," Billie sneered. "We don't give a shit. We have bigger problems to deal with."

My sister was right. The Ashfords didn't concern us. We lost the hospital, something that had been in our family for generations.

"I heard about the hospital," Marco muttered. "I didn't want to hurt you by bringing it up."

"How bad are the rumors?" I asked him.

He shrugged. "Not that bad. Desiré is being her usual tactless self." Billie growled next to me, clenching her fists. I gave her a barely noticeable shake of my head. "You want to come down?" Marco's voice penetrated my wordless communication with my sister. I forgot he was still down there. Glancing at my sister, I was fairly certain I knew what the answer was. She shook her head. Neither one of us was in the mood.

Billie's dream had been squashed. My dreams were on their way to being extinguished. Neither one of us was in the mood for anyone's company.

"Not tonight, Marco," I told him with an apologetic smile.

Before he could protest or say anything else, I sat back down in my chair. Billie rolled her eyes. "Why are you always so goddamn nice?"

I shrugged, my eyes locked on the moon. "It's good to practice my bedside manner for my future days as a doctor." Assuming being a surgeon was still in my future.

"Listen, soeur." Billie's voice suddenly got serious and I turned to look at her. "What if I got my hands on some money?" I raised my eyebrows. Neither one of us had any savings to talk about. "If I could... get a loan. That would help, right?"

"I don't think a loan will help Dad and his hospital," I

muttered. "Apparently they've already started moving patients. The building is no longer ours."

"But it will help you," she reasoned. "I don't want you quitting med school."

I reached over and squeezed her hand. "I don't want to quit either, but I'm not sure there's much choice. I don't want you to give up on your dream of working in Paris either. But here we are."

She waved her hand. "When you're a rich surgeon, you can front me some money."

I chuckled. "Gosh, Billie. I never knew your imagination was so wild."

She didn't laugh, her expression serious. It should have been enough to warn me. My thoughts bounced all over the place, unable to piece clues together.

"I'll make it happen," she vowed.

I shook my head. "How?"

Billie opened her mouth to answer when a single gunshot shattered the silence.

Chapter 14
Odette

"My condolences." Another voice. Another face. "He was a wonderful man."

I nodded, unable to find my voice. Billie and I held hands, and I wasn't sure whether she was holding me up or vice versa.

It felt like I was in a fog, lost and confused, as I tried to make sense of it all. Dad was gone. *Gone.* The buzzing in my ears, lack of sleep, Billie's hysterics—probably my own too, but I couldn't recall it—had me grasping for my sanity.

Billie's grip on my hand tightened, and I had to stifle my wince. It hurt, but I didn't want to complain. She needed me. I needed her. Jesus Christ. How did we get here? Was this Senator Ashford's doing too? Dad had put the gun to his own head, but the timeline said enough. Just days after the senator ripped the rug out from under our family, my father took his own life.

"My condolences." Another sad smile. Another nod.

The couple—whom I'd never seen before—moved to the left and Billie yanked me, forcing me to start walking.

"What's the matter?" I rasped, my throat squeezing so tightly it hurt to talk. "Where are we going?"

"I can't do this anymore," Billie hissed. "You can't do this anymore. We buried Dad. It's done. We don't need to put up with this after-party. It's morbid."

I let out a sigh. "I think that's the point."

God, I was tired. So fucking tired. This single week had sucked so much life out of me that I couldn't fathom how we'd carry on. I was due back at Stanford. They'd given me an extension due to *extenuating* circumstances, as they'd called it.

A shuddering breath rocked my body.

"You and I need fresh air," Billie muttered. "We need to be alone."

The door of the funeral home opened and fresh air hit us in the face. Yet, I couldn't draw in a breath. Dad was gone, and it was all my fault. I couldn't breathe.

I followed my sister, my black flats soundless against the pavement. Just like my guilt. I tried to smother the voices in my head—shut them the fuck up—and focus on the click of Billie's heels against the pavement. The sound of her black dress rustling against mine. My sister was only a year older than me. She'd always been the more reckless one, whereas I was the more responsible one.

But ever since Dad died, she seemed to be the rock. My rock. Hand in hand, we made our way through Villefranche-sur-Mer and down the promenade until we got to the sea. This was where we mourned our mother all those years ago. It was our first stop when we moved here. This was the spot Billie had cried her eyes out after her first heartbreak. This was where we were now mourning our father.

The sun slowly descended behind the horizon of our hillside village, the sea glistening with its last rays. Each minute extinguished another until there was nothing but dusk surrounding us

"He's gone." My voice was hoarse. My throat hurt, but it didn't compare to this pain in my heart. "How are we going to survive this?"

Billie's hands cupped my face. "I got the money to pay for your tuition and to set us up for a bit so we are not stone broke."

I blinked in confusion. That was a hundred grand. In U.S. dollars. She had already paid for Father's burial expenses. It all happened so fast, I never even got the chance to ask her how.

"How, Billie?" I rasped. "And I can't take it. You take that money and you go to Paris. Make your mark."

Her grip tightened on my cheeks. "No. Fuck no. You will finish medical school. I have enough for that. Then I'll follow my Paris dream."

"But—"

She cut me off. "I'm the oldest and what I say goes." When I opened my mouth to protest, she covered it with her palms. "This is what Dad would want. We have to do this." Her voice cracked. "For him."

A tear rolled down her cheek, shattering my soul into a million pieces. It was at that exact moment that I broke. We broke. A sob tore from my throat. Or maybe it was hers.

And as the moon made its way through the dark sky, our soft cries mixed with the sound of crashing waves.

We cried. Together.

Chapter 15
Byron

The day was dreary.

I was about to leave today when I saw the announcement in the paper. The death of the good Doctor Swan. I'd never made it back to see him at the hospital. My back was well enough, and Odette made it clear she didn't want to see me.

I knew when I wasn't wanted.

Yet, here I was. Both Winston and I.

He wanted to ensure I didn't do anything stupid. It didn't escape me how our roles reversed over the last two days. I drank myself into oblivion, and he ensured to cut me off. Lovely. I had hit rock bottom.

Standing in the back of the full church, I kept catching glimpses of Odette's red hair. She held hands with her sister, the black dresses making them appear even younger. The service finished and the line of condolences began.

Odette looked tired and pale, her eyes red from the tears she was now holding back, and my heart fucking hurt. She didn't want me here, but I couldn't help but come. I wanted to be here just in case—

The thought was stupid, yet here I was.

It was so appropriate that rain came and went all day, almost as if the sky was mourning too.

"They both look like death," Winston muttered.

The line of people offering their condolences grew by the second. Fuck, I wanted to talk to her, offer to help somehow. But most of all, I wanted to ensure she was okay.

"They just lost their father," I grumbled. "It's understandable they're upset."

He shot me a wry look. "If our father died, we wouldn't shed a tear. Not one of his children would."

My expression became hard. "Today isn't the day to discuss something like that."

Not while Odette was in mourning.

"Was their old man nice?" Winston asked curiously. "He seems to have a huge fan base from the number of attendees and tears. Even his daughters loved him, imagine that."

I gave a terse nod.

"The Swan family are close." I recalled the background check on their family. A close-knit family. Nothing like ours. "Were," I corrected myself. It was still hard to believe the old doctor was dead. The paper was vague on the cause of death, and it seemed inappropriate to bring it up here. I couldn't help but wonder who'd manage the hospital while Odette worked on finishing her degree. I'd offer to help, but I was certain she'd rather burn it all to the ground than talk to me.

I watched the two sisters whisper to each other and then make their way out of the room.

My heart beat, painfully. Alive.

Filled with sadness I hadn't felt in a very long time.

Not since I buried my own mother. Not since my baby brother was taken all those years ago. Even when he was returned to us, he hadn't been the same, and the pain from that loss lingered like I knew this one would.

My captain had us drifting away, leaving Villefranche-sur-Mer and the French Riviera behind us.

Sun bounced off the ripples of blue water. The glare was bright even behind my sunglasses. I stood on the upper deck, staring at the coastline that shrank with each minute that passed. The outline of the hospital on the hill was one of the last things I could make out before the entire coastline became a blur.

"I know you are worried about pollution." Winston's voice came from behind me. "I dove for that damn bottle. You'll be happy to know we haven't left our footprint behind."

"Except for the gas that we're currently using to power this yacht," I remarked dryly, turning to face him.

"There is that," he agreed, fixing me with a serious gaze. "You have been different."

My eyes returned to the horizon. "So have you. You've been sober for three days straight."

He shrugged. "I figured it's better to be sober rather than drunk when Father catches me. He'd rob me, take my clothes, and leave me naked. Literally and figuratively."

I met my brother's gaze once more. "What did he do when he came on the yacht?"

"Searched for you. He didn't believe you weren't here, so he stormed into your office. In fact, he stayed there for a while as if he thought you'd show up out of thin air."

"He was probably trying to break into my safe," I remarked dryly.

Except, he knew it was impossible to break into any safe I designed. He had tried it plenty of times.

So what exactly had he been doing in my office?

Three Months Later

113

Chapter 16
Odette

Kneeling over the toilet, I wiped my mouth with the back of my hand.

There were many reactions people experienced when seeing that pink plus sign. Puking their guts out while sobbing wasn't usually one of them. Well, it shouldn't be, anyway.

I got to my feet and brushed my teeth while Billie tapped her manicured nails on the countertop of our little bathroom. *Click. Click. Click.* The soft sounds felt like drums announcing an execution.

I. Fucked. Up.

The summer heat radiated through the air, sending a bead of sweat rolling down my spine. Gosh, it was on days like this that I wished we had air-conditioning in our home.

"How did you get preggo, *ma soeur?*"

She only called me soeur when she was worried. Her voice was sweet and soft, but panic filled her expression. Both of us stared at a pile of pregnancy tests, empty boxes, and way too many pink plus signs.

"Are you asking how—like in physical terms—or are you asking how I let it happen?"

She let out an exasperated sigh. "I guess both. What sexual position got you knocked up because I plan on avoiding it. And... didn't you use protection?"

My face heated.

"We used protection," I muttered. *For the most part.* There might have been a time or two that he slid inside me without a condom on. But he never finished. It was a stupid justification, and it was reckless. Yet, he'd felt so good that I kept forgetting. And so did he apparently.

Fuck, fuck, fuck. It was protection 101.

Just thinking about that man had my body going into a state of sexual shock. Yes, it was a medical term. Invented by me.

"Billie, what am I going to do?" I asked desperately. I was just about to enter my second year of medical school. I had dreams. Goals. Plans.

Tears burned in my eyes, threatening to spill. I refused to let them. I never used to fucking cry. Now, I cried all the time. Although it was understandable. We had lost our father. Our last parent. Now, Billie and I were all that was left.

And a baby.

My hands shook as I stood in front of the bathroom mirror of our home in Villefranche-sur-Mer. The summer break was in full swing, but cheer was nowhere to be found. Our home felt empty without Dad. My sister made some changes to it—especially the room *it* happened in—but it still felt off. I saw him in every corner. Sometimes I even heard his voice, his feet shuffling against the hardwood.

"Well, they say no method of protection is foolproof, except for abstinence. I guess they weren't lying," Billie remarked calmly, staring at one of the many tests I held in my hand. Foolishly, I hoped the plus sign would just fade away.

It didn't.

This couldn't be happening to me. All these symptoms had to be stress-related. *Plus signs too?* my mind mocked.

God, what a fucking doctor I would become!

My mind worked vigorously at the options I had. I had my period three weeks ago. Granted, my last couple of periods seemed lighter than usual—again, blaming stress levels—but still, a period was a period. Plus, I hadn't had sex with anyone else in almost three months.

I shook my head. No, I couldn't be pregnant.

Now, I almost regret taking the test. Except, I kept getting nauseous and sick every morning. I groaned out loud.

This was the last thing we needed. We'd just buried our father, his hospital foreclosed on—Dad was brilliant at saving people, but evidently not finances—and we were broke. Both of us had jobs for the summer, and if not for my scholarship—and Billie's miraculous deeds—I would have had to withdraw from Stanford.

A quiver started inside me—slow but strong—spreading through every single cell in me. It trembled in my veins and burned my eyes. My sister's gaze met mine in the mirror—my hazel eyes against her brown ones. My strawberry hair color against my sister's blonde hair.

We couldn't have been more different. But we always stood by each other.

"We'll figure it out. Together." She wrapped her hands around me and my boobs protested achingly. Another fucking side effect of pregnancy. "Are you going to tell him?"

Staring at two pink lines, I bawled like a baby against my sister's shoulder.

"I have to tell him, Billie," I cried softly. "It's the right thing to do." *I think.*

"Fuck the right thing," she hissed. "We do what's best for us. You, me, and the baby."

The tightness in my chest eased a bit at her words. *She included the baby.* My sister already saw this baby as ours. Part of our family.

Guilt pierced through my chest. I didn't deserve it. I didn't deserve her. The guilt I felt for bringing the Ashfords into our lives was a heavy weight in my chest. A constant companion. It squeezed my insides and stabbed at my heart with each breath.

Yet, I couldn't admit my sins to my sister. I needed her. I loved her. Without her, I'd fall apart. So I selfishly kept the events that led to our father's suicide a secret. My reasoning told me that I couldn't have possibly known what was going to happen, but that was the thing about guilt. There was no rhyme or reason when it came to it. It didn't listen to facts. It just ate at you, weighing you down. I hated it, the twinge of guilt in my gut, but I just couldn't force the admission out.

"Forget the baby's father, Maddy," Billie said. She knew who he was. Even without telling her about Senator Ashford, my sister held a grudge against the Ashfords. "We don't need him. We can do this alone."

We could, but it was wrong to keep it a secret. He had a right to know. Worry swarmed my mind. What if Senator Ashford found out and decided to hurt us? Surely, Byron would protect his child. Protect us. Wouldn't he?

"We tell him," I whispered. It was too big of a secret to keep. After all, it wouldn't be fair to keep it from him. It was up to him to own up to it or discard us. "If he doesn't want any part of it, we just carry on as if he never existed." None of the Ashfords.

I just had to hope the Ashford wrath wouldn't cause us more pain.

Chapter 17
Odette

I stood in front of the tall glass building in Washington, D.C. The wealth and power stared back at us, making us feel even smaller. Nausea swam in my stomach, whether from my nerves or the little life growing inside me. Or maybe it was this July humidity in this city that suffocated its residents.

The summers in D.C. were unbearable—at least, according to my standards. I'd take the French Riviera over this humid fog any day.

"Are you sure you should tell him?" Billie questioned again. Ever since those pink plus signs stared back at us, I'd fought with my conscience. I didn't want to tell him, but it felt like the right thing to do.

"What if he thinks you just want shit from him?"

"I don't want anything from him," I hissed, anger and hate slithering through my veins. Unfortunately, it didn't extend to Byron. I wished it did, but for some reason, I couldn't handle it. Maybe it was my stupid mind chasing fairy tales. "I'm just making him aware. What he wants to do with the information is up to him."

I'd be certain to tell him I wanted no claim on anything of

his, regardless of whether he wanted to be part of our baby's life or not. This was just a courtesy. Right? I refused to feed any hopes of happily ever after. Senator Ashford had made it crystal clear.

His kind and ours didn't mix.

Then why did the images of that night still haunt me? The way his touch felt. Those whispered words that I was his. His grunts. My moans. His hands on my hips. The way he owned me. It felt so fucking real. How could I have misread it all?

"Earth to my sister." Billie's voice penetrated through the reel of images swirling in my mind.

"I just need to get this behind us so we can move on." I glanced at my sister. "I'm so sorry we spent money we don't have to make this trip. I should have waited until next semester started. I just—"

I didn't really know why I felt the need to tell him right now. Maybe I thought I'd lose my courage and chicken out.

"You need to get this behind you so we can start planning how to move forward," my sister finished for me. I nodded. She was right. I needed to know where Byron stood, so I could make the right choices. For our baby. My job at the coffee shop on campus wouldn't be sufficient to raise a baby, nor would my summer gig back home. And med school—

"Oh. Guess what? You won't believe this shit." Billie rolled her eyes, emphasizing the words she hadn't spoken yet. The tension built inside me, and I worried I'd explode.

"What?"

She snickered. "Marco's here, in D.C. I swear that guy stalks you."

"Marco is the least of my concerns." Stalker or not.

She shrugged. "Apparently, he's dating a doctor that works at George Washington Hospital or something. Remember, she was at Le Bar Américain. Tristan's sister."

"Good for him," I muttered. Marco was a friend and I wished him all the best, I just didn't follow his life as closely as Billie apparently did. We'd touch base occasionally, but we all had our own lives to worry about. "Okay, wish me luck, soeur."

Billie's brown eyes sharpened. "You don't need luck. Show them who the fuck we are. That fucker is lucky he knocked you up. He's ugly. You're beautiful."

A choked laugh escaped me. Leave it to my sister to make me feel better, although Byron was anything but ugly.

Inhaling deeply, I stiffened my shoulders and steeled my spine. "Okay, I'll meet you back at the hotel."

Ten minutes later, I finally made my way to the top floor of the building. My heart thundered, and I held my breath as the elevator took me. Higher and higher. *Ding.*

I startled at the sound of the doors sliding open.

Stepping out of the elevator with feigned confidence, I made my way to the receptionist. Except, the desk was empty. I glanced around—left, right, left again—then made my way down the only corridor that held a large, gold "CEO" plate. Byron's office had to be that way. My reading stated he was CEO of the Ashford empire.

I strutted down the fancy marble hallway with trepidation and smoothed my palms down my pink summer dress. The color was at odds with this black-and-white building. It certainly made me stand out. Albeit, I wasn't sure if it was in a good way.

I found the desk of who I supposed was Byron's assistant and asked if I could see him. She said something about an appointment, but by then, faint voices reached me. Unease slithered through me, but I reacted too late. I turned on my heel to leave, and came face-to-face with Senator Ashford.

I froze. My eyes widened and my breath hitched.

This was not how I envisioned this going. I had the entire speech—or something resembling it—prepared in my head. For Byron. Not for his prick father. He pulled me away from the desk and out of earshot of the assistant.

"Well, well, well." It wasn't Senator Ashford who spoke. It was the woman next to him. I hadn't even noticed her until now. She was breathtakingly beautiful. Designer clothing from head to toe. I didn't care about brand name clothing, but my fashion-obsessed sister cared about them a lot. It kind of stuck. "What do we have here?"

With long blonde hair and big blue eyes, she looked like a perfect Barbie doll. Except, instead of a smile, this woman wore a sneer.

"This is Miss Swan." Senator Ashford's voice was cold, but it didn't compare to his icy gaze. I shivered, wanting to fold up inside myself until there was nothing left of me. I fucking hated this reaction to him. "I'll handle her."

"Yes, please do. I don't want anyone disturbing Byron today."

I barely had time to blink and Senator Ashford was in front of me. His icy hands clasped around mine and he clutched them, his nails digging into my skin.

"What did I tell you, girl?" he hissed.

I pushed my shoulders back. "I have to talk to—"

He didn't let me finish. "I delivered my threat. The hospital is gone. Your father's gone." A sharp gasp tore from my lips. It was one thing to know he was behind the hospital loss, but entirely different to hear him gloat about it. The room started to spin. I stumbled backward, trying to put space between us. Tears blurred my vision. I had to get away. I didn't care about doing the right thing anymore. I just needed to get away. "Do you really want your sister gone, as well?"

His cold eyes and vindictive words felt like fresh needles piercing my chest. My heart burned like someone set fire to it. Every heartbeat, every goddamned breath hurt. I couldn't drag enough air into my lungs.

He took my father from me. I couldn't let him take my sister too.

"Let go of me." I hiccupped, struggling to get air into my throat. I had to get away from him.

"I told you to stay away from us." Senator Ashford's voice was hushed, his expression dark. He pulled out something from his pocket and slammed it against my chest. "Here. Now be gone." He flicked a glance over his shoulder to the woman. "These gold diggers will resort to anything and drain you dry if you let them."

A stack of bills pressed against my chest, staining me. Without thinking, my hand flew through the air and connected with his face. *Smack.*

Someone's gasp shattered through the air. Someone screeched. But I was too stunned at what I had done to react. Staring at the red mark forming on the senator's face, I stood frozen and wide-eyed. I had never hated anyone before, but I hated this man. With every ounce of my heart.

It was only then that I spotted the security guards. The ghost of a menacing smirk flickered in his blue eyes. Two brawny men in suits stomped around me, each grabbing me by an arm.

"Take the trash out," the senator demanded. "My son's orders."

Someone cackled behind me. I didn't have it in me to see who it was. I fought tears as they escorted me down the elevator and out of the building, shoving me outside.

Once on the sidewalk, the sky cracked and I turned my face up to the cloud directly overhead. It was still sunny, the clear blue skies marred by the only dark cloud making its way across the city.

I reached into the small pocket of my summer dress and pulled out the sonogram picture, a choked sob wracking through me.

"I didn't get to show you to your father, but I think it's for the best," I whispered, walking aimlessly forward and keeping my eyes on the little black-and-white photo. "I'm sorry Daddy and his family are assholes." My eyes burned, and I wiped tears off my face angrily. They—the Ashfords—didn't deserve my tears. They didn't deserve a single thought from me, never mind a heartache.

I was such a fucking idiot to think doing the right thing would accomplish anything. Instead, it got me thrown out. Like trash.

Gosh, how could I have fucked up so badly? I never broke the rules, always did the right thing. And here I was—fucked. Literally and figuratively.

I wiped my face again. I had to get myself together. Get my shit together.

Holding the sonogram photo with one hand, I rubbed my flat belly with the other. It would be just the three of us. Baby, Billie, and I. We could survive this.

I wished I was back in the hotel room with my sister.

"We'll be the three musketeers," I rasped, trying to convince myself it was for the best. I would call all the shots in terms of raising a baby. It was better all the way around. I was aware of alarmed and concerned looks from passersby, but I ignored them.

I heard the shouts too late. I raised my head and my instinct took over. I twisted my body in an attempt to protect my stomach just as I went flying through the air.

Pain exploded through me and the world ceased to exist.

Chapter 18
Odette

Numbness. Emptiness. Pain.

Peeling my eyelids open, I blinked against the brightness. My surroundings registered. The white walls. The scent of bleach.

A hospital. I was alive.

I closed my eyes again and felt the memory come rushing in. I might have been angry—furious even—but I'd gone into his building full of hope. And I came out... empty. Broken.

My lids slowly opened, and I saw him. Byron's head hunched over my hand while he gripped it. My heart made a dull thump in my chest. Ache. In my body and my heart. He was here. How?

I tried to recall what happened. But the last thing I remembered was being escorted out of the building.

"How long was I out?" I rasped, darting my tongue over my bottom lip.

Byron's dull blue eyes met mine. He looked like hell. His hair ruffled and messy as if he'd been running his fingers through it. Stubble covered his face, and deep black circles surrounded his eyes. His shirt was bloodied, his tie hanging loose and crooked.

I saw pictures of him in *Forbes*—pristine, perfect—he was far from it now.

"Baby, you're awake." He cupped my face, his big palms gentle. So damn gentle that it brought tears to my eyes. "How are you feeling?"

Disoriented. Confused. Achy. Tired.

"Let me call for a doctor."

"No. I don't need a doctor." He was already on his way to fetch one, but my words stopped him. "How long was I out?" I repeated.

"A few hours." He took my hand back into his, and it was only then I saw it. My sonogram photo bunched up in his palm. Of our baby. My baby.

"Baby?" I barely managed to say the word.

His jaw pulsed, agony in his eyes matching what I now felt in my heart. The feeling that threatened to swallow me whole.

He shook his head. "The baby didn't make it," he croaked.

The baby didn't make it. The baby didn't make it. It whipped in my brain like the hollow cries of a windstorm.

My heart cracked and the first tear rolled down my cheek. His words—they felt like a stab in my chest. How could he say those words knowing he'd just used me, thrown me away like trash. Ruined my family... *taken my father.*

His kind and my kind didn't mix.

The words played on repeat, piercing my brain. His father. His fiancée. My baby.

No, there was no "my baby" anymore. It would seem God agreed. I was good enough to fuck as a side piece. Not good enough to love.

Overwhelming emotions whirled inside me. Suffocating me. Drowning me. The pain was too much to bear. I wanted oblivion.

"We need to talk," I whispered, my voice oddly calm.

"Not now, baby. We'll talk once you're better." He grazed his fingers over my knuckles. "Just get some rest."

I shook my head. I needed to rip off this Band-Aid once and for all. My eyes took him in, memorizing every inch of him. He was handsome, even when he was in this state. His expensive, white shirt bloodied. His sleeves rolled up, exposing his muscular forearms. His scruff gave him an edge. My fingers itched to touch him.

His eyes penetrated through me, down to the heart he broke. And I still craved him, even though I didn't think I could ever forgive him.

I loved his eyes. Intense. I knew how dark they'd turned when he buried himself deep inside me. Midnight blue. I hated them all the same, because they could so easily deceive me.

"Byron, I need you to do something for me." The words were heavy on my tongue. Or maybe that was the medication. They should have pumped me full of it to heal this ache in my heart.

"Anything, baby." God, when he looked at me like that, I felt like his entire world. One night with a man changed so much. It changed me.

I licked my lips. It didn't ease my tension nor ache.

"You and I were a mistake." My ears buzzed and the machine started beeping. Louder and faster. The pain piercing through my ears matched the one in my heart. "I need you gone. That one night is haunting me and destroying me. Every part of me and my life." My chest squeezed so tightly that each breath came out on a wheeze. "Please leave."

I saw pain flash through his blue eyes, but he averted his gaze.

"Is that what you want?"

The pain of losing him clawed at my chest all over again, threatening to open it. To break me. My heart screamed "no" but my brain had to be stronger.

Slowly, I let my pain morph into something else. Something dark and cold. Something irrevocable. Hate. Bitterness.

"Yes."

Barely above a whisper, the single word broke my heart completely.

Chapter 19
Byron

Six Years Later

Scout Island Scream Park in New Orleans.

My nephew Kol, Alessio—my slightly older half brother—and I boarded a train resembling a minecart that would take us through a ghost graveyard. Neither Alessio nor I were small men, our knees poking out of the cart, and poor Kol was almost smothered between us like lunch meat. He didn't seem to mind though, his eyes darting left and right. He couldn't wait for this damn cart to start moving so we'd get spooked.

My sister and her husband along with their kids were in the cart behind us, and they looked just as ridiculous as we did.

"Goddamn it, this is my first visit to an amusement park," Alessio grumbled. "I would have come sooner if I knew these seats were so comfortable."

I detected a sarcasm in his voice and chuckled. "Don't tell me you never snuck into the traveling fairs to hitch a ride."

Alessio gave me a dry look. It was all the answer I needed.

I lowered my eyes to Kol whose gray eyes glimmered with

excitement. My nephew's eyes had specks of hazel in them, much like his mother's. Sometimes it reminded me of another set of hazel eyes, except for the gold. I had never seen eyes like that since.

Pushing the thought out of my mind, I smiled. "I think we have to hold your dad's hand. Since it's his first ride."

Kol didn't even hesitate. Fuck, the kid was good. Kind too. His small hand grabbed his father's and squeezed. "I'll be with you the entire time. With both of you."

My brother's expression softened. "I appreciate that, buddy. I feel safer now."

Alessio had gotten his chance at happiness. I was happy for him, and I couldn't even muster up any jealousy. Our father had fucked his life up by never owning up to his offspring. But he came out the other side with a good woman beside him.

Kol's small hand took mine. "And I'll keep you safe too, Uncle Byron."

My brother and I shared an amused look. Fuck, our family was expanding and for the better. Although not for me. A small twinge in my heart reminded me of my chance. The single chance that ended before it even started.

I wouldn't have minded being a father. Especially not with a woman like that. After her accident, she moved on. Outside of her returning to Stanford, I hadn't kept tabs on her. It was too painful.

The ride started, and true to his word, Kol kept our big hands in his small ones. Except, he clutched our hands so hard, both Alessio and I winced. The little bugger was strong. Kind, but strong as fuck.

"What do you feed him?" I muttered to my brother. "Spinach?"

He let out a strangled laugh. "Yep, creating a Popeye here."

"I didn't know you watched cartoons." My voice was dry with just a touch of humor.

Alessio shrugged. "It's relaxing. You should try it sometime."

"I'm gonna have to borrow your kid more, so I don't ruin my

reputation. It'd be kind of weird if people found me watching cartoons by myself."

Silence followed while the ghosts surrounded us. Literal and metaphorical.

"Ever think about having a kid?" Alessio's question came out of the blue. We had gotten closer over the years, in particular during the time his wife got stuck in Afghanistan. It took us months of greasing palms and making deals to find a way into the country that had shut down its borders.

"Sometimes," I admitted. It'd be easier to have a child without the mother. I didn't want another woman in my life. I tried— fucking really tried—but it wouldn't be fair to tie the knot with anyone while my heart was still stuck on the red-haired French doctor.

"You'd be good at it. You have the patience for it." *Unlike our father.* We both knew it. Our father's selfish ways stretched beyond any normal politician. Although he had earned some points when he hired Kian—an old military specialist—to protect Alessio's wife. Autumn and Kian were both in Afghanistan during the chaos. The connection and timing always seemed peculiar, but it didn't matter. It saved my sister-in-law.

I smiled. "Maybe one day." Fuck, even I could hear the tinge of bitterness in my tone. "So. Kol, are we scared yet?"

Kol blew out a frustrated breath. "Where are the ghosts?"

I chuckled. "Up in the air?"

"They're supposed to come out of the ground and scare us."

"Well, I am glad they're not," Alessio chimed in. "I'm plenty scared. Thankfully, you're holding my hand, or I'd have started crying."

I shot my brother a look. "Too much," I mouthed.

Alessio just grinned, flipping me the bird over his head. So fucking mature.

"If you want to close your eyes, Dad, I won't tell anyone," Kol assured him.

I threw my head back and laughed. I couldn't even picture Alessio doing that. The guy who ran the underworld in Canada, squeezing his eyelids in fear to make it through the ride.

"But Byron will," Alessio answered in a feigned whiny tone. Geez, he was really enjoying this too much.

"I won't," I choked out, trying to keep a straight face. "Scout's honor. I never rat on our family."

Kol grinned. "Me neither. Even when my sister steals chocolate, I don't tell on her."

A choked laugh escaped both Alessio and I. "Is that where all the chocolate is going? Into your sister's belly?"

Kol gave him a serious look. "I don't know what you're talking about."

I couldn't hold my serious face any longer. Letting out a full belly laugh, I ruffled my nephew's hair.

"I'm proud of you, Kol."

And I was. I was so proud of our family.

Yet, a small ounce of loneliness—or was it regret?—lingered in a dark corner of my soul.

Three hours later, we all made our way out of the amusement park. Aurora and Autumn looked slightly green. Alessio, Alexei, and I all corralled the little ones. I had Kol sitting on my shoulders. Kostya sat on Alexei's shoulders, kicking him like he was a horse. Alessio held his daughter in his arms since it looked like the wives would be puking at any moment.

"Well, this was fun," Alessio remarked. "Let's not do it again for another year or two."

"Agreed," Alexei stated in a flat tone. "Kostya, for the last time, Daddy is not a horse."

I shook my head, then immediately winced. Kol tugged on my

hair like he was steering me. "Jesus, Kol. You know that's my hair, not reins. You'll make Uncle bald."

Kol and Kostya shared a glance and then giggled.

"Son, don't make your uncle bald," Alessio instructed Kol. "We still have to get him married. Then he can go bald."

Alexei snickered, and I flipped both of them off.

"I'll shave your heads bald while you're sleeping," I threatened half-jokingly. It wasn't as if I had never done it. In fact, I had shaved River's beautiful locks on one occasion. He cursed so loud, I was certain they heard him on all continents. Possibly all planets too.

"I'm never sleeping in the same room as you," Alexei stated matter-of-factly, while his eyes shone in amusement. Our father was so fucking wrong not to approve of him. This man would protect his family at the cost of the entire world.

"Good, because that would scar me for life. Sleeping in a room with you is not on my agenda."

"That's right," Alessio chimed in, barely holding in a snicker. "Your agenda is to sleep with a pretty doctor."

I glared at him while Alexei's eyebrow curved curiously. "Thank fuck you're not coming to our family lunch tomorrow," I muttered dryly. "I can only handle you for a few days at a time."

Alessio chuckled, unperturbed by my words. Nothing got to my brother. Except for his wife's and children's distress.

"I bet," he mused. "By the way, I heard the beautiful red-haired doctor is back in the States."

"I feel left out." Alexei's monotone drawl made it sound like he didn't give two fucks. The truth was that he rarely showed any emotions. But over the years, since he and Aurora had become an item, he started to express himself more with words. But only with people he felt comfortable with. Around my father, he behaved like he'd murder him at any moment. Not that I could blame him.

"Oh, Byron didn't tell you?" Alessio was more than happy to fill my brother-in-law in. "Not surprising. He keeps his love life a secret. But there's this beautiful doctor who can't stand him. She's been all over saving the world, but my intel tells me she's returned to the States."

"And why are you checking up on her?" I hissed.

He shrugged. "For your sake."

I glared at him. "So what do you know about her?"

"Aside from the fact that she's back in the States, not much."

"Did she get married?" The stupid question came out of my mouth without permission. I had security companies. I could check into all that myself. I just made a point not to.

"Don't ask me about her personal or love life, or any shit like that. I'm not keeping tabs on it."

"Then why do you know she's back?" Alexei asked the logical question.

Alessio shrugged. "For some reason, her and her sister's names came up on the dark web. Something to do with diamonds."

My brows furrowed. "That has to be wrong."

Alessio shrugged. "I think so too. She was in Ghana, working under WHO. Did you know?"

I shook my head. "No, I've made a point not to know." Then, because talking about Odette was the last thing I wanted to talk about, I changed subjects. "Are you sure you can't stay for our monthly luncheon tomorrow?"

Alessio shook his head. "No, Autumn has a gig for a photoshoot in the Ukraine. I'm not letting her go alone."

"Jesus, is it safe?" He shot me a "what the fuck do you think" look. "Was Afghanistan not enough?"

"She wants to make a difference," he grumbled. "She tried doing nothing and got too antsy. So we made a deal. She can take on assignments as long as I'm with her and in charge of security."

"That's probably wise," Alexei chimed in. "She'd eventually go with or without you. This way, you have some control."

"Do you want me to watch the kids?" I offered. "I could bring them back to you when both of you return."

My brother tilted his head. "I appreciate it, but we already made arrangements for Autumn's parents to watch them. Next time, it's definitely your turn."

"I'm counting on it."

I might never be a father, but I'd be the best uncle to my nieces and nephews.

Chapter 20
Odette

"These fucking heels," Billie muttered.

The cobblestone sidewalk of the French Quarter was uncomfortable in my flats, never mind the heels I saw women around me wearing. My sister included. She grabbed my arm every so often, using me for balance.

I helped steady her while my mind was on what we were about to do. "This better work, Billie."

Or we'd be dead. Dread washed over me, coiling tightly in the pit of my stomach. The last six months felt surreal. We'd been on the run ever since that fucking day. Every single day. I'd seen more of the world than I cared to. We left Las Vegas just last week where Billie managed to squeeze in a wedding dress fitting and make some extra money.

"It will work. They get their shit and our life will be back to normal."

My eyes darted to my sister, letting out a frustrated breath. I loved her; I really did. But at the age of thirty, Billie should have been smarter than to grab a bag of diamonds and think nobody would notice. Ten million dollars' worth of blood fucking diamonds from organized crime syndicates.

While I was performing surgeries, my sister had been busy robbing criminals.

Jesus H. Christ.

"You have everything in your purse?" I questioned. If she forgot them, I might have to murder her myself.

"All the diamonds are in the bag," she assured. "Glittering and expensive."

Her hand reached out again, grabbing my arm.

"Why in the fuck are you wearing heels?" I hissed. She'd never be able to outrun the men in those heels if it came to that.

Billie shot me an annoyed look.

"I wanted to look good." I glared at her. She knew what was at stake here. I couldn't fathom her appearance was more important to her than our safety. It was life or death here. Literally.

"You look good, Aunt Billie," Ares said, his small hand in mine.

My expression softened as I looked down at my son. Big blue eyes. Dark hair. My heart swelled with pride. At five, he knew how to flatter and capture hearts. He'd break hearts one day, even with his seriousness. My little boy was five going on ten.

"Only because I wore heels," Billie drawled, smiling softly.

I rolled my eyes. It was best not to comment on it, or it might turn into a full-blown discussion. Ares was the apple of my eye. Billie's too. The years had been difficult but worth all the hardship. It was the three of us. The three musketeers.

Unfortunately, we were in New Orleans instead of the French Riviera. But we'd be there soon enough. I could hardly wait until we were back home.

Elegant historic buildings surrounded us. A trumpeter played nearby, his sad tunes traveling over the breeze. The sweet, sticky smell of alcohol drifted through the air. Crowds of people meandered the streets, their laughter, dancing, and colorful clothing giving this city the vibrancy it was known for. Mardi Gras was about to be in full swing, although judging by the crowds all around us, you'd think it was happening now.

"There it is." Billie pointed and I followed her finger to the sign. St. Louis Street.

I lowered to a crouch, bringing my eyes to my son's level. "Ares, when we go into this restaurant, you'll go with Aunt Billie while I deal with some work stuff. Okay?"

He nodded. "Okay."

My son was used to my work. Except this time, it wasn't the normal work stuff that pulled me away. It was the accidental stealing of diamonds. By my sister. Big emphasis on *accidental*, which was still up for debate.

"Good boy," I murmured, pressing a kiss on his cheek.

"Don't worry, Maman," Billie chimed in. "Everything will be over soon."

I swallowed hard, my heart trembling in my chest. My biggest fear was something happening to him. I knew I'd never be able to forgive myself if Ares ended up hurt because of her or my own stupidity.

Straightening up, I met my sister's eyes. "Follow the plan, Billie. Do not deviate from it. No matter what. And if something happens to—"

"Don't say it," she cut me off. "It's bad luck."

I closed my eyes, praying for patience. I wanted to snap at her and tell her bad luck was stealing from criminals. Instead, I just stepped onto the sidewalk that was thankfully paved.

"Keep him glued to you," I said in a quiet voice. "And keep out of sight." She nodded. I loved my sister. The past five years of my son's happiness had been possible thanks to her sacrifices. This was the least I owed to her. I had to get us out of this mess.

I extended my hand and she reached out into her purse, pulling out a small, black velvet bag.

Ten million dollars in such a tiny package. It was enough to turn our life upside down.

I took it and shoved it into my own purse. We made our way down to the corner of St. Louis Street, stopping right at the entrance of The Sazerac Bar.

Billie picked up Ares, our gazes locking. She knew I was mad. She knew she fucked up. But until this was fixed, we couldn't exactly move on. The organized crime syndicate wouldn't let us live as long as we had those diamonds.

I just hoped once we returned the stolen goods, they'd forget about us. Although, my sixth sense warned me I was delusional. My gut revolted.

We entered the restaurant and I silently cursed myself. Billie was dressed appropriately for it. Me, not so much. My jean shorts, white quarter-sleeve shirt, and white ballet flats were too casual for this place.

Fuck! Why didn't criminals specify a dress code?

My eyes traveled over the expansive room. It had the ambiance of old New Orleans with walls painted in deep colors and decorated with old photographs. The sounds of the trumpeter carried through the large open windows. A crystal chandelier dominated the room.

"Hello." A hostess greeted us with a wide smile. "Do you have a reservation?"

Billie and I shared a glance. "Yes," I croaked. "Blood Diamond."

Those fuckers!

To the hostess's credit, she didn't even bat an eyelash. "Right this way."

We made our way through the space, bypassing tables and booths, when the hostess paused. I turned to Billie, giving her a nod. It was her time to disappear into the bathroom and hide there with Ares.

"Billie?" A vaguely familiar voice came from behind us. "Billie Swan."

My sister's face paled. My heart tripped, worried that we'd fucked up already. We were supposed to be here before Danso

Sabir, the killer for the Ghanaian and Corsican crime syndicate. Fear suffocated me, but I was more scared for my son than myself. Or even for my sister. He was all that mattered to me.

I forced a smile on my face as I mentally prepared for the worst. Slowly, I turned to face my fears.

Except the worst wasn't what I expected. Or rather, who I expected.

My heart constricted in my chest as I watched him. Byron Ashford was still the most handsome man I'd ever had the misfortune of meeting.

He watched me with that glimmering sapphire gaze, looking up at me from his table. The vision of him looking up at me with his head between my legs, his beautiful lips glistening with my arousal, had my body's temperature instantly spiked.

He'd broken my heart. I bit my bottom lip, focusing on the sting of that pain rather than the one that almost broke me six years ago.

God, forget it. Forget the memory. All of it.

But I still remembered the way he'd kissed me. The way he'd devoured me. I'd felt his passion all the way to my toes. I couldn't forget the way he'd cupped my cheeks with his strong hands and brought our faces close. The way he'd inhaled deeply, his eyes closing. As if he wanted to memorize me forever.

As if I was important to him.

Chapter 21
Byron

Six goddamn years.

I spotted her the moment she entered the restaurant. A flash of red hair, shorter than when I'd last seen her, falling down to her shoulders. She pushed a strand of it behind her ear as it caught the sun's rays and flickered with a golden hue.

It was impossible to see any golden colors and not think of her. Those gilded flashes in her eyes. Highlights in her hair. The image of her on all fours was ingrained into my memory.

My hand fisted, the burning in my palm throbbing with the need to wrap her hair around my fingers. Just like I did that night when she'd dropped down to her knees.

Six fucking years and I was still unable to move on from her. Six fucking years and she still held my heart. I left it right next to hers in that hospital when she begged me to let her go.

She looked just as beautiful as I remembered too. Graceful. Strong. Offering the hostess her polite and reserved smile, she uttered a few words, then turned to her friend holding a kid. Odette's expression immediately softened. She murmured something and they both nodded in agreement, then headed this way.

She was still at least ten feet away, but I swore the scent of crisp apples already drifted through the air, intoxicating me. My fucking cock hardened. After all this time I still wanted her with the same intensity as that day. That wild night.

"Billie?" Winston called out behind me. "Billie Swan."

My brows furrowed. Fuck, that was her sister. How did I miss it? I always noticed everything, but when it came to this woman, I might as well have been blind as fuck because I saw nothing but her.

Odette's spine stiffened and she slowly turned around, her eyes landing on me. Those eyes! They got me every time. Big hazel bedroom eyes that were temptation even for a saint. And I was a sinner through and through.

"Winston Ashford," Billie grumbled, her tone slightly disgusted. "Exactly the man I never wanted to see again."

It turned out neither Swan sister wanted to see us, because I could have sworn Odette mouthed "shit" under her breath, but it was hard to confirm. The restaurant was too busy and the music drifting through the air was too loud.

"Hello, Odette," I greeted the sister that mattered. At least to me. "Or should I call you Dr. Swan?"

My eyes dropped down her body. Fuck, she looked even better than I remembered. She was wearing tight blue jean shorts that hugged her hips and butt just right. Her long, bare legs had a beautiful bronzed tan. She must have been spending a lot of time out in the sun, which would make sense with what Alessio said about her work in Ghana.

She ran a hand through her hair, annoyance clear on her face.

"Dr. Swan," she answered tightly, her tone clipped.

It didn't escape me the way she fisted her hands, her knuckles white and her nails probably digging into her skin.

She wasn't happy to see me. Not. At. All.

"Congratulations. But then, you never doubted your skills, did you?" She narrowed her eyes at me, anger flashing in them. I'd bet my fortune there were words burning her tongue right now. She wanted to spit them out and probably slap my face. Instead, her gaze darted behind me to my family and my brothers-in-law's family. The Nikolaevs.

It was our monthly get-together. No matter what, we always made a point to see each other regularly. Alessio and his family, Aurora and hers, Winston, Royce, and my whole wild brother-in-law's family.

"Come on, soeur, we don't need this shit. Ashfords are a goddamn plague on this plant. Best to keep our distance so we don't catch anything."

Billie's words annoyed the fuck out of me, but I ignored her. I couldn't peel my gaze from her baby sister, drinking her in. I'd need it to jerk off for the next decade. She was still hot as fuck. Maybe even hotter. More confident. Just looking at her made me hard.

Other women could parade around me naked and nothing. Zip. Nada. But one glimpse of her, and I was fully erect.

The air crackled between us, and if one of us didn't leave, New Orleans would get to experience a different kind of fireworks.

"It's nice to see you." Fuck. Why in the fuck was I being nice? She was the one that ended shit between us—before they'd even had a chance to take off. What were her exact words?

A mistake. We were a mistake.

I had never thought the words from a woman's mouth alone could break my heart.

"Mr. Ashford." She tilted her head like a queen. Her eyes over-flowed with ice, the gold freckles in them suddenly frozen. "I'd say it's nice to see you, but it'd be a lie."

Jesus fucking Christ. Women fell down to their knees, worshiping me like a god. Not the other way around. Why couldn't she be like the rest of them? But then I remembered the things that had attracted me to her in the first place—her stunning looks. Her intelligence. And how goddamn stubborn she was.

Turning her back to me, she nudged her sister away from us. "Just stick to the plan," I thought I heard her mutter.

My eyes lingered on her ass, those jean shorts hugging her just right. Seriously, that ass was made for me. It fit my palms just right, and she fucking loved my palms on them.

"Who's that?" the little boy questioned, his blue eyes darting over Billie's shoulders to Odette, then to me.

Odette's answer sliced like a sharp knife. "Nobody important, baby." *Ouch.*

Stop looking at her, my reason commanded. *Look away.*

But my body never listened to reason when it came to her. I watched Odette take a seat, her back to me. Something wasn't right. The tension in her slim shoulders was obvious. Her back was stiff, and she was still fisting her hands.

Maybe I still impact her like she impacts me? One could only hope.

She said something to her sister, and with a frown, I watched her sister and the boy—who had to be Odette's nephew—scurry away.

"Who are they?" my sister Aurora asked curiously, interrupting my staring.

I let Winston take that one, but he just grumbled something under his breath. "I'm going to the bathroom," he announced, standing abruptly. "Unless you want me to grind against your dick, I suggest you move your ass."

Goddamn him. My cock was hard as a rock, and I really didn't need anyone witnessing this reaction I was having to Odette Madeline Swan.

Fucking booth seating. Whoever came up with it should be shot!

Winston disappeared in the direction of the restrooms while I took my seat back.

"Byron, who's that?" Aurora asked again. She was relentless

when she wanted answers. It was probably what made her a good FBI agent.

"A doctor. She treated me once." And I fucked her brains out. Or maybe she fucked my brains out. It was still up for debate. "She was still in medical school back then."

"You must have been a cranky patient if she had that reaction to seeing you again," my sister mused.

"And you're surprised?" Sasha Nikolaev, the annoying fuck that he was, chimed in. "She probably hated the fact she had to touch his ugly ass."

I flipped him off. "I'm better looking than you."

"Yet I'm married and you're not."

"If you don't want your wife to become a young, attractive widow, you'll shut your mouth," I deadpanned. Okay, maybe it pissed me off that Sasha—of all people—ended up happily married even with his annoying mouth, yet here I was, detested by the only woman I'd ever truly wanted.

You and I were a mistake.

Those fucking words would haunt me forever.

"Someone is waiting for me. Blood Diamond." A deep, accented voice traveled over the restaurant. "I see her. Don't bother walking me over."

I followed the voice and found a man, about six feet tall with dark skin and dark eyes. He wore a camouflage uniform, except it was—the catalog flashed through my mind of different military uniforms—it was Ghana's. Benefits of having a photographic memory. The question was what was the Ghana military doing here?

He prowled through the restaurant, uncaring who or what was in his way. And he didn't stop until he was at Odette's table. I watched fear flicker in her expression before a professional mask slid on her face.

She muttered something but she was too far away; I couldn't hear a fucking thing. The fucker in the uniform grinned—viciously

—his eyes lingering on her chest. Anger unlike anything I'd ever experienced before settled deep in my stomach, and I clenched my fists.

"What in the fuck is that guy doing here?" Vasili hissed.

My eyes darted to Vasili, then followed his gaze. His attention was on the man sitting across from Odette. I took in his face; something about him looked familiar. Yet I couldn't place him. I couldn't remember. I had a photographic memory, yet when Odette was around, my brain just stopped functioning and my cock took over.

Fucking bad!

"Who is it?" I asked Vasili.

"It's Danso Sabir. A contract killer for the diamond smugglers in Africa."

My brows furrowed. Why was he talking to Odette? Then my brother's comment from yesterday rushed to the forefront of my mind. The Swan sisters' names came up on the dark web in connection with diamonds. And here she was now—meeting a diamond smuggler. It couldn't possibly be a coincidence.

I returned my attention to her table, tension creeping up my spine. No wonder Odette was nervous. She tried to hide it, but I could see it in her shuddering breaths and each of her trembling fingers.

Danso leaned across the table, whispering something, his eyes flashing with something sadistic and dark. Whatever he said had Odette stiffening and leaning away from him. Reaching into her purse, she pulled out a black velvet bag and pushed it across the table, careful not to let her fingers touch him.

My ears buzzed, disappointment washing over me.

"Are you sure she's a doctor?" Alexei questioned, his voice sounding distorted. "And not a diamond smuggler?"

My jaw clenched, my teeth grinding as I watched the transaction. Odette went to pull her hand back, but she wasn't quick enough. The fucker grabbed her by the wrist. Anger simmered in my blood. It burned in my throat, in my chest, and covered my vision with a red mist.

He touched her.

Odette jerked her hand, trying to free herself from his grip, and before I knew what I was doing, I was on my feet, storming through the restaurant.

"Get your hands off her," I hissed, dark warning reverberating. Taking advantage of Danso's surprise, Odette yanked her hand back. She stood up abruptly, her chair falling behind her with a loud thud that brought everyone's attention our way.

The tension around us was louder than the music of the trumpeter. Louder than the drunken shouts swarming the French Quarter. Guests cast curious and cautious glances our way, but nobody dared move. Except the Nikolaevs. I didn't need to look behind me to know they'd shuffled their women behind them, and their hands were probably reaching for their weapons.

Danso's eyes darted behind me, confirming my suspicions.

"She's all yours," he finally said, standing up and brushing off his sleeves. As if he could see anything on that ugly uniform. He shot Odette a meaningful look. "For now."

Odette didn't move, frozen in her spot. Both of us watched the fucker walk away. Her hands trembled, mine were fisted at my sides. It took all my self-restraint not to go after him.

Once he was out of sight, I turned my attention to Odette. Her bottom lip trembled as she took it between her teeth as if she were scared to break down. She admitted to me a long time ago she wasn't much of a crier. The fact that she was close to tears attested to how upset she was.

"What in the fuck are you doing here meeting with a diamond smuggler?" I hissed.

As if my words snapped her out of whatever spell she'd been under, her eyes flashed and her lips thinned.

"Mr. Ashford, let's get one thing straight." She bent over to pick up her purse off the floor and fuck if my cock didn't respond to the movement. Her round ass was just a few inches away from me and images of her naked and bent over the bed, love-sofa, chair—every piece of furniture in that hotel room—as I fucked her flashed through my mind. Not helpful at all. She straightened up, squaring her shoulders and meeting my gaze head-on. "Whatever I do or don't do is none of your fucking business. Understood?"

I took a step toward her, but Odette stood her ground, her chin tilting up in her stubbornness. Just the way I remembered it. Except, back then she did it when she was flirting with me.

"He's bad news," I gritted.

"So are you," she said as she slid her bag over her shoulder. "Goodbye."

And just like that, she dismissed me, leaving me staring at her back.

What. The. Fuck.

Chapter 22
Odette

We're going to die.

The words repeated in my mind like a broken record. Over and over again.

If I wasn't so shaken, I'd strangle my sister with my bare hands. I loved her, but I loved my son more.

One million dollars!

Danso called it interest. I called it bullshit. But I was in no position to argue with a criminal. A renowned killer. *Jesus Christ.* For a split second, I even imagined killing him, but there were bigger fish than him, and they'd keep coming until they got what they wanted.

One million dollars! I thought again. We'd never be able to come up with that kind of money. We were dancing on the line between broke and stone broke.

A bead of sweat trickled down my spine, and it had nothing to do with the warm February temperatures of New Orleans. It had everything to do with the man I just saw. The combo of meeting with a criminal and seeing my ex-lover was enough to send me into a full blown panic.

Byron Ashford.

Butterflies erupted low in my stomach, even after all this time. This attraction to him burned—in more ways than one.

Good God.

Of all the people to run into today, why him? Seeing Byron rattled me more than I cared to admit. It cracked wounds open that I thought were sealed shut. Every woman went through one earth-shattering heartbreak. He was mine. End of story.

I'd moved on. He'd moved on. Obviously. He had a baby next to him. And a gorgeous woman. Not the bitchy blonde fiancée that I'd run into before. This one almost seemed nice. Truthfully though, she could have been a wife to any one of those men. And what *men*. Blond. Pale blue eyes. Scary looking. Nah, she had to be Byron's wife. He'd be her type. I mean, how could he not be?

A wave of something unpleasant slithered through my veins. *Envy. Jealousy.* It was ridiculous. But I couldn't help feeling the irrational anger that shot through my veins. He was out there getting laid, and I couldn't even remember the last time I had sex. Long, lonely years of no sex.

I groaned out loud as I rushed through the back hallway of the restaurant. My life was hanging by a thread, and I was pondering Byron's relationship status.

I didn't fucking care. I was content. Happy. My healthy and wonderful son and my sister were all that mattered.

Finally spotting the bathroom sign, I pushed on the door when I heard a painful grunt. My eyes roamed the bathroom, finding my son and sister unharmed. And then I saw it. Or rather, him. Winston Ashford.

"W-what happened?" My eyes locked on Winston's big body, sprawled on the bathroom floor.

"I had to knock him out," Billie snapped, her voice low. "Shut the door before someone sees us."

I shook my head. "Jesus Christ, Billie. You'll have every goddamn person after us by the time you're done. Why did you knock him out?"

"He wanted to take Ares," she whimpered.

I frowned. "Why?"

Winston Ashford didn't strike me as a man who cared much for children, much less kidnapped them.

"He thought Ares was his."

Surprise flared in me. I had never hooked up with Winston, unless—

"Billie, why would he think that?"

Her brown eyes found mine and a soft groan left her lips. "Because I hooked up with the jerk that night you hooked up with his brother."

My eyes widened. "I thought you couldn't stand him."

She shrugged. "I can't." Her eyes flickered to the unconscious body on the ground. "I still can't. Obviously."

Oh, Lord.

This day was getting worse by the second. "Step over him and give me my son," I ordered, my patience teetering on the edge of control. "Then let's get out of here before anyone finds him."

"Sorry, Winston," Billie murmured as she stepped over him. "You're lucky I didn't kill you, though."

We're both lucky she didn't kill him, I thought silently. I wouldn't put it past him to come after us. As if we didn't have enough trouble.

Once out of the bathroom, I took Ares into my arms and squeezed him to me. "I love you, baby."

"Love you too, Mommy."

He had seen too much crap over the last six months. His routine was pretty much nonexistent. He missed his kindergarten friends. Since we hadn't stayed put in one spot longer than a week for the past six months, I'd been homeschooling him. Ares being Ares, soaked up everything. All you had to do was show him—or read to him—something once and he remembered it.

"We're gonna have to move quickly. Okay, buddy?" I had to be the worst mother on this planet. "If bad people take Mom or your

Aunt Billie, you scream and you run. You run until you find a police officer. Oui?"

No child should be dragged through this shit. See this shit. And here I was, explaining it to my kid.

His blue eyes watched me seriously. "Oui, Maman."

Goddamn it, he deserved better than this. Every child did, but when it came to mine, I wanted to give him the best of everything. Not in terms of material items, those came and went. But in terms of quality of life. Our parents had given it to us. When my mother died, Dad ensured we had a good life. Wonderful memories.

What was I giving my boy? Nightmares. A life on the run.

I swallowed hard, pushing hair out of my face. We didn't have much time, surely Winston's family had already started to wonder where he was. "Okay, hold my hand. As soon as we push through the door, we run."

After a terse nod from my son, I stood up, holding his small hand in mine, and found my sister's eyes. She nodded too.

We headed toward the back, until we found the emergency exit. It was the only way out, unless we wanted to risk going back through the front. That wasn't an option. So I pushed the door open, feeling the sunlight hit our faces, just as the alarm sounded.

"This day is turning into a full-blown disaster," I muttered as I took off down the cobblestone alley, holding Ares's hand.

As we ran out of there like the devil was on our heels, the alarm blaring behind us and sending the entire building into commotion, one thought lingered in the back of my mind.

The one thing that never crossed my mind to do. But I might not have a choice now.

Chapter 23
Byron

Something set off the alarm, the shrieking sound piercing my eardrums, shaking the entire building.

Alexei grabbed Kostya and Aurora, ushering them from the table. Aurora refused to be rushed, always taking her time and rarely losing her cool. She was like me in that regard. Vasili had already left with his family and Sasha's wife. Thank fuck Royce wasn't here. He'd go busting through the building and probably shoot the fucking place up. Unfortunately, Sasha was here, and he was doing exactly that.

"Go with my brothers," he ordered his wife and plowed his way through the crowd trying to go the opposite way.

I shot to my feet and started to push my way through. *Odette's still in the back.* I had to get to her. I barely made two steps out when Aurora's voice came from behind me.

"Byron, you're going the wrong way." *My woman's still in the back.* "Byron."

I locked eyes with Alexei. "Take them out. I'll see you in a bit."

"She has my kid." Winston's voice came from behind me. "That's my son."

All of us turned to see Winston swaying on his feet. He stumbled forward.

"Your kid?" I hissed. "How would you have a kid with—" Suddenly, realization washed over me. That night in Le Bar Américain, they must have hooked up, despite whatever argument they had going when Odette and I found them at the table.

"Yes, my kid. Do you not understand English?" my brother spat as he swayed on his feet, his eyes slightly unfocused.

I gritted my teeth. I understood English just fine. I loved my brother—all my siblings—but I'd be lying if I said there wasn't a small part of me that was jealous of my brother right now. Odette and I would have had a child the same age right now if the accident—

Refusing to go back to that day, I focused on my brother who still looked disoriented.

"Were you drinking back there?" I gritted.

"She hit me upside the head," he mumbled, rubbing his forehead. It was only then that I noticed a purple bruise forming over his temple. "I wanted to talk to her about our son, but the maddening woman smashed my skull." Jesus, if Billie was anything like Winston, we'd have a disaster on our hands. "Then she took off. Billie and her sister set off the alarm." Then, noticing my look, Winston added, "I didn't touch the fucking alcohol."

I kept my expression blank, but relief slammed into me with an intensity that stole my breath. Winston had finally reached his sobriety, and it was preferable we kept it that way. Winston and I dealt with our wounds and scars differently. He numbed them—or used to—in a bottle, while I dealt with it by putting relationships and women at arm's length. Hence the sharing of the women. It was easier to let someone else take care of the emotional part than risk them getting close to me.

All except for one. Dr. Swan slipped through my defenses effortlessly and without even trying. It was as if she was my other half and I'd been waiting for her all along. Yes, it was ironic that she wanted nothing to do with me.

"What are you talking about?" Aurora's voice held disbelief that we all felt. "Byron's doctor hit you?"

"No, her sister knocked me out."

"Special Forces and a woman knocks you out," I muttered under my breath.

Winston grinned—the smile telling me he had a plan. And not a good one. Jesus, I wanted to wipe off the shit-eating grin with disinfectant. Or better yet, wipe it off with my fists. At least it'd match that bruise on his forehead.

Sasha returned before I could follow through. "Someone exited through the emergency door, that's what set off the alarm."

Someone finally turned it off and the silence was almost as deafening as the sirens.

Winston flopped back onto the seat of our table. "I told you. The Swan sisters escaped that way. They took my son."

Breathe, Byron. Keep your cool.

The restaurant was empty. Aurora and I sat back down, keeping our eyes on Winston.

"What makes you think that's your son?" I questioned my brother. He'd never indicated he had hooked up with the Swan sister.

Sasha and Alexei sat down too, Kostya on his father's lap. Nothing fazed my nephew. If a bomb exploded next door, Kostya would maybe glance at the damage, but wouldn't bat an eye.

"He's the right age and has the same colored eyes as mine. Exact same," Winston said, waving a waiter over. "Water. And some ice, please." The waiter was about to leave our table when my brother stopped him. "What do five-year-old boys drink and eat?"

The waiter gave him a blank look. "Umm, I don't know. Nuggets and apple juice maybe," he answered, his eyes tentative. "I don't have any kids."

"Just bring him water," I said, dismissing the waiter. "Maybe a functioning brain too," I added sarcastically.

Once the waiter was out of earshot, Aurora tried to bring some sanity back down to this insane family. "Winston, I don't think you should jump to conclusions. Lots of kids have blue eyes."

"He looks just like us in our baby pictures," Winston claimed. Although, now that I thought about it, he wasn't far off. And judging by the look on Aurora's face, she thought so too.

"Did you get any information from your woman?" Sasha asked.

My teeth clenched. "No."

"If either one of the women are involved in diamond smuggling," Alexei stated calmly, "it'll put them all at risk, and they won't hesitate to kill the kid."

Everyone's heads turned my way.

"Byron, can't you ask your doctor?" Aurora said softly, her hand coming to my forearm and squeezing gently.

Sasha answered on my behalf. Not very helpfully, if I might add. "She didn't seem keen on seeing him." I narrowed my eyes on the Russian. "Might be better to send someone else in. Someone more charming."

I fought the twitch in my jaw and the growing urge to lunge across the table. I wanted to break his nose and make that face a little bit less crazy. How his wife didn't scream every time she looked at him was beyond me.

Rather than punching Nikolaev in the face, I smiled serenely at my sister and brother.

"Don't worry. I'll drag the truth out of Odette."

Chapter 24
Odette

I made my way through the streets to the dingy little hotel on the outskirts of New Orleans. The pouring rain soaked through my clothes as I stomped through puddles covering the cobblestone of the French Quarter.

Bitterness slithered through me. Yesterday, I thought we'd be free of smugglers—finally able to start our lives. And yet, here we were, none the better. I went to five banks, hoping for a loan.

A million-dollar loan.

They pretty much laughed in my face. I had no permanent residence. Barely any activity under my social security number. Some even insinuated my identity was false. After my last failed attempt at a loan, I roamed the streets aimlessly. I didn't have it in me to go back to the hotel.

I just needed to come up with an idea to get my hands on a million dollars.

Except, my stupid brain kept circling back to Byron Ashford. I never expected to run into him again, least of all here. In New Orleans.

It was raining hard, drenching me to my bones. Yet, I couldn't feel the chill nor the rain. I was numb. To the rain. To my feelings. To everything.

Maybe I'd reached a tipping point.

I turned the corner into a dark alley, taking a shortcut to the hotel. It was dark, damp, and the scent of urine filled the air. I took two steps in when my head flew sideways, hitting the building wall. My cheek exploded as I felt my purse fall to the ground, landing with a loud thud.

I took a lungful of air and readied myself to scream, but before I could make a sound, a hand wrapped around my mouth. I bit into it with all my might and another slap landed across my cheek. Pain exploded, followed by a burning sensation. My eyes stung as I blinked my tears away, desperate to see around me. A shove and a thwack smacked against my skull. I fell to my knees, facedown. Gurgling sounds filled the air. Mine.

A sharp kick to my stomach followed and I collapsed on my front. I yelped, crawling on my knees, reaching for my bag. I had pepper spray, I just had to get my hands on it. Just as my fingers brushed against faux leather, a booted foot flattened over my fingers.

I screamed, but another kick in my stomach followed. "Make one more sound and I'll shoot you."

There were many times over the last months I'd worried we'd find ourselves dead, but it wasn't until tonight that my fear had a shape and a taste. His leg the only piece of his body within my reach, I wrapped my hand around his ankle and pulled myself closer. I didn't make a sound, but I sunk my teeth into his shin, like a rabid dog. It was a matter of life or death.

"You goddamn whore!" A shiny green army boot kicked me off.

The warm, metallic taste of blood filled my mouth. Adrenaline coursed through my veins, and I felt every cell in my body awaken with panic. Another kick followed, hitting my neck. My body throbbed. My breaths became shallow and my face ached like never before.

I started crawling away from him, my knees scraping against the cobblestone. A hand wrapped around my hair, yanking my head up with a violent jerk. Then he grabbed my foot, pulling me back toward him. He spun me around, bringing me face-to-face with him.

"Two weeks. Or I'll end you and your sister, once and for all."

He let go of my hair and my face hit the concrete with a thud. His footsteps echoed in the dark alley, softened by the raindrops that were coming back into focus.

I peeled myself from the ground and reached for my purse, grabbing the scattered contents. Then, I painfully made my way back to the run-down hotel that had suddenly become a haven. I had no idea how I made it back, past the lobby, and up to our room.

The hotel door shut with a soft click and I stood there, finding the room enveloped in darkness, two figures sound asleep on the bed. It was only then that I finally broke down. My back against the door, I slid down to the floor and curled into a ball.

I bawled like a baby, keeping my cries silent while my son and sister slept.

"Soeur." Sister.

I woke up to a soft voice and nudging. I issued a groan—wrapping arms around me—my entire body aching. I didn't want to wake up. I didn't want to feel all this pain.

The grip on me tightened. "Odette, what the fuck happened to you?"

My brain finally caught up. The reality of what had happened slammed into me, and my eyes flew open to see my sister crouched on the floor next to me. I must have fallen asleep crying, and now I had some explaining to do.

Wiping the back of my hand over my eyes, I murmured a weak, "Nothing."

"Don't give me that bullshit. Clearly something happened. You're black and blue."

I let out a heavy sigh and met my sister's gaze. "Is it bad?"

"Your hair is tousled. Your lip is split and swollen. Your cheek —" She gripped my shoulders. "Tell me who did this," she demanded.

For a split second, I debated lying to her, but I was too tired. I didn't have it in me.

"The diamond smuggler," I murmured tiredly.

She gasped and her eyes widened. "But why? We told him we'd find a way to get him the money. Right?"

I shrugged. "I guess he wants it sooner versus later. Or wants to show us he's serious."

"I want to murder him," she hissed angrily.

Ares's small body stirred on the bed and both of our eyes shot to him. I held my breath, hoping he wouldn't wake up. I didn't want him to see me like this. I had to get cleaned up. It seemed like we stayed frozen for hours, when in fact it was only a few minutes.

"Maybe someone does us all a favor and murders him," I whispered. "That way, we're not guilty of the crime."

"I fucked up so bad." Urgency colored her voice. We both knew this wasn't some simple robbery she'd committed. We were batting way out of our league, and it had become apparent this could get us killed. Drastic measures were needed.

"We need to fly to D.C. and reach out to Nico Morrelli," I told her. "With some luck, we'll get through to him."

She sighed. "We haven't had much luck lately, so I won't hold my breath for it." She was right; our luck had taken a downturn and there was no end in sight. It was one thing after another. "Let's get you cleaned up," she offered, helping me to my feet.

We made it into the bathroom and the reflection that stared back at me was gloomy indeed.

"Jesus Christ, I look like a battered wife."

"Get in the shower and get your cuts cleaned up." She moved

around the bathroom efficiently, starting the shower and getting the toiletries out.

"Billie?"

"Yeah." She reached for the towels.

"Why did Winston think Ares was his kid?"

She froze mid-step and for a few heartbeats remained like that. Then she got herself together and turned around, locking eyes with me.

"I told you I slept with him. Afterward, we had a scare and thought we were pregnant." My mouth shaped into a silent O while I stared at her with disbelief. She usually shared those details with me—whether I asked or not—-so I found it unusual that she had never mentioned it before. "I'd rather not talk about all that. He's my sore subject, like Byron's yours."

With a wordless nod, I stepped into the shower.

It would seem we both made some mistakes when it came to the Ashfords.

Chapter 25
Byron

I got two hours' worth of sleep last night.

Images of Odette Swan ran through my mind. All the memories of that single night flashed through my skull like a movie on repeat. The way I fucked her against the mirror in that hotel room while she moaned my name. The image of her on the bed with her thighs spread open, her long legs hooked over my shoulders.

Her moans and whimpers were an addiction no man could forget nor resist.

It had been a week and everything had spiraled out of control. I had men looking into her and her sister. Yet somehow, barely anything had come out of it. Either my men were getting sloppy or the Swan sisters were indeed working with diamond smugglers. It was the only thing that could keep their trail so fucking clean.

I might have to resort to Nico Morrelli's services. Although I preferred not to.

"What's wrong with you today?" my brother Royce asked, throwing himself into the dining room chair and propping his legs up on the table.

"Nothing." I eyed his expensive and dirty shoes on the shining wooden surface of the long table. "Do you mind?"

He cocked his eyebrow, then followed my gaze to his feet on my table. "Actually, I do. My legs hurt like a bitch."

Our live-in kitchen staff walked in carrying trays of food and coffee. I waited until they put it all out and departed before resuming our conversation.

"Have you been hiking in the woods?" I asked dryly. "Or maybe stalking someone in California? I know those Hollywood pavements are hard on your ankles and knees."

He promptly flipped me off.

"Why do you look like someone has stuck something up your ass?" Kingston, my youngest brother, asked coldly, showing up out of nowhere. He didn't frequently visit the States, and much like Alexei Nikolaev, Kingston liked to keep to himself. He loved us in his own way. Well, all of us but our father.

It was only after I assured him Senator Ashford wouldn't be anywhere near my estate that he agreed to stay under my roof whenever he was in town. He'd cut all ties with our father, not that I could blame him.

"He ran into his fling," Winston took the liberty of answering on my behalf. God, why were all my brothers under my roof today? "Dr. Swan."

"Didn't you have a thing with the Swan girl too?" Royce asked, reading his paper and sipping his coffee.

I growled. "Winston, I swear to God—"

"Her sister." Winston's tone conveyed annoyance. "Not the same woman," he hissed at Royce, then flipped him off. "Freak."

God, what a way to start the day off. Suddenly, I regretted my open-door policy. The penthouse I kept downtown was off-limits but this—the Ashford manor—was a family home. At least, I tried to make it so.

"She looked good," Winston stated pensively. "Better than I remembered."

"I sure as hell hope you're talking about Billie and not Odette." Otherwise, he'd be a dead man.

"I told you, Royce is the freak, not me," Winston answered seriously.

"I'm not the freak here," Royce deadpanned. "Can you two little bitches stop whining? You're older yet you whine the worst."

"Watch yourself." I glared at him.

"We can have a sparring session." Royce grinned. It was his favorite pastime and his way of releasing tension. I wasn't in the mood for it today. I had no idea what crawled up his ass, but considering his impulsive and crazy nature, it could be any number of things.

"I'm busy adulting," I drawled. "Besides, I know I can still make you cry. Now, stop talking so I can think."

"About what?" Kingston asked, disinterest clear in his tone. He couldn't give two fucks about our conversation. He probably had someone targeted as a hit for the Omertà organization, and we were his alibi. I didn't give a shit, as long as he was around.

"He wants Dr. Swan back," Winston answered unhelpfully. I shot him a glare. He'd better watch it.

"I'm going to kick you all out, onto your heads."

"Listen here, you little bitch," Royce said, ignoring my threat. "If you want a woman, then you go and get her." He laid out his paper. "Get your fill of her and then move on. I don't need to put up with your moody ass at breakfast."

"And that's working so well for you, huh?"

"At least I'm getting my fill of her while you're perishing in the desert."

"Will you shut the fuck up?" I muttered dryly before taking a sip of my coffee.

"Fuck, this coffee is strong," he grumbled. "I've had green tea for a week straight. Women and their green teas."

God, grant me patience so I don't murder my brother. "You can always leave without breakfast."

Royce sighed, rolling his eyes. "I need to take pleasure where I can. Like this breakfast, for instance." It was my turn to roll my eyes. "Do you know what hard times are?" he said.

"As if you do," I remarked dryly. "You've had a silver spoon in your mouth your entire life."

Royce ignored me as if I hadn't spoken. "My woman doesn't even know I exist, except when she wants to bang me. I feel used, Byron."

I cracked a smile. Royce's theatrics always managed to cheer me up. He had a way of exaggerating, and somehow, I didn't think he minded being *used*.

"She's still not giving you the time of day, huh?" I mused. "Except between the sheets, of course."

"Do we have any updates on the boy?" Winston asked, ending Royce's show for the morning. It was all he could think about—Billie Swan and her son. Except, there was no record of her having a child.

"No."

"How can that be?" he wondered. "You saw it yourself, Byron. That kid is the spitting image of me when I was a kid."

Kingston grabbed a paper and looked it over. "Why don't you just kidnap her and keep her?"

Bunch of "atta boys" traveled around the table while Winston looked like he was seriously considering it. My brothers were idiots.

"Oh, for Christ's sake." I exhaled heavily. "We aren't gangsters."

All three of my brothers shrugged. "Technically."

They referred to our mother who'd had connections to the Syndicate. To the Kingpins. She was just used by our father to get necessary funds to advance his political career. Unfortunately for him, when she was killed, all those funds passed on to me. I was the executor of her estate, and it burned our father.

My brothers exchanged looks. "Well, if that's the case, I'm

kidnapping Dr. Swan first." Yes, apparently I was an idiot too. "After all, I'm the eldest."

Royce and Winston high-fived each other. Bunch of immature boys.

"Find something she needs and use it against her," Royce said—always with the unhelpful advice. "You've been pining for her for far too long. Marry the woman."

I stared at them for a moment, ideas dancing through my mind. I could blackmail her. Maybe something to do with that diamond smuggler. That exchange had definitely been illegal. Or I could hack into her phone and find whatever else she had going on. Clearly she was involved in something.

"Big brother likes the advice," Kingston stated, his dark eyes on me. It was impossible to tell what he was thinking. Was he serious, or joking? The little boy Kingston was before he was taken from us had been carefree and happy. So protective of our sister. The brother we finally got back was... different. Slightly broken. Regardless, it felt good to have all my brothers here.

"Just do it, Byron. Take the woman and work out the details once you put a ring on her finger."

I threw my hands up in the air. "She hates my guts."

"Yeah, nothing new there," Royce deadpanned. "Women usually hate your guts. Just look at Nicki."

"Don't put Nicki and Odette in the same sentence," I growled. "Odette was the best sex of my life." I pushed my hand through my hair. "I've been walking around with a fucking semi-hard-on ever since I saw her."

All my brothers stared at me for a moment before bursting into laughter.

"You're fucked." Kingston chuckled. My brother *actually* chuckled. It was such a rare sight, I actually paused.

"What are you going to do?" Royce asked. "Maybe ask her if she'll take care of your semi?"

"I don't have time for this shit," I growled, rearranging the napkin on my lap. "I certainly won't be taking advice from the brother who can't get a date from the woman he's been pining after for decades."

For the remainder of breakfast, I ignored their jabs.

Rush hour in the city was in full swing by the time I walked into the restaurant to see my old friend Kristoff Baldwin. The place was crowded, but our spot was always reserved. It was where we usually met since it was conveniently located between our two office buildings. We called it the "meet in the middle" restaurant.

I made my way over to him at the back of the restaurant and took my usual spot. My drink was already waiting for me. Bourbon for me. Scotch for Kristoff.

"You look like shit," Kristoff deadpanned, looking me up and down. The comment was rich coming from the man who'd seen us through explosions and bullets. We'd served a few deployments together. He saved my life on his last deployment, just a few days shy from getting out of the military. It bonded us for life.

"Aren't you a cheerful and supportive friend?" My voice was clipped while my heart raced. Adrenaline from my workout an hour ago still ran fast through my veins. After my shitty breakfast with my brothers, I decided to take out my frustration and world of regret on the treadmill. I should have convinced her to give us a chance all those years ago. I should have dragged her out of the hospital and made us talk. Made everything, most of all us, work.

My mind drifted to that day. The last day I'd seen her—body splayed on the pavement, destruction all around her.

The scent of apples mixed with copper as I held her in my arms. The pent-up emotions swirled inside me, suffocating me. Fear mixed with anger.

"Ambulance!" I roared, my voice breaking. I couldn't lose her. Not like this. "Someone call an ambulance!"

Water flooded the street, spilling from the fire hydrant. Odette's body lay in a red puddle—water and blood mixing. Her hair sprawled, red tresses stained with blood.

My heart hammered against my ribs, fearing that she was gone. I had lost her again... except this time, she'd no longer walk this earth. The breeze swept through the street, but her wet, bloody hair didn't move. The buzz of the city was a distant noise.

"Open your eyes, baby." She lay limp, her eyelids closed and her chest barely rising and falling. I cradled her head, those hazel eyes I loved shutting me out forever.

My heart bled right alongside her. It twisted into knots that would never untie. It hurt to breathe, suffocating me. My throat clenched, each heartbeat painful in my chest. Each breath I took burned my lungs.

"Where is the fucking ambulance?" I shouted, panic lacing my voice while my eyes darted around for any sign of it. "Did someone call?"

A soft breath. Hers. Mine. I didn't know. All I knew was that her pulse was too weak for my strong girl. For my strong woman.

"There's a union protest blocking their passage," someone shouted. "It might take them an hour to get here."

I couldn't wait an hour. It could be a matter of life and death.

Evaluating the pros and cons, I decided to take matters into my own hands. I used my military medical training to ensure there wasn't a spinal injury before lifting her into my arms. Pulling her close to my chest, her blood staining my white shirt, I started running. The nearest hospital was three blocks away.

"Don't you dare die on me," I murmured, thanking all known and unknown saints I'd kept in shape even after getting out of the military. Gasps, chatter, honking—it was all background noise. Distant to the wild thundering of my heart and fear that she'd leave this world.

I'll accept a life without her, *I vowed silently as I ran through the busy, metropolitan city.* I won't even regret it. Just let her live. God, please just fucking let her live.

A soft, pained moan escaped her mouth and her graceful fingers moved to hold on to me. My grip on her tightened. Fuck, I should bear this pain. Not her. Never her.

"It's me, baby," I rasped, never stopping. "Just hold on. We're almost there." Her mouth moved but no sound came out. "Open your pretty eyes for me." A single whimper. Her eyes didn't open. "Please, baby. Let me see you."

Ice wrapped around my lungs and I ran even faster, ignoring the burning in my chest, my eyes, my heart. I just needed to get her to the hospital.

The blaring of the ambulance sirens carried through the breeze. The glimpse of the hospital and emergency entrance entered my vision.

"We're almost there. Hang on." *I prayed she heard my pleas.* "For me, baby."

The moment I stepped through the emergency doors, paramedics surrounded us. I answered a torrent of questions, yet couldn't repeat a single one. They rushed us into a room. Frantic movements. Hushed voices.

"For Christ's sake, will she be okay?" *I roared, my composure gone. Anxiety pounded against my chest, rattling the cage and ready to take over. I hadn't felt it since my mother was shot. I couldn't lose this woman. Not like this. God, I'll give her up, I prayed. Just let her live.*

They laid her still body onto the bed and slid an oxygen mask over her face.

"How are you related to her?" *The scent of antiseptic, bitter and full of reminders, filled my lungs.*

"I'm her husband." *It was the first thing that came out. I couldn't risk them kicking me out. I'd tear down this hospital if they took her out of my sight.* "Just save her. Do whatever. Just fucking save... her."

My voice broke, each word making the ache in my chest spread. My throat burned, each breath hoarse. How was it possible for a woman I barely even knew to mean so much to me? One night. It was only one night. Nobody fell that fast.

Nobody but you, *my heart whispered.*

Jesus H. Christ.

An hour later, the only sound calming me was the constant beeping of her heart monitor. She lay in the hospital bed; her face was pale, but her chest rose and fell rhythmically. The movements brought me comfort, right along with the beep, beep, beep of the machine. I could breathe again. It was the sign she was alive. She was still here, with me.

She had a concussion. Likely a result of hitting her head on the pavement after being hit by the car. But she'd recover. She would need rest and to take it easy for a few weeks.

I'd take care of her.

The bloodied sonogram photo crumpled in my hand. I gripped it like my life depended on it. Maybe it did. I needed answers. Confirmation. Assurances.

The door to the room opened softly and the doctor entered the room to check on Odette's vitals again. Her movements were quiet. Efficient.

She looked vaguely familiar, but I couldn't quite place her. I usually remembered names of anyone I spoke to, which meant I hadn't spoken to her before.

"She'll pull through," the doctor assured again.

"And the baby?" My voice was hoarse with the pent-up emotions swirling inside me. I almost broke at the pity in her eyes.

"I'm sorry, the baby didn't make it."

It was the last fragile thread connecting us, and it was being ripped from me. Our baby had been ripped from me.

When Odette woke up, she was done with me. She didn't want me. She'd called us a mistake. Her biggest mistake.

Fuck, I should have brought her back to my home and made her give us a chance. I should have fought her, convinced her I was everything she desired and forced her to stay with me until she saw how good we could be together.

But I didn't.

I needed to move the fuck on. It had been six fucking years. Screw her and her tempting body. That gorgeous mouth. Incredible brain.

Shit! Stop it, man.

"What's got into your ass, Byron? A dildo?" Kristoff mused, studying me.

I twisted my face in disgust. If he knew my sour mood was related to a woman, he'd never let me live it down. It didn't help that I pulled his leg when he was pining for his beautiful secretary. Of course, he was a happily married man now. Head over heels in love, working for baby number five or six. I'd lost fucking count.

"The fact that that word even came out of your mouth tells me you're doing some freaky shit with your wife."

He shook his head. "You need to get laid, dude."

"I fucking agree," I muttered. Except there was only one woman who could get me hard. Six fucking years. I needed her back in my bed.

"So, what's stopping you?" he asked casually, leaning back into his seat and bringing the scotch to his mouth.

"One single woman." I reached for my own drink. "If you can believe it. I can't get it up without her."

He frowned. "What woman?"

I shook my head, sipping my drink. "And she fucking says I'm nobody important."

Kristoff gave me a puzzled look. "Who?"

"Do you fucking listen to me at all?"

Kristoff smiled, amusement flashing in his gaze. "Honestly, you haven't said much, so you must be having a conversation in your head." He picked up his phone and checked for messages. "I'm sending my wife a message that we'll be late for dinner. You obviously need mental support."

He had become so damn dramatic and supportive since getting married.

"I don't need mental support," I muttered under my breath, before taking another sip of my bourbon.

His eyes never left his phone. "Yes, you do." He placed his phone back on the table. "Now, talk."

I pushed my fingers through my hair. I did that more in the last few days since I'd seen her than in my entire goddamn life.

"Talk about what?" I feigned ignorance. I had never told another soul about what happened with Odette. Winston knew some bits. Royce had some bits. But nobody had the whole story.

"Talk to me about the only woman who is able to give you a hard-on," he said, his expression serious.

A familiar laugh came from behind me. "You can only get a hard-on for one woman, brother? Man, that's a bummer."

"What in the fuck are you doing here?"

Royce's eyes widened in feigned distress. "Geez, what a fucking welcome."

I sipped my bourbon and shook my head. My younger brother had a knack for showing up at the worst time and saying the worst things. My best friend apparently agreed. I watched Kristoff put his hands on his temples. His personality gave him a headache too, evidently. Royce was chaotic. Kristoff was the exact opposite.

"You do know this lunch is by invitation only," Kristoff grumbled.

Unfazed, my brother threw himself into the empty chair and leaned back, signaling a waitress over. "I'll have what my big brother's drinking."

She offered him a beaming smile and scurried away, hoping to impress him. There was no chance in hell of that. There was only one woman he had eyes for.

"So tell us, brother, how can we help you get this woman?" The waitress came back with his drink, and he took it with a grin. "Thanks, lovely." She blushed crimson, then scurried away. I almost wanted her to stay so my brother wouldn't continue talking. No such luck. He returned his attention to me. "I cannot handle the idea of you going around limp-dicked."

Kristoff choked on his drink, stifling his laugh. Yep, my baby brother managed to give my friend headaches *and* make him laugh. The oddest fucking combination.

"Did you read that word in the dictionary?"

Royce grinned. "Some medical dictionaries. Basic anatomy, brother. Nothing to be ashamed of."

God, give me patience so I don't murder this guy!

"Why are you here, Royce?" I demanded to know. I loved him, but it required a whole different level of patience to deal with him, and I wasn't prepared.

"I need a favor from you," he answered. When I raised my eyebrow, he continued, "There's a deal in the works for Willow. I need you to kill it."

I rolled my eyes. "You've really got to give up on that one."

He snickered. "Like you gave up on your woman."

Touché, little brother. Not that I'd ever admit it to him. Although it seemed to be common knowledge at this point.

"Okay, let's ignore him," Kristoff interrupted, looking at me now. "This woman. Where did you meet her?"

Royce, that little prick, answered before I could even open my mouth. "In France. She treated a sunburn on his back."

"And how do you know that?" I grumbled at my brother, although I knew. My siblings were like gossiping grandmothers.

Kristoff held my gaze. He knew I rarely let anyone touch my back, and there weren't many women out there—for sure not in our social circles—that wanted to touch that scaly skin.

"She's a good nurse... doctor."

"Is she a nurse or a doctor?" Kristoff looked from me to Royce back to me.

My brother just shrugged. "I can't keep up."

"She's a doctor." I rubbed my face. "The best-looking doctor I have ever seen. I have to do something about it."

"Have her treat you? As a doctor," Royce suggested. "For limp dick and sunburn."

God, he was a prick. He was lucky we were blood; otherwise I'd punch him in the face and wipe off that grin. Maybe have it smeared all over this restaurant's floor.

"Kristoff, you're closest to him. Just smack him."

My friend didn't move. "I dealt with enough idiots while we served in the military. I don't feel like wasting energy on another one," he drawled. "Now, about this woman. Why can't you get over her? Just get another woman under you and fuck her raw."

"Now we're talking." Royce was determined to get his ass whooped today.

"Which part of not being able to get it up don't you understand?"

"Have you tried?" Kristoff tutted.

"No, I've just opted for abstinence these past six years because it's such a fucking joy." Wasn't he listening to me at all? "I'm obsessed with this woman. I need to figure out how to move on. I have no fucking skin left on my dick."

"I'd say. Six years of jerking off is a long time."

"You think?" My tone was dry as gin.

"Why don't you set up an *arrangement* with a woman you like, and ensure you both get what you need?" His suggestion didn't surprise me. Years ago, before he fell in love and married his wife, he had a similar kind of arrangement going with her. Well, sort of similar. He'd offered her a secretarial job with some *extra* duties. Of course, Gemma refused, and he chased her down, offering her a trial period. My buddy was obsessed with her.

I shrugged. "Much like Gemma, I'm fairly certain Dr. Swan would refuse me and then probably cut my dick off."

"At least it'll be professionally done." Royce was so damn unhelpful. "Regardless if she's a doctor or a nurse."

"Dr. Swan is actually a surgeon," I gritted. They both chuckled and I pinched the bridge of my nose. "Christ almighty." I put my head into my hands in dismay. "You two are not helping."

"Aurora said she's gorgeous." Royce was so fucking helpful today. At this rate, I might murder him in broad daylight. "Even the Nikolaev men agreed. And you know how those men have eyes only for their wives."

Kristoff's brow rose in surprise, but he remained quiet.

"The worst part about it is that I feel like I already know her."

"What do you mean?" My brother saw too much. Or not enough. I couldn't figure it out.

"I can't explain it. There's this connection I feel with her. The familiarity. It's like I've known her forever."

"Well, technically, only for six years," Kristoff pointed out. "How long were you together?'

Fuck, they'd laugh. They'd laugh and laugh until they keeled over. So I didn't answer.

"According to Winston, only for a day or two." Of course my brother knew. It was impossible to keep secrets in this family. Except really big ones. Those remained sealed and shut away.

Kristoff frowned. "What happened? Why only a day or two?"

I threw my hands up. "I don't know. The night we'd spent together was perfect. When I came back from the bakery the next morning with food, she was gone. I thought maybe she'd been called into work early. I went to look for her, and she gave me the cold shoulder."

"I can't imagine a woman giving *you* the cold shoulder," Kristoff remarked, taking another sip of his scotch. "Usually they fall at your feet."

"Well, this one fell at my feet like Gemma fell at yours," I retorted dryly. "You remember those days, right?"

A dark expression crossed his face. He'd almost lost his woman before he finally got smart.

"Listen, you two old fuckers," Royce interrupted us. Kristoff and I winced. We weren't that old. Older than him, but not that fucking old. "Stop reminiscing about the old days. Byron—find a way to get your woman."

"I have to agree with your brother. Not about us being old, but finding a way to get your woman." Kristoff flipped open the paper before he continued. "Find her weakness and reel her back to you."

"Unless you're bad in the sack," Royce cackled. "Then there's no amount of weaknesses that will bring her back to you."

Royce just couldn't help being a jackass.

I exhaled heavily. "Jesus, don't you have somewhere to be."

Amusement passed my friend's expression and his lips tugged up. He casually turned the page of his newspaper. Why in the fuck he was reading the paper today of all days, I couldn't comprehend. "The more important question is, what are you going to do about your dick?"

"He'll have to cut the fucker off."

They both snickered while I ignored them and sipped my drink.

The universe was trying to send me a sign. Or torture me—it was still up for debate.

Chapter 26
Odette

Days dragged on; nights even more so.

Twelve days. Twelve nights. The countdown to our doom. I'd set out to save lives and somehow managed to end them. If we'd never found ourselves in Ghana, my sister wouldn't have picked up those diamonds. If I hadn't gotten pregnant, Billie wouldn't have put her career on hold for me. Round and round we went. Like a vicious, never-ending cycle.

After med school, I got the opportunity to work my residency in Ghana with the United Nations. Leading the effort in Ghana was the World Health Organization, and just as Dad had, I jumped at the opportunity to make a change. And Billie, she was there with me every step of the way—with my son—ensuring I had the chance to fulfill my dream. The exposure in Ghana was amazing, and the WHO agendas covered all areas of the global healthcare spectrum.

My whole adventure turned out to be the best kind of experience. With the exception of the stolen diamonds. And here I was, back in my childhood country, beaten up and stone broke.

My bruises had faded, but the pain and fear remained. We were at the end of our road. If we couldn't get false identities and disappear, I had one last option. It would ensure my son's survival, but not my sister's nor mine.

I was on edge—every little noise startled me. Considering we were currently in a hotel in Washington, D.C., that was a problem. Doors opened and slammed all night. Toilets flushed. Voices traveled. So much for getting any rest tonight.

I hadn't gotten a decent night's sleep since we left Ghana. But since we'd left New Orleans, sleep downright eluded me. We used the last of our money to fly here and try to get in to see Nico Morrelli. The word on the dark web was that he could set us up with new identities. A new life. Maybe I could even find a way to continue practicing medicine.

My brain analyzed everything we'd done—from our plan to turn in those stupid diamonds, to how we'd run into Byron.

Byron Ashford.

God, he still looked as good as I remembered. There was no mistaking those muscles hidden under the expensive material of the three-piece suit. Rock-hard body. Goddamn it, he was so tempting. And abstaining from sex didn't help my cause. If he stripped his clothes off, I feared I'd totally be on board with having sex with him.

Not that sex with Byron was anywhere on my mind. He was currently the least of my problems. I had to figure out a way out of this clusterfuck.

Staring at the dark ceiling, lying still so I wouldn't wake up my son who cuddled into me, I couldn't come up with a solution to our problem. Our million-dollar problem.

What kind of interest is that, anyhow? I wondered.

There were two choices left; change our identity or come up with a million dollars. The latter we didn't have. The former was a possibility.

We had another forty-eight hours left to come up with a solution. Or we'd all be dead.

The back of my eyes burned. I wished Dad were still alive. I missed him. His quiet confidence. His wisdom. Although if he were still alive, he'd be disappointed. In Billie, and in me. It didn't matter that I'd busted my ass through medical school as a young mother. It didn't matter what I sacrificed; only how badly we fucked up. The year in Ghana should have been a highlight of my career. It turned into a nightmare. All because Billie grabbed that little black bag.

But I couldn't turn my back on her. It was only thanks to my sister that I finished medical school at all. She sacrificed her own career for me. It was the least I could do for her.

Bang.

Another slammed door.

My eyes darted to my son, worried he'd wake up, but he was out like a light. His navy dinosaur pajama bottoms had rolled up his legs, so I pulled them down, then brushed his dark hair from his forehead.

I swallowed hard. I'd managed to forget Byron over the years. Okay, maybe not exactly *forget*, but I did succeed in suppressing memories of our night together. *Barely.* He obviously had no issues forgetting me.

Slipping out of bed, I padded barefoot to my suitcase we'd been living out of for the past six months. I dug through it and pulled out my laptop.

"What are you doing?" Billie's voice was barely above a whisper, but it drew a startled whimper from my throat. I whirled around, finding my sister's eyes on me. She was wide awake too. She patted the spot next to her on the bed. "Talk to me."

I sighed, took three steps, and sat next to her.

"I'm sending an email," I told her, opening the laptop. "To Nico Morrelli."

We did some research. Per the dark web, Nico Morrelli was our best bet at getting new identities. New passports. New life.

One tiny problem. The cost.

I didn't know how much it cost to obtain new identities, but I was certain it was in the upper thousands, not lower thousands. Per person. And there were three of us. How did I plan to pay for it? I had no fucking idea. I hoped for some kind of payment plan.

"So we're doing it?" Billie asked quietly.

I met my sister's eyes. "I don't think we have a choice."

"I can't believe those assholes are charging us a million in interest," she muttered. "If those diamonds were so valuable, they shouldn't have left them sitting around."

I let out a heavy sigh. Silence buzzed through the tiny hotel room. And so, I asked the question. The one that had been burning on my tongue ever since we ran from Ghana, like fugitives in the middle of the night.

"Why did you take that bag?" I sputtered. "Even if you thought they were fake diamonds, why would you take them?"

The sounds of D.C.'s nightlife shattered the quiet that should have been a respite for us. The noise of honking, even shrill laughter and shouting, came through the closed windows. And then there was the constant whine of the police sirens slicing through the night.

The last bit was a reminder of how far we'd strayed from the right path.

Billie's brown eyes met mine. They glimmered with tears. "I thought we'd be able to buy Dad's hospital back with that money," she said, her voice full of anguish. "So you could treat patients, I could design clothes and jewelry, and we could raise Ares together. We were happy on the French Riviera."

My lungs tightened, and every breath closed them a bit more. Billie had done it for us, but it backfired. The guilt slithered its way through my chest. Billie knew who Ares's father was, but she didn't know that it was my fault we lost the hospital. I never told her about my encounter with Senator Ashford and his threats that he clearly fulfilled.

"We were happy there," I acknowledged. "You've done too much for me, Billie. Now, let me fix this."

We had to face the consequences. Not that it mattered, because I had already decided we'd meet Nico Morrelli. If that didn't work, I'd go to Byron Ashford.

But we'd do it together. We were in this together.

"I still can't believe he answered your email," Billie said, her voice suspicious as we stood in front of the building in downtown D.C. The Morrelli empire extended to both legal and illegal areas of business.

This building happened to be part of his legal business. Cassidy Tech. Worldwide Cassidy. And others, but who had the time or energy to be impressed.

Right now, we just needed a ticket to freedom. If it were up to me, I'd have been here at 8:00 a.m. However, waking Billie after we'd stayed up most of the night was a task in itself. Not that I could blame her. In fact, as soon as our life went back to normal, it was the first thing I'd do. Buy a comfortable bed and have a week with the same bedtime as Ares.

If I could have, I would have left them both sleeping at the hotel, but we had to check out or risk being charged another night. What the fuck we'd do tonight, I had no freaking clue.

My eyes roamed over my son, then to my sister. We all looked put together, wearing warm coats and our luggage trailing behind us.

Ares was dressed in navy pants, a white shirt with a navy blazer, and loafers on his feet. He looked like a little gentleman. My sister and I were dressed in business attire. She opted for a light blue dress. Mine was white. Not the best color for February, but it was the only dress I had. It was either that or scrubs. Why did I have scrubs in my suitcase if I wasn't working? I had no freaking idea. Maybe I hoped it'd all work out and I'd be able to get back to my career.

I took a deep breath in and then exhaled. "Maybe our luck is about to turn." I really hoped so, or we'd all be dead. "Let me do all the talking, Billie. We don't want to give him too much information."

She nodded, and we entered Worldwide Cassidy. Hand in hand. Prepared for anything but hoping for one thing.

A new life.

The grand lobby of the building welcomed us, in all its marble glory. TV monitors following stocks over the world markets were used as accents. Flashes of news sped across the bottom of the screen.

Billie and I shared a glance. This wasn't the world we were used to. Before our mother died, we'd spent our time in the back of the runway shows, admiring all the pretty clothes. When Mom died, we moved to France, and our time was either helping Dad in the hospital or hanging on the beach.

The corporate world was like a whole different universe.

The receptionist gave us one look and she knew we didn't belong here. Well, to hell with her.

"Hello, we're here to see Mr. Morrelli," I stated with the confidence I didn't feel.

"Do you have an appointment?" she questioned. I hesitated, and it was all she needed to make assumptions. "No appointment, no Mr. Morrelli."

I wasn't sure why she couldn't just call him and tell him someone was here. He wouldn't have replied and asked us to come in if he wouldn't see us. Right?

"Can you call him?" My voice shook. My words stumbled. This was our last hope. We couldn't leave without seeing him. "He sent me an email asking me to come today." The look she gave me clearly said she didn't believe me. "I can show you," I offered, pulling out my phone from my purse.

This time she hesitated, biting down on her maroon-glossed lip.

"Just call him." I jerked my chin toward the switchboard phone.

She did. The conversation lasted less than thirty seconds. "Head to the elevators. The top floor is the executive floor," she instructed. The surprise on her face told me she didn't expect that we actually were allowed to go up there.

A relieved breath escaped me, easing the weight on my chest.

"Mommy, are we going to take the elevator high up in the air?" Ares asked, tugging on my hand.

I smiled softly.

"Yes, we will. Do you see an elevator?" I asked.

His eyes roamed over the grand lobby and flickered with light.

"There," he exclaimed, pointing his finger across the lobby.

"Excellent, my little explorer. Lead the way."

My sister and I followed him as he eagerly tugged on my hand. Billie and I shared an amused look. Ares was nothing if not curious and eager for adventure. Our entire time in Ghana, it was impossible to keep him inside. He'd explore the vast land around the little hospital with Billie, or even inside the hospital, until he crashed at night.

Ares pressed on the button impatiently after I showed him which one to push, and it took no time for the elevator door to open. The three of us entered, and I smiled when Ares's blue eyes met mine, asking for permission.

I nodded. "The last button with the highest number," I instructed. He didn't need me to repeat it, because his little finger already found it and pushed it.

As the elevator shot up, I sent a silent prayer up to whoever was listening. Maman. Dad. Anyone. *Just save us.*

The elevator dinged and we strode out of it, one hand holding Ares's, the other smoothing down my dress nervously. The room opened up to the executive floor, and there was only one corner office in sight.

"Why can't we go to the movies with friends?" a whiny young voice traveled over the air.

"Because you're too young to go without an adult," a woman's calm voice scolded. "And you'll only go with Dad or me as chaperones."

"But—"

"That's not fair!" It had to be a teenager arguing with her parents. "Their parents are responsible too."

"I'm sure they are," a man's voice argued. "But like your mother said, one of us goes with you or nobody goes to the movies."

"Come on, Hannah. We can just watch a movie at home. I'd rather be in pajamas and comfortable in our home theater anyway."

It had to be her sister. Billie and I exchanged an amused glance.

A stomp on the floor and then the door swung open. Two girls, identical twins no older than ten, rushed out of the office and almost slammed into us. Their blonde curls bounced and the soft freckles over their noses were pronounced with their agitation.

I couldn't help but smile. Billie had the same thing going on with her freckles.

"Hello, girls," we greeted them. Their cobalt eyes studied us, and I wondered how anyone could tell them apart. Even their freckles seemed to be in the same spot.

Although my vision might be slightly impaired, thanks to a sleepless night.

"Hello," they both grumbled before disappearing into the elevator.

"Ah, the joys of the preteen years," Billie mused. "Remember my tantrums?"

"Like anyone could forget," I mused. Both of us lowered our gazes to Ares. "You'll be a good boy when you're that age, won't you?"

Before he could answer, a deep voice, cold and calm, greeted us. "Dr. Swan?"

Billie and I turned our attention in its direction at the same time. "Holy shit," Billie muttered.

Holy shit was right. Nico Morrelli was hot. Like *volcanic heat* hot. Older. Maybe mid-forties. With broad shoulders and an arrogant smile, he reminded me of Byron. Except for his eyes. He had a stormy, cloudy gaze under dark, thick lashes that were every woman's envy.

"Dr. Swan?" he repeated, and I got myself together.

"Yes, that's me," I said, closing the distance between us and extending my hand. "Mr. Morrelli."

He took my hand into his firm handshake. "Nice to meet you." His eyes traveled to my sister, then to Ares. "I've heard a lot about you."

The nervous knot in my stomach formed. He heard about me? Nothing I did was relevant in his circles, so he shouldn't have heard anything.

A petite woman with dark brown hair and soft brown eyes appeared by his side. I watched in fascination as his expression softened, those steel-gray eyes turned into molten silver.

That feeling came back—the one I had been avoiding to feel for the past six years. *Longing.* Longing to love and be loved. Longing to have *him*.

"Hi, I'm Bianca," she greeted me, extending her hand. "His better half."

I smiled. "Nice to meet you." I turned to my sister and Ares. "This is my sister, Billie, and this is my son, Ares."

Bianca's smile widened. She shook Billie's hand, then lowered down to her knees. "Hi there, Ares. I love your name." She extended her hand, and like a big boy, Ares took it, shaking it seriously. "Nice to meet you."

"You too, ma'am."

Pride swelled in my chest. I might not be the best mother, but I must have done something right because my little guy was making me proud.

Bianca rose to her feet. "Now I wish I had brought my boys with me," she said sorrowfully. "They could have all played together while you're talking to Nico."

"That's a shame," I agreed. "Ares loves to play with other children."

"Maybe next time," Billie chimed, giving me a meaningful glance. Usually, I had to remind her not to get too personal and here I was chatting with Nico Morrelli's wife.

Bianca must have picked up on it because she rose to her full height, then pecked her husband on the cheek.

"I'll leave you to it," she said. "I'm going to check on our girls before they start a riot."

As she disappeared into the elevator, Nico turned his attention to us.

"Ladies, after you," Nico said, extending his hand for us to enter his office.

With heavy steps, both of us made our way inside the modern office. Neat. Organized. Big.

As we took our seat, I realized one thing.

In my whole life, I had never violated a single rule.

Tell no lies. I obeyed. *Do no wrong.* I listened. *Follow the law to a tee.* Absolutely. *Save lives.* I gladly did.

Yet, as I sat across Nico Morrelli's executive desk, I was about to commit a federal offense. Just the attempt to fraudulently use a passport was a violation of federal law. In any country.

Ares sat on my lap and my hand tightly wrapped around him as I struggled to find the right words.

How did one ask for fake documents?

"So what can I help you with, ladies?" Nico asked casually.

The sharpness of his eyes didn't escape me. Neither did the tension in his shoulders. Could we trust him? I didn't think we had a choice.

"Umm, we heard that you can"—I searched for a diplomatically correct word—"help us. We need help."

I swallowed.

"With?" Nico clipped.

God, why couldn't he make this easier on us? Maybe he could recite the services he offered. Like in the movies.

I could feel Billie's eyes darting between Morrelli and me. I shifted in my seat uncomfortably. Something wasn't right, but I couldn't pinpoint what. Maybe it was my sixth sense warning me.

Or maybe I was being paranoid.

With a shuddering breath, I jumped to my feet, Ares sliding to his. Billie followed my movement.

"I'm sorry." I gulped. "This was a mistake."

Without another word, I picked up my son and tugged Billie out of the mobster's office.

Maybe everything wasn't lost just yet.

Chapter 27
Byron

I barely managed to keep my focus all morning.

It had been almost two weeks since I'd seen her and my body still burned. I managed to hack into Odette's phone. It was a burner and she kept little information on it. A few photos. Barely any contacts. And her note.

To contact Nico Morrelli for fake identification.

That was my ticket. I had a plan. A good one. Once she said those words—made that request—I'd have her. It was a federal offense. I even lined up a buddy of mine who'd bust into Nico's office and bring her to me.

The trap was perfect. I would have two things to hold over her. The diamond smuggler interaction and federal offense. Plan A and Plan B. She'd finally be mine.

Winston paced around my office frantically. He'd been on edge ever since learning about his son. The odd part, we couldn't find any trace of Billie giving birth. No trace of the boy. Although I did learn one thing my brother never shared with me. The most peculiar connection between him and Billie Swan.

I flicked a look at my brother. He'd changed over the last six years. Gave up the booze and drugs. Was it all for Billie Swan?

I shook my head. It turned out we both fucked up in some way six years ago.

None of the wealth, fame, or power could keep the Swan women with us. God, I fucking missed Odette. The thought of seeing her again clawed at my chest. My body had yet to cool down. The memories came back with a vengeance—of her writhing beneath me, her mouth wrapped around my cock, the feel of her soft skin under my fingertips.

My phone vibrated, dancing across the table.

"Morrelli." I hit the speaker button, my shoulders tensing. I'd been itching to dial him up all fucking day. It was fucking two in the afternoon. Agony.

"Dr. Swan and her sister left," he said, leaving it at that.

"And?"

"They were here for barely a few minutes. Whatever they were going to ask, they changed their minds."

I frowned. All that for nothing?

I ran a hand through my hair. Part of me wanted to go after Odette and kidnap her. Maybe all these mobsters had a point when they forced their women into marriage. If I had done it, I wouldn't be in this position now.

"Someone got their hands on Dr. Swan," Nico continued. "The bruises were faded and she hid them with makeup, but there's no mistaking it. Someone hurt her."

A deathly stillness fell over me. I had to take a second to swallow down the burning rage. *Someone hurt her. Someone hurt her.* A part of me—the irrational part—pounded at my chest, shaking the bars of its cage, ready to go hunting. To punish the one who dared lay a finger on my woman.

My woman. Christ, six years and I still thought of her as mine.

"I want a name," I snapped, but deep down I knew. I fucking knew.

"And the boy?" Winston demanded. "Was my son there? Was he okay? Safe?"

Nico's answer took a heartbeat too long, yet it felt like hours. And I wasn't even the father. Winston's eyes were glued on my phone as if he could force an answer out of Nico through the phone.

"Dr. Swan's boy is your son, Winston?" Nico's question changed everything.

My heart stopped. It fucking stopped beating. Now it was me staring at the phone sitting on my desk, as if it held all the answers. *Dr. Swan's boy.* No, it couldn't be. No fucking way.

The doctor said she lost the baby. How could that be? There was no chance that I misunderstood her.

I ran a hand through my hair. It fucking trembled. I survived burning flesh, deployments to war zones, SEAL training, and never once did I let my cool waver. Fucking. Ever. Yet right now, my hands shook.

There were only two other times that my hands shook. That day I sought her out at her father's hospital, after our one and only night together. And that last day I saw her—the day she lost the baby.

Before that day, I hadn't seen her for three months and that was even worse. Seeing her slumped body on the street shaved a decade off my life. The sheer terror that she was gone, forever. I was willing to sacrifice my happiness so she could move on, but not with the knowledge that she no longer walked this earth.

The fear that she wouldn't pull through tore my heart to shreds; learning she was pregnant and lost the baby on the same day felt like a sharp stab into what was left of it. It didn't matter that being without her was killing me, because living in a world where she didn't exist was worse.

Dr. Swan has a son. The meaning pierced through the fog of a million other scattered thoughts. The boy looked like me. How was that possible? The doctor clearly indicated that Odette lost the baby. Didn't she?

I opened the drawer of my desk and pulled out my wallet. There was a single sonogram photo in the sleeve of it, old blood-stains still smeared on it. I stared at it, as I had many other times before, except different feelings filled my chest now.

How many times had I stared at it, wishing we had a different outcome? How many times had I hoped against all odds that the baby had survived? That Odette, the baby, and I could have had a future together.

She came to see me the day of the accident, and I was fairly certain of what she wanted to tell me, if what I was holding in my hands wasn't proof enough. Then why did she leave? She came so close only to turn around. Why did she run? I thought back to the day in the hospital. Had I missed something? Had I done something wrong? Maybe I was too rough?

Goddamn it, I wanted to know. I could have seen *my* son grow up. I should have been part of his life from the moment he was conceived.

My mind conjured every single moment, trying to evaluate what signs I could have missed.

"Hello? Anyone there, or is this call over?" Nico's voice sent memories and thoughts scurrying into the dark corners of my mind where they'd hidden for the past six years.

A deep ache pierced my heart and grew with each heartbeat. It pulsed deeper and higher, thundering painfully in my ears. I raised my eyes and met Winston's. Same eyes as mine. His hair—same color as mine. No fucking wonder he thought the kid was his. Our baby pictures were almost identical.

"We're here," Winston answered, his eyes filling with apprehension, as though the realization was hitting him at the exact same time. "No, he's not my son. He's Byron's."

A light bitterness laced my brother's last words.

I never realized Winston wanted a kid. Not until he made the assumption—the wrong one—a few days ago in New Orleans. I searched deep inside me for regret. I couldn't find it. But I did find something else.

A sliver of resentment. Bitterness.

Was he mine? Or someone else's son? He looked like me, even Winston. Yet, a shred of doubt inched its way inside my brain. None of it made any sense. I fucking hated doubt and insecurities. I had seen the boy, and I couldn't deny the plain truth staring at me. He was an Ashford, which brought me to the next point.

Odette stole something priceless from me. *My son.*

It was time to teach Dr. Swan what it meant to cross an Ashford.

Chapter 28
Odette

A different building. A possible lifeline. Another billionaire.

We were still in downtown D.C., roaming the streets, while a single thought kept running through my mind.

Go to Byron.

Maybe I could beg for a loan. Maybe offer him... what? We had nothing.

Or you can tell him he's Ares's father, my reason whispered. Or maybe we could just say Winston was the father, since he'd already jumped to that conclusion in New Orleans anyway.

My heart revolted at that thought. Fuck, too many lies. Too much deceit. Those words his father threw in my face at the hotel, the money he had shoved my way, and his visit to the hospital all those years ago still plagued me. Was it the right choice to cut all ties with Ares's father at that point? Was it even smart to seek out Byron now? I didn't know.

I thought all our ties were cut when, by some miracle, my baby was safe. I hadn't lost it. Although I *had* lost Byron, once and for all.

I never sought him out again. I couldn't let his father hurt us. Not anymore, not when I had a baby to protect.

If the Ashfords came after Billie and me, we'd deal with it. The most important thing was that Ares would be safe. Protected from the diamond smugglers.

My mind drifted back to that day six years ago when I sought him out to give him the news of the pregnancy. It seemed like a different me. Different universe.

I stared at the door of the hospital room for hours after Byron left. A single scuff mark became my entire focus as I ignored this pulsing ache in my chest. Tears blurred my vision, but I refused to look away from that spot on the door.

What was I hoping for?

I didn't know. Maybe to wake up and realize it was all a nightmare.

I didn't know why losing the baby shattered me so badly. I was approaching the four-month mark and had started making plans. For the baby. For a family. So many "what ifs" played in my brain over the last weeks. This wasn't one of them.

I swiped at my cheek with the back of my hand, but it was utterly futile to stop the tears. My chest felt tight. I wanted to sleep, but I couldn't even muster the energy to close my eyes. Not that I could calm my mind enough.

Byron's words echoed in my brain. The baby didn't make it. His eyes weren't cold nor cruel. Nothing like his father's. Worst of all, Byron didn't seem repulsed. In fact, pain slashed across his face when I told him to leave.

Maybe I should have confessed what his father did to me. Maybe I'd fucked up and had no one to blame except myself.

The hospital door opened and my heart fluttered lightly, full of hope. I held my breath as one foot appeared. Expensive shoes. Expensive suit. Then the man came in full view.

The breath in my lungs was cut short.

Senator Ashford stood in the doorway, and suddenly, whatever I had in my stomach threatened to make a messy reappearance.

A shudder rippled down my spine. There was something about this man that creeped me out more than anything. Maybe it was the cold, calculating cruelty in his eyes.

In measured, even steps he strode over to my hospital bed.

My heart drummed against my ribs, cracking them with each beat.

"You can't be here," I rasped. Why did this man always show up whenever I was vulnerable?

His hand shot out and wrapped around my throat. My hands instinctively came up, both my fingers wrapping around his wrist, my nails digging into his flesh.

"You almost cost me everything." His grip tightened. My ears buzzed. The oxygen thinned. "You want to die, girl?"

I kept clawing at his hands, terror seeping through my pores and flooding my bloodstream.

"Let go of me," I croaked, my words barely audible.

His grip loosened—barely—but he didn't let go. "Do I need to wipe everyone you love and everything you have away for the message to get through your thick skull? Or maybe you want your sister to get a taste of my wrath?"

I shook my head, desperation and fear clawing at my chest. But there was hate too. It was such a strong feeling, I feared it'd suffocate me. I wanted to fight him. Maybe even kill this man. But my strength was nonexistent.

"I want nothing to do with you and your family," I choked out.

"Don't come around us again," he hissed. He tightened his grip around my neck once again for good measure. "Just remember what I can do to your sister."

He released my throat, my hands falling onto the bed. Greedily, I gasped for air. My nails throbbed from clawing at him. Oxygen seeped into my lungs, and I panted while the senator turned around and strode out of the room.

This time, I stared at the door and clutched the hospital sheets, fearing he'd come back. I never wanted to see him again. I never wanted to cross paths with him—nor Byron—again. One came with the other. They were a package deal, and I couldn't survive the senator. So I'd avoid the Ashfords at all costs.

The door opened again and I reached for the emergency button next to me. I didn't think I could scream loud enough. But before I pressed it, an old, familiar voice came through.

"Ma chérie. What happened?"

Marco stood in the doorway, as handsome as ever. His jeans hugged his hips and the button-down silky black shirt made him look like... well, like a gigolo or something. Yet, I had no energy to even give him a hard time about it.

"Marco," I said. My voice sounded strange to my ears. Low and hollow. Lifeless. Beaten. I didn't even wonder what he was doing here. I had nothing—no spark, no life—left in me. He closed the distance to the hospital bed and took my hands into his. "What have they done to you?"

My breaths seemed to take too much energy. Words even more so. "Car accident."

"Baby?"

A single tear rolled down my cheek as I attempted to take a lungful of air in. My breaths were shaky. My heart was achy. And my body... it felt broken.

"Lost." Why did it hurt to say it?

He shook his head. "Non. You're still pregnant." Hope and confusion fluttered in my heart. My eyes sought out his, and found nothing but a somber expression. No trace of a tasteless joke or maybe some mistake.

"How? Why?" I rasped. "I don't understand."

He took a deep breath, sadness and another feeling lingering in his eyes. I couldn't quite pinpoint what it was. "My girlfriend works here. Tristan's sister." I blinked, then remembered the serious woman I spoke to briefly all those months ago. "This was to protect you. From them."

At that moment, I couldn't quite determine if Marco had saved me, or stolen something from me.

But one thing was certain. I wouldn't risk my baby's life by staying close to the Ashfords.

Pushing the memory away, I focused on our current situation. I had no choice but to reach out to Byron. It was our last lifeline.

I squared my shoulders. I'd just ask for a loan. Ares couldn't get caught in the middle of all this shit. Revealing Ares as Byron's son would be my last resort.

"Tell me again why we didn't ask Nico Morrelli for false identifications?" Billie demanded to know. Desperation laced her words. I could see it in her eyes too. It reflected what I felt in my heart.

I let out a heavy sigh. "We both know we have no money to pay him for it. I doubt falsified documents for the three of us would cost less than ten grand. It's not like my Hilton rewards points would cover that bill."

"Maybe he would have given us a discount," she grumbled.

"Or called the feds and had us sent to federal prison."

"Now what?" She ran both hands through her blonde hair. "If we can't pay for the fake documents, we certainly can't come up with a million dollars in the next"—she glanced down at her watch —"thirty-six hours."

We stopped in the middle of the sidewalk, pedestrians never missing a step. They rushed around us, some even shot glares at us. My eyes traveled around us and a small shop caught my attention. A bookstore with coffee tables, and piles and piles of books.

"Let's go inside," I said, my eyes darting over Billie's shoulder. She turned around to see what I was looking at. "Ares can have hot chocolate and books to read while we talk."

A happy squeal sounded, and before my sister could even agree, we were being dragged into the store.

The minute we stepped inside, coffee beans and the smell of

books on the floor-to-ceiling shelves filled the air. The tension in my shoulders eased slightly, and we roamed around until we found an empty table, right next to the children's section.

"Who wants hot chocolate?" I asked.

Ares's and Billie's hands shot up at the same time. "Me, me, me."

I grinned at their excited expressions. It only took hot chocolate to make it all better. "Okay, you two find something to read, and I'll be right back."

They didn't need to be told twice.

I headed to the little corner of the store where the coffee shop was. The sound of coffee grinding replaced the hustle and bustle of the city noise that lay on the other side of the door. It felt like a different world here—away from danger and reality.

At least for the moment.

Five minutes later, Ares was lost in the vast selection of books, a dreamy smile playing around his lips. A little chocolate mustache lingered above his mouth. He refused to let me wipe it off, eager to get to his books. He was very single-minded when he had it set on something. Sometimes, I wondered if he'd inherited that from his father.

Locking eyes with my sister, both of our fingers curled over the sleeve of our coffee cups. I sipped my latte, working up the puzzle in my mind.

A lot hung in the air with whether or not Byron still wanted me like he did six years ago. I could pay him very slowly—in small increments—over my lifetime. If that didn't work, I'd give him what he asked for that day he'd come to me at my father's hospital.

My body.

"Okay, I can't take this silence anymore," Billie exclaimed. "Tell me the plan. I know you have one."

I knew her patience wouldn't last long.

"I'm working up the plan as we speak," I admitted. She raised her eyebrow, tapping her fingers impatiently against her coffee cup.

"And?"

"And I'm not sure if it's a good plan, but it's the only one I have." I took a deep breath and let it out. "I'm going to ask Byron for a loan."

A blank stare. Then she blinked, as if waking from a dream.

"A loan?"

I chewed on my bottom lip. "Yes."

"And how are we going to repay it?" she questioned hesitantly.

"You're not; I am."

I just prayed Ares didn't get caught up in this fiasco.

Chapter 29
Odette

Another grand lobby. This one represented the Ashford empire. My last visit here wasn't pleasant and that was putting it mildly. Shoving the memories to the back of my mind, I focused on the here and now. This was important.

"You two stay here," I said softly to Billie and my son, signaling them to remain closer to the elevators. Just in case we had to make a run for it. Besides, my son didn't need to hear me humiliate myself.

We made it through two different receptionists—one on the main floor, and now we were faced with this one. The last obstacle was on the management floor, accents of gold and wealth surrounding me. I flicked a look over my shoulder to my family as I waited for the receptionist's verdict.

It came swiftly. "No appointment, no Mr. Ashford."

I swore it felt like déjà vu. All on the same day. The executive assistant watched me with a sneer on her face. Her platinum-blonde hair screamed fake. Her scarlet lips screamed Botox, and her goddamn perfume was giving me a major headache.

"We are old friends," I said. I would not let her see my confidence waver, no way. "Just call him and tell him I'm here." When she made no intention of moving, I added, "He won't be happy if he learns I came and left without seeing him."

The venomous grin on her lips warned I wouldn't like her next words. "If you're friends, why don't you text him."

Now wasn't that the question of the century. I didn't have his number. Even if I did, he would have probably blocked my number six years ago.

"Well, I left my phone at the hotel." I smiled sweetly, when I actually wanted to lunge across this reception desk and wrap my fingers around her slim throat. "But don't worry, I'll gladly go back to my room—that he paid for—and let him know that I missed him since I'm flying out tonight. I'll give him your name, Miss—" I glanced around, looking for a name sign.

She swallowed, her expression finally cracking. I held my breath as she reached for the intercom.

"Mr. Ashford. I have Miss—" Then she realized her mistake. She hadn't even bothered to ask me my name. She had to be the worst assistant ever.

"Dr. Swan." It was petty, but I couldn't keep the snobbery out of my voice. I never thought myself better than anyone, no matter who they were or what they did, but this woman pissed me off so badly, I wanted to rub all my accomplishments in her face.

She hesitated, biting down on her Botoxed lips. I bet she wouldn't feel them if they were bleeding, she'd had so much work done. I jerked my chin toward the phone. "Tell him Dr. Madeline Swan is here for him."

I didn't know what possessed me to say Madeline. He was the only person on this planet to have ever called me by my middle name in full, and only when he fucked me. A shiver snaked down my spine.

How would I survive Byron?

We weren't even in the same room, yet I already felt consumed by him. By the memories of his scent, of his hands on my skin, by the sounds we made when we both came—grunts and moans.

"Sir, it's Dr. Madeline Swan."

I held my breath as I waited, my heart thundering in my chest.

"Yes, sir."

She hung up the phone and gave me a sour look. "Go ahead through that door. Wait in the executive lounge for his meeting to end."

I bet it killed her to say it.

Without sparing her another thought, I turned around and signaled Billie who stood with Ares by the elevator.

They rushed to me and the three of us made our way through the final door that would lead me to the one man I hoped never to see again. And now, I was seeking him out. Our footsteps were soft on the white marble as we made our way through to the office suite.

Everywhere we looked, gold accents, lush flowers, and beautiful paintings decorated the space. Sleek modern furniture mixed with old-fashioned elegance. Black lacquer was in such contrast to white marble, you could see the outline of the furniture reflected in it.

There was no doubt where Byron's office was. Even without the golden plate "Byron A. Ashford, CEO" by the door, it was easy to spot the biggest and best office. The corner office.

Of course. Nothing but the best for the liar.

I mentally slapped myself. None of it mattered. We needed that money. The endgame was getting out of our predicament and returning to our normal life. I'd get a job as a surgeon either here in the States or back in France. Ares would go to school, make some friends, and our life would go on.

"Should we wait in the guest lounge?" Billie whispered, her eyes darting to the right to a small waiting area. The golden plate next to it read "Executive Guest Lounge."

My eyes traveled to the heavy, mahogany double doors. Muted men's voices came through it. The meeting might go on for a while.

"Yes, I guess so."

Ares's eyes darted to where the wooden *Thomas the Train* table

209

sat, and his eyes lit up. Without prompting, he ran to it and fell down to his knees.

I folded my knees and sat next to him. "It's a beautiful train set, isn't it?"

His blue eyes lit up. "Can I take it home? Please, Maman."

Guilt twinged in my chest. My stomach hollowed.

Ares never complained, but I knew he missed his toys. We were only able to bring the bare minimum with us, and not to mention, we didn't have a home. At least, not here. Our father had left us his little home on the French Riviera, and while it wasn't worth much, we could settle there.

It'd be a roof over our heads.

"No, love," I murmured softly. "But one day we'll have one. I promise."

I vowed right then and there, I'd do whatever Byron demanded.

Just so I could see my son safe and happy again.

Chapter 30
Byron

My lawyer, David Goldstein, sat across from me in my office. Judge Duncan, who I had on speed dial if I ever needed him, was here too. I had never needed him.

Until now.

My son. She'd kept *my* son from me.

I still couldn't wrap my head around how that was possible when the doctor told me she had lost the baby. None of it made any sense.

"We can assign temporary custody to you," Duncan stated. "But considering the woman isn't a resident of the United States, that might be a problem."

"She has U.S. citizenship," I hissed. I didn't want excuses, I wanted results. My son belonged in my life. I'd lost so much already, and I'd be damned if I lost this chance to be part of his life.

"Yes, but she has spent most of her life living on foreign soil."

"She attended medical school here," I pointed out.

Fury boiled beneath my skin. Ever since I saw her again, it simmered, threatening to explode. She looked so fucking good. Her scent alone was enough to intoxicate me. But all the while, I pictured the men she would have touched over the last six years. The men who had touched her. And I wanted their names and their deaths, so I could be the only man alive to know how she felt underneath me. I could still hear her moans and feel her nails on my skin as I thrust into her.

Was I fucking furious? Yes. But even knowing I had missed out on raising my son, I couldn't hate Odette. Everything within me rebelled at the notion of hating the woman that so effortlessly captured me. I wanted to protect her. Own her. Fuck, I was obsessed. And still in love with her.

"So do many foreign citizens," he retorted dryly. It was a delicate situation and Judge Duncan didn't want to be obvious about his allegiance. Not that I gave a flying fuck. "I'm not saying it's not possible," he continued diplomatically. "Just that we should tread lightly."

"Your son was born in France. The jurisdiction would be questionable and could cause a problem for you." Why in the fuck was he so pessimistic?

"Does my son have U.S. citizenship?" I was met with a blank stare. "Surely he's entitled to it since his parents are U.S. citizens."

"But—"

I slammed my hand across the table, sending every single item rattling. "I don't pay you to give me excuses and reasons why we shouldn't."

Before I could ram into him further, my phone rang.

"What?" I barked.

"Mr. Ashford. I have Miss—" My executive assistant's voice trailed off and my infamous cool threatened to erupt like a volcano. Or like champagne under pressure.

"Well?" I'd have to fire that woman. She strutted around here like she was shopping for a husband rather than working with efficiency.

"Sir, it's Dr. Madeline Swan."

For a fraction of a second, I froze. Just fucking froze while my brain shouted, *She's here.*

My heart tripped, then started drumming wildly, like I was some kind of teenager. I jumped to my feet, ready to run to her. I'd drag her back to my office and bury myself inside her—seduce all her secrets from her.

My cock throbbed with excitement, totally on board with that plan.

But then realization slammed into me, and I fell back into my chair. Odette never referred to herself as Madeline. Fucking ever. She was sending a message. *Madeline.* One night full of passion and her name slipping from my lips. Over and over again.

Opportunity. This was my chance.

"Let her in. Have her wait in my lounge."

I hung up and met the eyes of the two men in my office. "Goldstein, I need you on standby." Then I turned my head to the judge. "And you, explore all options but do not act on any. A solution might have just landed in my lap."

"What do you mean?" my lawyer demanded to know. "I must advise you—"

"Dr. Swan is here," I cut him off. "My guess is she's here because she needs something. So I'll do what I do best." My smile sharpened and had the same effect as always. It dropped the temperature in the room by another ten degrees. "I'll trap her with a loophole in a contract. I'll get everything I want. And she'll have no way out of it."

I stood up, signaling the meeting was over, and escorted them out.

The moment I opened the door, I saw her, kneeling on the floor. She played with her son—our son—smiling at him softly. Her expression was full of love as she helped him build the ridiculous train set.

My chest squeezed and a snarling, protective beast rose in my chest. They were mine—both of them. I'd never let either of them go again.

"Can I take it home? Please, Maman." He looked at his mother pleadingly, his gaze darting back to the train set.

Odette's expression shattered a bit before she got herself together. "No, love. But one day we'll have one. I promise."

Tomorrow, I decided. They'd have it tomorrow.

The boy's eyes lit up and the smile on his face was bright enough to light up this whole planet.

My chest tightened unlike ever before. It was clear the boy didn't have much, but he had his mother's love. My flesh and blood had been forced to go without. My flesh and blood had roamed this planet without my protection.

"Dr. Swan," I greeted her.

She stiffened the minute she heard my voice, and I moved toward her. The scent of apples filled the air, making my dick stir. I fought the need to lean forward and bury my nose in her strawberry mane, then wrap it around my hand.

Odette shifted, rising on her knees. I inwardly groaned, the position sparking so many ideas. All she had to do was open my fly and her pretty, stubborn mouth. Fuck, none of these images were appropriate for the audience. And I needed to keep my head clear to play my cards right.

Odette shifted, giving me a glimpse of her cleavage, and instinctively, I blocked that magnificent view from my lawyer and the judge. My hand reached out and I grabbed her elbow, helping her to her feet. The softness of her skin seared through me and straight to my groin.

Jesus H. Christ. I wasn't a teenager anymore.

"Thanks." She avoided looking at me. Her eyes darted next to me, to our son, then to her sister who stood unsure of what to do.

While she shifted from foot to foot uncomfortably, I let my eyes roam over my woman—yes, she was and would always be *mine*—and I could see exactly what Nico saw. A faint yellow bruise on her neck, on her jaw. Her lip still had a little cut on it. Someone had hurt her. Badly. Someone had wrapped their hand around her neck. Rage rushed through me, drumming in my ears. *Boom. Boom. Boom.* Red crept into my vision, until every inch of Odette was covered in it.

Nobody—fucking nobody—was allowed to ever lay their hands on her. Except for me and only for pleasure. Never for violence.

"Thanks for seeing me." Her soft smile eased the raging beast inside me.

"Of course." I'd always want to see her. If the world were burning, I'd make sure to see her even then, one last time. To hear her voice one last time.

Glancing over my shoulder, I dismissed my lawyer and the judge. They knew their assignments. With a terse nod, they scurried away.

"Can I play a bit longer?" The little pleading voice brought all our attention to him. Winston was right. I was so blinded by Odette in New Orleans that I missed how much he looked like us. Like *me*.

I knelt down, bringing me to eye level with my son. My throat squeezed. I still couldn't believe it. *My son.* Our baby survived, and I missed it all.

"Hello, I'm—" *Your father. Your dad. Your papa.* I choked. The press would have a field day. I never choked. Never lost my cool. Around this woman, I was a different man. "I'm Byron."

I extended my hand and he took it without hesitation. His was so small and fragile in mine. A protectiveness rose in my chest again with such ferocity it stunned me. It rendered me speechless.

"Hello, sir. I'm Ares." My mask almost slipped. My eyes almost sought out the mother of my child. They didn't. I had to play this right.

But the beast in my chest pounded with pride. She might have stolen him from me—robbed me of years with my son—but I'd be lying if I said it didn't please me to learn his name. Odette gave him *my* name, although I wondered how she knew it. We never discussed my middle name, only hers.

"You can play here while I talk to your mother," I said softly.

Hearing me refer to her as his mother, Odette startled before steeling herself and brushing her fingers over Ares's hair. "Yes, you two stay here and play." Her eyes darted to her sister. "Okay?"

The two of them exchanged wordless nods, and I rose to my full height, towering over the mother of my child.

"Dr. Swan," I said formally, extending my hand toward my office. "You wanted to see me. Let's go into my office."

I led her to my office, then closed the door behind us. "Now, let's hear what brings you in, Dr. Swan," I drawled. "Considering your parting words the last two times we crossed paths, I'm guessing you're not here to see how I'm doing."

"Don't be a dick, Byron," she snapped, annoyed. That same blaze of fire when we first met in exam room number five returned to her eyes, and my dick throbbed painfully. Jesus Christ, how was I supposed to go through with my plan if every move by her gave me a full-blown erection? Then, as if she realized she made a mistake, her shoulders slumped. "Sorry."

She wasn't sorry, but she was desperate. There was a quiet confidence in her hazel eyes, but also something else. Panic. Dark circles under her beautiful eyes attested to her fatigue. And those damn bruises... I could strangle whoever gave them to her with my bare hands.

"Sit down." She hesitated, then took a seat as I took my own behind the desk. "How have you been, Odette?"

Truthfully, I wanted to demand the list of every man who had touched her in the past six years, so I could hunt them down and kill them. No woman—aside from my family—had ever brought out this possessive side of me.

"Fine." She chewed on her bottom lip; then, as if realizing her manners, she added, "You?"

I hated small talk, yet here I was. It was like when she came around, all I wanted to do was cuddle her and protect her. I'd always been protective of my family, but with her it flared tenfold. And now that I knew she had a son—our son—it amplified even more.

I still couldn't believe our baby survived. I was planning on finding that fucking doctor who told me Odette lost the baby and dragging the truth out of her. Why had she lied to me?

"Fine." My eyes glued to her, I studied every inch of her face. Those faded bruises had my fists clenching and every fiber of me itched to go hunting for the culprit. "Who touched you?" I growled, unable to keep a rough edge to my tone.

A light blush crawled up her neck marred with faded bruising and colored her cheeks. She tucked a lock of her red hair behind her ear. She could wear rags, be a hundred years old, and she'd still be breathtaking.

"It doesn't matter." It was clear she wasn't into small talk either. She straightened in the seat, her spine rigid. "That's not why I'm here."

"Then why are you here, Dr. Swan?"

She took her bottom lip between her teeth, a hint of fear creeping into her eyes. She took a deep breath, then exhaled. "I need your help." She gulped, twisting her hands in her lap.

"What kind of help?" I prompted when she didn't continue. Something so raw flashed in her eyes, it punched me right in my gut. It gutted my soul and sent anger rushing through me. The young, carefree woman was gone. In its place was a different woman. Still mine, but different.

"While in Ghana last year, we ran into some trouble." Her voice was faint and raspy, the hint of desperation bleeding into her expression.

"What kind of trouble?" I asked softly.

She blinked, clearing her throat and straightening her back. I watched her neck bob as she swallowed.

"We left Ghana with something that didn't belong to us."

It wasn't hard to guess. "Diamonds."

She nodded. "Yes, and now these criminals have been after us for months. Back in New Orleans, we returned them, but now they're demanding interest." She was squeezing her hands so tightly, her knuckles were turning white.

I leaned in and rested my elbows on the desk. The thought of my son in danger had my blood simmering, but I hid it behind my mask. I'd hide it all until I had her exactly where she needed to be.

"What do they want, Dr. Swan?"

She met my gaze, and a hint of that fearless young woman was deep in those hazel depths.

I watched her neck bob as she swallowed. The name fit her so fucking right. She was graceful and delicate, just like a swan. Everything about her just pulled you in and refused to let go.

"Please, Byron, I'll do anything—" Her voice broke and a single tear rolled down her face. Fuck, it tore at my heart, shredding it to pieces. And she'd already shredded it once.

"What do they want?" I repeated, my voice calm and even. She didn't need to know that I'd give her anything. Fucking anything! As long as she stayed with me. Odette, my son, and I. We'd be a family—just like the one she had.

She let out a heavy sigh, her long lashes wet.

"A million dollars," she breathed, her cheeks turning crimson. "I know it's a lot. I'll do whatever. Anything," she added quickly.

If she only knew I'd give her ten million, easy. As long as she promised to be mine.

Chapter 31
Odette

I held my breath as I dropped that bomb.

I wrung my hands that rested on my lap. Byron leaned back in his chair, his eyes studying me. Except, I couldn't read his expression. It was almost... calculating. His three-piece, dark gray suit molded to his body like a second skin. Wealth surrounded him. A million dollars was a drop in the bucket for him.

To me, it was a matter of life and death.

"You're a doctor now," he remarked coldly. "You're well off."

"No new surgeon is making a million dollars," I blurted. "And I spent my residency in Ghana earning the bare minimum salary."

My palms dampened. I performed life-and-death type of surgeries, and I never lost my nerve. Around this guy, I wasn't steady enough to hold a pen, never mind a surgical knife.

"How did you end up in Ghana?" Surprise washed over me at his question. Why would he even care?

"I worked for the World Health Organization. There was an opportunity to work for a cause while finishing up my residency. It was too good to pass up, and my father did something similar when he was my age."

That familiar ache in my chest pierced through. It didn't help that the misdeeds of his family caused it, yet I couldn't let that deter me. I needed the money.

"I heard what happened to your father." Byron's expression softened. "I'm sorry for your loss." I gasped, digging my nails into my palms. I wanted to lash out, but instead, I focused on the pain as my nails left crescents dented in my skin. "Did you go alone?" he asked casually, leaning back in his chair.

I shook my head, swallowing my pride and the words I wanted to throw in his face.

"No, I didn't go alone." I almost didn't take the opportunity. Bringing a small child to Africa wasn't the wisest decision, but leaving him behind wasn't an option. It was Billie who insisted I take the job, and we moved to Ghana together. As if she hadn't already sacrificed enough. I could never repay my sister for everything she'd done for me. "Listen, I didn't come to chitchat. Can you help me or not?"

It was ballsy and maybe even rude, but I couldn't stand to drag this on anymore. It felt like a slow execution.

"What will I get in return?" he drawled.

My heart shuddered, hope flickering.

"Please," I rasped. "I'll do anything."

Something flashed in his eyes and my self-preservation flared. But it was too late. The truth was, I would do fucking anything to get us out of this mess. My son deserved to have a good life. My sister too. She'd put her life on hold for me so I could finish medical school. So I could complete my residency.

It was the least I could do for them.

"How will you pay back this loan?" Byron ran the back of his fingers over his sharp jawline. The jaw I'd once kissed and licked.

"It might take me a while, but I will pay you back. I promise." He made no move to say or do anything. My desperation grew thick. Bitterness suffocated. "Please, Byron." In my entire life, I had never begged anyone for anything. And here I was, pleading with this man to save my family. "Y-you said once that you wanted me out of your system." It was my last option. My body buzzed with that old flame. It didn't matter what had happened. It didn't matter how badly my heart was broken. Or how scared I was for my son. All of it became background noise when he came around. The attraction sizzled and took control. The throbbing between my thighs became unbearable. The memories were even more so. "I'll be whatever you want me to be, whatever you need me to be for you," I choked out. "I'll do anything."

My cheeks burned. My body ignited. And my pride went up in smoke. Might as well. There was no room for pride here. If he wanted me as his whore, and it'd ensure my son's and sister's safety, I'd be his whore.

Something dark passed over his expression. Arrogant. Predatory.

"Starting now?" he deadpanned, those eyes burning with blue flames. Hope flickered with my next heartbeat. My tongue swept across my dried lips.

"Sure, starting now."

"How many men have you offered this deal to?" My cheeks burned with humiliation at his question. He thought so little of me. Six years and I hadn't moved on to another man. And for what? For this?

Angry words rushed through me, eager to leave my lips. I refused to let them. I wouldn't let my pride destroy this chance. If he refused, I'd have to play my very last card. I'd have to tell him Ares was his son and then pray for his mercy. Or maybe the man had already figured it out himself.

Because one thing I knew for certain; he'd make me pay for keeping this secret. Maybe even take my son from me. Byron was ruthless, undoubtedly like his father, and the latter had already threatened my life. I wanted to save all three of us—my son, Billie, and myself—but Ares came first. Billie and I always had agreed on that. We had to do whatever necessary to ensure his protection.

"I don't know any other multimillionaires, Byron," I retorted dryly while my heart drummed against my ribs.

"Stand up, Dr. Swan." Uncertainty slithered through me, but I pushed myself to my feet. A smoldering look in his eyes set me aflame, but my reason warned. "Come here."

My stomach fluttered at his command and my heart tripped. *Stupid, stupid, stupid.*

"Byron—" The words caught in my throat. Not that I knew what to say.

"Come here, Odette." Displeasure colored his voice and memory rushed forward. He'd call me Odette when I was being a bad girl and switch to Madeline when I pleased him. Was it dumb that I wanted to please him? Yes, it totally was. Yet, I couldn't control my body's response to him.

Pulling my gaze for a fraction of a second to the door, then back to Byron, he must have understood my concern. He pushed a button and a soft click sounded. And then it was just the two of us, cut off from the world.

I walked around the desk and came to stand in front of him. His hands came to my knees, wrapping around them. The raw need that flashed in his eyes sent a jolt to my core. The hungry touch of his hands as he pushed them further up my dress caught my breath.

The air sizzled and sparked.

His hand reached for my nape, pulling me close to him. Our faces were inches apart and my eyelids grew heavy, inhaling his masculine scent into my lungs.

"Who hurt you, Madeline?" he growled. It was right then that I was lost to him. When he said my name. *Madeline.* He was the only one who ever called me that.

I shook my head, unable to find the words. My brain grew hazy, the need for him overwhelming everything else. Pain. Desperation. Terror.

"It doesn't matter," I murmured. Despite this fucked-up situation, I wanted his hands on me. His mouth on me. "Just kiss me already." My tongue swept across my lips, wetting them, and the next thing I knew, his mouth crushed against mine. All bets were off. All reason gone. Our mouths molded together, frenzied and frantic.

His groans. My moans as he slipped his tongue into my mouth. Kissing Byron was explosive. Urgent and desperate. Our bodies ground against each other with carnal need. My hand went to his crotch to stroke the outline of his hard cock. He was as big as I remembered, my pussy clenching greedily.

His feral grunt ignited me into flames. The throbbing between my legs intensified. I was drenched already, and we'd barely gotten started.

His lips never leaving mine, he tore off his jacket, then returned his hands to my inner thighs, tugging my dress up to my waist. I moaned into his mouth, my fingers working on his buckle. I needed him inside me.

A million dollars be damned. I *needed* him.

As if reading my thoughts, he pushed my panties aside and slid two fingers inside me.

"Fuck." We both grunted at the same time.

My head fell back and my eyes fluttered shut. It had been so damn long since someone touched me. His touch felt better than I remembered. Everything about him felt so right.

"Look at me," he hissed, and I instantly obeyed.

My throbbing core clenched around his fingers. He was my last lover. Six years without a man's touch was a long time. Six years without *this man's* touch was an eternity. His hands gripped my ass for a mere second before the cold surface of his desk hit my flesh, his fingers never once leaving me.

His hard ridge pushed against my entrance. My hands came around his neck, and I hooked my ankles behind him, bucking my hips to feel him against my pussy. My hips arched, grinding against him shamelessly. My core pulsed with an ache only he could ease.

I was on the verge of an orgasm, shivers rolling down my spine, when he suddenly stopped.

"Ass up," he ordered, hooking his fingers into the flimsy material of my panties. I fell back onto my elbows and lifted my ass, eager to have them off.

Apparently, being older didn't necessarily mean being smarter.

He pulled my panties down my legs, his palms skimming my bare legs. I thanked all the saints I didn't have pantyhose to put on earlier this morning. The cold was worth feeling his touch on my skin.

Tucking my panties into his pocket, he moved on to undoing his pants. I reached out to help him, pushing his pants and boxer briefs down far enough to let his cock spring out.

Then without warning, his hands came to my hips and he drove in.

He grunted. I gasped.

I forgot how good he felt inside me. How big he was. My pussy clamped down around him so tightly that his next thrust was shallow. My head fell back at the intensity of it all. I spread my legs wider, needing him deeper. He slid in all the way, filling me to the hilt, making my eyes roll.

My fingers clutched him to me, gripping the fabric of his expensive shirt.

He didn't move, as if he'd found home and wanted to stay buried inside me forever. Or maybe that was just wishful thinking from somewhere deep in the back of my thoughts. My muscles shook. His eyes found mine and his nostrils flared. He reached behind me, pulling the zipper of my dress down, then pushing it lower over my hips to expose my bra, which was gone the next moment.

At the sight of my heavy breasts, Byron's breath hitched. He pulled out, then drove into me. Hard. I whimpered.

His mouth came to mine, smothering my sounds. "Did your pussy miss me?" he hissed, his lips moving against mine.

Thrust. Thrust. Thrust.

My muscles squeezed around his hardness, begging for more. Tremors danced along my skin and down my spine.

"Did." Thrust. "Your." Thrust. "Pussy." Thrust. "Miss me?" My head fell back as stars shot behind my eyelids. I moaned. "Answer me!"

"Yes, yes, yes," I whimpered, the pitch of my voice getting higher and higher.

"Good," he groaned. "Now you're going to scream my name, Madeline." *Thrust.* "Good girl."

Shit, why did that turn me on even more? His praise. The way he called me "Madeline," letting me know he was happy with me.

His fingers dug into my hips as he tilted me to get a better angle, hitting that sweet G-spot. He picked up the pace, his thrusts turning wilder. More erratic.

He was losing control. So was I. My whimpers became louder. His name on my lips became more frequent. He covered my mouth with his palm and my tongue darted out, licking his palm and then between his fingers. He felt so good. So perfect.

The tension built in my body. My thighs quivered. I grabbed one of his hands and placed it on my bouncing breasts.

"Your greedy pussy is strangling my cock," he hissed, pinching my nipple. Hard. "That's right. I own this pussy. I own you, Madeline."

Thrust. Thrust. Thrust.

The orgasm unfurled in the pit of my stomach, violent and consuming. It slithered down my spine and my muscles tightened around his shaft, milking him of everything. Reason warned about something, but I couldn't grasp it. I was too far gone. Desire licked every inch of my flesh, burning through me, as my body shook.

A harsh growl vibrated through Byron's chest. He grabbed the back of my thighs and threw my legs over his shoulders, then began plowing into me hard and fast.

I clawed at him. To push him. To bring him closer. I didn't

know. The sensation was too great, overwhelming me. Every single feeling dissipated in the wave of his passion. His possession.

He robbed me of my breath. He fucked me almost desperately, penetrating me deeper, harder, and faster. Each thrust hit my G-spot, making stars burst behind my eyelids. My second climax caught me off guard as it exploded through me at the same time his hot cum shot inside me, the violent ripples rolling through Byron's strong, muscled body between my thighs.

He slumped over me, still mostly clothed, his lips finding mine while his cock still twitched inside me.

It was then that realization sunk in.

"Byron." I panicked, pushing against him. "We didn't use a condom."

Chapter 32
Byron

My plan went askew. A slight detour.

She distracted me, fried the circuits in my brain the moment she offered to be mine, to do with what I wanted. Instead, the moment she offered herself to me, my dick took over. Holy fucking Christ. I should have maintained control and steered the conversation. Something short-circuited, though, and I was zeroed in on one thing and one thing only.

Having her. Owning her.

All I could feel was the consuming, feral need for her. Six years of distance and separation all dissipated into thin air. Still buried deep inside her, my face in her neck, I inhaled the familiar scent of crisp apples. I hadn't been able to stomach anything with apples for so long that my mouth was now salivating.

Her small, delicate hands that saved lives started pushing on me and dread pooled in the pit of my stomach. Did my desire blind me, making me think she wanted me too?

"Byron, we didn't use a condom." Panic laced her words while I couldn't help but smile smugly. We'd come full circle.

I straightened up, helping her into a sitting position. I snatched a handful of tissues from the box on my desk and helped her get cleaned up. My cum on her pussy was enough to get my cock hard again, but this time, I ignored that little shit. Instead, I helped with her bra, then her dress, before I cleaned myself up.

She remained sitting on my desk, those hazel eyes following my every movement. She looked thoroughly fucked—her hair tousled, her mouth swollen from my kisses. I'd never be able to sit at this desk without seeing this image.

"We won't be needing condoms," I told her calmly, leaning back in my fancy chair. Unable to keep my hands from her, I brought my palm to her thigh and squeezed. "Because you, Dr. Swan, will marry me and give me heirs." She stared at me in confusion, shaking her head. "Yes, that's my condition," I said coolly while my heart thundered. I was so close to having what I wanted. I couldn't fuck it up. "I'll give you a million dollars today, and you'll marry me. When we leave this office, you'll go to my home. My bed."

You and our son will be in my home where you both belong. But I wouldn't tell her that I knew her little secret. If I knew her well enough, she'd insist her son and sister come along anyway.

She swallowed. "Marry you?" she whispered, blinking in confusion. "But you... Aren't you married already?"

Jesus, hadn't this woman looked me up at all? The press deemed me and my brothers the most eligible bachelors on this planet and this woman didn't even know my marital status.

"Unless you know something I don't, I've never married," I stated calmly while agitation grew inside me.

"But I thought... y-you already have an heir," she sputtered.

Okay, now she was really pissing me off. "I do?" I raised my eyebrow. Maybe she'd come clean and tell me about Ares, although somehow I doubted it. "Where is that heir, pray tell?"

"In New Orleans?"

"New Orleans," I repeated. Then I remembered. My nephew

was sitting next to me when we ran into each other. "That's my nephew. Kostya."

"Oh."

I waited for her to say something else. Anything else. I gave her a chance to come clean. My heart raced. I needed my ring on her finger. I needed her in my bed for the rest of our lives.

"Tell me you'll marry me, and I'll take care of all your troubles."

She kept shaking her head, the look in her eyes telling me she'd rather do anything but that. Too fucking bad.

"Can't you just help me"—she licked her lips and my cock throbbed, eager to have her again—"out of the goodness of your heart?"

I scoffed. My heart. The very same one she shattered. The very same one she'd stomped all over without a second thought.

"No." For a split second, I saw pain flash through her hazel eyes, but she averted her gaze. A small sigh left her lips, and she started to twist her graceful fingers.

"I can't marry you," she muttered.

"Why not? As far as I know, you're not married."

"We're incompatible." She raised her head, meeting my eyes head-on. "My family is nothing like yours. Your father destroys people. Mine saved people." My brows furrowed at the odd comment. Why would she care anything about my father? She'd never even met him. Not that her comment was off base though. "We have nothing in common. We never had anything in common. Not six years ago, not today."

Aside from our son. The knowledge danced through the air. Except she didn't know that I knew her secret. Or did it not even cross her mind that our son would bind us forever? Unless—

No, it would be impossible for Ares to be anyone else's son. He was the spitting image of me. I was a rational man, and I'd trust evidence, despite my trust in said evidence having been betrayed once already. But I would get to the bottom of that soon enough.

"We're plenty compatible," I told her. "After all, I was just buried deep inside of you, and it seemed to me we fit just right."

She let out a frustrated breath. "Don't be an asshole."

"Asshole is my middle name." *Or Ares, like our son,* I added silently. It made me wonder whether she knew my middle name or if this was just a lucky coincidence. "You will marry me, or I'll hand you over personally to the diamond smugglers."

"You wouldn't dare!"

I shrugged, my pulse racing. She single-handedly managed to raise my blood pressure. "Try me, Dr. Swan," I gritted.

She stared at me, weighing her options. Of course, she had none. If I'd known she was pregnant six years ago, I'd have dragged her to the altar.

"If we get married, we live separate lives?" She tried to frame her words as an ultimatum, but it wavered just enough to make it a question.

"No, you'll move in with me."

"I—I can't move in with you." Then she straightened her shoulders, fixing me with a glare. "I won't move in with you."

"Why not?"

That stubborn tilt to her chin came back. That same one that could drive me wild and crazy at the same time.

"I don't want to."

She let out an exasperated breath. "Because I have other people that depend on me. My sister and my—" She hesitated for a moment. "My son."

Bingo.

"They can move in with us," I assured her. "My place is big enough."

The gold in her eyes shimmered, drowning out all the hazel, and I could see her brain working it all out. Weighing the pros and cons. Looking for her way out. There wasn't one.

I was her only lifeline.

"Fine." Her sigh was soft, exasperated. Defeated. "Help me get those diamond smugglers off my back, and I'll marry you." Relief, unlike anything I'd even felt before, rushed through me. This was what I wanted, above all else. Now more than ever. She'd be my wife, and our son would finally have both parents—like he should have from the beginning of his life. And I wouldn't risk any chances that something would change that outcome. Not with her. Not with our son. "A longer engagement will be prudent."

"You'll marry me today," I told her calmly. I'd waited six fucking years, I wasn't about to wait another minute longer.

Above all else, I wanted Odette Madeline Swan as my wife.

And this time, she wouldn't slip through my fingers.

Chapter 33
Odette

The media referred to him as a heartless billionaire who ruled his empire with a cool head and an even colder heart.

I could see the ruthless part. The calculating aura he had. But never cold. Everything about Byron screamed passion. A single glance his way had me melting like the polar ice caps. A single touch and I was putty under his expert hands.

Bottom line, Byron Ashford was another heartbreak waiting to happen. My beautiful disaster. And unfortunately, my best bet at staying alive.

Locking gazes with his blue eyes, I tried to figure out his angle and failed. He had one, I was sure of it. But what? He didn't have to marry me to have my body. I made that perfectly clear. Yet, he insisted on it.

I knew from his father and his fiancée—apparently she never graduated to being Byron's wife—that I didn't fit in their circles. I wasn't good enough to marry a future president's son.

Well, the joke was on Senator Ashford, wasn't it? The old man was still not president. If his election hung in the air by a single vote and my vote was a determining factor for him winning the election, he'd be screwed.

Byron stared at me, calculatingly, refusing to give me a reprieve. I was only ready to give him my body. He wanted a lot more. Way more.

Freedom was within my grasp, but so were the chains. Chains of love? More likely lust. And lust didn't last. I'd be bound by the shackles of a loveless marriage.

I didn't want that. Seeing firsthand what our parents had, my sister and I always refused to settle for less. Our goal was to have it all or none of it.

"I don't want to marry you." Six years ago, it would have been a different story. Back then, I was a blind, infatuated woman in love. Thanks to his father, the blinders fell off and my heart was broken. I wouldn't repeat the same mistake. I refused to go down the same road again with him.

Byron smiled coldly. "That's what makes you perfect for this marriage of convenience."

I blinked, confused. "Huh?"

The concept was foreign, although I knew what it meant. It was just mind-boggling that anyone even did that anymore.

"Marriage of convenience," he repeated. "You get something you need, and I get something I want."

The look in his eyes told me he was serious.

I swallowed. "Like what? What could you possibly want from me?"

He made no attempt to answer. What did I expect? After all, he was a ruthless billionaire. Just like his father. A shudder rolled down my spine. This wouldn't just impact me. It was about my son. My sister. I had to make the right decision for them. How could I possibly marry Byron and bring them around someone like Byron's father? Yet, marrying Byron was currently my only option at saving the remains of my family. So I'd do what I must.

"My time is precious, Dr. Swan. Let's get going."

His hand on my lower back, Byron led me out the door and into the lounge where I found my sister and son, playing with the *Thomas the Train* set. Leaving Byron's side, I rushed to my family. The two people I'd do anything for.

"Hey, guys." I lowered myself behind my son and kissed the back of his head. "You ready?"

My sister's gaze burned the side of my cheek, but I couldn't meet her eyes. I feared that if I said anything, my voice would betray me. My desperation. I also feared she would see in my eyes how thoroughly spent I was after what we'd just done in Byron's office.

Ares's big blue eyes met mine, gripping the blue train. "I don't want to go, Maman."

I smiled and gently brushed his hair away from his forehead. He needed a haircut, but we'd been on the move so much, it hadn't been a priority. Staying alive was. And then there was the fact that Ares hated anyone giving him a haircut. He tolerated me and Billie, but our skills were sad.

"I know, baby."

"Why don't you take your favorite train car from this set, and we'll go shopping for your own train set?" Byron said gently. Ares's gaze lit up and darted over my shoulder. I followed it to find Byron leaning against the wall, his hands tucked in the front pockets of his suit pants.

"Really?"

Byron smiled, extending his hand out. "Ready?"

Ares nodded eagerly, but wouldn't move from my side until I inclined my head. The fact he wanted to go to him made my chest heavy. Light. Sad. Happy. So many damn emotions swirled inside me that it made it hard to process them all.

But one thing was certain.

I wouldn't allow the Ashfords to hurt my son the way they had hurt me.

Byron opened the back door for us. Billie and Ares climbed inside, and I followed.

"Take us home. Once you drop us off, I'd like you to run some errands so we can ensure our guests feel comfortable," he ordered the chauffeur. Upon his acknowledgement, he clicked the remote to raise the partition. I didn't have the emotional bandwidth to consider what he meant by that.

Billie flicked me a curious look, but I gave her a barely noticeable shake of my head. "Not now," I mouthed. Not that I had many answers. Byron said he wanted to marry me today, yet I couldn't fathom how that would be possible. He didn't have a marriage license. Nothing was making sense.

My gaze darted to my ex-lover. He looked just as handsome as he did six years ago. His dark suit highlighted his broad shoulders and looked like it had been sewn directly onto his body. Everything about him screamed wealth. Sophistication. Self-confidence.

Next to him, I felt like a scrawny little mouse. That was the result of his father's words from six years ago. The lasting impact he'd obviously left on me. I hated him for it.

Byron cracked his knuckles, then pulled out his phone and started typing. A *swish* filled the enclosed space every time he sent off a message. It was as if he readied for war. World domination was not out of the realm of possibility for this man.

Tension danced through the air, and it was only thanks to Ares that it didn't suffocate me. If it weren't for him, the drive to the Ashford home—a mansion, I realized—would have been uncomfortably tense and quiet.

Another *swish* filled the air and Byron put the phone on the seat, next to him. His gaze landed on Ares who was rattling off his imagination while playing with his train. To my surprise, Byron's expression softened.

I swallowed, turning my head to look out the window.
How would I survive him again?

Chapter 34
Byron

I led my son, my soon-to-be-wife, and Billie into my home.

I had already sent a note to Winston who'd ensure Billie was out of my way. Those two had their own shit to figure out. Odette and my son were my priority.

Mrs. Watson, my housekeeper, took Billie to the opposite wing of the house. She'd have to hike her way back to my side, which would give me plenty of time to work out my deal with Odette.

The atmosphere was tense between us as I led them into my home office. Ares's expression fell. He expected to find a Thomas train set here too. I'd ensure there was one here tomorrow.

I squatted in front of him. His eyes took me in, so much like Winston's. So much like mine. His hair was tousled, probably in need of a haircut. But if he was anything like me, he hated haircuts.

"Ares, is it okay if I talk to your mom?" My son's eyes darted to his mom. She smiled softly—assuringly—and that was enough.

"Okay."

I stroked his dark hair. I wanted to pull him to my chest, but that would probably alarm him. Never mind Odette. Was it normal to feel such strong attachment only on the basis I knew him? Our father wasn't the affectionate kind, so it was hard to know how a good father should be.

Ares headed to the window, flattening his palm against it. He was so small, making my chest squeeze with worry.

"Make this quick, Byron." Odette pulled my attention away from my son. "I don't have all day."

Everything about Dr. Swan managed to make me feel edgy.

A single look. A simple word. A smile.

If she knew the power she had over me, it'd have her running away and accepting her fate with the Ghanaians. Everything she did sent a zing of electricity up through me.

And her backbone only made my cock harder.

She was what I wanted above all else. Making her my wife would prevent her from leaving me again, and it'd keep my son with me. I'd keep them both safe. Having her in my bed would be a nice added bonus.

"Please sit down," I told her, my tone disgruntled as I grabbed a blank sheet of paper and held it up. "We'll make this arrangement a bit more formal."

Odette crossed her arms and sat in the chair, her spine stiff. "Right, let's not forget NDAs and prenups."

My pen froze midair. Fuck, it never even crossed my mind to draw up a prenup. I was one of the richest men in the world—not having a prenup was risky. To my family and my empire. With anyone else, it'd be the first thing I'd take care of. Yet, with her it felt wrong to do it.

I shook my head ruefully. "Tell me if there is anything else you want in return for marrying me, Odette." Her eyes roamed over my face, her expression slightly appalled. I wondered what she saw. The young Odette was easier to read than this one. She masked herself way too well, hiding her emotions. Unlike when we first met six years ago. That young woman hadn't been afraid to take risks. To take what she wanted.

"I just want you to get the diamond smugglers off our back," she muttered, avoiding looking at me. Being filthy rich meant people were eager to flock to me and our family. To cling to us, like we were their salvation. But not Odette.

The only woman to ever walk away from me. The only woman who wanted me for me. Money, wealth, and status meant nothing to her. Maybe it was that which pulled me to her. She seemed to see *me*. Not to mention her body molded into mine like an ocean to a beach. We fit perfectly. Even those damn scars on my back didn't repulse her. It didn't matter what my front looked like, women cringed when they saw the scars. I could never distinguish whether it bothered me or not. None of them had ever looked at me and seen *me* nor had they cared who I truly was. They saw wealth, prestige, and the Ashford name.

In the end, a transactional marriage would work best.

"Is that it?" I asked her.

Odette hesitated, and I involuntarily tensed. "Are you sure you want to take it as far as marriage, Byron? Whatever you want, I'll give it to you—" Her eyes flickered to our son, then back to me. "You don't need to marry me to get it." When I remained silent, hope entered her expression. "We could pretend we're dating, and then amicably go our own way when you're finished with me."

I smiled at her and started to draft our contract, ignoring her comment. "Marriage or nothing, Odette. You will give me exclusivity, fidelity, your body—" And heart eventually, I added silently. "—and heirs. Occasionally, I'll require your presence during certain social events."

Her eyes flared with wrath and, at the same time, what might have been fear. It made the gold specks shimmer, pulling me into their web. "Excuse me?" She was on her feet, her palms sprawled on my desk as she leaned closer to me.

"You will give me exclu—"

"I heard you," she snapped. "Why do you need heirs anyhow?" She flickered a worried look to our son who was still mesmerized with the window and the garden it overlooked. He dragged his train up and down, probably scratching the fuck out of the glass. I didn't give a fuck, as long as he was happy. "If I give you heirs, I won't be able to—" *Leave.*

The word hung heavy in the air and fuck if it didn't piss me off. I smiled coldly. I knew her brain already worked up ways to get rid of me. To fucking leave me again.

"There'll be no leaving," I cut her off dryly. "No divorce. Marriage is for life, and I'm no quitter. I want a big family with you. If we have issues, we work them out. Together." Odette fell silent. Her mouth opened, then closed—the gears in her brain turning. "Are you a quitter?"

I watched her delicate neck bob as she swallowed. "No, I'm not," she whispered.

Desperation laced her tone, mirrored in her expression.

"Do I have your word, Dr. Swan?" She nodded hesitantly, and sat back down with a resigned sigh. I glanced down at the empty sheet of paper in front of me. "Tell me your requirements, aside from taking care of the diamond smugglers. Consider them taken care of."

The way she stared at me made me wonder if she was determining whether to trust me or strangle me. She brushed her hair out of her face and inhaled deeply. Whatever it was, she resigned herself to her faith and to me.

"If you want my fidelity, I want yours too."

"Done." Surprise crossed her expression at my fast response. Cheating wasn't my thing, and I'd seen plenty of what my father's infidelity did to our family. I didn't want to repeat his mistakes. "What else?"

She hesitated for a flicker of a moment, then steeled her spine and smiled. "I'll continue my work, and if it requires travel, extended stays out of the country, you won't stand in my way. My son comes with me, of course."

My son. God, how it irked me to hear it stated that way. I wanted to announce it through every channel—to the entire world

—that Ares was *our* son. He was an Ashford. But there'd be time for that.

"We'll discuss it together," I stated diplomatically. "If you're pregnant, certain areas of the world won't be safe. If I can accompany you during your travels, I will." Her jaw tightened but she gave me a terse nod. "Then you have my full support, Dr. Swan."

I knew I couldn't forcibly hinder her career. If I held on to her too tightly, I'd only end up crushing her. It'd only push her further away.

"One last thing," she said, her tone firm. The look in her eyes intrigued me, so I straightened my back. Whatever she was about to demand was clearly non-negotiable. "My son's name is to be kept out of the public. I don't want him dragged through the mud, alongside your—" Her tone faltered for a moment as she searched for the right word. "Your father's political career." *Interesting.* She must have kept tabs on my family if she knew about my father's political career and the continual scandals that always seemed to follow him. She sighed and looked away. "I don't want our marriage broadcasted and impacting any of our children. My career, either."

I didn't like the sound of that. I wanted the entire world to know she was mine.

"Understood. I'll do what I can to divert media attention."

Chapter 35
Odette

Something about the way Byron watched me had me on pins and needles.

No matter how this went, I feared there'd be no getting out of this marriage of convenience—fancy word for forced marriage—unscathed. I'd be a fool to lie to myself.

There was no denying the way he affected me from the moment I laid eyes on him. Six years apart almost amplified the attraction. Much to my dismay.

In the short time he'd known me, he'd hurt me more than anyone. How much would be left of my heart when he was done with me?

"If we do this—and I mean if—I want nothing to do with your father." Surprise flickered in his eyes. He couldn't really be surprised. Could he?

"Okay." He agreed too easily. "If that's what you want. You'll always be my first choice. Forever. But in return, I have a few requirements of my own."

He said forever, my heart sang. Except, I couldn't blindly trust him. He had lied before. He had deceived me before. I had to keep my reason and keep my feelings to myself. Yes, my body melted for him, but it didn't mean my heart had to lie on a platter for him.

"Tell me your requirements," I murmured, annoyed. "Aside from bestowing you with heirs. Assuming you can deliver."

I couldn't resist the jab. Although judging by his grin, it didn't have the desired effect. I realized my mistake the moment I heard his next words.

"To ensure I can deliver, Madeline, you'll be in my bed every single night." I opened my mouth to protest, but he didn't give me a chance to. "Sometimes during the day too."

X-rated images flashed through my mind, flustering me. The thought of sharing a bed with Byron—night in and night out—made me lose that very reason I was struggling to keep hold of. The last time I spent a night with him, I had lost all my restraint. Even just hours earlier, I barely recognized the woman splayed out on the desk in his office.

Heat rushed through me as memories flooded in. The same ones I kept at bay in order to survive my broken heart.

I bit down on my lip, a pulsing ache throbbing between my thighs matching the one in my chest.

"There's no going back after this. From this day onward, your body and your essence are mine. I want all of you, and I won't settle for anything less."

The intensity of his gaze made me feel vulnerable. I wrapped my arms around myself, as if it could shield me. The craving in my body worried me. No, it actually terrified me. How could I want him after all that he and his father had put me through?

Yet, I did. Maybe in the grand scheme of things, I was my own worst enemy. If only I could hate him, I'd save myself a world of heartache. Six years ago, I'd have given him everything without a second thought. Today, I was a different woman. I had to put on a mask of indifference and protect myself.

"Do we have an agreement?" I nodded. "Words, Odette. I want your words."

"We have an agreement, Byron." My heart and soul ached. He spoke of desire, of heirs, of owning me. But there were no words of love and devotion. The thing I craved the most when I imagined a future for myself. "The only promise I want is fidelity on your part too."

He looked at me as if he were reading me, digging up all my secrets.

"I will never cheat on you," he vowed. "You're the only one I'll touch. You're the only one I'll desire. I will make this agreement between us worthwhile; this doesn't have to be a punishment, for either of us. I'll fulfill all your fantasies, Odette." Heat rushed to my cheeks and I averted my gaze, finding my son. He was too far away to hear our conversation. "But there'll be no sharing. You're mine alone."

At that, an inferno blazed through my veins. He'd laugh—or boast—if he knew I hadn't had sex with anyone else in all our years apart.

"Okay," I agreed, resigned to my destiny. I could almost taste the bitterness on my tongue. I could almost see my dream of finding the same love my parents shared extinguished in front of my eyes.

"What do you mean you're marrying him?"

Billie spit her water all over her clothes and mine, the liquid shooting through both her mouth and nostrils. She coughed, waving her arms like she was drowning. I came behind her and patted her on the back.

The countdown in my brain was as loud as a grandfather clock, reminding me I was down to minutes before I'd be Mrs. Byron Ashford. A sudden storm broke outside, knocking against the windows. As if it warned against the impending doom.

"It was the condition he required before he agreed to settle our debt. I didn't have a choice now, did I?" I discarded my clothes, my eyes darting to the dress laid out on the bed in my temporary bedroom. The room was connected to Ares's bedroom and would be turned into a playroom. *Tomorrow*, Byron said. It seemed ridiculous that I'd been given this one at all. If anything, it symbolized my waning freedom that much more.

Nobody could call Byron inefficient. He certainly moved fast.

Billie's eyes darted to Ares to ensure he wasn't listening. His attention was on the toys that had awaited him in his bedroom, and I knew he'd be distracted for the foreseeable future. I had already changed him into a suit—who knew Armani made three-piece suits for children?—and he looked dashing.

"Does he know about—" I shook my head and she let her question trail off. We agreed we'd never utter those words out loud. I'd been worried that Byron would suspect Ares was his, if not for his age fitting the timeline of my accident, then for his resemblance. But if Byron knew about Ares, he would have exploited that piece of information too. Perhaps he wasn't as attentive as I'd once thought him to be. "You can't marry him," she whispered, yanking me from my thoughts. "Delay the wedding until he pays off the Ghanaians, and then we can take off."

"So we exchange running from smugglers for running from the Ashfords?" I stared at her, standing in my panties and bra. The consequences of their wrath had already taken so much from us already. She still didn't know the full extent of the mess I'd brought onto our family, but I hadn't forgotten. It was a risk we couldn't take, not when so much had been lost the first time. "I'm sick and tired of running, Billie. It's not good for Ares. It's not good for us. When was the last time we had a good night's sleep? Or even three meals a day?"

Billie flinched as if I'd slapped her, shame filling her expression. "I'm sorry."

I shook my head, laughing bitterly. I needed to steer the conversation away from her guilt and shame, knowing it wasn't fair for her to carry alone. Knowing the role I'd played in landing us in the situation with the diamond smugglers. Billie would have never acted out of such desperation, had I not become involved with Byron.

Everything always led back to the Ashfords, and I was tired of this web of deceit I was constantly weaving. So, I tried to lighten the situation, and to hopefully convey to my sister that we were going to be okay. "I'm starting to think what our parents had was exceptional and as rare as finding a Melo Melo pearl."

When we were children, Billie was obsessed with jewelry. Obviously, she still was. A Melo Melo pearl was known to be the rarest pearl in the world and one of the most expensive ones. What our parents had was incredible, while it lasted. It was cut short by Maman's death.

A tense silence stretched between us. The only sound audible was Ares's constant humming as he played with his toys.

Billie looked beaten down. Tired. She looked like I felt. "I'm sorry."

I took my sister's face between my hands. "We have taken care of each other. You did something for me and Ares that I'll never be able to repay. Don't apologize. Ever. Even when I'm mad. You're my sister. My family. There are things that I've done... things we've never spoken about—"

She shook her head, cutting me off. "None of it matters. I did what Dad would have done." There was that pain again at the mention of him.

I swallowed down all my emotions and pecked my sister's cheek. "You have done more than any normal sibling would have done. I finished med school thanks to you. You were there when Ares was born. You took care of both of us. Now, let me take care of you."

"With his money," she retorted dryly. "It always goes back to the damn Ashford money."

"What do you mean?" I asked her. She didn't know that the Ashfords were responsible for the ruin of Father's hospital.

Her eyes flickered and her cheeks flushed. "Winston Ashford is an entitled prick too," she mumbled.

My brows scrunched while I watched her pensively. "What do you mean?" I asked again.

She waved her hand exasperatedly. "I don't like the fact it's their money."

"I don't care whose money it is at this point." It might have been wrong, but I really didn't. I was marrying Byron to save my family. My sister and my son. Frankly, I'd have done a lot worse for the two of them. Up until now, my sister had taken care of us. It was my turn. She'd never said it, but I suspected she saw the diamonds as an opportunity to kick-start her dream. It was the reason she took them, never thinking it'd backfire so badly.

"Let's learn from this and move on." I took her hand into mine. "Maybe we can finally focus on our careers. You can move to Paris, work with designers, and start your own jewelry line. And I can finally practice medicine without looking over my shoulder."

With that, I slipped on a pearl-hued Dior mid-length dress with three-quarter sleeves that hugged my silhouette like it was made for me. Knowing Byron, it *was* made for me no matter how ridiculous that sounded.

"Okay," she agreed reluctantly.

"How do I look?" My tone was dry as gin as I twirled in front of my sister.

Her eyes flashed, stopping me in my tracks, frowning. Did I look that bad? "Byron said he wanted you to wear this."

She reached for a blue, leather-bound case from the table and handed it to me. Wondering what was inside, I lifted the hinged lid and my sister's gasp filled the space.

"Holy shit." Her voice was hushed and her eyes gleamed like the jewelry in the plush velvet setting. "It's stunning. Even more so in person."

My eyes darted between my sister and the necklace. It was beautiful, that was for sure, but she acted like this necklace was famous. The only famous jewelry I had ever heard of was the Hope Diamond—a 45.52-carat diamond extracted from the Kollur mine in India—but I knew for a fact *that* necklace was stored securely in the Smithsonian Institution.

"What is it?" I questioned.

"It's a Harry Winston," she said, her tone hushed and reverent. "It would be worth at least twenty million."

The diamonds, set in a way to look like vines covered in ice, wreathed the whole necklace until it reached a single stunning emerald.

"The story is that this piece was designed for the Queen of England, but Harry Winston couldn't bear to let it go, so he made another piece for her while holding on to this one."

"How does Byron have it?" I asked in a hushed tone.

She shrugged. "We'd certainly be set for life with that necklace," she said wistfully.

I groaned. "Don't even think about it, Billie. Diamonds have gotten us into enough trouble. Just put it around my neck and throw me overboard so I can drown with it if you're tempted to steal it."

Billie grinned. "I just might, soeur."

The two of us laughed—a strangled and humorless laugh—while the wail of the wind and the hail pounding against the windows warned of impending doom.

Chapter 36
Odette

An hour later, I stared at our marriage certificate in my hand with disbelief.

Such a plain piece of paper, yet it held so much weight. Depending on who you were, it represented love, promises, arrangements. Never in a million years did I think it would be a cold business arrangement for me.

But here I stood, dumbfounded and numb, staring at my future. Ares's hand gripped my dress, his eyes studying me. He reminded me so much of his father when he did that. I ruffled his hair affectionately, the golden band catching the light and mocking me.

"I'll keep this safe. And the mayor will file it first thing in the morning."

Byron tugged the paper out of my grip, his voice penetrating the haze in my brain. I lifted my eyes to find him and our witnesses —Winston and Billie, along with the mayor who married us— staring at me.

The mayor cleared his throat uncomfortably, shot me a smile and said, "Congratulations again."

My smile felt unnatural. "Thank you."

Byron's hand came around me, holding on to me, as if he worried I'd take off. Maybe he was worried about the necklace that weighed more than me.

"Beautiful necklace," the mayor complimented.

Billie's eyes were locked on the piece around my neck, but I didn't think much of it. After all, jewelry was her passion.

"I hear it's famous for its attributes," she muttered.

Byron stiffened and I shot him a curious look. He didn't say anything, so I turned my attention to Billie.

"What attributes?" I asked curiously.

"It either brings happiness in marriage or doom." My eyes flicked to my husband. Jesus, maybe he planned to kill me. Although the way he looked at me, I didn't think so. At least not until I gave him heirs. *More* heirs. Good God.

My sister, on the other hand, might be a dead woman with the way Byron's eyes turned icy as he stared her down.

"I don't believe in superstition," I commented, hoping to ease the tense situation. "Although my sister could have mentioned it earlier."

She smiled sheepishly. "I didn't want to add to your distress. Besides, Byron should think twice about using the necklace."

"Do you ever not have an opinion?" Byron growled.

Billie shrugged, refusing to be intimidated by Byron. "Up to you, soeur. But from what I know, this necklace dated back three generations of the DiLustro family before it landed on your neck." My brows scrunched. Who in the fuck were DiLustros? "Rumor has it that they are part of the mafia." She waved her hand in the air like that little piece didn't matter and the necklace story was more important. "Anyhow, this little 'Hope Diamond wannabe' has brought the DiLustros unhappy marriages."

"I didn't know you're such a diamond expert," Byron remarked dryly. I should be thankful he didn't call us diamond thieves.

"There are a lot of things you don't know about me. But not to worry, soeur. There is hope, because before the DiLustros, this necklace was designed for royalty. It is said to bring happiness and love to all those before them."

"I guess we just have to hope we have some royalty in our bloodline somewhere along the way." My tone was dry. I didn't like that story nor the odds.

The mayor cleared his throat uncomfortably. "I'm gonna get going. See you at the fundraiser, Byron."

My husband nodded, tucking the marriage license into his jacket. The old mayor disappeared through the door while Byron's gaze remained on Ares and me. He seemed calmer somehow, while the tension in me grew tenfold.

"Everything okay?" he asked. I guess he thought me superstitious. I didn't think I was, but at least my sister might rethink stealing the necklace now. I looked up at him, catching a hint of concern in his blue eyes.

"Yes," I assured him, staring at his strong jaw. The same one I'd traced with my lips. His expression consumed and stirred something deep inside me. Something I thought I buried long ago. It terrified and thrilled me at the same time.

We'd said our vows and signed the papers. There was no going back. We were past the worries and regrets. I'd have to make the best of this. It was bittersweet how it all started, but I couldn't exactly say I regretted it. All I had to do was look at my son to know I'd do it all over again. Every tear shed and all the heartache—I'd endure it all again for him.

It was past eight and Ares's yawn reminded me of his bedtime. Byron must have noticed it too, because he squatted down right alongside me.

"Tired?" Another yawn as he nodded.

"Off to bed, then, buddy," Byron said, lifting him up onto his shoulders. A wide grin spread across Ares's small face and Byron laughed—soft and... happy?—while I memorized this moment. Father and son.

Over the years—in rare, quiet moments—I often wondered how

Byron would be as a father. Now, I was getting a preview, and it made me want to see the entire movie.

It made me want the fairy tale even more.

"You all right?" Billie's hand landed on my shoulder.

My heart thundered. Unable to peel my gaze away from my son and husband, I croaked a trembling, "Yes."

"I don't know about this," she muttered under her breath. "I don't have a good feeling about any of it."

I shot Billie a glance. She wore a blood-red dress. She said it was a choice between either red or black. She wanted to wear black for mourning, but we finally settled on red. *So much better*, I thought wryly.

"Hello. Earth to my sister."

I rubbed my nose. "Everything will be fine," I uttered automatically, like so many times before. It had become my motto when shit was bad over the last six months.

"If you say that one more time, I'm going to lose my temper." Billie held a glass of champagne, studying me intently. I guess I should be grateful she wasn't going all cavewoman on Byron. She wasn't happy about any of it—especially being connected to Winston—but it was unavoidable. Whether we were willing to admit it or not, from the moment I gave birth to Ares, we were connected.

"It's too late for anything else." I leaned over and pressed a kiss on her cheek. "Just, please, no more stupid decisions. Let's just focus on the good. Ares is safe. We're safe."

"Except, we're now in a completely different mess."

I sighed, suddenly feeling exhausted. Today had been a whirlwind, and I didn't know how much more I could take. Feeling eyes on me, I turned my head to find Byron, Ares, and Winston studying us. Identical blue eyes. Identical hair color. Identical expressions.

"Time to tuck Ares in," Byron observed smoothly, his eyes burning with blue flames that promised carnal pleasure to come after we put our son to bed. I should fight him. Keep my distance.

But I didn't have any fight left in me. It was as if the six years of grinding, sacrifices, and pain all caught up to me.

"Did you know Ares is Byron's middle name too?" Winston addressed me for the first time tonight.

I stiffened, but kept my composure. I did know it. It was part of Byron's medical chart, but neither Winston nor Byron knew that. And I'd been practicing what I would say if this ever came up. So I was totally prepared.

"No," I lied. "What a weird coincidence." When I learned I'd have a son, a part of me had wanted to tie him to Byron regardless of the way we parted. I fell for my one-night stand and letting go was so damn hard that I had to keep part of it alive. It came in the form of his name. "Mythological names became popular, and I jumped on the bandwagon."

Winston arched an eyebrow, as if to say *you are so full of shit*.

Well, he had nothing on me and no evidence. Byron and I never discussed his middle name.

With a last peck on my sister's cheek and a terse nod, I joined my son and new husband. Byron led me out of the living room by the small of my back and toward the wing of the house where his private rooms were. Where *our* private rooms were.

Byron's lips were curved as Ares kept shaking his head when I offered help. Leaning against the door of the private bathroom, he watched us with an indescribable look in his eyes.

"Thank you for keeping his room close," I murmured as my heart thumped wildly. Ares was brushing his teeth, insisting on his independence.

"Of course. This is where he belongs." His cryptic answer didn't help to ease my anxiety.

After Ares's teeth were brushed, we changed him into his favorite set of pajamas and read a book. Much to his delight, Byron and I alternated the dialogue pieces and something in my chest cracked hearing Ares's happy giggles each time we switched voices.

But all the while, my body buzzed in anticipation of what was to come.

My heart drummed against my ribs as I sat on Byron's large, comfortable bed, wearing what he had chosen for me. A satin, white babydoll with matching panties. The set was still in the delicately wrapped package when he'd handed it to me.

The sound of the shower running filled my ears. I took one first, hoping it'd settle my nerves. If anything, it kept them teetering on the edge. Byron's home was luxurious and expensive, nothing I was accustomed to. We grew up comfortable but not rich. But we were happy. This home felt... too big. Too empty.

My jaw clenched, knowing my choices were limited in terms of home and future settings. I'd have preferred to raise Ares on the French Riviera, surrounded by warmth, love, and happy memories. Not in a metropolitan city. Washington, D.C., was never on my list of dream cities to visit, never mind living in.

"What are you thinking about?"

I startled, pulling my knees closer to my chest. Byron stood in the doorway in nothing but a pair of black boxers. Involuntarily, my eyes roamed over his body and my face flushed. Much to my dismay, he had the most magnificent body. I'd hardly had the chance to fully take him in earlier in his office, but now I did, he looked better than I remembered. My eyes settled on his tattoo of the elements, remembering how fascinated I was with it when I first saw him naked. I gulped, letting my gaze travel down his chest, then abs, to where a deep V was clearly visible below his waistband.

I finally tore my gaze away from his body and met his eyes. It was then that I realized he had a new tattoo. Right on his chest. It was done with a light hand, almost as if he didn't want it noticeable.

"What's that tattoo on your chest?"

His gaze on me, he walked up to the bed, and I swallowed hard. The look in his eyes told me there'd be little sleeping tonight. There was such a burning desire in those blue depths that I feared it'd consume me alive. What worried me most was knowing the same look was reflected in my own eyes.

"Byron, I asked you a question," I murmured, my whole body humming in anticipation.

"It's a date." Okay, it wasn't what I expected. "The date we met."

A soft gasp tore from me as I stared at him, dumbfounded. He had the date we met tattooed on his chest. Why? What did that mean?

As if he didn't just drop that bomb on me, he got into bed and turned to face me, his back against the headboard, leaving his torso exposed. My desire kicked up a notch, matching his and urging me to touch him. Maybe it was his admission, or maybe it was just the fact it was him. Either way, my fingers trembled with the need to feel him. He looked so ridiculously attractive, I was losing my resolve to keep myself detached. After what felt like the longest day of my life, I could feel the fight leaving my body.

"Come here," he murmured, looking at me through heavy eyelids. Before I could even process his words, I shifted to my knees, crawling to him over the ridiculously large bed. "You're as beautiful as I remember." He took a strand of my hair between his fingers and lifted it to his nose, inhaling deeply. "You smell the same too."

Byron reached for me, drawing a soft yelp from me when he lifted me into his arms and positioned me so I was straddling him. He placed his hands on my thighs and looked into my eyes, his gaze moving leisurely, as though attempting to memorize every inch of my face.

My heart raced, wild and hard, threatening to crack my ribs.

"My Madeline," he whispered, his voice husky. I was in his good graces if he was back to calling me by my middle name. "Look at me, wife." I bit down on my lip, my entire body burning at hearing those words. I did as he asked, my heart hammering in my chest. The tips of his fingers brushed over my temple gently. "Thank you for marrying me." My eyes widened at those words. I expected anything and everything, but not that. "I'll be a good husband, I promise. I'll make you happy."

The sincerity in his gaze sent a shudder rolling through me. The gentleness of his touch had my skin burning desperately. I felt the words *you left me no choice* on my lips but couldn't bring myself to say them. Gone was the cold man who stood in front of me with an offer I had no choice but to accept, given the situation. Gone was the man with such fierceness in his eyes, such bitterness. It was as though signing that marriage certificate had softened him and reminded him of the way we'd been that first night together.

"Thank you for agreeing to take care of our problem," I murmured.

He ran the back of his hand over my cheek, his eyes on me. Chemistry and lust sizzled between us. My body leaned into him of its own free will as he cupped my face, his thumb brushing over my bottom lip. His gaze lowered, inhaling deeply.

"Kiss me, wife." His order made my heart skip a beat, but it was the longing in his eyes that had me obeying. We'd always had this incredible pull—this chemistry—that was impossible to resist. My gaze dropped to his lips, and he hardened underneath me.

A whimper slipped through my lips while the throbbing between my thighs pulsed, needing his length inside me. Yet he didn't move. He just waited, my lips hovering over his.

"I hate you." *And I love you.* For the pain his father and he caused me. For the dreams they took away. For the years we lost.

Byron's hand threaded through my hair, and gripped tightly. "Despise me as much as you want, but don't you ever fucking leave again."

I closed the distance between us, my lips brushing against his. Byron groaned and tightened his grip in my hair, his touch rough as he forced my lips open, deepening our kiss. His hands roamed my body with a hunger and urgency I could taste on my tongue.

His lips moved to my neck. Even if I had the energy left to resist him, I wouldn't be able to. The effect he had on me was indescribable, but one thing was clear: I wanted him. Even with the knowledge that his every touch promised impending heartache.

Just like it had before.

Chapter 37
Byron

I threaded a hand through her red mane and she wrapped her arms around my neck. She shifted in my lap, repositioning herself so my cock pushed against her panty-covered pussy. My wife's hot entrance brushed against my hard shaft, sending shudders down my spine. Her body was as I remembered, just slightly curvier. Softer. More beautiful.

My hands moved down from her waist to her ass, and I kneaded her curves, enjoying the feel of her. Our kiss turned urgent, and her breathing hitched as her hips rotated in my lap.

"Byron," she whispered, grinding herself against my cock. My name on her lips and her body at my mercy were a dream come true. I moved my hand up and cupped the back of her neck, my lips devouring hers.

Impatiently, I pulled her babydoll nightdress over her head, breaking the kiss.

"Fuck," I groaned when I saw her nipples, hard and ready. For me.

I knew enough to know she never played games; her desire

written unapologetically all over her face. Her hands roamed hungrily over my abs and torso. This was the woman I remembered. I leaned in for another kiss, my touch rougher now. I forced her lips open, swallowing her every moan, every pant.

My cock started to throb—painfully. It wanted her—my wife, my lover, *the mother of my child*. A million years wouldn't be enough. Earlier today, things were too urgent. My need was too great. Now, I needed to savor her. Taste every inch of her.

I wrapped my hands around her waist and pulled her up onto her knees, her tits right in my face. My lips wrapped around her nipple, and my name left her lips on a moan. Her hands tangled into my hair, and my eyes locked with hers as I flicked my tongue over her sensitive buds.

Her eyes shimmered like a golden sunset, full of desire. My hands moved down from her waist to her panties, pushing them aside, as my thumb brushed over her pussy. Her head fell back and her hips bucked.

"Byron," she whispered, her voice laced with desire. "Oh, God."

Years of fantasizing about her didn't come close to reality.

"Whose pussy is this?" I rasped, teasing her soaked pussy. I circled her clit, her breathing speeding up. "Whose pussy is this, wife?" I repeated.

"Yours," she breathed, grinding her hips against my hand. "Oh, God, I need... more."

My wife reached for my boxers, her fingers somewhat clumsy. I lifted my hips and pushed them out of the way, lost in the moment with her. The need for her clawed at my insides, frantic and demanding. She sat back down in my lap, my cock perfectly positioned against her pussy as she wrapped her arms around my neck, her breasts pressing against my chest.

My fingers wrapped around the thin lace fabric of her panties and tore them off. She moved on top of me, grinding eagerly and chasing her own pleasure.

"Just like that," I moaned into her mouth as she ground herself on top of me. My hands gripped her ass, jerking her back and forward. Up and down. Each move pushed the tip of my cock into her. "Show me how much you want my cock, Madeline."

My brain always switched to her middle name when she was so compliant and so eager to please.

"I want it," she whimpered breathlessly, her hands in my hair. Our kiss turned harder, my sanity and control slipping into nothingness. She lifted her hips, then brought them back down, taking the tip of my cock into her entrance once more. "Please, Byron."

My control snapped and I turned her over onto her back roughly, her tits bouncing with the impact against the mattress. My eyes roamed over her naked body, tempting me. Her hair spread around her like a fan and she stared at me through her lashes. Her gaze was hazy, hungry, and needy. Her lips bruised from my mouth.

Yes, I was fucking obsessed with Odette Madeline Swan. Correction, Ashford. She was finally mine. My ring on her finger.

I spread her legs and moved between them, her eyes settling on my cock as I rose to my knees. Leaning over her, I grabbed her wrists and pinned them above her head with one hand while using my other to line my cock up to her soaking entrance.

Pushing the tip into her, I groaned. "You're heaven," I murmured. "My own personal heaven when you're here, and hell when you aren't."

She darted her tongue out, sweeping it over her bottom lip. "Byron, you feel so good."

I pushed in a bit further, her inner walls clamping around my dick. My heart started to race, thundering against my rib cage. I pushed further inside her, her pussy strangling me.

A soft gasp escaped her lips, and her eyes rolled back. Her hips bucked under my weight.

"You're so fucking wet. Is that for me?"

"Yes."

"Such a good girl," I murmured, pinning her down with my weight, our gazes burning into each other. She arched her back, her breasts grazing against my chest. "My woman. Say you're mine."

"Yes. Yours."

Her eyes shimmered, pulling me under her spell as I inched in deeper. "Your tight pussy takes my cock so perfectly." I skimmed my mouth over her graceful neck, down her jaw and over her lips. "Look at us, Madeline."

"Let me touch you, Byron," she whispered, her voice trembling. My eyes found hers, and my heart skipped a beat. "I want to feel you."

Right now, it was as if six years had never passed. I released her wrists, and her hands wrapped around me, her palms roaming over my scarred back.

"You ready?" I rasped, my muscles shaking with the need to bury myself deep inside her.

"Give it to me," she demanded, arching herself against me. Her moan vibrated right into my heart, and I couldn't hold back any longer. I thrust, filling her to the hilt.

"Fuck," I grunted. I kissed her neck as I pulled nearly all the way out and pushed deep inside her again. "Your pussy is so tight."

My mouth traveled from her neck to her ear, to that sensitive spot. She moaned, her eyes on me. That was all I ever wanted. For her to be as consumed by me as I was consumed by her.

Her fingernails curled into my back as I murmured sweet nothings. I kept moving in and out of her, slowly at first, giving her a chance to adjust herself to me. Her hips moved with me, our mouths molding together.

"More," she panted, begging me. The softness of her touch along my scarred skin sent shivers down my spine. Desire consumed both of us, but it was more than that. It was two hearts beating as one. Two bodies moving as one. "Give me more, Byron."

She didn't have to ask again. I slammed my cock all the way

into her only to pull out, earning me a disgruntled growl. I took her thighs in my hands and wrapped her long legs around my hips, giving me a better angle. Her hips raised, I pushed back inside her, deeper. My thumb rested against her clit as I powered in and out of her.

"Good girl," I whispered as I pushed back in, earning myself another gasp from her. She moaned and writhed underneath me, every inch of her on display. "This pussy is mine. Every fucking inch of you is mine."

I circled her clit as I slid in and out of her, my movements jerky and harsh.

"Oh... Oh..."

"Look at what you do to me." I thrust in and out of her, my control nonexistent. "You want to come?"

Her pussy strangled my cock greedily, and I feared I wouldn't last much longer. Every flick of my fingers against her clit matched my movements perfectly. I pushed my cock at the right angle, pushing against her G-spot. Her moans turned frantic. Louder.

"Byron," she breathed, her eyes watching my cock slide in and out of her pussy. "Please, I need to... I need—"

She rotated her hips, trying to get my fingers to move where she wanted them. She rode my cock and hand in sync, unraveling by the second.

"What do you need, baby?"

"You." Hearing her admission was a rush. It'd never get old. "Please, give me more. Make me come, husband."

Fuck.

Hearing those words out of her mouth had me ready to spill inside her before she could even find her pleasure. I increased the pace of my thrusts and the pressure of my fingers on her clit, teasing it harder and sending her over the edge.

I pushed deep inside her, harder and faster, my eyes closing in bliss as her pussy contracted around me, milking me for all I was worth. Her eyes met mine, glazed over from her orgasm. I was fucking her with desperation. Obsession. I pulled back and thrust back into her, harshly and roughly.

"You take me so well, wife," I murmured, pounding into her again. I fucked her, moving in and out of her, again and again. Her legs wrapped around me, she moved with me, her nails scraping over my back. "You feel so fucking good, baby."

I fucked her savagely, like it was our last time. Like it was our first time. My wife's mouth found mine in a messy kiss, swallowing my grunts as I spilled deep inside her. Six years of abstinence and the end result was my cum painting my new bride's pretty pussy white.

Her nose brushed over my neck, pressing soft kisses to my throat.

One lifetime wouldn't be enough with my wife.

I blinked in the darkness, reaching for her. Again.

I lost count of the number of times I'd reached for her throughout the night, losing myself in her body and her moans. Reaching toward the other side of the bed and feeling nothing but sheets, something jackknifed straight through my chest and jerked me up into a seated position.

Holding my breath, I listened for her footsteps. Anything. Glancing at the clock, 5.00 a.m. glowed in ugly red. I got up and slipped on a pair of pajama pants before leaving our bedroom in search of her.

I found her in our son's bed. Wearing long, checkered pajama pants and a black T-shirt, she slept on top of the covers, her arm around him. They slept in identical positions, with Ares tucked in tight under the sheets.

A smile touched my lips and my chest grew full, seeing them

like this. After a lifetime of searching, I finally felt at peace. My world was reduced to this room. These two human beings.

I debated whether or not to take her back to my bed, but decided against it.

Only because I had a diamond smuggler to deal with.

Chapter 38
Odette

The next day I woke up to a knock against the door.

I startled, rubbing my eyes, wondering what hotel room we were in. Then I remembered. The Ashford Manor. Byron's place. Maybe I imagined the knock on the door too.

But then it came again.

I slid out of the bed and rushed to the door, my feet silent against the plush rugs in Ares's room. My son's room. It was the most luxurious room I'd ever seen. The Bocote wood furniture—I only recognized it thanks to my father's hobby of wood carving—paired with the luxurious bed was not only inviting but also comfortable.

Crossing the large sitting room, I rushed to the door before the knocks turned into pounding. Opening the door, I came face-to-face with Winston. He looked like sin in a striped navy suit.

"Winston, what are you doing here?" I hugged the door, stifling a yawn. Gosh, didn't he believe in sleeping in?

"I'm wondering the same thing," he retorted dryly, then flicked a glance over his shoulder. "This way."

He shouldered past me, soldiering into the adjoining sitting area of my son's bedroom. He always seemed grouchy, but since we barreled into them in New Orleans, I wondered if maybe he wasn't upset. That Ares wasn't Billie's son. Or maybe he was relieved. I had no fucking idea.

"What are you doing?" I asked, flabbergasted when two more men plowed through behind him.

"Put it here in the playroom," Winston ordered them, ignoring my question. "When my sister-in-law leaves the room, I'll call you to assemble the piece."

"What are we assembling?" I inquired of the men, watching them haul two large boxes into the room.

"A *Thomas the Train* set." My heartbeat paused, and I stared at the boxes as if they would reveal themselves. "Mr. Ashford wanted them delivered first thing."

I swallowed, emotions swirling inside me. He noticed how much Ares loved the set. It shouldn't surprise me. There wasn't much that usually escaped him, but something about this hit differently. Somewhere deep and tender.

The two men left, leaving me alone with Winston. He shoved a yellow envelope into my chest. "My brother suddenly thinks I'm his delivery boy. He wanted me to give you this." I took it and peeled it open. "It's a list and a credit card. He also needs you to fill in a few documents. Our family lawyer will handle your legal name change and—"

I blinked, then shook my head. "I'm keeping my name."

Winston just shrugged. Very much like his older brother, his presence had a way of stirring the air around him. Except, Winston didn't impact me like Byron did. My heart never missed a beat around this man.

"You'll have to battle that out with your husband." Telling him it was non-negotiable was futile. *Husband.* The word hadn't sunk in. Not yet. I wasn't sure if it ever would. "What is it with you Swan girls and keeping your name?" he muttered.

I cocked an eyebrow, my gaze zeroing in on him. I had no idea what he meant by that comment. There were only two Swan girls—Billie and me. Only one of us was now married.

"Are you upset because Billie knocked you out?" I asked, hesitantly bringing up the incident in New Orleans.

He scoffed. "It wasn't the first time." Huh? "But then, you probably knew that."

It was clear he wouldn't discuss anything with me. Not yet. He clearly didn't trust me. It didn't really matter. I didn't trust him either. And I wanted him out of here before Ares woke up. I wanted to ease him into all this. The shotgun ceremony left him slightly confused. He kept asking if we'd be going back to the hotel. There was no need for him to hear Winston's odd conversations.

"Can I have my—" I stopped myself from saying *husband*. It was terrifying how easy it came. And we'd just gotten married. A marriage of convenience. Or maybe it was a forced marriage, though that didn't sound right, either. I shook my head. None of it mattered now anyhow. "Can I have Byron's cell number?"

"It's already in your phone," he said as he turned around to leave. "See ya."

"Wait!" I called out. "What about... the diamond smuggler?"

He stopped at the door. "Already handled."

And just like that, all my problems disappeared, but brand-new ones made an appearance.

The dining room was too big—too formal—for my taste.

My sister, Ares, and I stood in the doorway, feeling way out of place. Winston was already in the midst of his breakfast, drinking his coffee and reading a paper. Yes, the actual paper.

The big French window covered the entire south wall of the room, letting natural light pour in. The scent of eggs and sausage drifted through the air, making Ares's stomach rumble.

"Hungry?" I smiled at him.

He nodded. "Oui."

Darting a glance my sister's way, I noted her clenched jaw, her usual soft brown eyes flashing with anger. Loathing. Bitterness.

Winston lowered his paper onto the table, his eyes traveling over us. They paused on Ares and I swore for two heartbeats, his gaze softened. There was something resembling longing there. It had been almost two weeks since our incident in New Orleans, but my sister's words only now registered.

Winston Ashford had thought Ares was his son. I wondered how he'd felt when he discovered he was mine, and not Billie's. My eyes found my sister. Her lips pressed in a thin line.

"Are you going to linger at the door or come in?" Winston grumbled, reminding me of the day I met Byron.

"Billie, are you okay?" I asked quietly, ignoring my brother-in-law.

She gave me a terse nod before the three of us made our way to the table. Just like me, Billie wasn't chatty about what happened between her and Winston. Somehow, I had a feeling there was a lot more to their story than what my sister told me.

The three of us made it to the table, and the moment we sat ourselves, the servers came around. It was like being at a restaurant. Ares's wide eyes tracked their movements, mesmerized by their efficiency.

A plate full of egg casserole and bacon was placed in front of us. My stomach tightened. I hadn't eaten much last night—or yesterday in general—but I was starving now.

Ares's big blue eyes met mine, watching me as if he could sense my tension. I smiled, stroking his head. Clearing my throat, I fed my son some of the casserole. He made a soft *mmm* sound, and I couldn't resist pecking him on top of his head.

"That good, huh?" I teased. "I better try it before you eat it all."

He grinned and Billie gave me an amused look. "Since when do you eat breakfast?"

"It seems neither of the Swan sisters eat breakfast," Winston commented, confirming my suspicion. "It's a good thing we boys know how important breakfast is. Right, Ares?"

Two sets of blue eyes met. Ares gave a quick nod, then reached for his own fork and took a forkful into his mouth. He chewed and swallowed, then went for another.

"He likes to eat," Winston remarked. "Must take after his—"

He cut himself off, and I wondered once more whether he realized that Ares was an Ashford. Or maybe, just like his father, he'd never accept us—Billie, Ares, and I—as part of the family. It was clear Senator Ashford had different plans for his son and preferred he married someone of a similar caliber.

Winston stood up abruptly, his eyes finding Billie. Dark midnight, shimmering like the deepest oceans.

He left without another word, while something in my chest twisted. Old wounds opened. Old words his father and that woman threw in my face came rushing back, but I steeled my spine. None of it mattered. Nobody mattered to me but my son and my sister. They were my entire world.

After breakfast, we attempted to make our way back to the bedroom. Ares ran left and right, eager to see it all. Eager to touch it all. The manor was large, with four wings, a family hall, a large library, and the grand marble foyer that could easily house fifty people. Why Byron would ever need a place so large was beyond me!

Billie sighed. "I can't stay here."

We were in the grand foyer, obviously lost on our way through the large mansion. At least we always ended up in the grand lobby instead of some scary dungeon.

I tilted my head, watching her. She had been with me through thick and thin. Yes, she fucked up stealing those diamonds, but she was the reason I was able to keep my son and finish medical school. My sister was the reason that my residency and year in Ghana were possible.

"Tell me what you need."

She sighed. "That's it? You're not going to scold me?"

"You never scolded me," I pointed out. "You stood by me, no matter what. If you want to talk about you and Winston, I'll listen. If you don't, I won't ask you questions. Just know that I'm here for you. Whatever you need."

She stepped back. "You mean it?"

I smiled, nodding my head. "It's time for you to shine and thrive, just the way I always knew you would. My big sister is the best."

It was the truth, and I needed her to see it.

Billie gulped, shaking her head. "I've always wondered whether you're the older one."

I grinned. "We're only a year apart. That's not that much older. You were always the more fun one. Now, I want to see you do everything you've wanted. Your bucket list."

Surprise flickered in her eyes. "How do you know about my bucket list?"

A chuckle filled the grand foyer. Mine. For the first time in months, I could chuckle. There were different worries plaguing me now, sure. But in the grand scheme of things, they didn't compare to the life-and-death shit of the past six months.

I had Byron to thank for that.

"I saw you typing into it," I admitted. "Now, tell me what you need so I can ensure you can start checking things off from it." Ares started climbing the stairs, and I tugged her along. "When are you leaving?"

"The sooner, the better." I nodded.

"I'll miss you," I admitted softly. "But I know you have to do this. I'm just sorry I can't go with you."

Billie eyed me curiously. "Will you and Ares be okay? I'm worried."

I gave her my most confident smile. "The two of us will be okay. I promise."

She glanced around us to ensure the coast was clear before she whispered, "Do you think Byron knows about *him*?"

Sometimes I wondered, but he hadn't called me out on it. Byron was many things, but he didn't shy away from conflict.

"I don't think so. Why do you ask?"

She shrugged. "It just seems odd that Winston isn't bringing up what happened in New Orleans and the fact I knocked him out cold."

It was odd. "Maybe he was drunk that day in New Orleans," I suggested.

She didn't look convinced. "Byron seems good with him. Ares that is." It was true... he was good with Ares. Better than I could have possibly imagined. It made me sad that my baby boy had to miss out on it for the past six years. "Are you falling for him again, soeur?"

The question caught me off guard. Billie scanned me with eyes that seemed to see too much. I didn't want to admit to her that I had never fallen out of love with the man. I came to terms with the fact our lives would be separate, but it would seem one night of amazing, mind-blowing sex fucked all sense and reason out of me.

"I'm fine." I rolled my eyes. "I feel about Byron the way you feel about Winston," I answered vaguely.

"Uh-huh." I found her gaze, and suddenly, I worried how deep my sister was in with Winston, but before I could ask, she continued, "You'll call me if something goes awry?"

I nodded, taking her hand into mine. "I don't want you to worry about us. We will be fine. I want to see you happy. Now, let's go shopping, take care of the cash so you can travel in comfort, and when we get old and frail, your adventures will entertain us for the rest of our lives."

It was time for Billie to chase her own happiness.

Chapter 39
Byron

Danso Sabir peered inside the three large black duffel bags. "A million dollars?"

"Count it," Vasili sneered, spitting on the floor. Alexei stood stoic next to him, his arms folded over his chest, a vein throbbing in his temple, the only thing betraying his fury.

Leaving my son and wife safe at home, I flew to New Orleans where the Nikolaev family had gotten their hands on Danso Sabir. The diamond smuggler who dared touch my woman. The surveillance Nico was able to retrieve played on repeat in my mind. Over and over again.

There was no chance in hell Danso Sabir would leave this place in one piece. I'd get his boss's name before I gave him back what he'd given my wife.

Danso began to sift through the money, bound in stacks of ten thousand. He didn't seem worried, his posture lax and confident. It took him ten minutes to figure out all the money was there. Either that, or he didn't know how to count.

"Pleasure doing business with you." He zipped the last bag, then smiled. A sharky, menacing smile. "I almost hoped that bitch wouldn't come up with the money. I bet that pussy's worth a pretty penny. It'd have made me twice as much."

Vasili and Alexei shared a glance before turning to the door. Alexei locked it with a soft click. I purchased the building an hour ago, so if I wanted to, I could set it on fire.

"*That pussy* is my wife," I told him. "The mother of my child." Danso's eyes flared with surprise. I took a step toward him, Vasili and Alexei blocking his only way out. It was my turn to smile maniacally. "Now you'll get a taste of what you gave to my wife."

He tried to wrestle his way through Alexei and Vasili. A big mistake. Alexei grabbed him by his neck while I calmly went to grab a bucket of ice water. He shoved him onto a chair and chained him to it, then shoved a cloth over his head. Slowly, I poured ice water over his head and over the cloth, waterboarding him. There were quite a few things I learned during my time in the military.

"Stop," he spurted, pleading.

"More, you say? Of course. Let's do it again."

And so we did. Again and again. Then I watched Vasili hang him by his arms from a hook in the ceiling where the chandelier had been two hours ago.

My phone rang and I pulled it out of my pocket. Glancing at the screen, I saw Odette's name flashing.

"A peep and I'll slice your throat," I threatened, then answered the phone, putting her on speaker. "Wife, is everything okay?"

Danso opened his mouth, and before he could let out a sound, I punched him in the mouth.

He grunted and I balled my fist again, ready to silence him. He instantly clamped it shut.

"What was that?" she demanded to know.

"A rat. Is everything okay?"

A beat passed.

"Yes, everything's fine," she assured in that soft voice that could easily get me off just from hearing it. "And my name is Odette. Just in case your memory's short-lived."

Vasili's stifled snicker came from the back of the room. I flipped him off without a second thought.

"I like calling you wife. But if it bothers you, baby, I'll find another pet name."

A frustrated soft growl filled the room. "Whatever." I chuckled. "The reason I'm calling is this list you left me."

"Yes?"

"Why am I going shopping? For a gown, nonetheless."

I grinned. "Because you married a wealthy man, and I want to spoil you."

Silence stretched for a few seconds, then a heavy sigh. "If that's your idea of spoiling someone, you need to learn a thing or two from French men."

This time I growled. "Mention other men and there'll be hell to pay when I get back."

"Get back?" Fuck, I slipped. "Where did you go?"

"Nowhere important. I'll be back for dinner." I could only imagine the face she was making. "Go shopping. Go to a spa. Spend some money. Buy clothes. Get some toys for Ares."

She let out a frustrated breath. "You're joking, right? It will take me days to drag him away from that train set."

I smiled. "He liked it?"

Fuck, I wanted to see his face when he opened it.

"Yes, he liked it." She cleared her throat. "I took a few photos. Umm... I can send them over."

My heart hammered in my chest. I could hear the vulnerability in her voice. There were so many secrets she was keeping, some I knew and some I couldn't even begin to guess at. The carefree young woman I'd known had become an enigma, but I'd solve this mystery. Then I'd show her that she was mine. That she had always been mine. Words wouldn't assure her, but time would.

"I'd love that," I said. I'd taken her numerous times last night, yet I still hadn't had my fill. I feared it'd never be enough. If the last six years without her hadn't cured me of her, nothing would. I'd want her until my dying day.

My phone buzzed. Once. Twice. Three times. "Okay, pictures sent," she announced, her tone soft.

"Thank you."

I kept her on speaker as I checked out the photos she sent. Instantly, my lips tugged up. Ares's face beamed, an ear-to-ear grin stretching wide as he stared at the new *Thomas the Train* set.

"Is Ares's room okay? You can change anything you want. In any of the rooms."

"Yes, it's fine. Perfect."

"Something must not be good enough in our room though," I stated.

"I couldn't sleep." Another deep sigh. "I'm not used to sharing a bed with an unfamiliar person."

I switched off the speaker so the others couldn't hear. "Bullshit." She didn't have that problem the first night we spent together. I still remembered how she'd tucked herself into me, dozing off, only for her to wake up with my face buried between her legs. "Now tell me what the deal is. Mattress not to your liking?"

"It's fine, Byron."

"Then what?" I challenged. "You know every inch of me, so don't give me the 'unfamiliar person in your bed' excuse."

"Or else" hung in the air.

She let out a frustrated breath. "Ares usually doesn't sleep well the first night in an unfamiliar place. I wanted to make sure he was okay."

Okay, that made a little more sense. Aurora, my little sister, was like that too when she was a kid. "I'll get a baby monitor. We'll need it eventually anyhow."

Especially because I planned on fucking her every chance I had. Six years of jacking off. She had a lot to atone for, whether she knew the role she'd played or not.

"Yeah, you're crazy," she muttered.

I chuckled.

"You're right. I'm crazy about something. Or someone, rather." Shit, did that make me sound too whipped? I was too old for this crap. I just wanted things back to the way they were before. There was no holding back. The Odette I knew didn't hesitate to tell me what was on her mind nor what she wanted—in bed or outside it. "Anything else?" I inquired.

There was something different about the strong-willed woman I fell for. It was almost as if she feared something aside from this diamond smuggler. But for the life of me, I couldn't quite figure out what. It couldn't be me. Right? I had never given her reason to fear me. For Christ's sake, I couldn't stand seeing her in pain. It was the main reason I respected her wishes when she asked me to leave that day in the hospital. I didn't want to be the cause of her pain.

She remained on the line, quiet, almost as if she needed to say something else but couldn't think of a way to. "Take him to get more trains and accessories for it." When she didn't answer, I continued, "There's a toy store downtown. He'll like that."

Still no response, but this time I let the silence linger.

"Your note said to use the card for whatever," she finally stated softly.

"I did."

She cleared her throat. "Can I use it to withdraw money?" I stilled. The first thought that slammed into me was that she'd try to run. That she'd leave me. "Umm, Billie has things she needs—okay, wants—to do and..." She trailed off, letting out a sigh. "I'll pay you back as soon as I get a job. I just... She's done so much for Ares and—"

"That card is yours to do as you please." *Except leave me.* "It doesn't have a limit. Withdraw as much as you need."

"I'll pay you back."

A sardonic breath left me. Had she already forgotten that I didn't make her sign an NDA or prenup? With any other woman, it'd be the first thing I'd do. With her, I never worried she'd take me for my money. If anything, she was reluctant to touch it.

"It's your money, Odette. You can do whatever you want with it."

I could hear her frustrated sigh through the phone. "I bet if our positions were reversed, you wouldn't be saying that."

I chuckled. "When you're a famous surgeon, you can pick up the check at dinner." I could practically see her rolling her eyes. "Did you just roll your eyes?"

She coughed. "Do you have cameras here?"

I did have cameras around the house, but I didn't need them to read her mannerisms. "You better use that card by the time I'm back. I fully expect a dent in it."

"Sure thing, hubs. I'll wave it all around D.C. like a white flag. And I'll hit every ATM from here to the toy store."

"That's a good wife."

"You are just as arrogant as I remember," she said, then ended the call.

A deep chuckle came from behind me.

"You got it bad," Vasili tsked, shaking his head. "Welcome to married bliss."

I laughed. Today was a good day. One of the best days I'd had in far too long.

Returning my attention to the guy in front of me, I grinned. "Let's wrap this up, shall we?"

"We should have taken him to the basement of my other building," Vasili said. "There are so many tools I'd enjoy using on him. For entering my city without my permission. For beating a *woman* in my fucking city."

"Please," Danso sputtered, teeth chattering, chest caving in. "I didn't know she was under your protection."

"Stop begging," Alexei declared coldly. "It doesn't matter whether she was under our protection or not. Nobody is to lay a hand on a woman in our city."

"And it just so happens, I'm not the forgiving type," I seethed, the images of Odette trying to fight him off rushing through my mind.

An hour later, Danso was tied to the chair, his face and body covered in bruises as he gasped for air. He looked like a purple pig. My hands were just as bruised and bloodied.

Alexei tsked, turning his head in my direction. "Are you thinking what I'm thinking?"

"Indeed I am, brother-in-law," I deadpanned. Alexei dumped the towel back on Danso's face and emptied another bucket of water on it.

Reaching for a baseball bat, I swung it through the air and it smashed against his face, crushing above his nose. He let out a scream, fighting against the chains. Unsuccessfully. I hit his ribs next. His back. Then his cheek. Back to his knees.

"Keep the money," I told him. "Your boss knows you have it. If you don't catch your flight, it will be on you." I pressed the bottom of my shoe to his broken knee and pushed him over, his head slamming against the wooden floorboard with a loud thump. "If you so much as breathe in my family's direction, I'll wipe your entire bloodline from the face of this earth."

The scent of sweat, blood, piss and violence perfumed the air. It reminded me of the war.

Even back in the civilized world, violence always surrounded us.

Chapter 40
Odette

B illie shimmied into a pencil skirt, silk blouse, and sheer black tights. At least she went for flats rather than heels this time. She would lose her toes otherwise.

Her eyes landed on me.

"He has a whole new wardrobe of designer clothes for you and you are going to wear this?" My sister's tone was exasperated as her eyes roamed over my chosen attire. White jeans with a Lilly Pulitzer bright pink sweater with pink flats.

I shrugged. "I went for comfort. We'll be doing a lot of walking." Glancing at my son, I smiled. "We'll have to see lots of stores, starting with the..." I made the sound of drumrolls as I waited for him to fill in.

"Toy store," Ares exclaimed, his eyes glimmering like the sea under the bright sun. Dressed in dark jeans, a crisp white polo shirt, and a blazer, he reminded me of a mini-Byron.

"Then let's go and have some fun."

"And the best part is—" Billie grinned mischievously. "It's with someone else's money."

I rolled my eyes. "I was gonna say that's the worst part. But beggars can't be choosers."

She waved her hand. "You'll never be a beggar. Besides, Byron Ashford married you without a prenup. He's either a fool or so in love that he's blind." *Or "no divorce" is part of his stipulation*, I added silently.

My sister stared at me as if she expected a response. I didn't have one. Truthfully, I agreed with her. It was reckless for Byron not to have a prenup. He was loaded and I was... well, I wasn't.

Billie opened her mouth, but before she could say anything else, I tried to deflect. "Okay, let's get this party started."

And with that, we made our way down the stairs and out the door where Byron's driver awaited, ready to take us anywhere we desired.

If only he could take us back home to the French Riviera.

By the time noon came around, we had bought every train in the toy store and Billie had two hundred grand in her purse.

"Are you sure you won't be in trouble?" my sister asked for the tenth time. "That's a lot of money."

"Yes, I'm sure; I asked him. And don't worry, I'll pay him back."

She shook her head. "How? With your body?" I leaned against the shelf, watching my son play. For the first time in six months, he was truly happy. Ecstatic. Relaxed. He was having a good, normal day. "What if he breaks your heart again?"

I shook my head. "I won't let him. And you cannot lecture me on this money. You paid to get me through school."

"Part of it," she corrected me. "Your scholarships paid for most."

Only half, but hey, who was keeping track?

"Anyhow, I'll get a job," I said. I checked the postings this morning. There seemed to be many vacancies in this city. It wasn't exactly what I'd wanted to do—my dream was still to get back to the French Riviera and raise Ares there—but considering my latest arrangement, that wouldn't be happening. At least, not for the foreseeable future. I met my sister's gaze. "He won't hurt me," I murmured. "I'd have to love him for my heart to break again. And I don't."

The lie was bitter on my tongue. Honestly, I didn't know why I loved him. Maybe because despite everything, he'd given me the most precious gift. Our son. He didn't know it, but he saved us. Saved him—our son. If he hadn't run back to the hospital with me in his arms, I would have lost him.

Billie shot me a look that told me she didn't believe me. "Are you sure about that, soeur?"

"Yes, I'm sure." I returned my attention to Ares, watching him play with another boy. "All that matters is that we survived. That Ares is safe."

Except, I didn't know who I was trying to convince. Her, or myself.

Neither one of us ever felt settled in half-assed relationships. Seeing our parents deliriously happy ruined us. Or maybe gave us a brand-new perspective on love and relationships.

"He's safe and happy," she said in a low voice. "But you need to be happy too. It's been so long since I saw the old you."

"The old me," I murmured. "I don't even remember the old me."

My sister's arm wrapped around me. "Don't you think it's time to try?" I shrugged, unsure how to even answer that one. "Before *he* broke your heart. Before Dad died. Before it all went south."

My chest squeezed. It seemed like a different lifetime. Everything had happened in the span of a few months. We went from being happy, to our whole life falling apart. And Senator Ashford ensured it would all be taken away.

I could forgive a lot. But not that. Never that. Father had been everything to me. *To us.* And the senator's cruelty robbed us of years with him.

A single gunshot. I had never heard the sound until that night, but I knew—deep down, I fucking knew—it could only be one thing.

Billie and I jumped to our feet, the chairs falling backward with a loud thud.

We ran in the direction of our father's study. He always spent his evenings there.

"Dad?" Billie banged on his office door, panic lacing her voice.

No answer.

I stepped forward, pressed the handle, and pushed the door open. After the loud bang, it was eerily quiet. Too quiet. With dread in the pit of my stomach, my eyes roamed the room.

Stepping through the door, I froze.

Father's slumped body, his head on the desk, was the first thing I saw. A hole in his temple was the second thing that registered. Blood was the last. So much blood, seeping over the shiny surface of his pristine white desk.

The scent of copper entered my lungs. I'd been around it often enough to recognize its smell. Billie screamed. It sounded distant, like I was underwater and somewhere far away where only this pain existed. The ache in my chest spread, wider and deeper, until each breath sent shuddering pain through me.

I hadn't moved from my spot, my eyes following the river of blood spreading across the desk. Crimson against white. My sin—my mistake—caused this. I caused this.

I took a step, then another, my limbs stiff and my heart heavy, until I reached my father. Billie still screamed in the background, but I could barely hear her. The buzzing in my brain drowned out all the noise. All except for one voice.

Mine. "You did this," my guilty conscience whispered. "You did this. You did this."

Dad's usually warm eyes were vacant. His gaze was focused on something in his hand. Bu-bum. Bu-bum. *My heart thundered achingly and pain hammered through my bones, seizing my breath as I stared at the last thing Dad saw before he took his life.*

I fell down to my knees, blood trickling from the desk and dripping onto the hardwood.

Drip. Drip. Drip.

Blood soaked my knees as I stared at the photograph of our family.

The last photo of Maman, Dad, Billie, and me together, laughing happily in front of the private clinic.

My mistake put the final nail in the coffin and cost Dad his life.

I shook my head, chasing the memories and anger away. My chest ached. God, I missed him. Even after all this time, the raw pain of losing him stole my breath away. I always dreamed of practicing alongside him. Tag-teaming and traveling the world on medical missions. Always coming back home, to the French Riviera.

Letting out a heavy breath, I tugged my sister. "Let's go," I said, heading toward the table where Ares played. "I have items to purchase. My husband's list."

With Ares's hand in mine, we spent the next two hours shopping. From Hermès, to Dior, Chanel, and ending with Valentino. Byron's black American Express and his last name opened every door and made every salesperson eager to assist.

Although I didn't think I'd ever get used to spending someone else's money.

The little cafe in Georgetown buzzed with life. The beautiful weather—like an Indian summer except in the winter instead of fall —drew people out of their homes and out into the open. The outside seating was at full capacity, soft music drifting along with the chatter and laughter of Washingtonians.

"Those people are leaving," Billie exclaimed, tugging me and Ares along like our redemption sat at that table. We must not have been fast enough because we got there at the same time as another gentleman.

We turned to face the stranger, when surprise coasted through me. I never would've expected to run into him here.

"Marco," Billie and I exclaimed at the same time.

"Maddy. Billie." Marco's smooth drawl filled the air. I hadn't seen him since my last visit to D.C. when he came to visit me at George Washington. The day that altered the course of my life in such a major way. The day Byron believed I lost the baby because of a not-so-small lie told to him. His girlfriend at that time worked there and he was visiting her. His modeling career took off right around that time, and he married shortly after. We kept in touch for a few years and then life just got too busy. I hadn't talked to him for years now.

His hands came around my waist and I squealed in delight as he lifted me into the air. He landed a loud smooch on my cheek, his lips lingering a heartbeat too long.

"Girl, you're looking good," he told me in French.

"Oh my gosh, what are you doing here?" Marco was still gorgeous. I'd seen him over the years in different fashion magazines. "I thought you were in Rome or Paris."

"I came back last week. This is my home base."

"I always thought you'd live on a yacht, lounging around in your speedo," I joked.

He threw his head back and laughed. "Speedo, huh?" His sculpted cheekbones, dark eyes, and dark hair pulled a lot of women's attention our way. "Trying to get me naked?"

I rolled my eyes. "You wish." He grinned. "So what made you pick D.C. for your home base?"

"Remember, my wife works in the city." I remembered her. She treated me after the accident. She was Tristan's older sister. "I travel to New York, L.A., and Milan, but always come back here."

"So you're a big shot," Billie said lightly, completely unimpressed. "A famous and sought-after model."

"What she's *trying* to say, Marco, is we're happy for you. Congratulations."

The cafe was bustling, and, emphasizing just how cutthroat people were about snagging a seat, another couple came up to our table. "Are you leaving?" the woman asked.

"Actually, we just arrived." Marco signaled for us to sit down while I offered an apologetic smile. Once I had Ares settled in his chair and we were all seated, it took no time for the efficient server to take our order.

"Now tell me, what are you doing here? I'm surprised to see you in the city, Maddy." It felt like a different lifetime when my friends called me Maddy. Not even my sister did anymore. "Your annoying sister, yes. She was always the one for the big-city life." His hand landed on mine, covering it completely. I stiffened and counted until five before pulling my hand back with the pretense of fiddling with Ares's menu.

"I avoid the cities you're in," Billie deadpanned. "But you have a tendency to stalk my sister, so here we are."

"You're just jealous nobody is stalking you." Marco's tone was on the colder side, which didn't really surprise me. Billie never did have much patience for the guy.

"Actually, nobody at this table wants to be stalked," I remarked, jumping to my sister's defenses. "Billie has been by my side. But she'll be chasing her dream now."

"By the way, did you hear Odette got married?" Billie grinned like a shark that caught her bait. She just couldn't help herself.

"He's great," Ares beamed.

Marco's eyes snapped to me as I took a sip of my sparkling water. A hint of displeasure or something like it flashed in his gaze. He could be slightly overprotective sometimes.

"Really?" he questioned, his tone not as friendly. I nodded. "What? How?"

"It just happened." *Literally.* The words felt foreign on my tongue, like it was someone else's life I was telling him about. I swallowed, then smiled. "I'm looking for a job, actually."

"Well, you might be in luck," Marco stated, grinning smugly. When I gave him a blank stare, he continued, "My wife is the head of George Washington Hospital now. She treats patients occasionally, but her main concerns involve having the most qualified staff in her hospital."

My eyes widened. "What? No way! Good for her."

The last time I was at that hospital, she was working her way through the ranks. It was only a matter of time before she became the head of the hospital.

One thing we never discussed was the age of Marco's wife. She was about seven years older than him, but it seemed to work for them. No judgment, as long as they were both happy. He talked about their homes in the city, on the Riviera, and even a vacation home in Colorado. That was one thing Marco could be counted on for. The guy could *talk.*

"Wow, that's impressive." I didn't really give a crap about material things, but he seemed happy.

He shrugged like it was nothing. "I married big."

"I'd say." Billie couldn't keep the sarcasm from her tone as she bit into her sandwich.

"Maman's married big too. He's bigger than Aunt Billie and Maman." Ares grinned, his little fingers wrapping around his ice cream cone and shoving it into his mouth before I could stop him. Then he reached for my pastry. His appetite could easily bankrupt us.

Marco's eyes found mine, narrowing to slits. Almost as if he was displeased at being reminded. "When was the big day?"

I shrugged. "Yesterday," I answered, averting my eyes. Unfortunately, I caught Billie's snickering gaze. The corners of her lips twitched, and I could only imagine the words burning her tongue.

"But never mind that. Tell me, how long have you been married? Do you have any children?"

Marco shook his head. "No. We don't want any children. We're too busy with our careers."

"Sounds like you're too busy with your pretty-boy career," Billie mocked. I knew she couldn't hold back for too much longer.

"Well, it sounds like modeling is going very well," I noted, ignoring Billie. "We even saw you in the papers in Ghana."

Smiling confidently, he pushed a strand of his hair behind his ear. It almost felt rehearsed. He'd always been slightly vain, but it might have gone overboard over the last few years. Or maybe, after not seeing and talking to him for years, I noticed it more.

"I heard you were in Ghana," he remarked. "I tried to find you, but that place is a mess."

"Why am I not surprised to hear you tried to find us?" Billie's tone was dry and laced with sarcasm.

"We were probably in a remote location at that time." I smiled tightly, shooting a small glare at my sister. Her response was an eyeroll. "We stayed in huts, mostly, in the local villages."

The horror that passed Marco's expression was almost comical. His hand clasped over mine and he squeezed tightly. I was starting to get uncomfortable with the constant touching. I slid my fingers away from his clammy ones and placed both my hands on my lap.

"But now we live in a mansion," Ares chimed, bragging with a happy smile.

"Do you like it there?" The eager nod by Ares was unmistakable. "Do you like Maman's husband?"

The way he said "husband" sounded off. Almost as if the word was dirty.

Ares tilted his head pensively. He had just met him, I couldn't fathom my five-year-old having any kind of opinion on him. The three of us watched him, waiting, but I was the only one holding my breath. Why? I had no freaking clue.

"I like him. I want Byron to be my dad."

Billie's mouth dropped. Marco's eyebrows shot to his hairline and his gaze found me. The look in his eyes appeared almost angry but not quite.

And me?

I tipped my head back and drained my glass. I had a fucking problem. My son seemed to have fallen for his father's charms—just as I did six years ago.

Chapter 41
Byron

I boarded the plane, tugging my tie, ready to relax for the next two hours—one of the many benefits of having my own private jet and pilot.

"Take us home, Oliver."

Taking my seat on the cream sofa, I pulled out my phone to check through my messages as the pilot made his way to the cockpit.

I flipped through my work emails when an email came through. Nico Morrelli.

"Ah, perfect timing," I muttered under my breath. I had asked him to keep tabs on Odette and Ares. It might be morally questionable, but it was for my peace of mind, so I'd kept surveillance on them. Besides, she had unlimited access to my money now, and I still couldn't help but worry she'd take the money and run. It was easier to disappear when you had money.

I slid the message open and the recording started.

Marco's hands on Odette's waist as he lifted her up in the air, then pecked her cheek, lingering for far too long. My teeth clenched. For the next five minutes, I watched the recording play out, scenes from their apparent lunch date compiled, including a series of images that made my blood boil. It seemed he kept finding ways to touch her. Red mist marred my vision. Anger crept beneath my skin, slow but searing. I had to take a second to swallow down the burning jealousy that raged inside me, so strong, I could barely form a coherent thought.

The recording showed my wife having a cozy lunch with her ex-buddy, Marco. And his hands were on my woman. *My* fucking woman.

The irrational part of me—the obsessive, jealous one—pounded at my chest, shaking the bars of its cage. I wanted to shout "get the fuck away from her" to the world and to fucking Marco. But I was three hours away.

The sound of the plane's engine was distorted by the rage rushing through me. I had to close my eyes and take a deep breath to clear my head. She might have been in a cafe surrounded by people—her sister included—in the middle of the day, but I was far from comfortable having him anywhere near my son. And I sure as shit did not like how close he was sitting to *my* wife.

I dialed up Nico and he answered on the first ring. "Let me guess, you want my guy to follow Dr. Swan home."

"She's not to be left alone with that guy," I gritted. "Not for one minute."

"Sure thing."

My next call was to my brother-in-law.

"Didn't you just leave here?" was Alexei's greeting.

I got straight to work. "I need a favor."

"I have a feeling it has something to do with your wife."

He was fucking right. I never asked for favors and here I was—asking for one from Nico Morrelli and, probably worse, Enrico Marchetti.

"I need Tatiana's husband to get a name to Enrico Marchetti."

The perks of his sister Tatiana marrying Illias Konstantin were never lost on me in times like these. Konstantin had vast connections in the underworld and, most importantly, to the owner of one of the major fashion houses. Enrico Marchetti.

"A model candidate?"

"Wrong." So fucking wrong. I still stared at the recording of my wife having lunch with Marco, who was now holding her hand. "I want a certain individual to be blacklisted from all runways and fashion shows."

Jesus fucking Christ. I was so in love with her, with each breath she took... with her smiles, her backbone, and her strength. Every. Single. Fucking. Thing.

I adored every piece of her. She had been my kryptonite from the moment I met her.

She was finally back in my life, and that fucker wouldn't take her away from me. Odette and our son belonged in my life. I belonged to them. The three of us would be a unit forever.

And Marco...

He'd get the beating of his lifetime if he got anywhere near them again. My knuckles itched to hunt down the fucker now and punch him. Break that pretty face so she would never look at him. Never smile at him.

Exactly like I did to that drunk asshole who drove into her.

My memory drifted to the past.

*The drunk glared at me, his face bruised and bloodied. He looked the way my soul felt, but I couldn't think about **her** right now.*

We were a mistake.

Anger flared through me and I hit him again. His head snapped back, and a pained groan filled the air. I wanted to punish him. For hurting my woman. For taking our chance at having a baby. For stealing my chance at having her. My happiness.

It had been two days since the accident. Two days since she asked me to leave. I walked away from George Washington Hospital, leaving my heart behind. It was broken anyhow—forever damaged— and the only woman who could heal it wanted nothing to do with me.

A mistake. I hated that fucking word.

So I took it out on the fucker who hurt her. On the fucker who had his hands on her. No one threatened what was mine. And, fuck it, Odette was my woman.

I walked over to the table, put on my brass knuckles, and returned to my victim.

Yanking his head back, I hissed, "You have cost me something priceless."

The stupid drunk grinned, his teeth crimson. "You look like you can afford to buy another of whatever that was."

A moment later, an agonized howl ripped through the air.

By the time I was done with him, his face was unrecognizable, and he was missing more than a few teeth.

My woman might have left me, but the agony remained.

But I wouldn't let her leave me today. Or ever.

Once we arrived back in D.C., I had my driver take me straight home. I made my way to my office and locked the door behind me.

I put the code into the safe and then pulled out two passports, skimming through the pages until I stopped on the one I was looking for.

Odette Madeline Swan. Ares Etienne Swan.

I hadn't taken Billie's. That woman could stay or go for all I cared.

Without hesitation, I shoved the passports back into the safe, slammed it shut, and I locked it once more. Nobody had the combination code but me. It was my insurance policy that would keep them both here.

I couldn't risk her leaving me for that French blast from the past.

Chapter 42
Odette

We arrived home with a car loaded with bags, the driver not far behind us as he wheeled in our shopping bags. Ares gripped his bag full of trains with a big grin on his face.

"Now here is a sight for sore eyes."

My head whipped around to find my husband waiting for us at the top of the staired entrance leading into the impressive mansion. It still felt surreal that we lived here, and I wondered if the grandness of it all would ever cease to shock me.

"You're home early," I remarked. "I thought you said dinnertime." I glanced at the time on my phone. "It's only three."

Something dark passed his expression as he stood with his hands in pockets, sending a wariness through me.

He didn't answer me, but he smiled at Ares. "Hey, buddy, you liked the train set?"

Ares nodded eagerly, running over to him to show him what he got today. Byron lowered to his knee, bringing the two of them to eye level.

"Maman said you bought it for me." Ares beamed, happiness

evident on his face and in his words. "Thank you." My son's small hands wrapped around Byron and I froze, watching the two men I loved in an embrace. Byron scooped Ares up and rose to his full height. Although he was tall for his age, in Byron's arms, he looked so small. Almost tiny.

Suddenly, my mind conjured up images of what could have been. Byron holding Ares when he was born. Or feeding him. Holding his hand as he took his first steps. My throat squeezed, and for the first time, I wondered, *Did I do the right thing?* I shook away my self-doubt. Everything I did was to protect my son and my sister. We wouldn't have survived the senator's wrath.

"Let's go see your train set, buddy," Byron remarked, throwing me a dark look over his shoulder.

The two of them disappeared into the house and Billie came up to me. "Why is he mad?"

I swallowed. "I don't know."

"Maybe we spent too much money?" She reached into her purse and pulled out the envelope that held her cash.

I shook my head. "I don't think it's the money. Put it away."

"I don't want—"

I shot her a warning look. "Put it away, Billie. I mean it."

Sighing, she put the envelope back into her purse. "Want me to stay a few days?" she offered. "Just in case the fucker turns crazy like his brother." My brows scrunched at her words, and she must have realized she'd slipped, because she immediately added, "All of them are crazy."

As Byron's staff took care of bringing all our bags into the house, I headed toward Ares's playroom. I could hear my son's excited voice explaining to Byron his logic in building the train tracks. It was another resemblance he had to Byron—his brilliant mind. Billie was artistic and creative. I had a knack for the sciences. But Ares—even at his young age—overachieved in everything.

The moment I entered the playroom, two sets of identical blue eyes—one young and one older—rose to greet us.

"Hey, Maman." I smiled as he returned to tearing open his packages so he could place every train on the table.

I met Byron's eyes, the same dark expression lingering on his face. I hesitated, chewing on my bottom lip. I didn't think he was mad about the money, but I couldn't even fathom what else it could be.

"Did I spend too much money?"

My heart raced looking at him and remembering last night. Whenever I was in his presence, my body went into hyperactive mode. It was impossible to switch it off. Even when my heart was breaking six years ago, I wanted him. All of him.

"You didn't spend enough," he replied, rising to his full height.

"I didn't?" Then what had made him so moody? Maybe he missed me. *Yeah, right.*

Byron smiled at our son, and my heart twisted. I couldn't deny he was good with Ares. Each smile and kind gesture now made me question my decision. A decision I believed to be the right one at the time, but was now apparently spiraling over.

"Ares, we'll have dinner in an hour," he told him.

He didn't even bother glancing at either of us. "Okay."

"Let's go talk." Byron's fingers wrapped around my arm. I could barely keep up with his long strides as he walked toward our own bedroom. The moment the door slammed behind us, Byron's hand left my forearm and came up to curl around my throat, my back hitting the door. "Where have you been, baby?"

He applied gentle pressure, tilting my face up so our gazes clashed while I blinked in confusion.

"What are you doing?" I tried to push him away, but Byron was a solid wall of muscle.

His lips hovered a breath away from mine. "I'll ask again. Where have you been, wife?"

My body warmed, feeling him pressing against me. My lungs grew intoxicated from his scent. And my pussy—that traitorous body part—throbbed, the evidence of my desire soaking my panties.

"Shopping. That's where I've been. Getting shit from the list you left for me."

"Liar." Byron's jaw locked, his pressure around my neck increasing. Not enough to hurt, but enough to threaten. "You had lunch with that playboy. Marco." Unease slithered down my spine. It seemed like Byron was as jealous as ever, which still surprised me, given how much confidence he oozed. It looked the same as it had all those years ago in that tight elevator; dark and possessive. Byron never did like to share when it came to me. He applied pressure on my neck, his mouth skimming over my skin. "Answer me, Odette."

There it was. He never called me by my first name when he touched me, kissed me. Unless he was displeased. Well, tough shit. I wasn't exactly in heaven either.

"Get your hands off me, Byron." My tone was calm. Cold. Yes, I still wanted him. But not like this. Never like this. And I'd be damned if I let him manhandle me. Fucking ever.

Seconds stretched, feeling hours long, until he tore himself from me. He stalked toward the bathroom. But this wasn't over. We'd talk this out, if it was the last thing we did. I would drag it out of him. If there was one thing my father said about marriage, it was that you had to talk shit out. Otherwise, the problems would only grow bigger.

So I trailed after him, determined to bring this to a head.

"We were shopping and then stopped for lunch. It's where we ran into Marco." His steps faltered right before reaching the bathroom. He faced me, angst sweeping past his eyes. But something else lurked beneath the surface too. I couldn't read what it was, but it felt important I found out. "We're old friends. Marco's wife is the head of the George Washington Hospital. He offered to pass my name on to her, and I couldn't miss the opportunity. I need a job."

He gave me a look, and I knew what his next words would be.

"You don't have to work."

I closed my eyes, pinching the bridge of my nose. I wished I understood why he insisted on marrying me. Have heirs with me. I bet he had a harem of females ready to do his bidding. Anything he wanted. So why did he want me?

"I *want* a job," I finally said. "I didn't work my ass off getting through med school just to have a pretty resume."

Our gazes held. My pulse thundered in my ears. There were so many words—said and unsaid—that danced between us. That night with him was the first time I'd fully let go. And then it backfired so fucking bad that it nearly destroyed me.

Yet, I loved every minute of that night with him. Every touch. Every kiss. Every word he whispered in my ear.

It was the intimacy I'd been craving. He gave me a taste of something amazing and then it was ripped away, leaving a gaping hole in my chest—a hollowed-out vacuum—that I knew only he could fill.

"What do you love about it?" I blinked before recalling what we'd been talking about. My job. My career. I let out a sigh, a small smile curving the corner of my lips.

"I love the chaos of the emergency room. I love performing surgeries and seeing the look on people's faces when I let them know they'll be all right. It—" My tone faltered for a moment, but then I continued, "It almost feels like my dad's right there, shadowing me. I **love** doing it, and I won't give it up. I've already given up too much."

He stilled. "What did you give up?" Goddamn it! I slipped. "Odette, answer me. What. Did. You. Give. Up?"

He was so damn demanding. I squeezed past him, scurrying to the bathroom. He followed me, his steps unhurried, his broad shoulders tense.

"I won't stop until you tell me," he stated dryly. His intense stare met mine through the mirror's reflection. A memory flashed in my mind, and judging by the way his eyes heated, my husband remembered it too.

I sighed, hating and loving this intensity between us. It was so

305

easy to let myself fall into that web and ignore everything else. God, I wanted to ignore everything else. But I also wanted... more. What my parents had, however short-lived.

"I miss home," I murmured.

He frowned. "You *are* home."

Gosh, he couldn't be so dense. "The French Riviera. My dad's place. His hospital. It was our little world. Small and modest, but cozy. It was ours."

A blank look of confusion on his face alarmed me.

"Why did your father get rid of the hospital?" he asked. I stiffened, confusion swirling inside me. His tone seemed genuinely curious. "I would think it'd make sense for you to carry on his legacy."

Either Byron was excessively cruel, or he didn't even know the lengths his father went to six years ago. He might be ruthless and arrogant, but I didn't take him to be cruel.

"I wanted to carry on his legacy," I rasped, locking eyes with him in the mirror. "I still want to. But the bankers took the hospital." *And your father helped to speed it up.*

"Bankers? He defaulted on it?"

"Yes, he was bad at finances. He just wanted to help people, not run the hospital like a business. Unfortunately, one cannot go without the other. And your father leeched onto it."

The confusion in Byron's gaze was evident. "My father?"

I swallowed hard. I still didn't understand their father/son dynamic. I didn't dare to trust Byron explicitly, despite our marriage of convenience. So I settled for a half-truth.

"Your father is a dick," I grumbled. "And apparently, he had some connections with the bank to pull some strings."

Fury flashed in Byron's blue gaze. It was lethal. "Why would he do that?"

I shrugged, done with this conversation. The day started off too good to ruin it with this conversation. "Because he's a dick. And not the good kind."

Byron's jaw clenched, and I watched him gather himself together as various emotions passed his expression.

"I'll get it back," he vowed. My heart fluttered despite knowing it was impossible. Okay, maybe not impossible, but it'd be pretty damn hard.

I gulped.

"Don't do that." My voice was a whisper.

Byron was flush against my back all of a sudden, his hands trailing down my thighs. It was amazing how quickly my body submitted to him. His touch seared through even my jeans, craving skin to skin. Needing him inside me.

"Do what?" His breath warmed my skin. His lips brushed against my earlobe, and I tilted my head sideways to allow him better access. His teeth dragged along my neck, nibbling at the sensitive hollow along my shoulder blade. And all the while, his eyes were locked on mine in the mirror.

"Make promises you won't keep," I breathed.

He stilled. "I never make promises I don't intend to keep," he grunted. His eyes flashed with something dark. Maybe even angry. I couldn't pinpoint it. "All you have to do is ask, baby, and the world is yours." His voice was deep and husky. I glanced behind me, finding his desire-filled gaze on me. His large erection pushed against my backside, and I quivered from the top of my head to the tips of my toes.

"What do you mean?" I breathed.

He turned me around, bringing us face-to-face. Nerves fluttered in my stomach. Every fiber of me drummed in anticipation to have him again. Last night, he took me so many times, my thighs still ached from it. It was the sweetest kind of pain.

"What I mean is, the world is at your feet." Arousal danced like fire in his eyes, and he took my bottom lip between his teeth. I didn't break the kiss. I wanted him. "Raise your hands."

I instantly obeyed, and he yanked the sweater over my head. My bra was unfastened and discarded onto the floor next. Trailing his mouth over my jaw, reaching my ear and nibbling my earlobe. He expertly unbuttoned my jeans and shimmied them down my legs as he dropped to his knees. I raised my left foot, letting him slide my flats off. He did the same with my right foot.

Without another word, Byron tore my underwear off in one fluid motion, then dragged his tongue up my slit. I gasped. He growled.

My husband's teeth grazed my pussy as my head fell back against the mirror. "Ohhh."

He thrust his tongue between my lips, striking my nerves. My hands came to his head, gripping his strands.

"Byron," I whispered, while he laved me in a sensual rhythm, his growling noises vibrating through me. "Don't be rough. I'm sore from last night."

"I'll take care of you, baby," he murmured against my pussy and my knees turned to water. His lapping turned into languid French kissing. Heat simmered in my core, threatening to send me into a spiral.

My nipples hardened the moment Byron took my clit between his teeth, sucking on it lazily. An orgasm curled in the pit of my stomach, spreading down to my toes. Ache forgotten, I fisted his hair and rode his face. Desperate. Needy.

"Ahhh... Byron."

He drove his tongue back into me, massaging my clit with his thumb and tearing me apart. My moans shattered the air, his name a constant on my lips. His tongue sank deep inside me, and I arched my back, holding on to him. I trusted him to have me. Again and again—like he did last night.

It was so counterintuitive. He broke my heart six years ago, but I trusted him to have me now. At least, my body did. He nipped my clit. Gently.

I moaned so loud, skating on the edge of orgasm, that I thought I'd die if he stopped. I gripped his hair so tightly, my knuckles turned white. I was slick with arousal, grinding shamelessly against his face, needing him more than I needed air to breathe. The thrust of his tongue. And another. My orgasm shot through me, shudders seizing every muscle in my body.

I rocked against his face, unraveling inch by inch and letting the most beautiful sensation flood my body. It felt like floating on a cloud over the warm waters of paradise.

Byron rose to his feet, wiping his mouth with the back of his hand while his other hand curved around my neck, drawing my ear to his lips.

He gave me a slow, satisfied smile, but his eyes darkened. "I see Marco sniffing around you again, and I'll end him. His career. His family. His entire world."

His eyes burned, his mouth still glistening with my arousal.

"You touch him, and you won't see me again," I said, my tone slightly breathless from the orgasm he gave me. "I told you, he's married and it's strictly a friendship."

He cupped my face, leaning in and pressing a slow kiss to my lips. His tongue swept through my parted lips.

"Maybe for you, but not for him," he whispered.

He kissed me again, deep and hard, swallowing my protest. My eyes fluttered shut in bliss. Kissing with Byron was almost as good as sex. The way he devoured me, like I was a luxury he wasn't accustomed to. Every touch and grunt covered my body in goose bumps, and I could orgasm from this alone.

He gripped my hair with his one hand, tilting my head so he could taste every inch of my mouth. He trailed his lips down my neck to my bare shoulders, turning me around.

The reflection of the two of us. Byron towering behind me, his eyes hooded as his hands roamed my body. With his lips on my neck and his teeth scraping my skin, he brought his hand around and parted my wet folds, sliding his fingers through them.

His cock was hard against my butt. He'd just given me an orgasm and here he was, taking care of me again. Our arousal pumped thickly between us, bouncing off the bathroom wall. I could taste it—his need—and I wanted to take care of him. The way he took care of me.

"Byron, I want to—"

The words died on my tongue as he slid two fingers inside my clenching pussy while his other hand cupped my breast.

He slid another finger in and the burn of three thick fingers fucking me felt hot and addictive. The sound of my wetness echoed through the air. Filthy and erotic. I lifted my leg, propping it on the corner of the luxurious, freestanding bathtub. Fuck gentle. I needed his fingers inside me deeper and rougher.

"Byron," I whimpered. "Please, I want you inside me."

I pushed my bare ass against him, grinding so he knew I meant it. He hissed.

"You're sore, baby."

"I'm not anymore. Please, please. I need you."

I'd barely taken my next breath before he was shedding his clothes. It had to be a record for the time it took him to get naked. I looked over my shoulder to see his thick cock, dripping with precum and ready for me.

In one swift movement, he pulled my hips back and pushed my back down, bending me over. My hands sprawled on the mirror and my butt jutted out. He slammed inside me. Hard. I moaned. His hands gripped my hips as he pulled out almost all the way, only to thrust back inside me.

"Fuck," he grunted.

"Don't stop," I moaned, grinding against him. Then he rode me, hard and unapologetically. His skin slapping against mine. Flesh against flesh echoing in the bathroom.

I caught the image of us in the mirror. My orgasm coiling, building. The sight of him was magnificent. So big. So powerful. All mine.

His tanned skin glistened with perspiration as he dug his fingers into my hips. The look of sheer ecstasy as he watched me through hooded eyes—both of our gazes locked in the mirror—had me spiraling. This man made me lose my head.

"Harder," I moaned.

He slapped my ass hard and growled, "I make the demands here."

But his pace picked up and his thrusts came deeper and harder. I cried out, my insides clenching around his shaft. The orgasm that shattered through me stole my breath away.

"Fuck, fuck, fuck." Now it was his turn to scream out.

My body contracted around him as his cock jerked deep inside me. I shuddered with the intensity of it, both of us gasping for air.

My body still bent over, palms splayed against the mirror, Byron's chest came down to cover my back as his lips brushed against my earlobe.

"Anything you want, baby," he murmured, nuzzling my nape. "All you have to do is ask."

I looked into his eyes, my heart bleeding and glowing at the same time. It scared me so much the control he had over my heart. Like no time had passed.

Chapter 43
Odette

I showered for dinner, wrapped the towel around me, then skimmed through a fully stocked closet at a loss for what to wear. I preferred wearing casual, but Byron always seemed to be dressed in his Brioni—or was it Armani—suit.

A knock sounded and, gripping the towel around me, I padded to the door and opened it.

"Billie?" My eyes roamed around. "Is everything okay?"

She waved her hand. "Yes, just peachy." She entered the bedroom, her eyes curiously skimming the room. "Wow, this room is much bigger than mine."

My sister was dressed in a black Valentino dress with golden accents around her waist and on her shoulders. She looked gorgeous.

"Want me to ask him to give you his bedroom?" I joked. Her answer was an eyeroll. "You look beautiful."

Her smile softened. "You can wear rags and you'd still shine. Your beauty is timeless."

I chuckled. "You're biased because you're my sister."

Her eyes traveled to the walk-in closet and she made her way to it. Her fingers skimmed over all the beautiful garments Byron had secured in the matter of a few hours. I had no idea who or how he did it.

"Did Byron yell at you?" she asked casually. The realization sunk in. She was worried about me. Her eyes found mine. "About the money."

I shook my head. "No. I told you, he said he's okay with it."

"Are you sure?" I nodded. "He seemed off when we got back."

Letting out a sigh, I said, "He wasn't mad about that at all. I promise you."

Her eyebrows scrunched. "Then why was he upset?"

I threw my arms in the air, almost causing my towel to slide off me. I quickly grabbed it and secured it back up. Thank God for reflexes.

"He must have had me followed because he knew we had lunch with Marco." She gave me a blank stare. I shrugged. "I guess he thinks I like him. Heck if I know."

She blinked at me in wonder as a slow grin spread over her face. "Oh my gosh."

"What?"

"He's jealous," she purred, smiling like a cat that just ate a mouse.

"I wouldn't go that far," I muttered.

"He totally is." She was convinced, and I knew there was no changing her mind. "Do you think he realizes he was stupid for letting you go?"

The brief conversation I had with my husband played through my mind. He genuinely seemed interested in what happened in the hospital. If he truly wasn't aware of his father's intentions, maybe all the sacrifices over the last six years were for nothing. Absolutely nothing.

"I don't know, Billie," I murmured, sitting down on the plush rug of the walk-in closet.

Lifting the hem of her fancy dress, she lowered down and sat next to me. "What exactly happened between you two?" I shot her a look. "Aside from sex," she groaned. "I don't need to know those details."

I chewed on my bottom lip. I owed her the truth. "I have to tell you something," I whispered, keeping my eyes on her. "Y-you might hate me."

My heart twitched in my chest. She was my sister. The thought of losing her was unbearable.

Worry entered Billie's expression. She took my hands into hers and squeezed them tightly.

"I will never—fucking ever—hate you. If you committed murder, I'd have your back. If you burned the entire world, I'd be your alibi and claim you didn't do it."

"I killed Dad." The admission was barely above a whisper, but it might as well have been as loud as an atomic bomb.

Billie stared at me with confusion. "What are you talking about? No you didn't. You were with me when the gun went off."

I swallowed the lump in my throat. "Not like that." Every cell in my body trembled. "After the night with Byron, I woke up and found his father, Senator Ashford, in the room." A shudder rolled down my spine. I hated thinking about it. "He wanted me gone and out of Byron's life. At first I thought he was just crazy, but then he got meaner and scarier. He threatened the hospital, vowing he'd destroy everything Dad built."

Understanding entered Billie's light brown gaze. "Jesus Christ, Maddy. All this time, you... you have been blaming yourself?"

"How could I not?" I sputtered. "If I hadn't messed around with Byron, Dad would still be here."

"Look at me." My sister's voice was strong. Unwavering. "You. Didn't. Do. It."

"But—"

"Repeat it, Maddy. Or I swear to God, we'll have it out."

My tongue swept across my lips. "I didn't do it."

"That's right. Now, does Byron know?"

I let out a heavy sigh. "I thought so. All these years, I was convinced he was playing me too and knew what his father did." Except, now that I was thinking about all the events, some things didn't add up. "But earlier when I said something about the hospital and his father, he seemed surprised. Then he said he'd get it back."

Billie watched me pensively, and I could almost see wheels turning in her head.

"If Byron had a part in it, I don't think he'd care whether you have it back or not." I nodded my agreement. "And he can thank his lucky stars because if he had, I'd murder him. Cut his balls."

I blinked, confused. "Why aren't you mad at me?"

"Because you didn't take Dad's hospital. You loved that stupid building as much as Dad did. It's like that damn thing was a part of you. Just like it was part of him."

My eyes burned. Gosh, I never even understood how much my sister knew me. Probably better than I knew myself.

"I am going to miss you so much," I muttered, pulling her into a hug. "So fucking much. But we'll text and talk. And you'll find your happiness, because you are the most amazing human being on this planet."

Her body shook lightly as she chuckled. "I wouldn't go that far. I don't save people, although I'm pretty good at destroying them."

I pulled away, finding her eyes. "You still planning on leaving tomorrow?"

She nodded. "It's for the best. You work shit out with your husband. Find your happily ever after. It's likely that the past six years were wasted. I was mad at him for knocking you up, but I'd be lying if I said I still felt that way now. I couldn't imagine my life without that little bugger."

I smiled, my chest feeling so much lighter. "I love you, Billie."

She stood up and extended her hand. "I love you too. Now, let's get you dressed in one of these gorgeous designs."

And that's exactly what she did.

Half an hour later, dressed in a beautiful, satin Givenchy dress in a pale yellow gold, I made my way out of the bedroom and down the hall. Billie left my room to make her way downstairs ten minutes ago.

Faint voices traveled from Ares's playroom, and I followed the sound. I found Byron and Ares there together in serious discussion.

"They were really yours?" Ares asked curiously, his eyes gazing at Byron like he was God himself.

Byron was sitting on the floor next to Ares, wearing gray slacks and a black button-down shirt. Both of them worked intently on setting up the train sets and mountains with soldiers surrounding them.

"They were," my husband said seriously. "They were my favorite sets. So when I was too old to play with them, I let my brothers use them. But I warned them if they didn't take care of the soldiers right, I'd take it all away."

I leaned against the doorframe and watched them.

"So they did a good job taking care of them?" Ares stated.

"They did," Byron confirmed. "I had to keep an eye on them a little bit, but mostly your uncles did pretty good."

I couldn't help all these warm feelings dancing deep inside my chest at seeing them together. The way it should have been all along. Had I done wrong by not going back to see Byron again? When I saw him in the hospital and he told me I'd lost the baby, I was devastated. Too young to have a child, but I was still devastated.

I never quite forgot that moment at the hospital. The way his chest visibly shook. The way I held my breath as I watched him walk away. But I... I couldn't go back and seek him out. Not after what had happened.

"My uncles?" Ares's voice was soft and small and his eyes wide as he watched his father. "Because you married Maman?"

Byron's hand came to Ares's head, the touch almost reverent.

"Yes, Ares, they are your uncles. And your family. Both you and your mom."

I didn't think there was a comeback from this free-falling. I didn't even want to come back from it.

I just wanted *him*. Ares, Byron, and I. My own happily ever after.

"I like you," Ares beamed. "You're just like grand-père. Maman always says he was the best dad."

My son's words made my heart hurt, in a good way.

"I didn't know your grand-père well, but from the little I knew, he was a very good man. He helped take care of my scars."

Ares's eyes widened. "You have scars?"

Byron ruffled his hair, his expression soft. "Yes, but they don't hurt. Thanks to your grand-père and your maman."

He leaned forward and pressed a kiss on Ares's forehead. My breath caught, and my heart squeezed at the sight of my husband being this way with him.

The gesture was simple, but so caring.

I cleared my throat and two sets of the same shade of blue eyes met mine.

"Hey, guys," I said softly. "Are we ready for dinner? I'm starving."

They both grinned and swiftly got to their feet. Byron's eyes were dark pools as they coasted down my body, leaving a trail of fire and ice in their wake. A shiver rocked my body, and I took a shuddering breath, waiting for him to say anything.

"You look stunning, my wife."

I tucked a strand of my wild hair behind my ear. "Thank you for the dress, husband."

He closed the distance between us in two large strides, his hand wrapping around my waist.

Lowering his head, he brought his lips close to mine and murmured, "Say it again."

Desperation coated his words. His blue eyes shimmered, and I wanted nothing more than to drown in them.

"Thank you for the dress," I breathed softly.

He nipped gently on my lower lip. "Not that. The last part."

His voice was hoarse. There were truths in his blue eyes that I was scared to decipher.

"Husband," I murmured, pressing my lips against his.

Ares wiggled himself between us and wrapped his arms around us both. "We're a family now."

Satisfaction, dark and lazy, flared in Byron's eyes. "That we are, son. Forever."

Forever.

Chapter 44
Byron

As I made my way out of our bedroom, leaving my wife soundly sleeping in our bed, I ran into my sister-in-law. She was on her way to catch a morning flight out, ready to take off on her "bucket-list adventure," as Odette explained to me last night. It was obvious from the little she told me, I owed a lot to my sister-in-law. She helped raise my son and supported her sister through med school. For that, she'd forever have my gratitude.

"Good morning, Billie," I greeted her. "Leaving already?"

She nodded. "I hate goodbyes, and if I see Ares's face, I might never leave."

I nodded in understanding. I had only just met him and I hated leaving every morning. Early retirement suddenly seemed like an appealing choice. I wanted to spend my days with us together as a family. It was clear she wanted to work, though, and I was determined to find a way to be okay with it. I could be the caretaker so she could focus on her career. I could already picture it, Ares and I picking her up every day, telling her all the things we got up to.

"Want me to give you a ride to the airport?"

"No, thank you," she answered quickly. "I'm sure you're busy."

"I'm never too busy for my family."

She shook her head. "I'm not your family."

I smiled. She walked into my trap so beautifully. "But you are. And you've been family through marriage, even longer than your sister." She stumbled and my hand shot out to steady her. Then I took her suitcase out of her hand. "It'll give us time to talk."

"This feels like blackmail," she muttered.

"Take it any way you want, dear sister-in-law."

She shot me a suspicious look but said nothing else. Five minutes later, we were in the back of my car, sipping on our travel coffees. My driver made his way through the city toward Reagan National.

I leaned back in the seat, studying Billie. The sisters were close —clearly—and I wanted her on my side, but it was clear from the occasional glares she shot my way that she wasn't happy with me.

"So what are your plans?" I asked her.

She shrugged. "Not sure yet. I'll make them up on the way."

The thought of going through life without a plan threatened to break me out in hives, but I kept the comment to myself.

"So how was seeing Marco again?"

She shot me a look. "Are you jealous?" she scoffed.

Fuck, was I that transparent? Unfortunately, when it came to my wife, all the jealousy and possessiveness rushed to the forefront, and it was hard to control it.

"Maybe," I deadpanned.

Billie gave me her first sincere smile. "You probably have every reason to be." Red mist covered my vision, which she must have caught because she rushed to add, "No, not because my sister likes him. She's never considered him anything more than a friend. But Marco is nothing if not a persistent bastard."

The red slowly faded, and I focused on her words. "Elaborate." When she glared, I gritted, "Please."

Both Swan sisters would be good for our family. They were normal when we were definitely not. Exactly what we needed.

Well, Odette was exactly what I needed. I wouldn't make assumptions about Billie and Winston.

"Marco has always drooled around my sister," she finally answered. "He was there after every breakup, waiting and hoping she'd choose him. She never did—and she never will—but somehow the guy can't seem to get the message."

"I thought he was married," I remarked casually.

"Oh, he is." She leaned back into the seat, getting comfortable. "It doesn't mean jack crap. If Odette gave the slightest hint that she was interested in him, he'd drop his wife like a hot potato. You should have seen the way he was all over her when she was in the hospital, his woman all but forgotten."

I stiffened, awareness shooting through me like a lightning bolt. My mind worked vigorously, trying to connect the dots. *The doctor who looked familiar.* I could remember where I saw her now. She was seated at the same table as Odette at that bar all those years ago.

"In the hospital?" I asked. "That doctor in the hospital is Marco's wife."

She must have realized she'd slipped, because she straightened up, and her lips thinned in determination.

My gaze narrowed. I'd always had a knack for reading body language. It was useful in running a business, particularly when there were enemies trying to take you down at every corner. And Billie's tight posture and expression told me she wouldn't say another word on the matter. So I did her a solid and changed the subject, storing the sliver of information away for another time.

"Ares is my son." I dropped the bomb on her and her gaze shot to me, turmoil swimming in those eyes. She had such different eyes from my wife, but there were similarities in their mannerisms.

"How do you know?" Her voice was barely above a whisper. "A-are you going to take him away?" She leaned over, pleading in her eyes. "Please. Please. It will destroy her and—"

"Nobody is taking Ares," I told her firmly. "And you're not

asking the questions here, I am. I want to know how it happened." Her eyebrows shot up, and she stared at me like I was crazy. "I was the one who brought her to the hospital. The doctor told me Odette lost the baby."

I had to hear her say it out loud.

My sister-in-law shrugged. "I have no idea. She was bawling her eyes out when I got there, telling me she thought she lost it, but then Marco told her the baby was alive, healthy."

Uneasiness crawled up my spine. "And you said Marco visited her while she was in the hospital?"

She nodded. "Yes, he saw her being brought in. I guess he happened to be meeting his woman for lunch. He must have seen you too, didn't you carry her all those blocks in your arms?" Agitation flared in her eyes as she continued. "Anyway, I was so fucking pissed, the fucker waited hours to tell me she was there. I was going crazy in the hotel room, waiting for her."

If my suspicions were correct, that fucker and his wife would be history by morning.

"Why are you grinding your teeth?" Billie questioned, studying me curiously. "It's like you're preparing to murder someone."

Billie's expression and words told me she didn't share my suspicions. Neither did my wife, for that matter.

I forced my jaw to relax.

"I want to thank you," I told her.

Her eyes flashed in surprise. "So you're grinding your teeth because you want to thank me?"

I let out a forced laugh. "Maybe I'm not accustomed to thanking people."

Billie snickered. "Yeah, I believe you there."

My clenched jaw loosened some, and I gave her a sincere smile. Billie didn't hold back her opinions. Neither did her sister, but Odette was more subtle and had much better manners. Probably due to her profession.

Billie was a different breed of a person, but something told me it was what attracted my brother to her.

"I want to thank you for watching over my son and your sister." My tone was serious. "You have my gratitude, and I'm forever in your debt. It means a lot to me that they both had you."

Billie waved her hand nonchalantly. "They're my family. Of course I'd do anything for them. Besides, I fucked up plenty. Just look at what happened with those diamonds." When I cocked my eyebrow, Billie's smile turned sheepish. "Well, it was me who took them. Obviously."

I shook my head. Jesus, those two sisters were thick as thieves. My wife led me to believe it was she who'd done it. Not that I would have refused her either way.

"I see. Well, I won't hold it against you if you don't tell your sister that I know Ares is mine."

Somehow we'd come full circle and made it back to the negotiation phase.

Billie tilted her head, watching me, and I could see her mind working something out. What? I couldn't tell.

"Fine," she agreed. "But if you make my sister cry ever again, I'm going to find you and kill you. I'll cut you into tiny little pieces and scatter your remains all over the world." Well, that was rather specific. She must have thought about it a lot over the years.

"What has Odette told you?" Honestly, I'd like to know why Odette pushed me away too.

She shrugged. "My sister never told me fully what happened between you two. That's between the two of you. It won't be, though, if you make her cry again." Her eyes narrowed on me. "Because, again, I'll kill you."

I chuckled. "Duly noted. And since you are so heartwarming, a piece of advice about my brother." Billie's cheeks stained pink, and she actually averted her eyes. "He thrives on a challenge, and somehow, I think you've inadvertently become his."

We spent the rest of the drive in a somewhat surprisingly peaceful silence.

The idea had been playing on my mind ever since I dropped off Billie at the airport. By noon, I'd decided on the perfect wedding gift for my wife—no matter how much it cost me.

I dialed Kristoff. He owned Baldwin International and had connections in international real estate, among other things.

"How's married life?" was his greeting.

"How did you hear?"

"Winston told Royce. Royce called me. We had a bet going."

Surprise coasted through me. "Bet about what? And since when are you a betting man?"

He chuckled. "I couldn't pass up the opportunity to teach your brother a lesson and make him a hundred grand lighter."

"Jesus, what the fuck was the bet?"

"That you'd make that woman marry you within two weeks," he deadpanned. "Royce said you'd need a month. But obviously, I know you better. When you set your mind on something, you are all in." I shook my head. They were both idiots. "So? How is married life?"

I fucking loved it, but something was missing. Odette gave me her body freely, but she was still holding back. She refused to fully open up to me, and damn it, I needed all of her. I craved it.

"It's good. I have a son."

"Wow, that is some speedy marriage you got going. Is it on fast-forward?"

I rolled my eyes. "It's a long story. I think someone fucked with me. He'll be dealt with soon." A dark chuckle came over the line. Kristoff would have done the same thing. "I need a favor."

"I'm all ears. But if you want the guy dead, call Morrelli."

I chuckled. "If anyone's going to do the killing, it'll be me. I want to buy a building on the French Riviera."

"Tell me your requirements."

"It's simple. I have the address. I want the entire piece of property around it and that specific building. It was once a castle."

"Shoot me the address, and I'll see what I can do."

"Thanks." My intercom buzzed. "Okay, duty calls. Price is no object. Just make it happen. I want it as soon as possible."

"Text me the address," he repeated before hanging up.

Another buzz through my intercom.

"Yes?" I answered as I typed the address of the building.

"Your brother's here," my secretary announced.

Clicking the send button, I let out a silent sigh. Didn't that woman know after so many years, I had so many brothers it was hard to keep track. Retirement was sounding more and more attractive. Or working from somewhere sunny and warm.

Like the French Riviera, my mind whispered. I hadn't been able to forget Odette's words. She wanted to raise our son the way she was, after she and her sister had left the States as children. Back in Villefranche-sur-Mer. I knew Kristoff would make it happen. It'd be the perfect wedding gift to my beautiful wife.

"Sir?" My secretary's voice reminded me it wasn't time for daydreaming.

"Which brother?" I asked.

"Alessio." Surprise washed over me. While my brothers were full of surprises, Alessio usually gave me a heads-up whenever he visited.

"Send him in." It didn't take long for a knock at the door to follow.

The door opened and Alessio came into view, his son, Kol, trailing behind him. "Hello, Uncle Byron."

"Hey, buddy!" I stood up and strode to him. "This is such a good surprise. I missed you."

He grinned, letting go of his father's hand and running over to me. I lifted him up and swung him around.

He spread his hands wide open. "I'm a plane."

I chuckled. "And what a pilot you will be. How are your pilot lessons coming along?" I asked, lowering him back to the ground.

Kol wrinkled his nose. "Daddy won't let me fly a real plane."

"And the world is grateful to your dad for it."

My oldest brother—well, half brother—threw himself into the chair and spread his legs. "God, you have the most comfortable chairs ever here. I don't know how people leave your office."

"Sometimes I have to kick them out," I remarked dryly. "I wasn't expecting you."

He shrugged. "Wife's meeting Aurora. We're here for the family dinner the day after tomorrow." Fuck, I forgot. "And let me guess, you forgot."

"Of course I didn't forget." The look he gave me told me he didn't believe me. I sat back down and pushed my hand through my hair. "Yeah, I forgot."

His lips twisted into a smile. "And I bet I know why too."

I leaned back into my desk chair, studying my big brother. It was hard to believe how far we'd come in the last few years. From not speaking, to being closer than I'd ever have imagined. The grumpy brother turned into a contented husband. He gave it all up for his woman, and he didn't seem to regret it at all.

"And why is that, my all-mighty and all-knowing brother?"

He gave me one of those smug smiles. "It's got to do with a very specific French woman."

Jesus, how the fuck did he know?

But then his words from way back rushed to my mind. It was during one of my visits to his place in Canada. What were his exact words? *I bet you a specific woman is demanding you stay out of her sight too.*

He wanted me to get off his back, and the best way to do it was to hit me where it hurt. Except, how in the fuck had he known?

"Let me guess," he drawled. "You're wondering how I know

about her."

"It'd be nice to know," I grumbled. "Considering it was only Winston who ever saw her, and he barely remembered her."

Alessio chuckled. "She's not exactly forgettable, but then Winston was busy getting wrapped up in her sister if I'm not mistaken."

I shook my head. "I honestly never saw you much as a stalker."

"You had to be in my profession or you'd end up dead." He was referring to his days in the mafia, running drugs and gun smuggling through Canada. But like I said, those days were behind him.

"So how did you learn about her?"

Alessio shrugged. "I kept tabs on you. Honestly, I wouldn't have picked up on her, but then you went and beat up the driver who ran into her."

"The drunk fucker almost killed her." Just thinking about it had a cold sweat forming under my skin. I had never been so terrified in my entire life. "He touched something that didn't belong to him."

My big brother didn't seem bothered by the fact I had put the man in a coma. Okay, so he might have lost a few fingers and his face was all but unrecognizable, but he almost killed my woman. And I thought he killed my unborn baby.

"You don't have to justify yourself to me."

I scoffed. "As if I would." My big brother had done a lot more than just beat up a fucker here and there. "Do you ever regret it?" I asked him, changing subjects abruptly. When he raised his eyebrow in question, I added, "Do you ever regret leaving all your businesses to just be a father and husband?"

He didn't even hesitate. "Not fucking ever."

We sat in silence for a bit while Kol busied himself with the train set I kept on hand for exactly these visits. He was right outside my office, but he left the door open and his small chattering voice traveled through the air. He still alternated between English and French a lot.

Kind of like my own son, come to think of it.

Chapter 45
Odette

S tanding in the changing room of the designer dress shop, I watched my reflection but couldn't recognize myself.

I played the role he wanted. Except, I wasn't happy. This world wasn't for me, but I swallowed my protests and complaints, because I'd sold myself.

Jesus, I sold myself.

My only consolation was seeing Ares's happy face. Whenever I fought the urge to pick up and go back to Villefranche-sur-Mer, I'd look at his happy face. It took no time for Ares to fall for his father's charms. I mean, what was there not to like?

"How do you like the dress?" the salesperson asked.

I forced a smile. "It's beautiful."

And it really was. But it'd bring everyone's eyes to me. It screamed of money, power, and that "look at me" vibe. None of it was me.

I didn't know Byron had scheduled me in for an appointment to be seen by this supposedly famous designer. I itched to text my sister and ask her to come back. But I didn't. Instead, I smiled and nodded, accepting exaggerated smiles and compliments.

Byron sat on the couch in the lobby of the store, looking annoyingly sexy and entertaining Ares. He'd come home straight from the office, then dragged us here. His blue suit and tie were immaculate, his eyes darting my way every so often, as if to ensure I was being adequately flattered.

"Why are we doing this again?" I made a face. I hadn't meant for it to come out so sharp, but I was tired and cranky. Billie would be in heaven right now. But I was in hell.

He smirked, unfazed by my tone. "I need to know you're taken care of, and we need to coordinate colors."

I rolled my eyes. "Something blood-adjacent sounds pretty tempting right now."

"Red *would* look gorgeous on you, but I was thinking emerald."

Byron liked having control—I'd known from the moment I met him—but picking out my clothing was going a bit overboard.

The designer returned with another dress and I groaned. "No more. Please, no more."

She chuckled like I'd just uttered the funniest joke. Her head was full of wispy white hair, and despite its silver qualities, she moved surprisingly fast. She was slender and the collection of bracelets around her wrist jangled with each move she made.

"My spring collection would be perfect for you," she said, nodding to herself. Her assistant followed behind her with a rack of dresses and I stifled a groan. There was no chance in hell of me trying them all. "With that skin tone and that magnificent red hair, you'll shine above all others."

It was exactly what I didn't want, but that didn't seem to matter. So I just gave her a terse nod and a pained smile. What had I gotten myself into?

"Yay." Sarcasm dripped from that single word like melted ice cream, but the woman purposely ignored it. I sighed, trying not to dampen everyone's mood. Retrieving my phone from my purse, I snapped a picture of the rack of gowns and sent it to my sister.
Shopping with Byron and Ares. Miss you.

When I raised my head, everyone's eyes were on me. I shrugged. "My sister is a fashion fanatic."

"The green strapless number will be your dress." Her eyes sparkled. "Trust me on this. You save lives. I save fashion."

The comparison made no sense, but I didn't bother pointing it out.

"Okay, then, let's try that one first," I said, feigning a smile. I just wanted it over with. I hurled my phone into my purse as she handed me the dress.

Byron and Ares still sat on the cream-colored couch and gave me encouraging smiles. God, the two of them were so alike it was terrifying.

I returned inside the dressing room, and once the door shut behind me, I felt my face fall as I rubbed my cheeks. They hurt from all the fake smiles. I should have been excited. This was basically every little girl's dream—everyone's but mine—but somehow, I felt trapped.

Everything seemed fabricated. Well, everything but our sex life. But our relationship couldn't last with just the physical connection. I needed more. Would my relationship with Byron grow to become more than just sexual tension and overpowering chemistry?

My gaze landed on the emerald dress. I might as well put it on. Green was my favorite color, so maybe it would be okay. I emerged from the fitting room wearing the strapless number and went up the steps to stand on the platform in front of the mirrors, taking it in from all angles.

When I raised my eyes to the mirror, my breath caught in my throat. The gown was the color of power and envy. The rich green fabric gave out various sparkling tones. Below the waist, the corseted bodice burst into tulle rosettes in shades of emerald and moss, flowing down to the floor and trailing behind me in a short train.

Byron's gaze met mine through the mirror and my heart fluttered; the hunger in his eyes a barely diluted form of desire. He held my gaze so long my knees softened, and my cheeks warmed with a flush.

Fog spread through my mind, everything fading except for the two of us and our son. As if we were in our own bubble.

"Do you like the dress?" he asked me, his voice deep.

I nodded and his lush lips curved into a most beautiful smile.

"This is the one," he told the designer without looking away.

"Maman, you look like a princess."

Byron's lips lifted into an effortless smile, but his gaze remained on me. "No, son. Maman looks like a queen."

Chapter 46
Byron

Days flew by. Nights even more so.

And it was as if we'd always been together. The three of us.

Billie left with the cash my wife gave her, and I knew Odette missed her. If Billie knew I'd have given her ten times that amount, she would have probably come back to collect. Winston had disappeared for a few days, probably chasing after Billie, but he was back for our regular sibling night and I was glad for it.

The whole family was coming for dinner tonight. Well, except for my father. If it came down to choosing between Kingston and my father, my brother would always win. If Father was around, Kingston wouldn't be. Senator—never would be President, if I could help it—Ashford learned of my marriage just like most of the world. By reading the paper. The only ones I bothered calling were my siblings.

I pulled up in front of my house not a moment too soon. It seemed as though everyone had arrived at the same time. My siblings and their spouses. Well, that would be only Aurora's and

Alessio's spouses. And now mine. Kingston was here alone and Royce was yet to convince his woman to wed him.

The moment I was out of my car, another one pulled up. It stopped barely ten feet from me with screeching brakes, and I cursed under my breath. It was Father.

My gaze flicked to find my youngest brother, but he'd already disappeared. Kingston was good at sticking to the shadows, whereas my father forever craved the spotlight.

The car doors opened and slammed. Father stormed toward me. He always lost his head, while I never lost mine. Well, almost never. My wife was the exception.

"Married," he hissed. "Fucking married. I thought you'd marry Nicki."

Among many things, my father was delusional. Even after six years, he wanted to connect our family name to the Popovas. I'd rather cut my dick off than let that happen. Besides, she was nothing but a nauseating memory, and the only way that would happen was if he married her.

"You thought wrong." I sauntered past him and pressed a kiss to Aurora's cheek. "Hey, sis. How's it going?" I gave Alexei, her husband, a nod in greeting—he was never one to appreciate any form of physical contact unless it came from my baby sister.

She winked. "This dinner will be fun," she muttered under her breath. I knew she'd have rather skipped this evening altogether and not see Father, but it was our family tradition, and she'd come here for us. Her brothers.

"We can always stick to speaking French and pretend not to understand your dad," Alessio's wife, Autumn, muttered. She was French Canadian. "He pretends he understands, but he doesn't."

A round of chuckles followed while our father still fumed with rage, waiting for us to get a move on and head inside.

I high-fived Kostya next. "Hey, buddy. Long time no see."

Aurora rolled her eyes. "You saw us three weeks ago."

I grinned. "Like I said, long time."

"Who's starving?" Royce announced. "I'm so hungry, I could eat a horse."

"You are a horse, Royce." My father was a fucking asshole, but at least the rest of us had enough curtesy not to call him out on it. Royce hated his guts and didn't even stop to acknowledge him as he made his way inside my home.

"Show us your wife, Byron," Royce said, ignoring Father. "I can't believe another Ashford bites the dust. It's just Winston, Kingston, and myself left."

I didn't bother correcting him. Winston would have to do that himself.

"Father, I believe I made it clear this dinner was for siblings only." My voice was calm, but my fury wasn't. I promised my wife to keep my father away from her, and I was a man who kept his promises.

He waved his hands dramatically, his gray hair flying all over the place. "I gave you all life. Don't you fucking forget it."

"We have repaid your sperm donation many times over," I grumbled.

Suddenly, Father grabbed his chest as his knees wobbled. "My heart," he whimpered. "My doctor told me to keep stress levels low. Aurora, I don't know how much longer I have." I studied him with disbelief. This manipulative, crazy son of a bitch.

Aurora extended her hand reluctantly and supported our father by his elbow. "Should we call you an ambulance?"

Father shook his head. "No, no, no. I just need to rest for a minute. Could you take me inside? I don't want to keel over in the driveway. Can you imagine what a field day the press would have? Senator Ashford died in front of his son's house while he was inside having dinner with his siblings."

She let out an exasperated sigh. Aurora had a backbone but also a soft heart. She didn't care for our father, but she didn't wish him harm either.

"Okay," she caved. She shot me a pleading look. "Let me take you inside for a little bit." Then as if she could read my mind, she added, "Just for a little bit."

Fuck, fuck, fuck.

"Take him into the barroom." Nobody went into that room. I'd have preferred to shove him in the broom closet, but my baby sister wouldn't approve. There were limits that she wouldn't allow us to cross, although she didn't care much for our father either.

We made our way up the marble, tiered cake-like stairs and entered the foyer. Loud music drummed with a bass, shaking the chandelier. Alexei cocked his eyebrow and all of us followed the sound of music. I failed to remind Odette we had dinner obligations, and I was starting to regret it. She liked to strut around the house wearing skimpy shorts and a tank top. Normally I didn't mind it, but I didn't want anyone else to see her like that.

I paused in the living room doorway where my wife usually spent most of the time and found her and my son laughing, some ridiculously loud song blaring through the Bose speakers. Ares and Odette were jumping around, dancing and screaming the words of the song. I glanced at the screen of my Bose system. "HandClap" by Fitz and The Tantrums scrolled across it.

I smiled. The words weren't bad, but my wife and son butchered them.

As the two of them jumped, the whole first floor shook with each bass note blaring through the stereo. All the pillows lay discarded on the floor as if they'd had a pillow fight. One of them was ripped, its feathers scattered across the carpet. It was comical.

"Father, I told you no." My sister's angry voice came from behind me, and I turned around to find Father and Aurora standing a foot away. I glared at him while Aurora shot me an apologetic look.

"He feels better," she mouthed.

Imagine that. All of a sudden, he was cured. That manipulative snake.

I gritted my teeth, wanting to lash out, but I didn't want to appear heartless in front of my new wife and my son. My siblings knew who and what our father was, but it'd be different with my son. He only projected kindness and love, because that was how my wife and Billie raised him.

My father ignored me, his eyes locked on my new family as he looked like he'd been struck.

So with a clenched jaw, I turned my back on my father and focused on the good in my life.

Odette jumped up and down, and I thanked all the saints that she was wearing a bra, otherwise I'd have to blind my brothers. She was wearing a black chiffon designer dress with silver straps that matched the ones on her new pair of Gucci boots. Despite the forced arrangement—for her, not me—my wife was glowing. She looked healthy, rested, and happy.

Was she though? I pondered. It was hard to tell.

Royce let out a soft chuckle next to me. Aurora grinned, watching my family dance. Were my wife's moves sexy and sensual? Probably not, although she still managed to get my dick hard. Even after a week of taking her body every night, I couldn't get enough of her.

"She's dancing like she's on a trampoline," Father hissed, clearly displeased. He could always leave. He knew where the door was.

I couldn't care less how she danced, as long as those smiles and happiness remained on their faces. Her face was flushed, her red hair whipping through the air as she held Ares.

My chest warmed, the sensation swimming through me.

She threw her head back and laughed, a big grin on Ares's face lighting up the room. It was the best feeling in the world seeing them happy.

My wife stopped jumping. "We need some water. Right, buddy?" She sounded breathless.

He nodded, and she whirled around. When she spotted us, she stiffened immediately.

"Having fun?" Her eyes darted around, that happy smile still frozen on her face. Her eyes slowly traveled over my brothers— Winston and his grumpiness, Royce and his grin, my baby sister along with her family... until her eyes landed on my father. Any remaining happiness on her face was wiped clean.

Smoothing my hand over my waistcoat, I walked over to the stereo and turned it off. The music stopped, and the silence that followed was deafening as she stood frozen with Ares in her arms.

"Jesus, it's like a zoo here," Father declared.

Ignoring him, I moved toward my wife. I leaned down and kissed her cheek, watching the color rising on her porcelain skin. Then I turned to Ares and ruffled his hair. "Hey, buddy. Did you take good care of your mom today?"

My son's eyes darted over my shoulder, then back to me, before nodding.

"Remember, tonight is our family dinner night," I said coolly. "My father decided to invite himself since he's a sore loser."

She blinked, her eyes darting to my father and then back to me. "I guess I didn't realize you meant your *entire* family."

I suddenly realized the misunderstanding. I told her we were having a *family dinner*. She took it to mean just the three of us. I'd be lying if I said it didn't make me happy. If she already thought of us as family, we were moving in the right direction.

"Here, let me introduce you to my siblings aside from Winston, whom you know." I led her to where my family still stood. "Okay, the youngest and probably the nicest is Aurora."

My sister didn't waste time, she wrapped them both into her arms. "Welcome to the family. As fucked up as it is, some of us are okay."

Odette looked at me, probably wondering if Aurora was joking. Unfortunately, she wasn't.

"Nice to meet you." Odette shifted Ares on her hip. He was too big to be carried, but for some reason, she refused to let him go. "This is my son. Ares."

Aurora's brows shot up. Maybe I should have given them all a warning. To her credit, my sister didn't comment on it. Thank fuck. The last time we'd had this conversion, we all thought he was Winston's son.

Instead, she brought Kostya forward.

"This is our son, Kostya."

Odette smiled and reached out her hand. "Nice to meet you. I really love your name." Kostya sputtered a few Russian words, grinning wide. "Hmm, I'll teach you French, and you can teach me Russian."

A round of chuckles followed, and suddenly I knew—not that I'd doubted it—my wife would have no problem fitting in with my family.

Seeing another boy, Ares wiggled out of his mother's embrace and slid down her body. While the two of them started whispering, Aurora turned to the man at her side. "This is my husband, Alexei."

Odette smiled and extended her hand. "Nice to meet you."

This time I stiffened. There was no way she'd know Alexei didn't touch people. For a few awkward seconds, her hand hung in the air, but it was what happened next that had everyone gasping. Alexei took her hand in his and shook it.

"Dr. Swan, nice to meet you."

My brother-in-law just became my all-time favorite person on this planet.

"Okay, the eldest brother and his wife. Alessio and Autumn." I ruffled my nephew's hair. "And this guy is a future pilot and artist. Kol."

Odette shook their hands, then bent, resting her left hand on her knee and offering her right one to Kol. "Nice to meet you, Kol. I can't wait to see your artwork." My nephew's eyes lit up and he nodded eagerly. She switched to French and said, "And maybe one day, you can fly me around the world. I bet you'll be the best pilot ever." I feared my wife had gotten a new, lifelong fan because my nephew beamed like a hundred-watt light bulb.

"You and Kostya are Ares's age. I think you three will get along nicely."

The three boys left the adult circle and made their way to look at the trains Ares had lying all around the living room.

It was Royce's turn and, of course, he wrapped his big bulky frame around her. "Careful, brother," I warned. "Don't get any ideas."

He chuckled. "Don't worry. Your wife's safe with me." He took a step back and his gaze traveled over her. "It's too bad you saw him first. I think you and I would be better suited."

A choked laugh escaped my wife, and I promptly growled. Royce's easygoing manner always attracted women, and I had never been jealous of it. Until now.

"You're married to me, so don't get any ideas," I warned her.

He waved his hand. "Easily remedied. We can just get rid of him." He winked at Odette.

"But I like Byron." Ares's voice pulled everyone's attention back to him. "I don't want to get rid of him."

Royce watched my son with an untelling expression—his gaze coming to me, then back to my son—before a wide smile spread across my brother's face. He kneeled down, then extended his hand.

"Ares, right?" My son nodded somberly, his hand pushing into my own. "I think you're right. We don't want to get rid of him. I like him too." He grinned. "He's my brother, so I like to tease him."

Hesitantly, he shook my brother's hand, and my chest beamed so brightly, it just about powered the entire corrupt capital city.

It was time for my father's introduction, and instantly, Odette's eyes turned stormy. Her lips thinned, and I swore contempt flashed across her expression.

"And this is my father," I introduced him. "Senator George Ashford, who wasn't supposed to be here."

My displeasure was evident in my voice, although it didn't deter my father at all. Selfish prick.

To my surprise, Odette didn't move. She didn't smile nor extend her hand as she had with Alexei. She didn't say anything.

She waited. For what, I wasn't sure, but tension filled the space, and suddenly, I had an uncomfortable feeling.

A whisper in the back of my mind told me my wife had met my father before.

Chapter 47
Odette

From the moment Byron proposed his marriage of convenience, I knew we'd eventually cross paths again. Even with Byron's assurances that he would not bring him around, I knew it was inevitable we'd cross paths with his father.

The senator's eyes turned cold as he evaluated me, but I refused to move. I wouldn't be the one to make the first move. As far as I was concerned, Senator Ashford could drop dead, and I wouldn't move a finger. Hippocratic Oath be damned.

"Dr. Swan."

My pulse charged across my skin while my heart thundered so hard, I feared it'd explode into red confetti in my chest. Why was I so anxious? I had nothing to hide. I didn't do anything wrong. But this man, on the other hand, I'd begun to realize, did plenty wrong. And not just to me and my family, either, but through his position in politics. It rippled off his greasy stature and made my skin crawl.

"Senator," I bit out. I still hadn't extended my hand to shake it. I didn't want to touch the snake. Even after six years, his words stung. Even after six years, his threat while I lay scared and helpless in the hospital—because this man didn't care whether he hit people when they were most vulnerable—still felt fresh.

His kind and my kind didn't mix. He was right. Because his kind was rotten to the core.

The senator extended his hand and held it out for me to take. I made no move to do so. I didn't forgive, and I wouldn't forget. And I definitely wouldn't pretend nothing had ever happened between us.

After a few moments, he slid his hands into his pockets, observing me with detached dissatisfaction. As if I were a speck of dirt under his boot. As if he had never wronged me. Like he hadn't taken something precious from me. My chance at happiness. My son's chance at having both of his parents, together.

My father, I thought, feeling the familiar sadness creep into my heart.

"Dinner is ready," Maria, Byron's cook, announced and not a moment too soon.

Byron took my hand, then Ares's and led us into the formal dining room while everyone else followed behind us. The tension filled the manor, and for the first time since Byron brought us here, I hated this place.

All because of him. His father.

"You okay?" Byron whispered.

I nodded. By now, I was certain that Byron truly had no idea what his father had said six years ago. Or done.

And in this wretched moment, I was so mad—so upset—that I wanted to lash out and make Senator Ashford suffer. Make him pay, like he had made me pay. He took my father from me. Maybe not physically, but he drove him to take his own life. Senator George Ashford needed a taste of his own medicine in this twisted universe.

"Well, we can use this dinner to celebrate your marriage," Aurora stated as Maria scrambled to place another setting for the uninvited guest. Once she was done, we all sat down. Aurora was pretty with dark hair and even darker eyes. Her appearance was contrasted by her tattooed husband's, with his unnerving pale blue eyes and his blond hair that was so bright, it almost seemed bleached. I doubted it was, though. Back in New Orleans, I saw two other men who looked just like him and their hair was bleach blond.

"That's an excellent idea," Byron agreed. "Winston and Billie— my wife's sister—were the only ones there for the ceremony, so this will make up for it."

"Where is Billie, anyhow?" Winston asked me.

I shrugged. "Chasing her dream." This was her time, and from Billie's texts, it was clear she didn't want me to tell anyone where she was.

I could tell by Winston's gaze that he knew something. Not that I expected him to reveal it.

The food was brought out and the conversation stilted. Byron filled the uncomfortable silence with safe topics. Sports. The children. *Even the weather*. All the while, his father's eyes never left me. Kostya, Kol, and Ares sat next to each other, oblivious to the tension dancing through the air. I pushed my food around on my plate, studiously ignoring the man with the cold eyes, barely paying attention to the conversation. I felt out of my element.

"Byron says you are a surgeon." Royce aimed his question at me, trying to pull me into the conversation.

"Yes."

"Where do you practice?"

"I spent the last year in Ghana with the UN, offering health-care through one of their organizations. You might have heard of it, it's the World Health Organization."

"Wow, that's impressive," Aurora chimed in. I shrugged. "And you did all that with your son by your side? Or did your family keep him in the States?"

Lowering my gaze to my plate, I answered. "My sister helped. She came along with my son and me. Both my parents are dead."

Resentment built in my soul, slowly but surely. It brought back the hate and bitterness toward the man who'd driven my father to suicide. A part of me wanted to make him pay, punish him, so he'd feel the pain of such a loss, just as my sister and I had.

"Are you working now?" Royce asked, almost as if he could sense my anger building up. "I want to make sure if I ever need surgery, I'm worked on by you."

I shook my head, bringing water to my lips and taking a sip. I put my glass back on the table. "No, not yet. I'm talking to the head of George Washington for a possible opportunity. But since we're family now, I wouldn't be able to operate on you anyway. I'd lose my license."

From the corner of my eye, I could see—and feel—Byron stiffening. I hadn't told him I heard from Marco again. George Washington made me an offer to join their emergency surgical team, on Marco's wife's recommendation. She ran my credentials and touched base with my WHO and UN contacts. It turned out, she was eager to have me on her team, but I was dragging my feet with my final response.

"I don't think you'll have any problems getting a job," Alexei stated coldly. Man, that guy could be scary. Haunting secrets lingered in his pale blue gaze. I suspected that man hadn't had an easy life.

"Agreed," Alessio declared. "With your experience training with the World Health Organization and the UN, hospitals will fight over you."

I gave them a tight smile. None of the opportunities excited me. I had dreamt about working in my father's hospital since I was a little girl. Even before we moved to France.

"We could use her UN work to our benefit," the senator chimed in. My head snapped his way, my eyes clashing into him. "My reelection campaign is about to start." Was this guy for real? Anger bounced through the room, playing ping-pong between

Senator Asshole and me. "After all, she has no other political connections."

I shot to my feet, anger flaring through every cell in my body. My eyes found my son who was now staring at me, wide-eyed.

"Are you for fucking real?" I hissed, my hands slamming against the long table and sending all the silverware rattling. I *never* lost my temper. It could mean life or death when it came to my profession. But the nerve of this guy was incomparable. Noting my son's startled expression, I inhaled a calming breath, then forced a smile on. "Baby, can you go and play with your trains? Mommy will bring your dinner upstairs."

Ares's eyes darted around before landing on Kostya and Kol. He didn't want to leave his new friends.

"Kostya, buddy, go with your new friend and Kol," Alexei instructed, and I offered a grateful smile.

The moment they disappeared from view and the sounds of their little feet faded, I turned my wrath back onto my new father-in-law.

"Spare me your self-righteous crap, Dr. Swan," he spluttered. "Everyone's for sale."

My cheeks burned, fury flaming through my veins. The worst part was that I couldn't dispute it, because I'd sold myself to Byron. To save my son, my sister, and myself. Had Byron shared that detail with his father?

"Men like you should never be allowed into positions of power," I hissed. My ears buzzed with anger that simmered through my veins. "You will not, under any circumstance, use my name or anything about me for your fucking campaign."

"All the members of Ashford—"

Everyone watched in shock as I cut him off.

"Use my name, or my son's, and I'm warning you, I'll be sure the world knows exactly where I stand with you." My body was roiling with the anger I felt trickling down my spine.

Senator Ashford didn't seem concerned. He leaned back and

tipped his glass up, draining it in one mouthful. "And where's that?"

"That I'd never vote for you, for one. If your reelection hung by a single vote—mine—you'd lose. Nobody needs your fucking corruption."

He laughed. Fucking laughed. "Good thing you're not an American, then. Your vote doesn't count."

"It seems you didn't do your homework the first time you threatened me." Rage was a powerful adrenaline rush but also the best way to slip up. "Both my sister and I were born in the States, Senator Asshole." Royce started clapping his hands, but I was too mad to think anything of it.

"Baby, don't upset yourself. I'll handle this," Byron said, and it had the exact opposite effect. It made me see red.

"Upset?" I growled. "Are you serious? I am way past the point of being upset. This man is fucking nuts and destructive."

Senator Ashford sneered. "*This* is why you're inadequate, just like you were then. *This* is why certain people don't belong in our family."

For a fraction of a section, his eyes darted to Alexei and there wasn't an ounce of doubt in my mind that Senator Ashford didn't approve of him either. Not that it looked like Alexei gave two shits about it. I had a feeling the man could snap his father-in-law's neck and not lose any sleep over it. Good for him!

I scoffed, even though this conversation was starting to veer toward dangerous territory. "Nobody sane would want to be part of your fucked-up family."

And with that, I left the room and all the Ashfords behind me.

Chapter 48
Byron

My wife disappeared and the tension ticked as I ran through all that had been said.

It was clear from her reaction that my father had done something. Something terrible.

My grip on my glass tightened, and I was surprised it didn't shatter. I had to take a second to swallow down the burning rage so I wouldn't lunge across the table and wring my father's neck. Could that fucker leave any of us alone to live our lives without constantly meddling?

My eyes traveled around the table, but my next words were aimed only at my father.

"No one will ever disrespect my wife." Then I narrowed my eyes on the man who had given me life but was as close to me—and my siblings—as a perfect stranger. "I don't give a shit that you're my father. If you ever speak to my wife like that again, I will end you," I said calmly. "Your career will be over before you can say 'fuck you.'" It was the only warning he'd ever get. "Now you're going to tell me what you did." My voice was colder than polar temperatures. "And I will find out if you're lying," I warned.

My words had the desired effect. Father shifted uncomfortably, then coughed, scratching his ear.

Winston didn't bother moving, reaching instead for his glass of water. Royce gave our father a disgusted look. Alexei's face portrayed nothing, but I knew he didn't care about our father and that was putting it mildly.

There was a long silence as I waited. Father's cheeks blotched and his chest heaved. That fucker was so selfish, he never even spared Ares a glance. If he had, he'd notice he had another grandson. But then, he was never really around when we were kids to remember how we looked. Even now, he barely spared Kostya a glance.

After he helped Alessio, his illegitimate son, get Autumn back, I thought he'd finally seen the error of his ways.

But now, I wondered whether he did that with an ulterior motive too. I never understood why Kian was in Afghanistan on Father's assignment, but I knew I wouldn't get an honest answer out of my father. And Kian wouldn't betray a client's trust.

"I won't ask again, Father. What have you done?"

He ground his molars.

"I warned her off, that's all."

My jaw clenched. A burn radiated in my chest. "When?" I gritted.

He leaned back into the chair, in my fucking house, and flashed me a sly smile. The one that every single child of his was familiar with. The one he put on when he used us to get what he wanted. He was the reason my youngest brother had been kidnapped, and why we'd mourned him for two decades, not knowing whether he was alive or dead. I couldn't even fathom the abuse Kingston underwent. It'd haunt him for the remainder of his days.

Did my father learn his lesson?

Fuck no!

I slammed my hand against the table, silverware and crystal rattling for the second time tonight. "I asked fucking *when!*"

My sister just shook her head, and I let out a bitter laugh. The truth lay just beneath the surface, as I realized slowly what this meant. How could I have been so stupid? So blind? *Of course* my father was the reason for the fucking agony all those years ago.

"What did you use against her?"

"You're thinking with your dick, son, and—"

My pulse quickened and my vision narrowed. "No," I roared. "You are the one that has been thinking with your dick, destroying everyone in your path for decades, you power-hungry son of a bitch."

A sinister smile lifted the corners of his lips. "And you're just like me."

"You're delusional, Father," Aurora chimed in, glaring at him. "And you don't even deserve that title. You're a stranger to all of us. I thought you'd started to make amends, but in truth, you're just trying to figure out the best way to use us to your advantage. All of us."

"Over my dead body," I stated coldly. "There'll be no more of that. It's clear you have no scruples, Senator Ashford. You're ready to destroy your family for your own benefit."

"How could you cost Byron his own son?" Aurora hissed.

Father waved his hands in the air, like it was no big deal. "You don't know that's his son. That girl is French. They get around."

My nostrils flared, and I stared at this stranger through a mist of red fury. "What the fuck do you know?" I bellowed. "You are single-handedly destroying this family."

"I am your father. Remember that."

I gazed into the eyes of the man who was practically a stranger to me. A sperm donor. But that was not who I would be. I'd be an important part of my son's life. I *should* have been part of his life for all these years.

"I've heard enough," Aurora said, shooting to her feet. "And you wonder why your youngest son wants nothing to do with you."

She gave her head a shake, her lips curled with disappointment at our father.

I agreed with the sentiment completely.

"What. Did. You. Do?" I asked, my voice oddly calm. One of my kitchen staff came around and handed me a glass of scotch. I took it and brought it to my lips. "And don't forget, I have a way of validating your story."

Tension pulled at my muscles. It suffocated the air. The images of Odette six years ago played in my mind—exam room number five, our first night together, the next day, the terror when I saw her bleeding in the street, those hours when I held her hand in the hospital.

My brothers held their breath. I knew something bad was coming. I fucking knew it.

"My buddy in Deutsche Bank pulled some strings and fore-closed the loan on her father's hospital."

Even though my wife had hinted at it, Father's words hit me like a punch to the chest, and my grip on my control slipped. No wonder she was so gun-shy around me. Maybe she even hated me. She certainly couldn't stand me when we'd run into each other again. Suddenly, her anger after we spent the night together made sense. My father destroyed her beloved family. My mind was already connecting the dots; it didn't take a genius to figure it out. According to the information I pulled up, her father committed suicide not long after Odette and I spent the night together.

My grip tightened and the glass in my hand shattered. Fury— unlike anything I had felt ever before—shot through me, igniting the rage.

I let out a humorless laugh as I stood up. I should have known he'd go so far as to destroy something so pure. So good. After all, I'd seen it many times before. But still, it managed to shock me every fucking time. Shame on me for giving him more credit than he deserved.

"Well, Father. Let me reciprocate the favor. You're bankrupt now too." I'd fucking make sure of it. And all his donors would be a thing of the past. "You know your way out of my house. Don't ever come back." *Or else* hung in the air.

With that, I went in search of my wife.

Chapter 49
Odette

A nger had my hands shaking as I made my way upstairs. As if on cue, thunder rolled through the clouds and a harsh wind whipped against the windows. It mimicked my inner turmoil. The growling thunder shook the skies above, but thanks to Byron, we had a shelter over our heads.

I didn't know whether to let my heart love him or detest him. *Him* and his entire family, but especially his father.

My pulse drummed hard in my ears at the audacity of that fucking man. Rage simmered in my blood—years of guilt and blaming—threatening to spill over and create chaos. Images of my father's dead body played in my mind, the way his body slumped, blood seeping out of his skull, while he clutched at that single photograph.

Senator Ashford had driven him to suicide. But I was also to blame. I should have never touched someone like Byron. He oozed power, wealth, and—most importantly—ruthlessness. But then again, maybe it was exactly that which pulled me to him.

The moment I entered my son's room, a quiet kind of relief swept through me. He hadn't noticed me, nor had his new friends.

Family, I should say. They were playing with the trains, chatting among themselves. I released a shuddering breath, trying to calm my racing heart, and leaned against the door.

This was what I needed to come to terms with it all—seeing my son happy.

I closed my eyes, inhaling deeply and hoping for peace. The one that had evaded me ever since Senator Ashford woke me up in Byron's room that morning. Memories pricked at my skin. Regret—or something like it—danced in my soul. Would it ever go away?

"We're not all fucked up." A soft woman's voice startled my eyes open. I swept at the tears on my cheeks, hoping she wouldn't see the torment I was trying so hard to bury. Byron's sister and Alessio's wife stared at me with an all-too-knowing look. My eyes darted behind them, down the hallway, where both their husbands seemed to be deep in conversation. "My father has done so much shit that it doesn't surprise me to hear what he did to you and Byron. All I ask is that you don't hold it against us. Or him," Aurora added softly, and she didn't need to say his name for me to understand who she was referring to.

They crossed the threshold and approached me, as though one might approach a startled doe. I wasn't a wide-eyed young woman anymore, and truthfully, a weight had lifted off my chest with the confrontation. I was starting to think it was something I should have done years ago. For my peace of mind.

The boys startled and paused their movements, finally noticing us.

"Is the house gonna fall?" Ares asked, his cobalt gaze darting around at the sounds of the storm raging outside. "Like that other one?"

Beside me, Aurora and Autumn eyed me at the odd remark, clearly confused. I sighed. Back in Ghana, we stayed with a tribe for a week, caring for their sick. We were given a modest little hut to stay in, but unfortunately a storm swept through. It caused landslides and destruction around the area. We got out of our hut seconds before it crumbled in front of our eyes. Needless to say, it left a mark. On all of us, but it was particularly scary for my little boy.

"No, baby. There's nothing going to make this house crumble." Except for the lies and deceit of Senator Ashford. "Keep playing with your friends."

"Family," Aurora chimed in. When I shot her a curious look, she added, "We're a family. My father isn't, but you'll come to find that my brothers, half sister—" My brows furrowed. I didn't know Byron had another sister. She waved her hand in exasperation. "Long story. No surprise, my father was the culprit. Anyway, what I'm trying to say is, my brothers will always have your back. No matter what. You're part of our family now and nobody—fucking nobody—will dare mess with you, or they'll suffer the Ashford wrath."

This family was so different from anything I had ever encountered. Maybe I was too trusting, but I believed her. She was too outspoken and to the point to believe she was deceiving me.

"Yeah, too bad it doesn't apply to the senator," I muttered under my breath.

"Oh, it will. He has crossed the line many times before, but this time, Byron will hit him where it hurts the most." Her response sent a shockwave through me.

Maybe I'd made a fundamental mistake all those years ago. Maybe I should have told Byron what his father had said. Instead, I'd made the two of them out to be one and the same.

Autumn remained quiet through the whole ordeal, and I wondered if maybe she disagreed with her sister-in-law's assessment.

She must have read my mind, because she smiled softly. "I don't know Senator Ashford well. There are certain things that I'll never forgive him personally, but he did one thing right for Alessio and me. He had a lethal man watch over me while I was in the

Middle East. Kian Cortes. While I'm grateful to him for it, forty years of wrongdoings doesn't just get washed away."

Good God, maybe Senator Ashford *had* truly fucked with his entire family.

I was yet to finish the first paragraph of the medical journal I'd been trying to read for the past thirty minutes. My thoughts bounced off the library walls, hiding in the shadows and corners of this beautiful room.

After tucking in Ares, I let Byron figure out the sleeping arrangements for his siblings. I felt out of my element, and it made no sense to pretend I knew where they usually slept. So I let Byron be the host with the help of his staff while I focused on Ares and then found a corner to hide in.

The smell of leather-bound books and the soft buzzing of the dimmed lights were the only sounds in this wing of the house. The storm still raged outside, mirroring the one inside me as I curled up in the corner of the soft couch with the journal in my hands.

"There you are." Byron's voice, deep and strong, mixed with the sounds of thunder rolling through the sky. I raised my head to find him leaning in the doorway of the library, wearing nothing but black sweatpants and a white T-shirt. "Are you hiding from me?"

That familiar warm feeling danced through me, pushing me to him. His father was in this house somewhere—his whole family stayed—and knowing that man was under the same roof had my skin crawling.

My eyes roamed over my husband, wondering if there was ever a time when he didn't look seductive. No matter what he wore— suit, casual daywear, sweatpants, *nothing*. Although there was something especially hot about seeing Byron so relaxed. It had my heart beating a little faster and the butterflies in my stomach fluttering harder.

I shook my head to snap out of this daze that seemed to fall over me every time my husband was around me.

"Should I be hiding?" I asked instead.

Byron pushed off the wall and strode toward me, his gaze focused on me. In fact, there was an intense determination on his face that put me on guard.

He sat on the couch next to me, then swiftly picked me up and placed me back down on his lap. He glanced at the book in my hands—*Journal of the American College of Cardiology*—then took it and set it on the table next to him.

"You and I need to have a conversation." His arms wrapped around me, positioning me in such a way that I was forced to face him. I attempted to move off him, but his grip only tightened. "No, no more hiding. No more running. We need to talk."

I didn't know if I could go there. Just the memory of the ripple effects from that night we spent together had me in a chokehold.

"Byron, I'm tired."

He tilted his face, his lips brushing against my neck. "Are you worried about my father?"

I froze on his lap, surprised he could read me so easily.

"I hate him," I snapped. The words escaped me, my tone biting. "I hate that—" I couldn't finish, all the emotions I suppressed over the years were suffocating me.

"Do you hate me?" he asked softly.

I blinked, swallowing hard. It would have been easier if I did hate him, but I didn't. It felt wrong to hate someone who had gifted me with something as pure and beautiful as our son.

I shook my head. "Good," he murmured, brushing our noses together. "We can work with that."

"Please don't ask me to work things out with your father." I almost expected him to laugh me off, but he didn't. Instead, he cupped my face, his eyes boring into me and rendering me speechless.

"Never, baby." I inhaled sharply at his hard tone. "He will

never come around us anymore. He's gone for good, and if he ever approaches you or Ares, I'll kill him."

My emotions had been in turmoil ever since we left Ghana in the middle of the night, but since I married Byron, it was even worse. I loved him; I didn't want to love him. I craved him; it'd be easier if I didn't. I hated all these conflicting emotions.

"He's here now, though," I murmured.

He shook his head. "No, he's not. He's gone."

I stared at him in shock. "You sent him out in this storm?"

My husband's expression hardened. "Yes. He's never welcome here again, and I wasn't going to put up with him for a single moment more."

The truth rang in his tone and his eyes. Then why was I so scared to trust it? *Trust him*, my heart whispered. But that night, I trusted blindly, and it brought me nothing but angst. Even worse, my family had paid for it.

He must have read something on my face, because he let out a heavy sigh. He seemed tired, just as I was. Maybe he just wanted a simple life too.

"I'm glad he's gone," I rasped. "I like your brothers and sister. Their spouses too."

He smiled softly. "They are good people. Nothing like our father." I nodded. I could see it although it was difficult to trust my instincts anymore. Not after they failed me six years ago. Or did they? "I want us to have a clean slate, Odette. For Ares. For our future children. For us." He gently grabbed a strand of my hair and wrapped it around his fingers. But it wasn't his gentle touch that had my heart squeezing. It was the torment in his gaze. As if he were scared of losing me. "Please, talk to me."

I took a deep breath and looked away. It felt easier to tell him without looking into his eyes, like I was baring my soul to him.

"When I woke up after—" After that amazing night. After you fucked me and then made love to me until dawn flickered across the horizon of the French Riviera. "I woke up to your father sitting in a chair next to your bed. He said you were engaged, and I was your 'last hurrah' before settling down." His sharp exhale had me turning my head to seek out his cobalt blues. Such anger simmered in those eyes, promising retribution. But it wasn't aimed at me. I could see it now. "He said your kind and my kind didn't mix. I didn't know what he meant. I'd never heard of 'Senator Ashford' beforehand. He called me a whore and threw money at me. At first I thought he was crazy and I dismissed him, but then he started to threaten my family." I swallowed, knowing how this would end. "By the time I got to work that day, it was already happening. Dad lost the hospital." My voice cracked and he pulled me closer to him, his grip tight on me. "A few days later, Dad committed s—"

It hurt so fucking much to talk about it, yet with each word, the tightness in my chest slowly eased. The knots in my heart unraveled and hope started to boom.

Maybe this was what I needed all along. Him.

Chapter 50
Byron

Her voice broke, and she buried her face in my neck, her little body shaking.

"Shhh." Her tears stained my skin and seeped through my pores, making my soul ache for her. I should have been there for her. That whole goddamn time, I should have been her rock. Instead, those words I said to her—

Fuck!

I rubbed her back, murmuring soothing words. I didn't know if I was doing it right, but it was what I remembered my mother doing. My father hadn't comforted a single soul in his whole goddamn life.

"It was my fault, Byron." Her voice was full of anguish. "I messed around with you and my dad paid for it. I might as well have been the one to put that gun to his head. I'm surprised Billie doesn't hate me."

I cupped the back of her head and locked our eyes. "Your sister will never hate you. Firstly, I forbid it." A strangled laugh-slash-sob filled the space between us. "And more importantly, because she'd die for you. She loves you. Even threatened to murder me if I hurt you." She sniffled, her lips trembling as she smiled. "Do you think we could start over? Put the damage my father has done behind us?" My voice was soft, but my heart thundered so hard and loud, there was no way she couldn't hear it. "Fuck, baby. You're all I ever wanted, from the moment you walked into that exam room to cure me of my goddamn sunburn. There was never an engagement. There was never a woman that made me want to even have a long-term relationship." I let the words sink in, pressing a kiss to her forehead and inhaling the scent of fresh apples. "Until you. I don't remember anyone before you, and there has been nobody after you. Just you, baby. You are it for me."

Her sharp inhale traveled through the dark library. "Y-you haven't been with anyone else since—"

I could lie and tell her I didn't wait for her. That I didn't hope her path would lead me to her. Instead, I bared it all for her.

"I couldn't stomach another woman after you," I admitted. Fuck macho shit. Life was too fucking short to feign indifference and pretend I wasn't head over heels in love with my wife. "I hoped —against all odds—that we'd find a way to each other. You felt perfect. You felt like *mine*, unlike anyone else. And it felt like I belonged to you and only you. I fell in love with you. I couldn't stop loving you even if I'd wanted to, and frankly... I don't want to stop. You are the best thing that has ever happened to me."

Her palm came to rest against my cheek, and I leaned into it. "There hasn't been anyone else for me either." A soft admission. But it thundered as loud as my heartbeat. "I tried. I really did, but I realized no matter where I was or who I was with, I loved you and I couldn't forget. I will always love you. Truly. Completely. It's always been you, Byron. But after what had happened with your father, I stopped trusting myself."

Lights flickered, mirroring the beginning we should have had six years ago. With a snarl, I slammed my mouth against hers. I felt so hopeful about how the rest of our lives looked. Being happy. Having a house full of little girls and boys. But most of all, I couldn't wait to spend time with my woman. The woman who should have been mine all those years ago. The woman who gave me a son.

Mine. Forever. My lover. My entire life.

Holding her jaw in both hands, I broke off and pressed my forehead to hers.

"What if your father—"

I stopped her. "He'll only have power if we give it to him. Leave me to handle him. And trust me, he will pay for what he has done. He cannot and will not destroy us. You alone have the power to destroy me. I am nothing without you, absolutely nothing. And I will never, ever let you go."

Her hands wrapped around my neck as she poured her soul into our kiss. I hardened beneath her, and she shifted in my lap so my cock pushed against her pussy. My hands moved down her back to her waist, loving her curves. She was softer than she'd been all those years ago, and I loved that the reason for it was our son. She'd given birth to a life we'd created.

"What else has my father done?" I questioned. I had no doubt there was more, and I didn't trust my father to be completely honest.

She sighed, her grip on me tightening. "When I came to see you, he was there at your office and sent me away." My teeth clenched, but I didn't interrupt her. "He called me a gold digger. But then he showed up at the hospital, after you left." Her neck bobbed as she swallowed. "He threatened Billie. I felt so weak and couldn't fight him. I thought I had lost the baby and couldn't bear losing one more thing."

She thought she lost the baby. She'd slipped and hadn't realized it but I wouldn't call her on it. I'd wait for her. She'd tell me—I was certain of it—when she felt safe.

My chest burned with fury at my father and clenched with sorrow for my wife. My father would pay, in the way that hurt him the most. He cost us years. Fucking *years* wasted. He robbed my son of his father. He robbed me from having a good woman in my life.

"Trust me, I'll make him pay." My lips brushed against hers, the taste of her so addictive.

"Now that I have you, it's pointless. Let him be a lonely old man." She nipped at my bottom lip. "You, Ares, and Billie are all that matter to me." She smiled sheepishly. "Your brothers and sisters too."

I pulled slightly and locked eyes with her.

"I came," I said softly. Her brows scrunched. "Winston and I came to your father's service. I didn't know what happened, and I knew you didn't want me, but I wanted to make sure you were okay." My forehead came to rest against hers. "I wanted to make it all better for you. I wish I'd known."

She licked her lips, her breathing slightly shallow. "And I wish I'd trusted my gut. I should have known you weren't that type of a man. Maybe a little grouchy, but not vicious and cruel."

"My father played us both."

We'd have to talk about our son too. She just admitted that she hadn't been with anyone since that night, but part of me needed her to say the words, to tell me Ares was my son. To trust me with that information. But I knew she needed time. She was opening up to me and that was all that mattered.

My hands moved down from her waist to her ass, gripping her curves.

She would tell me—eventually. She needed time, and I'd let her get there. After all, we had the rest of our lives.

"I missed you so goddamn much," I murmured, my lips brushing against hers.

"Ditto," she breathed, her cheeks flushed and her hazel eyes glimmering.

I kissed her again, this time slowly. Devouring. As if we had all the time in the world. And we did. We would. I'd ensure it

Her breath hitched and her kiss turned urgent. It turned me on like nothing else. She gently rotated her hips in my lap, making me fall even deeper into this addiction.

Her hands roamed over my T-shirt, never breaking the kiss, until they came to my biceps, then her fingers traced my tattoo. Slowly. Reverently.

"You never told me why you have a chemical molecule as a tattoo," she panted, breaking the kiss.

"It's a combination that makes bombs. It was the mixture of the two that burned my back," I said. "It's my reminder never to fund assholes who make this shit."

Her touch was featherlight as she traced my tattoo. "But if you didn't have those scars, your sunburn that day may not have been bad enough to seek medical treatment, and you'd have never ended up in my dad's hospital."

She had no idea how many times that little fact crossed my mind. After she broke my heart, I cursed my burned back more than ever because it led me to her. But as the ache in my chest eased and settled deep inside my heart, I knew it wouldn't have made a difference. The two of us would have found a way to cross paths.

After all, life without her would have been bleak. A blank canvas. But now, there would be colors splashed all over it. She was the best thing that had ever happened to me.

She tugged on the hem of my T-shirt and pulled it over my head. Her gaze turned heated as she stared at my abs, and it had my lips curving into a smile. I remembered the same look six years ago when she beamed at my abs.

"I guess some things never change," I teased softly. She never played coy or pretended with her desire.

"You still have the most magnificent abs," she purred.

"I'll have to ensure I work out until I keel over to ensure you're happy with my abs."

She waved her hand in dismissal while a soft smile played around her lips.

Her desire was written all over her face, and she was owning up to it. Finally! I'd take this as a good sign. We were moving forward.

I leaned in for another kiss, my touch rougher now. Hungrier. Thrusting my tongue into her mouth, I explored every inch of it. I swallowed her moan hungrily. I pushed her robe off her shoulders, letting it slide down and fall behind her. My hands wrapped around the hem of her silky nightgown and pulled it off impatiently, breaking our kiss just long enough to pull her babydoll nightie over her head.

"Fuck," I groaned, seeing her breasts. If she was obsessed with my abs, I was fucking obsessed with her breasts. "You'll be the death of me," I rasped as I pulled her closer, so I could have her tits right in my face. Where they belonged.

I bent my head and took her hard nipple between my teeth. She moaned my name, her back arching into me and her hips rolling back and forth, grinding herself against my hard erection.

Her hands brushed through my hair, and I looked up as I flicked my tongue. Her hazel eyes met mine, dark with desire and something else that had my chest squeezing in the best way possible.

"Byron," she panted softly. "I need you inside me."

I grinned at her demand.

My hands slowly moved down from her waist, until they disappeared between her thighs. I pushed her wet panties aside, brushing my thumb over her pussy. Her eyes fluttered shut and her lips parted while her hips bucked.

"Oh, God... Please..."

My wife reached inside my sweatpants and wrapped her delicate fingers around my cock and squeezed. "If you're going to tease me, then I'll do the same."

I chuckled, although it was slightly strangled. "So demanding," I murmured, biting her earlobe.

"You started it, so finish it."

I chuckled as I lifted my hips and pushed my sweatpants and

boxers out of the way. Both of our movements were frantic, as if it was our first time together. And in a way, maybe it was. For the first time in six years, there were no emotional barriers nor were there any ghosts of my father's wrongdoing hanging between us. It was our admission that we had waited for each other.

My wife sat back down in my lap, my cock perfectly positioned against her opening. With her breasts pressed against my chest, she wrapped her arms around me.

"Rip the panties you bought me, husband," she murmured. "I need you inside me."

My lips came down on hers, and in one yank, the sound of material shredding filled the space. It was just the two of us. Our heavy heartbeats. Our labored breaths as our souls danced to the tune of our movements.

I wanted—no, needed like my life depended on it, to feel her pussy fully. My hands on her hips, I brought her down onto my cock. She gasped. I groaned. It felt like the first time with her, every fucking time.

She started to grind on top of me, our mouths molded together as we lost ourselves in each other. In this kiss.

"Yeah," I moaned into her mouth. "Just like that, baby."

Her hands threaded through my hair while I gripped her ass, kneading, playing. With each roll of her hips, my cock pushed deeper inside her, filling her to the hilt. I kissed her harder, her little whimpers undoing me.

I lowered her onto the sofa roughly, her back hitting the cushions. With her hair fanning out around her, she looked beautiful. She watched me through her thick lashes, her lips slightly parted and red from my kisses.

My eyes roamed over her naked body. "Fuck, baby. Every time I look at you, you take my breath away."

She blushed, and my heart skipped a beat. My wife. Odette Madeline Ashford. Fuck, yeah! It sounded perfect. Together, we were perfect.

I spread her legs and moved between them once more, her eyes settling on my cock as I rose to my knees. I leaned over her and grabbed her wrists, pinning them above her head with one hand.

"I want to touch you too," she protested softly, her eyes on my cock.

I brought my free hand to my cock and wrapped my fingers around my throbbing erection.

"Later, baby. I want to last and spill inside you." My heart raced in my chest as I lined my cock to her hot, drenched folds. "You're so fucking wet."

Moving both hands around her wrists, I thrust all the way back in.

She arched her back, her nipples grazing my chest. "You feel so good," she rasped. "So, so good."

As I slid out of her wet pussy, I pressed my lips against her neck and kissed her, only to thrust back into her again.

"You're taking my cock so good, Madeline." I sucked on her sensitive skin on her neck, making her moan for me.

"More," she whispered, her voice trembling.

My eyes found hers, and my heart sang. It fucking *sang* seeing the way she looked at me. It had my heart skipping a beat and falling deep under her spell. I pulled nearly all the way out of her before slamming back in.

She was all mine. She owned every one of my thoughts and my entire heart. Now I wanted to own all of her.

Letting go of her wrists, I murmured, "How is this, baby?" I thrust in and out of her, feeling her insides clenching around my cock.

"Yes," she moaned, her hips moving with me. "Oh my gosh... yes, Byron."

"Your pussy is milking my cock, baby," I praised as I pushed back in, deeper and harder, earning myself another gasp from her. I kissed her hungrily as I continued to fuck her this way, driving myself completely fucking insane with desire. I fucked her so hard I was afraid I'd break her, but when I tried to slow my thrusts, Madeline growled in disgruntled warning.

I kept her hips raised at an angle as I pushed back into her, my thumb resting against her clit, as I slid in and out of her.

"This pussy is mine."

My eyes locked on her pussy, watching my cock disappear into her. She felt like heaven, her face flushed as her pleasure-glazed eyes locked on me. Her drenched folds strangled my shaft, and her moans urged me to go faster and deeper.

"Yes, Byron... Oh, oh, *oh*."

I circled her clit, keeping my cock at the right angle to push against her G-spot. I loved my name on her lips, the way she moaned it. The way she gave me all her desire. All of *her*.

It was as it always should have been.

She rotated her hips in an attempt to get my thumb to circle harder, desperate for more.

I chuckled. "My greedy wife wants to ride both my cock and my hand."

"Byron," she moaned. She was desperate for it, the orgasm only I could grant her.

"Tell me who this pussy belongs to," I murmured, toying with her and torturing myself.

"It's yours," she panted, her tone pleading. "My pussy has always been yours. I've always been yours."

Hearing her admission was a rush unlike any other. It was six years in the fucking making. We deserved this.

I increased my pace, thrusting all the way in, my eyes closing in delight as her pussy contracted around me, milking me for all I was worth. My thumb on her clit moved harder, and I watched, mesmerized, as my wife shattered beneath me.

Her eyes still glazed over from her orgasm, she pushed her fingers into my hair. She arched her hips and wrapped her slim legs around me, moving with me. Her moans urged me to go harder until I came apart in a powerful orgasm that rippled from the base of my spine.

Slumping over her, Madeline's mouth came to my temple and she kissed me—softly—while my cock still twitched, spilling deep inside her.

When my breathing slowed and I came down from my high, I met my wife's gaze. She smiled softly, her expression relaxed.

"That was—" She sighed dreamily. "Just amazing."

"Only because it's you." I dropped my forehead to hers with a sigh. I already wanted more of her.

I'd make everything right. I'd be worthy of her and fix it all. Starting with what my father had wronged.

I'd make all of my wife's dreams come true.

Chapter 51
Odette

Distractedly, I listened to the principal of The River School list all the amenities and extra-curricular activities they currently had for their first graders. Except, I couldn't find an ounce of enthusiasm for anything she had listed. Well, maybe French being taught as a foreign language, but my son already spoke French.

"Our students thrive here. We have children of some prominent political families in attendance, and I'm sure—"

This time, I outright stopped listening. Ares clutched my hand, unwilling to let go. I didn't need to ask him to know he didn't like the school. After spending years with Billie, the free spirit, and then a year in Ghana, this place seemed too stuffy.

I smiled and nodded for another twenty minutes until I found my window of opportunity to sneak out. The principal was distracted with another mother who protested about her son playing with a certain kid who liked to eat popsicles that weren't "sugar- and dairy-free."

Like, seriously?

"Ready to get out of here, buddy?" I asked Ares in French. He nodded eagerly and started dragging me toward the exit. Byron's driver—Bernard—was already waiting for us and immediately opened the door as we approached.

"Mrs. Ashford," he greeted me. "Little Ares. How did you like the school?" Ares's grimace was his answer. Bernard chuckled. "Not to worry, little man. You'll find the right one."

I didn't think there would be one in this city though.

Ares slid into the seat with me right next to him. Immediately, he reached for his train and turned to me.

"Mommy, can I have little soldiers to ride on trains?"

I cocked my eyebrow. "I didn't know you liked soldiers?"

He shrugged. "Byron said he had soldiers when he was little, and they rode trains to get to war." He put the train against the car window, holding it up. I assumed so the train could see where it was going. "Did you know Byron was in a war?" He shot me a look and widened his eyes as if to drive his point home. "A real war."

I smiled. "Yes, I did."

I turned to look at the busy streets of D.C. out the window. The residents of this city always seemed to be rushing to get somewhere, rain or shine.

"Mommy?"

"Yes, buddy."

"Can Byron be my daddy?"

I froze, my eyes widening. Slowly, I turned to look at my son. His expression told me he was dead serious.

I couldn't say that it surprised me. Byron had a way with Ares. And then there was the little fact that he *was* Ares's father. I sighed. I needed to tell him. I should have told him. Yet, the words refused to leave my lips.

Why?

I had no fucking idea. Maybe I didn't want to ruin the moment. Maybe I feared he'd hate me for keeping his son away from him. I did try to tell him, but Nicki and his father had gotten in the way. Then the accident happened, and he thought I'd lost the baby.

"Maman?" Ares's voice pulled me out of my thoughts and I sighed.

"Yes, of course. You can call him daddy." *Because he is your daddy.* God, I'd have to talk to both Byron and Ares.

My phone buzzed, and I pulled it out.

I read the message. ***Bouillabaisse for dinner and crème brûlée for dessert.***

An incredulous breath left me. It was the last thing I expected. Bouillabaisse was a French dish. My sister and I grew up on it. We loved it, but I didn't think Byron would. It was a classic French fish soup with seafood, but if not prepared right, none of us would be eating it.

I typed a message back. ***Are you sure? We're starving. Bouillabaisse and crème brûlée are tricky to prepare.***

The reply was instant. ***Have some faith.***

I chuckled. "Okay, then," I murmured under my breath.

As we made our way back home, my thoughts reverted back to the five-year-old-boy-sized secret. The knot in my stomach twisted. It felt like—unintentionally or not—I'd stolen something precious from my husband, and just as things were starting to improve, I was about to ruin it with my admission. But there was no way around it. I had to tell him.

The car came to a stop, and before Bernard had a chance to open the door, Ares was already out the door, running up the stairs. I shook my head, trailing behind him.

"Thank you, Bernard."

He nodded and gave me a small smile. Making my way reluctantly up the stairs, my stomach twisted at the thought of sharing my secret with my husband. I had to do it. Had to!

Voices drifted through the home as I walked into the house. My heart thundered as I followed the sounds of Ares's and Byron's voices.

"Oh my gosh, can I have some?" I heard Ares ask.

"I don't know," I heard Byron mutter. "It looks kind of mushy. I'd never seen it mushy before. Where is the cook?"

I walked into the kitchen to find both of my men standing there, staring at the pot. Byron had a wooden spoon in his hand and was frowning.

Every so often, he'd shake his head, muttering, "This is wrong."

"It looks like puke," Ares remarked, his face slightly twisting. I didn't think he'd eat that dessert if his expression was anything to go by.

"Ugh, buddy. I don't think cooking is my strength. I'm better at running businesses."

My lips curved into a smile. It was hard to picture Byron not being good at something.

Ares patted Byron's big, strong hand gently. "It's okay, Daddy. You are good at everything else." Byron froze for a moment and Ares continued, unaware of the turmoil he probably caused. "Besides, Maman is good at cooking, and she's terrible at business. At least that's what Aunt Billie says." Byron turned to look at our son. Shit, I had to tell him. Stat. Ares's eyes—wide and vulnerable—stared up at his dad and he smiled sheepishly. "Is it okay if I call you that?"

A strong emotion flickered on his face, and I watched him swallow hard. There was something powerful about seeing someone so strong be impacted by such a small boy.

"Yes," he croaked, smiling at our son. "I'd be honored."

Byron's gaze found mine next, shimmering like sapphires, and my heart clenched.

"Are you okay with it?" Byron's question was soft, his voice raspy and thick with emotion.

I should tell him now. It was the perfect moment, but I was so fucking scared to ruin what Byron had planned for dinner. Swallowing the lump in my throat, I nodded. I wanted to tell him—just rip off the Band-Aid—but Ares was here, and I didn't want to have the conversation in front of our son.

As if Byron could read my thoughts, he looked at him. "Hey, buddy. I have a surprise for you in the playroom. Want to go check it out?"

Ares zoomed out of the room, bouncing up and down and squealing happily. All the way up the stairs, his words echoed through the mansion, "I have a daddy. I have a daddy."

I let out a heavy sigh. This was it. It was now or never.

"He's yours, Byron," I rasped, holding his beautiful gaze and holding my breath. My pulse raced while my heart drummed against my ribs so hard, it threatened to crack them. "Y-you saved us by getting me to the hospital in time." My voice trembled as I drowned in his gaze. "Please try to understand—"

Dropping his wooden spoon on the floor, he strode to me as I held my breath. His hands came to my hips and he lifted me up into the air. My hands flew to his strong shoulders, holding on.

"Fuck, Madeline." He buried his head into my stomach, showering it with little kisses. I thanked the saints I was wearing a light dress so I could feel his mouth through the material. "You just made me so fucking happy."

"You're not mad?"

"Considering what my father put you through, I have no right to be mad."

I sniffled, so many feelings swirling in my chest and squeezing my throat. "I—I tried to come see you at your work. I had every intention of telling you," I admitted softly. My eyes burned, trying to keep the tears at bay. I pushed my hand through his thick hair and tugged on it so I could see his eyes. "I promise I did. But then I ran into your dad and he had me escorted out. Called me trash and—"

The first tear rolled down my cheek, and soon, more followed.

His expression turned murderous. "I'm going to fucking kill him."

I shook my head, wiping my face with the back of my hand.

"He's not worth it." I gave him a wobbly smile. "And no cursing," I said through tears.

Byron nodded. "That's right. Not in front of our boy." He grinned so wide, I could see the crinkled lines around his eyes. "No more cursing."

I chuckled. "Just not in front of him."

"Or our future kids."

I rolled my eyes. "You said you wanted an heir. I delivered."

"Your negotiation skills are getting dangerously close to ruthless," he murmured as he gripped me by the hips and slid me down his body. "I might have rubbed off on you." His lips came an inch from mine. "Don't you want any more kids?"

I tilted my head. We still had some unknowns to figure out, but surprisingly, I wasn't opposed to more kids.

"I'll be a good husband and a good father." The look on his face was gut-wrenching, his expression tormented. As if he thought I would reject him all over again. "I take my vows seriously." His eyes suddenly seemed ancient. "I just want us to have a future together. I want to make you and our kids happy. All of us. Everything else will fall into place."

I cupped his face, my eyes roaming as my heart skipped a beat. Maybe I'd finally get my fairy tale. My father used to tell me how he felt about my mom, and this felt so much like it.

"I do want more kids, but let's take it slow. We only just found each other—"

He silenced me with a kiss on my lips. By the time he broke away, both of us were breathing heavily.

"I love you," I whispered as I wrapped my arms around his waist. I rose on my tiptoes and brushed my lips against his. I couldn't stop touching him, feeling him against me. He groaned as he cupped the back of my head, his tight grip betraying his desperation.

"I love you too," he murmured, his lips hovering over mine. "So much. Living without you was just existing, but with you—it's fucking thriving."

A soft sigh escaped my lips at his beautiful words. "So much time wasted." I sighed.

He kissed the edge of my lip. "Let's not waste any more. From this moment going forward, we start living." When I pulled away to find his eyes, he smiled with a smug expression in his gaze. "All I ask is that you don't take the job at George Washington Hospital."

I frowned. "Why?"

He grabbed my chin and dropped his forehead to mine. "Because I'm a jealous and possessive prick." I couldn't help my lips twitching at that admission. "And I tend to go overboard when it comes to you," he admitted in a whisper. "Trust me this time, baby." He pressed a sweet kiss to my cheek, his touch lingering. "I have better things in store for us. My sole purpose in life is to make you and our children happy."

God help me, but I trusted him to come through with his promise.

Chapter 52
Odette

As we strolled into the White House, we heard the announcement and the smattering of applause, as though we were celebrities.

Byron didn't even flinch while my shoulders tensed, and I let out a tight breath. Instinctively, my hand came to twist the large diamond necklace around my neck. It was my second time wearing it, and it still sparkled like all the stars in the sky.

My husband squeezed my hand.

"They are just people." His smile was sweet. Comforting. "Most of them are jackasses, so just ignore them. And remember... You're an Ashford. Practically American royalty."

A strangled laugh left me. "Humble much?"

This time, he grinned. "I came with a queen. Why would I be humble?"

His tone was smooth and warm, like vintage red wine.

A coordinator waved us through the grand room. We made our way across the enormous stone balcony—slowly, thanks to my heels and dress—and when we came to the top of the stairs, Byron's hand gripped my waist, stopping us.

Murmurs and whispers traveled through the air, every pair of eyes on us, and my heart raced in my chest. I hated being the center of attention, and at this moment, hundreds of faces were turned in our direction. It wasn't just the local political world, there were celebrities and socialites from all over the world. Some I recognized —thanks to my sister—others I didn't, but there was no mistaking them with average working-class individuals.

"Mr. and Mrs. Byron Ashford."

The voice boomed from the speakers and the applause broke through, filled with cheers and whistles.

I peeked at Byron. "Very subtle."

He gave me a charming smile. "Nothing about this place is subtle, baby."

No shit.

My husband's hand remained around my waist as cameras flashed, but I kept my eyes on him. It was a better option than staring back at all the unfamiliar gazes.

"You ready for this shit show?" he said under his smile, his lips barely moving.

I scoffed softly. "No."

Byron offered his arm and I took it, while grasping my full skirt with my free hand. I might have thought the dress was too elaborate, but I was glad for it now. All the dresses I'd picked out were beautiful, but subtle. And like Byron mentioned before, there was nothing subtle about this party.

My chin lifted, and we made our descent down the staircase, its stone steps covered with a plush red carpet. You'd think we were celebrities, not just little old me and—I peeked a look at my handsome husband—not-so-little Byron.

We wandered over to the gardens where tables had been set up on the lawn around an intimate dance floor. Festoon lights hung overhead, giving the space a warm glow while diamonds and dresses glittered beneath.

"Jesus Christ," I muttered. "Tax dollars at work here."

"Unfortunately," Byron agreed.

Our feet had barely touched the grass before people rushed at us. Someone handed me a glass of champagne, which I accepted and eagerly downed. I'd need something stronger to endure this crowd. A waiter passed me, and I placed my empty glass on the tray before reaching for another.

Men and women chatted at the same time, but I couldn't understand a single word. Not because they were speaking a foreign language, but because they spoke at the same time. I snickered. Even my son knew it was poor manners to talk over others.

My lips curved into a soft smile thinking about Ares. The way he grinned, telling me he was a big boy. I hadn't wanted to leave him with Byron's old nanny, Mrs. Bakers. The elderly lady seemed kind and competent, but I'd never left him with a stranger before.

I itched to make my way back to Byron's car and retrieve my phone so I could call to check on him.

As if he read my mind, Byron extended his phone to me, and I raised my head, meeting his gaze. "He's good. Look at this."

I leaned over the screen and smiled. He and Mrs. Bakers were playing chess, and Ares was kicking her butt. Both of them had big grins on their faces.

"At least he's having fun," I murmured softly.

"More than we can say." *Huh.* So he wasn't having a good time either. This was business, though, so I'd endure it. For him.

"How come you still have your nanny around?" I asked him curiously. When he suggested she watch Ares, I was floored that he was even in touch with her anymore.

He shrugged. "She did a lot for my siblings and me. I wanted to return the favor. She took care of us, and now we're taking care of her."

Well, shit. If that didn't make me love Byron just another notch more. At this rate, I'd have hearts in my eyes, swooning until my dying day. *Or until he breaks your heart again*, a nervous voice whispered.

"That's nice of you and your siblings." More than nice.

Suddenly, the sea of people around us parted as an older gentleman made his way to us. He looked familiar, but it wasn't until he stopped in front of us that I realized why.

It was the freaking President of the United States. Needless to say, the poor guy looked much older up close.

"Well, well, that was unexpected." The president shook Byron's hand. "Are you lining yourself up for the next elections? Might as well cut your father out of the way."

Byron gave him a tight smile but didn't comment. I could see him as the next president, though I selfishly didn't want him to have that aspiration.

"Mr. President, this is my wife, Odette," Byron introduced me.

I nodded, extending my hand. "Nice to meet you."

The president shook it so firmly, it rattled my bones. "Dr. Swan, I've heard a lot about you." I stilled, confused at his statement. Had Senator Ashford already badmouthed me? "Or should I call you Dr. Ashford?"

"Dr. Swan is fine," I murmured. "What have you heard about me?"

"It's standard protocol to check every plus-one coming to the White House. But I've got to say, no other plus-one is quite as impressive as you. Served alongside the World Health Organization as a surgeon in Ghana. You've done a few things for the United Nations too. Graduated medical school at the top of your class. You could have ended up at any top hospital, and yet, you went to Ghana. Why?"

I shrugged my bare shoulders, trying to set a mask of confidence I was not feeling in place. "My father did something similar in his youth, and I always wanted to follow in his footsteps. He said it was one of the best things he could have ever done for himself."

"So why didn't he stay with it?" he questioned curiously.

I smiled. "He fell in love with my mother, a model. She said Africa wasn't her runway."

All of us chuckled while fond memories danced in my mind. I missed him so much. I missed my mother too, but it was always my dad for me. Billie was more of a mama's girl.

The president moved on to talk to someone else. I still could not believe he'd given me his time and attention. It might have been the most complimented I'd ever felt. For the next little while, people came and went while Byron played his role flawlessly. I smiled and nodded, half of the time not even hearing what people were saying to me. But I carried on like I was having the time of my life, for Byron's sake and the kindness he'd shown me since I told him about Ares.

After an hour of listening to politics and holding a smile, my cheeks hurt like a bitch. And so did my head. Seeing a window for a break, I took it. Fuck, I grabbed it with both hands.

"Excuse me, I have to use the ladies' room."

Byron brushed a kiss at my hairline. "Don't get lost."

I gave him an assuring smile. "I won't. After all, my ride's right here."

I weaved my way through the crowd, pausing as strangers pulled me into conversation like we'd known each other forever, until I finally found my way inside the White House. I walked upstairs, past security, and toward the bathrooms on the second floor.

I pushed the door open, and my steps faltered. I almost turned straight back around, because Nicki—the ex—stood at the sink washing her hands. Her gaze flicked to me, full of hatred and something else. Straightening my back, I headed to the furthest sink away from her, and washed my hands.

We stood side by side there. She applied lipstick, while I waited for her to leave. This was supposed to be my escape and breather time, not fucking ex-fiancée drama.

Once done with her lipstick, she brushed so much powder on

her cheeks, I feared for her lungs. It created such a large cloud of white smoke around her, that even I had to clear my throat.

"He'll realize you're a mistake."

So much for a little zen time in the bathroom. I sighed, never stopping my movements. "And eventually, you'll realize it's time to move on from Byron."

She was unfazed. "He and I are the same. Same background. Same wealth. Same friends."

God, she was actually going to go there. I turned off the water and reached for the stack of luxurious, warm, one-time-use towels. Grabbing one, I dried my hands with painstaking detail.

"Maybe that's the reason he decided to marry me instead of you."

I'd rather die than tell her this thing between Byron and I had started out as a marriage of convenience, or whatever the fuck he'd called it. Let her believe it was a love fest. He was head over heels in love with me, and I was head over heels in love with him. Our affection had been there from the very first moment. It would not fade with time. I wouldn't let it. This time, I'd fight tooth and nail if anyone tried to tear us apart.

"Or maybe you trapped him."

I felt an odd pang in my chest. Why? I had no fucking idea.

I raised a brow. "And how would I have trapped him?"

"Well, he's a man. And you're probably good on your knees."

Jesus, were we really having this conversation in the White House bathroom? I was either too tired, or I simply didn't care about this woman whatsoever. Six years ago, this would have upset me. But today, my heart didn't even blip. Maybe it was true what they said; as you got older, you grew into your skin and who you were as a person. On second thought... maybe it was only true for most people. This woman was as insecure as they came.

"As a matter of fact, I *am* good on my knees," I stated calmly as I made my way to the door. My hand on the doorknob, I glanced over my shoulder, assessing her. "But my husband is even better."

I left the bathroom, but I barely made five steps down the corridor when someone shoved me. Instinctively, I reached out and my palm pressed against the green wall for balance. Thank God, or I would have fallen onto my face.

"You ruined us." *Are you fucking kidding me?* I turned around slowly, and wondered if beating a woman in the White House would get me arrested.

Nicki's eyes locked on my face. "You're a fucking frog." I raised my eyebrow. She really went there—resorting to some ridiculous insult. Gosh, she must be getting desperate.

"And you are pathetic, pining after a man who clearly doesn't want you."

She raised her hand, and before I could even move, thick fingers wrapped around her wrist, twisting it behind her back.

"You weren't just trying to hit my wife, were you, Nicki?" Byron's tone was smooth, but his expression was as cold as ice.

"N-no."

"I didn't think so." My husband's lips twisted into a smile. "And what did I hear about a frog?"

Nicki's eyes widened and her cheeks flushed, likely from embarrassment. "I didn't—"

"Don't insult my intelligence with your fucking lies," he snapped, his voice like a whip. Even I stiffened at the tone of it. "You will leave this party. Right the fuck now. If I see you anywhere near my wife, my son, or any of my family—or hers—I'll make you regret ever looking their way." My heart glowed like Fourth of July fireworks. He'd included Billie. "And I don't mean your inheritance, because you forfeited that tonight. This is your first and final warning."

I swallowed thickly. I focused on the material of his suit. The cobalt-blue, three-piece suit. Stuart Hughes Diamond Edition. It fit him perfectly, and according to my sister, it cost six figures. I stared at it, wondering what made it so expensive, working through various stupid scenarios in my brain to keep myself distracted from his wrath.

For Pete's sake. It wasn't even aimed at me.

"Leave us," he barked, and she scurried away.

Finally alone, I raised my head and met his gaze. The anger in his eyes slowly faded and the tightness in my chest eased. My father never fucking raised his voice at me and my sister. And even when we drove him nuts, he never lost his cool. He'd sit us down and talk us through our hormones, citing the scientific reasons behind what drove us to misbehave. By the end of it all, we'd be either confused, or—in Billie's case—asleep.

"You okay?" I nodded. "Did she hurt you?"

I shook my head. "No, but I probably hurt her pride."

His soft chuckle filled the space between us.

"How so?" This time, it was my cheeks flushing with embarrassment as Byron's eyes sparkled. "Seeing how you're blushing, now I have to know."

I gave him a sheepish smile. "She accused me of being good on my knees." The meaning registered and I could see the storm already brewing in his eyes. "I told her I was, but that you were even better."

His stare was as intense as the sun. Too hard to look at, yet its beauty so blinding you couldn't look away. Then he closed the distance between us, wrapping his hand around my neck as he brought our faces so close, our noses touched.

"You are fucking damn right I am," he murmured, brushing his nose against mine. "But you're the only one I get on my knees for." I gasped, and he took advantage, slamming his mouth on mine. When he pulled away, his eyes glittered like the diamonds around my neck. "I'm the luckiest man alive when I'm with you, baby. I want it all, but only with you."

"Byron," I breathed, my eyes stinging with happy tears that threatened to ruin my makeup. I couldn't believe the journey that had brought us here. After all these years, I was finally his and he was mine.

I laced our fingers together, smiling at him.

"I want it all with you too."

I had loved him for so long, it was impossible to stop.

My love for him had become an integral part of me.

Chapter 53
Byron

O dette was quiet as we walked into our bedroom. She was clearly upset by Nicki's behavior. The entire experience was unexpected, even for me. Although she handled it like a pro. It was what I always loved about my wife. Her backbone.

"I'm sorry about Nicki," I said, watching my wife slip her heels off and placing her shoes next to mine. There was something so fucking calming and right about seeing her stuff next to mine.

She shrugged. "I'm not sure what I was expecting, but this is probably good. It's behind us."

"It's far from over. Tomorrow, Nicki will wake up to a whole different world."

She shot me a puzzled look. "What do you mean?"

"I mean that nobody—fucking nobody—talks to my wife like that and walks away unscathed." I tugged on my tie and she turned to me, helping me loosen it up. I was surprised she was so calm. It didn't seem to bother her at all, while I was here fuming for the both of us. Nicki was lucky she was a woman, or I'd have murdered her. Right there and then.

"She's just a sad woman who has no purpose in life," she said, oddly perceptive. "In Dad's hospital, there were plenty of those coming and going. They expected the whole world to bow to them while they treated everyone else like shit." Her lips tugged up. "Besides, you're here with me, not her. So who cares about her?"

Pulling my tie through my collar, she handed it to me and walked barefoot toward our bed, throwing herself backward on it. Her slim body bounced up and down, and she let out a relieved sigh.

"I could go without another function like that for the rest of my life," she muttered to herself, wiggling her toes.

"Then that's how it will be."

I hated that I pulled her into a world she didn't want to be in. But even more, I hated the way she hid her pain from me. I wanted to be her comfort, her consolation, her confidant. Yet she kept herself at a distance, guarding her heart like the treasure it was, even after telling me she loved me. Well, fuck it—I wanted to own that treasure.

She propped herself on her elbows, watching me through hooded eyes.

"You know, I can't even blame her," she murmured absent-mindedly.

I raised my eyebrow. "For?"

"Wanting you," she remarked. "I mean, what sane woman wouldn't want you."

My movements froze, and I watched my wife as she stretched lazily on our bed. "Do you want me?"

"So much, Byron." Her knees lifted, her dress falling to her waist and she shimmied her panties down her thighs, giving me a glimpse of her arousal. Her fingers brushed over her pussy and I was lost. Her scent. Her moans. I was in heaven. "I'll always want *you*." I closed my eyes for a brief second, grunting as relief washed over me. She could say it a million times and I'd still never tire of hearing her say that she wanted me. Loved me. "Now, please, husband. Come and fuck me."

I undid my trousers and settled myself between her spread legs. She was so fucking wet, it dripped between her thighs and onto our bedding. So damn erotic.

"You want me to fuck that tight cunt of yours until you scream, Madeline?"

"God, yes."

I grabbed her hips and pulled her to the edge of the mattress. Then I plunged inside her with ruthlessness and possession.

"Ohhhh... Yes, Byron..." She moaned as I fucked her, her body bucking off the bed. I thrust inside her with intensity that should worry me. I was too rough, too demanding, but I couldn't slow down.

"Harder, Byron," she gasped, and the last thread of my control snapped.

"Say you're mine," I grunted, my movements harder, wilder.

"I'm... yours... Only yours, Byron."

I started thrusting into her, faster and faster until the only sounds were my grunts mixed with her moans. Our ragged breaths. Flesh slapping against flesh. I was so rough I thought she'd beg me to stop. I feared I'd break her. She never asked me to ease up, though. In fact, her moans and pants begged for more.

My hand came around her throat and I gripped it, slamming into her. She felt like heaven. Every. Single. Time.

She shattered underneath me, her pleasure-glazed eyes and sighs urging me to pick up my tempo. To fuck her faster, harder, and deeper until I came apart, a powerful orgasm rippling through me.

I fell on top of her, and her life-saving hands clutched my shoulders.

Once our breathing slowed, I sought out my wife's eyes.

"Not too rough?" I pushed her damp hair from her forehead, then brushed my lips over hers.

"Never," she murmured. "Don't worry, husband. I'm not one to put up with abuse in the bedroom."

A choked laugh escaped me as I kissed her forehead. I put my forehead to hers with a satisfied sigh, feeling more relaxed than I had in years.

"Then get ready for another round. We haven't even gotten started."

Chapter 54
Byron

The iron gates slid open, and I drove through.

The long driveway lined with weeping willows—my mother's favorite—stretched in front of me. My father's house—mine, really, since I paid for it—stood tall behind the trees.

I hadn't wanted to drag my wife and son here for this shit show, so I came alone. Besides, I promised my wife she'd never have to see my father again. So I'd settle this unpleasant affair myself, then I planned on meeting with Kristoff and Alessio to close out the deal on the purchase of Odette's hospital.

Despite the unpleasant task ahead of me, I grinned. I couldn't fucking wait to give the news to my wife. It would signal the official beginning of the rest of our lives.

I found my father in his office, smoking a cigar while having his dick sucked. Grunts. Fake moans. Balls slapping against a chin.

Jesus fucking Christ.

This was not an image I ever wanted to see. I was officially mentally scarred for life.

"Byron." The woman on her knees stiffened, preparing to stop, but Senator Ashford's hand landed on her back and kept her in place. "To what do I owe this surprise?"

I shook my head. "I'll wait for you in the den. Depending on how many little blue pills you took this morning, this could take a while."

Turning around, I left him and the gagging sounds behind me.

I didn't bother sitting down, I wasn't planning on staying any longer than necessary.

Just as I was about to check my watch, a grating voice filled the room.

"Ahhh, there you are." My jaw tightened. Slowly, I turned around and found my father standing there, fixing his buckle.

"Your fly is open," I pointed out.

He chuckled like it was the funniest thing he'd heard all day.

"To what do I owe this surprise?" he questioned again. "Considering you threw me out of your house in the middle of a raging storm only a few days ago, I wasn't exactly expecting you."

I stayed silent, studying the man who was supposed to be a father figure and had somehow failed at that. For all of us—his legitimate and illegitimate kids. He was a sperm donor, nothing more.

"I came to discuss your future living arrangements and finances."

He stilled, his arrogant mask slipping for a fraction of a moment.

"This home will be liquidated. I have arranged for a condo for you that will be adequate for your living standards. Also, all the sponsors that have been backing you—for my benefit—have decided to back a different candidate. One to be determined at a later date."

I stayed silent, letting the words sink in, and watched my father's blue eyes turn dark and stormy. I'd labored over my siblings and our empire since I was a teenager. I tried to be a good brother, give us all what I thought we needed, while this man—who was supposed to protect us—whored around and put our family in jeopardy time and again. He wreaked havoc on every single one of us with no concern but himself.

Enough was enough.

"This is all because of that French whore."

My knuckles turned white. "Careful, Father. Or you'll find yourself truly penniless." My voice was calm, my face and posture relaxed. "I know your income working for the Senate is not enough to support your *habits*."

He had dealers as well as high-priced escorts on speed dial. The allowance I set for him was spent without a single thought to how hard we all worked to grow our empire.

Needless to say, my father—the great Senator George Ashford —was pale, male, and stale. Who in the fuck would ever want him without money?

"You should have stuck to Nicki."

I scoffed. "She was never my choice. Never would have been. Unlike Dr. Swan, Nicki was a mistake." My father would never understand. He was a selfish bastard and only cared about wealth, power, and status. "At this point, both you and Nicki are lucky to be alive after the shit you've done. So do yourself a favor and shut the fuck up."

"I'm still a senator and I have some pull. Don't forget that, Byron." He smiled—that no-good, cruel smile he used to give my mother when he humiliated her, over and over again—and sauntered over to me, his eyes intense. "I could do some damage too."

Oh, I knew! I fucking remembered his fuckup costing my mother her life.

The familiar clawing pressure in my chest grew, remembering the day my mother died.

Screams and shouts made my blood run cold. What I saw next had my blood outright frozen, roaring at the sight of my mother. Her mouth was parted, a shocked expression etched onto her face. A bright red stain blossomed on Mama's cream Valentino dress, spilling onto the concrete around her.

She lay there, still and unmoving, the light completely gone from her dark eyes.

I shouted for an ambulance. I threatened to destroy them all if they didn't produce one right away, even though I knew it was too late.

She was gone. The only true parent we had. My baby sister would grow up without knowing her love and my heart clenched for her.

It was time for me to step in, because I knew my father never would.

I blinked the memories away and tamped down the irritation I felt toward the stranger in front of me. Tension rocketed down my spine at his threat. He had no qualms about destroying his own family for his personal gain. But he'd never succeed. It'd be him against all his children.

"Your funds have been cut," I told him, my voice cold and detached. "You'll have to lower your spending and your living standards. Thank God on your knees that I'm letting you keep your position in the Senate. Trust me when I say I have enough evidence against you to get you thrown in jail, never mind getting you kicked out of a government job."

I wanted to take everything from the man who'd stolen my chance at watching my son grow up. But still, he was my father. This would be his last chance. One more attempt at fucking with my family, and he'd go down faster than shit down a flushed toilet.

My blood still raged two hours later as I sat with Alessio and Kristoff at a Thai restaurant downtown.

"Congratulations." Kristoff handed me a folder with a wide grin. "I fully expect my family and I to be treated at your wife's hospital whenever we vacation in Croatia. Every time we go, I have my yacht and helicopter on standby. I love it there, but their health care system... Yeah, not so much. I might go in for a cut on my finger and lose my whole goddamn hand."

"You got it. You and your twenty kids."

A round of chuckles traveled around the table. "As my best friend, I expect you to know how many kids I have," Kristoff joked, and I was reminded of the many times his sense of humor had saved me during our stints in war zones.

I waved my hand. "You'll get to twenty at the rate you're going."

"Don't be jealous."

"That's some wedding gift," Alessio chimed in, leaning back in his seat. "I think you might have trumped us all. You'll probably end up having more kids than all of us combined."

Kristoff and my brother snickered, sharing glances. Ignoring them, my eyes scanned through the deed to the hospital Odette's father used to own, plus five additional properties around it. Ready for us to use and make our dreams come true.

"I have a lot to atone for."

"It was all him, not you," Alessio remarked. "I'm sure your wife sees that too."

I nodded, but it still didn't make it right. My father had destroyed hers. He'd driven him to suicide. So, yes. There were many wrongs I had to make up for.

"Thanks for making this happen," I told Kristoff, then turned to Alessio. "Were you able to pull some strings in France to get the medical facility and all licenses there reinstated?"

Alessio grimaced. "Yeah, I got it done. And trust me, it wasn't easy after the shit I pulled with the Corsicans, chasing them out of Philly."

"I never doubted you." Long story short, my big brother had to turn over Philadelphia and chase the Corsican mafia out of there to secure his way into Afghanistan and save his wife. He did it without hesitation, but any time you burned a bridge, shit would eventually happen and you'd end up needing those same people. "Tell me what I owe you."

Alessio smiled. "This one's on the house. After all, we're family."

"That we are."

I couldn't wait to give the news to my wife. I reached for my phone, eager to send her a note and tell her we were celebrating tonight. I found a message from her already waiting for me.

Smiling, I slid it open. ***Meeting Marco and his wife at Tortino Restaurant. Won't be long. Ares is with your nanny. I think he loves her more than us.***

The last part of the message had me smiling, but the first part had unease slithering through my veins. I rubbed a hand over my face, worry making its way into my heart.

I shot to my feet.

"What's the matter?" Kristoff was surprised to see me leave already. Usually we hung out for hours bullshitting.

"I have to cut this short." I had a bad feeling about this. "My wife's meeting the guy whose career I destroyed mere days ago."

She'd be too easy a target for him. He could use her to take his revenge.

"I'll come with you."

My brother at my back, I rushed out of our restaurant and headed to the Tortino Restaurant.

There was one thing I'd never have to question: my brothers and sisters would always have my back.

Chapter 55
Odette

I made my way through the large room, my eyes roaming the fancy Italian restaurant. Ares assured me he wanted to stay behind with Mrs. Bakers, but I suspected it was because he didn't want to part with his new toys. Smiling, I shook my head. His dad was spoiling him rotten.

A hand shot up, and it was then that I spotted him. He sat alone at the table and I groaned inwardly. He said his wife would be here too. Smoothing my hands down my simple green dress, I made my way to his table.

"Maddy." He put his hand over his heart, "You look gorgeous." I bit my lip, forcing a polite smile. Byron didn't like Marco and was convinced he was in love with me. He and Billie were in agreement when it came to that. I inched toward the table. "Thank you for meeting me," he stated.

I nodded. "Where's your wife?"

He didn't look at me. His eyes darted somewhere behind me, but when I followed his gaze, I didn't see anybody there.

"She couldn't make it."

I lowered myself into a chair across from him. "This should be quick, then. Like I said over text, I'm not going to take the job with George Washington at this time."

He stiffened, an expression flickering across his face. But it disappeared as quickly as it came.

"It's a mistake," he stated. I studied his face until suddenly, an alarming feeling shot through me. Marco looked weary. His hair was a mess and his clothes were wrinkled, sporting a few stains. I had never seen him look this way before, so unkempt.

"Are you okay?" I asked, ignoring his comment. It wasn't a mistake. Byron asked me to trust him, and I would.

He shook his head. "I lost my job."

He lifted a hand and delicately wiped it under his eye. Was he seriously crying? He had to be fucking with me.

"Okay... I'm sure you'll be able to find another. What is it that we used to say? One step forward, two steps back. Your next step will be forward."

"I remembered you like the raspberry tea. I ordered it for you before you arrived." He gestured to the cup in front of him.

"No, it's yours." I wanted to get out of here.

"Nah, I ordered it for you. I have my drink." He pointed to his mug of beer.

"Sure, then. Thanks."

He handed it to me, and I smiled uncomfortably.

"I'll try to find another job," he started casually, but his shoulders were tense. Too tense. "I have a few opportunities in Europe. Has your husband talked to you about it?"

I took a sip of my tea and made a face at the bitter taste. I swallowed the disgusting liquid out of politeness, then answered him. "No, I don't think any of his businesses are in the fashion industry."

Truthfully, business endeavors weren't my thing, so even if he had mentioned something, it probably went right over my head.

His eyes appeared sad as they settled on me. "I miss you." My smile fell a bit. I missed home, but not him. Life had changed so much, and so had we. "Remember the good old days? Things were easier then. "

My fingers traced the handle of my mug. "We had to grow up eventually."

His expression turned dark.

"Yeah, some of us grew up sooner than others." I took another sip of my tea absentmindedly. "The Ashfords ruined us all." I froze mid-sip, wondering what he meant. As far as I knew, he'd never met any of the Ashfords apart from that one night in the bar all those years ago. "I saw his father pay you a visit in the hospital. He even tried to bribe me to ensure you stayed away from his family."

Anger flared in my chest, and I had to clench my teeth to stop my words from spewing out. But I didn't interrupt, waiting for him to spill the beans. "He even put in a good word with my then girl-friend. It was the only reason she agreed to marry me. That and the engagement ring I was able to buy her with the money Senator Ashford gave me."

I gritted my teeth. Somehow it didn't surprise me that Senator Ashford would go so fucking far, but Marco succeeded in surprising me. I never imagined him to go that far. Even when he was broke and working three jobs to help his family, I always pictured him honorable.

"Hmm," was all I could find to say from under my mug while my rage simmered. I drank my tea, trying to wash it away, swal-lowing back my grimace at the taste. But it was better to drink bad tea than spit all the mean words that seared my tongue.

"You and I could have been so much more." His dark eyes were full of turmoil and irritation. My pulse quickened, but still I stared at the woodgrain in the table and tried to remain calm. "If only you'd given me the time of day."

My stomach churned, while a dull ache throbbed in my chest. "How could you? We are... were friends." That was definitely a thing of the past now.

"I can't see you, not with him," he said. "He ruined my career."

I frowned, not following his rambling. "I took you from him once before, and I'll do it again." My temples throbbed, not liking the threat laced through his tone.

"What do you mean?" My voice sounded dull. Far away. The room shifted.

Marco smiled. His face went so cold, it was nauseating. "Why do you think I convinced my wife all those years ago to tell Byron Ashford that you lost the baby? He didn't deserve you. You are mine."

The statement hung there for a long while, leaving us sitting in silence. My heart had an odd beat to it, causing a strange sensation. It was like I was running on a cloud and my feet couldn't touch the ground.

Marco is batshit crazy. How did I never see it before?

I blinked my eyes as two Marcos entered my vision. I started blinking rapidly, my heart out of sync with my body.

"I don't feel right." It took every ounce of strength to rise to my feet. Nausea rose in my stomach, and the world started to turn.

"No, I wouldn't think so." He rose to his feet as well, moving effortlessly, and taking my hand in his. Things moved around in my vision and I pushed him, stumbling away.

I must have knocked into a table as I registered the sound of silverware and plates slamming to the floor. Ignoring it all, I reached for anything to support myself, struggling to catch my breath.

"My wife had too much to drink," I heard Marco say to someone.

Somebody laughed. I wanted to scream, tell them it wasn't true. My mouth was too dry, though. The room was spinning out of control.

I hurled myself toward the front door. Someone opened it and I tried to rush for it, knocking one of the chairs clumsily. My stomach curled, threatening to empty its contents. Time slowed, and my insides burned. Tears welled in my eyes, and the pounding in my head threatened to crush my skull.

My legs quit working. I stumbled, down and down, until a set of strong arms wrapped around me. He smelled familiar. He smelled good.

"Odette!" a male voice shouted.

"You came," I thought I said, but I couldn't be sure. I dug my fingers into the warm material of his sleeves, anchoring myself to him. Hands scooped me up, while shouting and screams echoed all around.

"Odette, open your eyes!"

I forced my eyes to crack open before I let the darkness overwhelm me.

Byron came into view, and I knew I was safe. I reached up, wanting to touch his face.

"I love you," I croaked, dark dots dancing in my vision.

The world blurred as I sensed him place me down on his lap. He was yelling something, but I couldn't distinguish any words. The frantic expression on his face sent panic racing through me. Except, I was in such a state that I couldn't even feel my heart thundering in my chest.

"N-no," I whimpered. I didn't want to die in my husband's arms. I didn't want to die now, after finally finding a way back to Byron. I couldn't leave Ares without a mother. My thoughts were rambling, sifting through incoherent sounds. I wanted to claw out of this state back to consciousness. We had just found our way back to each other, and we deserved at least a few years of happiness. Surely destiny wouldn't be so cruel as to rip it all away from us.

"Odette." A cool fingertip gently brushed a lock of my hair back out of my eyes. I blinked, disorientation growing by the second. "What happened? What did that fucker do to you?"

My brain rapidly started to shut down. I opened my mouth to tell him something must have been in my tea, but no sounds came.

"What the fuck?" I thought I heard the voice of one of his

brothers coming from behind me, but I couldn't turn my head. It was too heavy.

"Break his legs if you have to, but find out what he gave her." His voice held a dark order. He rose to his feet, carrying me with him. "I'm taking her to the hospital."

"I'll meet you there." Whose voice was it?

"Don't... w-want to... die," I croaked, tugging Byron's jacket with the remnants of my strength.

"You're not going to die." I heard the quiet horror lingering there. A pained grunt slipped from my lips as an ache shot through my whole body, centering in the pit of my stomach. "Hang in there for me, baby."

Byron spurred into action. Wind swept through my hair, sending a shiver through my cold body. I felt sluggish, every blink and breath demanding too much energy. My heart beat slower and slower.

The sound of a car door opening, cool leather on my skin. A big warm body cradling me.

A door slamming shut.

"Nearest hospital," Byron yelled to the driver. "I don't care if you break every single traffic law. Get there as fast as you fucking can."

The sounds of tires squealing against the pavement filled the air.

Pushing myself, I reached out. I needed to touch him. I had to tell him something, but I could feel my vision slowly fading. I could feel his strong body wrapped around mine, but I couldn't see him.

"Byron," I whimpered. "Where—"

His hand wrapped around my wrist, pressing his face against my palm. "I'm here."

"Keep... our... son—" I broke off, struggling to form the words. "Safe. Happy."

He kissed the center of my palm. "*We'll* keep him happy and safe. Together. Just hang in there. Please, baby."

A shiver rolled down my spine. The car took a sharp turn and tires wailed against the asphalt. My stomach coiled, nausea bubbled, and I turned my head away from him as my stomach erupted. I retched, liquid spilling from my mouth.

Byron didn't let go of me. His hand shot to my hair, pulling it away from my face.

"Jesus Christ," he whispered. "Hang in there." He stroked a hand over my hair, all the while murmuring softly, "Everything will be okay. I got you."

His words and his hands trembled. I wanted to comfort him, but I was too weak to speak. My husband used the back of his hand to tenderly wipe my lips as he held my head, stroking my cheek.

A ringing sound filled the small space inside the car. "Yes."

A deep voice came through his headset, calm and collected. "He put shit in her tea. Have her tested for every drug."

A string of curses left Byron's mouth. "I want that guy dead."

Someone's scream pierced through the headset. "He will be. Also, he had an accomplice."

I retched again, more of my stomach's contents emptying. I tried to think, but all my thoughts bled together. Unsure whether I was lucid or dreaming, I kept peering at my husband's beautiful face. The anguish in his eyes pierced me right through my chest.

"It's okay, baby," Byron murmured softly. "Let it all out. It's better if it's not in your system."

"Byron." My throat was raw, but I pushed through. "I'm dying."

"No," he rasped. "You're going to get better. I'm going to save you again. This time, nobody walks away. We stay together."

The chaos in his eyes gutted me.

"How is she?" the voice on the phone asked.

"She's strong. She'll pull through." Byron's hand on me tightened, as if he were scared I'd slip away. "Who helped him?"

"Nicki Popova and—"

Another scream echoed through the headset.

"You fucking end her." A cold and detached order. "And who else?"

"Just—"

I didn't get to hear the answer as I slipped into unconsciousness.

Chapter 56
Byron

"**I** need help, now!" I yelled as I ran through the door and into the emergency room of George Washington Hospital.

It was such fucking déjà vu, sending anxiety ripping through me.

A whimper slipped through Odette's lips and her body started to convulse. Turning her head from me, she threw up all over the floor of the emergency room, heaving and shuddering. Gasps traveled through the air as people shifted away from us, parting like the Red Sea.

She was wheezing and her shortness of breath was alarming. My reasoning told me it was good that she was throwing up, but my soul shuddered at seeing her in pain.

"Sir, this way, we'll take her straight in."

I followed the male nurse down the corridor, cradling my wife's body close to me. "She was drugged. Don't know what substance, but she's having a bad reaction to it."

"We'll get a doctor in here right away."

The nurse opened the door to the room and pressed a call button.

"B-Byron—" Odette struggled to breathe. "Penicillin."

I blinked, studying my wife's face. Hives broke over her skin, ugly red and rashy looking. "You need penicillin?"

She whimpered, shaking her head. "Allerg—"

Retching again, her words were cut short. I met the nurse's gaze. "I think she's allergic to penicillin."

Still vomiting, Odette lifted her hand weakly and gave us a thumbs-up, telling us that we got it right.

"Good, good," the nurse muttered. "We can work with that."

The next hour was a whirlwind of activity. I refused to leave her side, but I ended up being in the nurses' and doctors' way. I had no idea when Alessio showed up, but he had to pull me away from her bed.

"We can watch from here," Alessio stated calmly. "We'll keep an eye together. Just let them do their thing so she can get better."

"She has to be okay," I muttered more to myself than to my brother. "She has to be okay."

"She will," he said with a conviction I didn't feel. "You smell," he remarked calmly. I pushed my hand through my hair, the stench of puke lingering in the air. I didn't give a shit. I refused to move from this spot until she was healthy again.

"I still smell better than you."

Alessio shoved his shoulder into mine. From the outside, you'd never guess that we'd only gotten close over the last few years. I hadn't known about him growing up, and I regretted that. He grew up a Russo, abused and battered by his stepfather while trying to protect his half-siblings. Father should have been man enough to step in and protect him. But yet again, he failed. Just as he did with every single one of his children.

The doctor approached us, disapproval in his eyes. He protested at having two large men crowding the room. Well, tough shit. My expression challenged him to try and remove us.

"Sir, we've administered a strong dose of antihistamines. Your wife will be fine." Relief washed over me, and I sighed. "She might experience fever and some other side effects over the next few days, but she'll recover."

I took the doctor's hand and gripped it tightly, shaking it. Poor guy made it look like I was shaking a ragdoll. "Fuck, thank you. Thank you so much."

"You did the right thing by bringing her in straightaway. Your wife's body did most of the work by emptying the contents of her stomach, but the antihistamine will continue to ease her symptoms." His eyes darted to Alessio, then back to me. "Keep her stress at a minimum. She might be in and out, some high fever coming and going, but it's all normal. You can even take her home tonight."

"Thanks again"—I looked at the name stitched on his scrubs— "Dr. Chen."

"You have the emergency line if anything changes. I'll be back one more time before she's cleared to go home. Excuse me," he said.

He walked out of the room and my eyes shifted back to the bed where Odette slept, her breaths even. She'd stopped throwing up, but the hives and rash were still there. As long as she was alive and breathing, everything else I could handle.

"Nicki and Marco were working together." Alessio's statement sent anger through me, but I kept it under control. "Marco was planning to impregnate her—fucking moron—and Nicki was convinced you'd marry her if Odette was *permanently* out of the picture, if you catch my meaning."

My jaw clenched. "So one had a plan to kill her and the other to—"

I couldn't even finish the statement. Adrenaline surged through my veins. Red mist covered my vision and every muscle in my body screamed to go punish those fuckers.

"Was our father involved?" Truthfully, at this point, it wouldn't surprise me if he was.

"This time they worked alone. Maybe they thought the senator would give you a heads-up."

The sad part was that I didn't think he would have.

"What do you want to do with those two idiots?" I wanted to make them suffer. Kill them, slowly and painfully. Peel the skin off their flesh and listen to both of them scream. My brother must have read my thoughts, because he added, "I can make it happen, you know."

Fuck, I was tempted. More than anything, I wanted to make them pay. Marco stole years of my son's life from me. I should murder Marco and his wife—instead, I'd make them regret ever crossing me. Marco and Nicki would regret the day they laid eyes on my wife. In truth, I wanted to kill them. See the light in their eyes extinguished.

I shook my head. If I went down that path, there'd be no stopping. It was too easy to let the lines between right and wrong blur.

"I want to press charges," I finally said, hoping it was the right decision. "But first, I want to rough them up. Then, they'll suffer being locked away for attempted kidnapping and murder."

Chapter 57
Byron

I descended the basement steps to where the head of the Maryland mafia conducted most of his interrogations. The location belonged to Nico Morrelli. Alessio's friend. As well as mine. The lines between our worlds had been blurring with each passing day.

Odette was sound asleep in the hospital, and I planned on taking her home as soon as she was released. Kristoff and his wife were keeping an eye on her and would send me a message as soon as she woke up.

A strange kind of calm washed over me. It was the kind of detachment I hadn't felt in a very long time. Not since I was in the military.

Nico and his right-hand man were leaning against the stone, their eyes meeting mine.

"Any problems?" Alessio asked while my eyes found the woman and man who dared come after my wife.

"None." Nico's cold voice and even colder gaze sent whimpers through our two guests. "Though I have to say, these two take the cake on all my past prisoners. They are bigger cowards than my infant son."

Grinning, I neared our two prisoners. Nicki's face was smeared with tears, her makeup running down her cheeks. Her hair was a tangled mess. Marco, on the other hand, was quiet, his face a mask of indifference, but stank of piss.

They were both tied to a chair, but neither of them gagged.

I grabbed a chair and pulled it over, letting the grinding of its legs screech over the floor. I sat facing them and clicked my tongue.

"So I hear you planned on impregnating my wife?" I tsked my tongue, barely holding on to my cool. The thought of that fucking bastard touching my wife had the blood in my veins boiling. "How were you planning on doing that, Marco? By raping her."

"No!"

I shook my head. "In over a decade that you've known her, she didn't want you. What makes you think she would today?"

"She's confused. You got between us six years ago and now again. She's my whore, not yours."

He wanted to make me angry. To make me lash out. But I intended to draw this out and take my sweet time making him scream in pain.

"She is my wife, mother of my child, which means she's off-limits. She's mine today and she was mine six years ago. I let your wife off easily for lying to me about the baby. She'll only lose her medical license, but you, Marco... You will suffer for what you have done."

"You already ruined my career."

I scoffed at that. "What career? The one where you prance around in your skimpy bathing suit shorts?"

He sneered at me. "She'll never be yours again. Your father ruined anything she had for you. I should have made my wife abort your bastard while she was unconscious."

I didn't think, just lunged. My fist swung out and I punched him in the mouth, then his eye. Marco's lip was split open and blood coated his chin.

"Your wife is lucky she didn't or she'd be here." I turned my attention to Nicki. "And you have crossed my path for the last time. I warned you last time you approached my wife. You didn't heed the warning. Now, you'll pay the consequences."

"What are you going to do, huh?" She screamed at the top of her lungs. Not that it would do her any good. These walls were thicker than medieval castle walls. "You're going to beat the shit out of me. The great Byron Ashford, beating a defenseless woman." I wouldn't beat her. I wouldn't torture her, but I'd make her pay by using her vanity against her.

Glancing behind me, I called out to my brother. "Let's give her a proper haircut and prepare her for her long stay in prison where she'll meet a lovely crowd. Shall we?"

Alessio was already on the move. He grabbed a pair of dull scissors from the table and strode over leisurely.

"Should I?" he offered. Upon my nod, he got straight to work. She snarled and struggled against her rope, but it was all in vain. Nobody ever got away from Nico Morrelli's tight ropes.

"Should we gag her?" Nico asked, causing Nicki to instantly stop. "I can't stand her screeching. I think I have a piece of cloth here somewhere. Although I think it might have blood from the last victim."

The next hour was their worst.

But it didn't even scratch the surface on the six years that Odette and I have spent apart. It wasn't punishment enough nor compensation for the fear I felt when I held my wife as she lay limp in my arms.

However, I'd make sure the rest of their life would pay for all they had done.

417

I sat with the detective, watching the footage of Marco and Nicki spiking the tea and conspiring prior to Odette's arrival and then as Marco handed my wife the drugged tea. Furious didn't even begin to cut it.

"This is all the proof we need," the detective said. "And you're saying you have them secured?"

"Yes, they are in my warehouse."

He shot me a weird look. Yeah, we both knew it wasn't customary to take people and lock them up in a warehouse. Not unless you were my brother who dealt with this shit by taking matters into his own hands.

"Just out of curiosity, why did you wait two hours to call us, Mr. Ashford?"

Because I contemplated murdering them while conducting some torture techniques.

"I was more worried about my wife's life than those two idiots." Alessio threw an amused glance my way. He'd tried to convince me to let him handle it and make them disappear. I was starting to think he might have been right. This cop was asking way too many questions. "My brother secured them so they wouldn't flee. They are both a flight risk."

The detective pulled out his phone. "Send a patrol car to go pick up a male and female at this address. Apparently, they're locked up in a secure location." He recited the address, then hung up. "I have to ask. Did you kidnap them?"

Alessio shrugged casually. "I convinced them it was better to come along than go with the police. It was their dumb assumption they wouldn't be turned in."

Translation: *I planned on killing them, but my brother changed his mind.*

"I want both of them charged and locked up tonight." He wrote a note in his little pad as I spoke. "They are a flight risk, you have to trust me on that. I want it known that we're against any provision for their bail." My eyes found my wife's sleeping form in the hospital bed. "In the highest-security prison."

The detective exhaled heavily. "We'll do our best."

He would, but I'd also pull my strings and ensure they were put in the worst cell.

Chapter 58
Odette

It was hours since Marco had drugged me, but it felt like days. Slowly, the side effects were tapering off, but the rash remained. Fever came and went, making me slightly delusional. All the while, Byron fussed over me, bossing around the doctors and nurses.

The doctor examined me one more time, checking my vitals prior to my release. He was exactly what I would have expected. Older and seasoned looking, with smart eyes and a serious demeanor.

"You're improving," he declared. "The high dose of the penicillin you were given caused your cardiac arrhythmia, but we've got that under control now."

I nodded. "Can I go home?"

He pushed his glasses up his nose. "I can release you with specific instructions to your husband in case your fever spikes again."

I nodded, my lips burning. "Yeah, I want to go home."

I could practically feel the wave of relieved sighs traveling through the room—Byron's, but also those of the nurses. Needless to say, the staff at the hospital were happy to be rid of Byron and his attitude. His tone was sharper than a whip and colder than ice.

Ten minutes later, I sat slumped in the back seat of the car, my throbbing head resting on Byron's shoulder. I was so full of meds and delirious from my ordeal that my focus wavered. Kind of like this low-grade fever. All I had on was a thin hospital gown beneath Byron's suit jacket, and a throw blanket pulled from the hospital. A shiver rolled through my body, my skin clammy.

Byron's lips pressed against my forehead. "Cold?"

My teeth chattered, making an awful sound. He pulled me tighter against him, his heat seeping into me. I was grateful for his warmth and that he'd shown up at the right time.

"Thank you for saving me," I croaked. "Again."

"Always."

He kept touching me, as if worried I'd slip away. Funnily enough, it also grounded me. The sun had set long ago, painfully reminding me that we'd spent all afternoon in the hospital. I was exhausted.

My husband must have felt the same, judging by his expression. His tie was undone, as were the top buttons of his white dress shirt. His hair was ruffled from raking his hands through it over and over again. The image reminded me of that day six years ago when he'd thought I lost the baby.

Except this time, we were going home together.

"I talked to Ares and explained you weren't feeling good. I didn't want to scare him. He wants to make sure we take good care of you tonight."

I smiled tiredly. "I'm feeling better by the minute."

"Better we don't tell him that," he chuckled, interlocking our fingers. "He wants us to watch a movie together."

My gaze traced over his long fingers and the muscles twisting along his forearm and disappearing beneath his rolled-up sleeve. He had such strong forearms, those veins and expert fingers.

"I love your hands," I murmured. "They're so sexy." Byron gave me a strange look, but my brain was still mushy from the drugs and fever. "When I was in Ghana, all I had to do was think about your hands when I touched myself and I'd orgasm."

Byron's soft chuckle had my chest glowing. "I think you might still be a little bit high."

I brought our connected hands to my lips and traced his knuckles with my lips. "Maybe, but it's better than throwing up." Then I frowned and lifted my eyes to meet his gaze. "Do I stink?"

He shrugged. "You always smell like the most delicious apples to me. Besides, Alessio already told me I smell like puke, so we'll be stinky together."

I smiled dreamily. "Yes, I like that."

"You want to know how I got myself off during all those years we were apart?" he asked softly, his lips skimming my forehead.

I locked eyes with him, despite the aching headache and blurry vision. His eyes were dark, like a turbulent ocean. So beautiful. So vulnerable.

"How?"

"By using your Hermès scarf. You left it behind in the hotel room."

"Huh?" It took a few seconds too long for the meaning to sink in. Surprise slowly washed over me, my delayed reaction a result of the drugs. "Ahh. I wondered what happened to it."

Images of Byron with that scarf around his cock played in my mind, and even in my pitiful state, my insides warmed. Not that I had any energy to do anything about it.

The car came to a stop in front of our home, and before I could move, Byron scooped me up and made his way into the house with me in his arms.

I pushed my palm against his chest where his heart thundered. "I can walk."

"I know. Just let me do this. I need to hold you."

Ares was sitting on the bottom step of the grand staircase

waiting for us when we entered. The moment he noticed us, he jumped up and ran over.

"Hey, buddy," I murmured slowly as he wrapped his hands around Byron's legs and buried his face into my hip. I brought my hand to his head and ruffled his hair, my movements slow. "Are you okay?"

"I was worried."

Byron lowered to his knee, still keeping me in his strong arms. "Mom is back home and feeling much better. But we still have to take care of her tonight. You up for it, buddy?"

Ares's worried gaze locked on me, and I smiled softly. "I promise, I'm better."

"You don't have purple stuff on your face." My heart clenched. The last time I got hurt, I had bruises all over me from that fucking asshole who'd cornered me in the alleyway.

"No, I ate something bad this time. Everything's going to be okay; I just have to sleep it off." I leaned over and pressed a kiss to his chubby cheek. "First, we'll put on a movie. Just be warned, I might doze off."

He nodded seriously, his little brows furrowed. "Not to worry, Maman. We'll take care of you."

Chapter 59
Byron

Another shiver wracked Odette's body.

Ratatouille played in the background, and Ares's attention was on it as he watched with a smile and wide eyes. He was okay, but Odette wasn't, so I focused all my attention on her.

Her hand trembled as she wrapped the cardigan tighter around herself. Ares snuggled against her, and I caught her wince a few times as he shifted. She leaned back against the cushions, putting some space between Ares and herself.

I frowned.

She had to still be in pain. Usually, she was pulling him in closer. But every time I asked her if she was better, she assured me she was. I started to suspect she was lying to me; while my wife was a great doctor, she was a terrible patient.

I studied her face. She was pale. Her eyes were glassy and there were dark shadows under them. She could barely hold her eyes open, which considering today's events was to be expected, but her fever worried me. I'd called Dr. Chen twice already. I feared after the third time, he might outright block my number, and then I'd have to go and be an asshole.

"Are you okay?" The movie playing in the background captivated all of Ares's attention. When we agreed on family movie night, both Odette and I voted against *Thomas and Friends*. There was only so much of Thomas we could bear, day in and day out.

"Ares, buddy." My son's eyes immediately found me. "Want to come sit with me and help me with this movie? I can't tell what's happening." He had trained me on Thomas's good and bad friends, but this movie I'd never seen.

I didn't have to say it twice. Ares jumped up from the little love-seat, leaving his mom's nest, and padded over to me. His blue pajamas had trains all over them, matching the one he gripped in his hand. He climbed onto the couch and scooted over close to me. His small body snuggled close and my chest tightened. He was so tiny. So innocent.

"See that—" he started, pointing to the large screen.

For the next thirty minutes, he animatedly explained everything about the movie. I listened, smiling at his enthusiasm while keeping my worried attention on Odette. She took up the love-seat and was curled into the fetal position, a blanket pulled over her body.

My chest pinched seeing her in pain. She could try to hide it, but it was fruitless. It was clear as day with the way her eyes drooped. I couldn't take it anymore. She'd have to suffer through me taking care of her.

"Ares, I think Mommy is not feeling well," I whispered softly. The fact that Odette didn't even register I was talking was sign enough that she was worse than I thought. "I'm going to get some medicine for her. Can you keep an eye on her for me?" His blue eyes immediately darted to his mother, full of worry. "Don't worry, buddy. I won't let anything happen to her."

He nodded seriously, his movie completely forgotten and all his attention on Odette. "I'll keep watch."

I stood up and headed for the closest bathroom. Each bathroom was stocked with a first aid kit and some essential medicine. I scanned the contents of the medicine cabinet. I could have sworn there was—*aha*. Found it!

Ibuprofen.

Dr. Chen said it was safe to give it to her. I returned to the family room carrying the bottle of pills and a glass of water. Ares's eyes were still trained on his mother.

"She hasn't moved," he whispered.

"Good. That means she's resting and that's exactly what she needs." He nodded, a serious expression on his face. "We'll finish the movie, and then it's bedtime. Okay, buddy?"

"Okay."

He was a good kid. I might have been robbed of years with him, but Odette raised him well. I placed all the contents from the bathroom onto the coffee table, then kneeled down, bringing my face closer to her.

"Odette." My voice was low as I touched the back of my hand to her forehead. My hand was too cold or her forehead was too hot, I couldn't figure it out.

A soft groan vibrated on her lips. "God, that feels good. Keep your hand there."

If this were any other circumstance, my dick would be hard as a rock. As it was, her response only had me more worried.

Removing my hand from her forehead, I replaced it with my lips. Her skin scorched my mouth.

"You're burning up," I rasped against her forehead. I reached for the ibuprofen and handed her two pills. "Take this."

She peeled her eyelids open, the gold specks in them dull looking. "I just want to sleep," she murmured, not moving. Another shiver rolled through her.

"Open your mouth," I instructed. This time she obeyed, and I put two white pills on her tongue, then lifted her head and brought the glass of water to her lips. "Now drink."

She did as I said before I got up to fetch another blanket from the sofa and cocoon her into it.

"I can't go to sleep," she murmured as her eyes fluttered shut, sweeping her tongue over her lips. "Ares needs a bedtime story."

"Don't worry about that. I'll read him a story and make sure he brushes his teeth."

I watched her every night do her routine with him, even when I wasn't at home. There were a few nights where we did it together. I was good with it. I could handle it.

"He likes to have one foot off the bed," she muttered, her voice heavy with sleep. "So he can escape his bad dreams faster. Don't force him... to... put it... under the covers."

Odette was barely hanging on to her consciousness.

I kissed her head. "Sleep," I told her. "I got this."

She didn't stir after that. Not when Ares kissed her goodnight or when we left the room. I left the television playing while getting my son ready for bed. My first time doing it alone. Definitely wouldn't be the last.

After he brushed his teeth, he ran to bed and jumped on it, his tiny body bouncing against the mattress. The clouds Odette had painted all over the ceiling glowed in the dark. I had to admit, it was a nice touch.

"Okay, which book do you want to read?" I asked him as I sat on top of the duvet covered in trains and planes. I scooted back and crossed my legs.

"Thomas and the trains."

I couldn't help but chuckle. "Not tired of it yet, huh?" He shook his head, his eyes eagerly on the specific book. "Okay, then. Here we go."

As I read the words about the imaginary friends, memories of my own bedtime stories so long ago flashed through my mind. Unlike my brothers and sister, there were rare times during my childhood our mother was able to sneak a story or two into our routine. They were few and far between—my father's power-climbing agenda leaving her little time for anything—but those moments remained ingrained somewhere deep.

Just as promised, I left Ares's foot dangling off the bed and out of the covers. He listened intently, his eyes drooping, until he was out with an innocent and happy smile on his face. He might be my spitting image, but Ares's smile was all Odette.

Soft and sincere. Kind.

I returned to Odette and found her sound asleep. I brushed my knuckles over her cheek, and they seemed cooler now. Not as flushed. Even her rash had cleared.

Lifting her up into my arms, I carried her into our bedroom. Dr. Chen said to give her a cool bath if the fever spiked too high, but she didn't seem as warm now.

"No bath. I think you need to sleep more," I whispered, although it was clear she couldn't hear me.

I tucked her into our big bed, pulling the covers over her shoulders. Every time she was in my bed—our bed—my chest swelled. She looked small and vulnerable, but I'd be lying if I said I didn't love the sight of her in it. It felt right having her in every part of my life.

Letting her rest, I went to take a quick shower. When I slid back into bed, my phone buzzed on the nightstand. It was a message from Alessio.

Both are detained. No bail.

All would be well in the world. Soon.

Chapter 60
Odette

Three days had passed.

The penicillin passed through my system, and I was back to normal. More or less. I still couldn't believe that Marco—the boy who was our first friend when we moved to the French Riviera—had tried to kidnap me. Possibly kill me. He would have known about my allergy; it was a well-known fact when we were growing up.

It was him—with the help of his wife—who'd told Byron I had lost the baby six years ago. I thought he was protecting me. He wasn't. He was sabotaging my happily-ever-after. He and Byron's father had cost us—more importantly Ares—years without Byron. It was unforgivable.

It was barely six in the morning when I woke up. I reached across the bed to find it empty, and frowned. Where was he?

I made my way into the bathroom to wash up before padding down the hallway in search of my husband. I held my breath, listening for the sound of his voice. I found him in his home office. He stood against the large French windows, reading something with so much focus that he missed me standing there entirely.

I leaned against the doorway and let my gaze travel over his body, shudders coursing through me. The desire that I felt was a definite sign of my complete recovery. My eyes lingered on him, wearing nothing but gray sweatpants, his upper body bare. It was surprising he had no shirt on. I gathered six years ago he didn't like anyone seeing his bare back. I didn't mind it. In fact, I thought he was the most beautiful man I'd ever seen—all his perfections and imperfections. They made him the man he was.

And then there was the little fact that no man had ever made my heart race like he did. Sometimes I wondered when it was that I fell in love with him. Was it six years ago during that one night of sex and lust? Maybe it was when our son was born.

"You should wear sweatpants more often," I said softly.

His eyes lifted and the serious lines on his face instantly disappeared. "What are you doing awake so early?"

"I'm done with sleeping," I told him. Yesterday, I'd slept the entire day away. The only time I'd woken up was to take a shower in the evening. Today, I felt refreshed and like a brand-new woman. A lust-infused woman. My eyes roamed over my husband's gorgeous body, soaking in every inch of him. "So will you wear sweatpants more often, or what?"

My tone was husky and my heart thundered in my chest.

"Are you feeling okay?" He closed the file and threw it on the desk as I padded across the room.

"Never better, husband."

My eyes flicked down to his sweatpants again, lingering a second too long on his crotch area. Fuck, no wonder women went bananas for men in sweatpants. The throbbing between my thighs pulsed and an idea shot through me.

I brought my hands up to his defined abs, his skin warm under my palms, and I gently nudged him back until he fell into his seat.

Surprise flickered in his eyes, but he didn't say anything, just watched me with a hooded expression. When I dropped to my knees between his spread thighs, heat flared in his gaze.

"Madeline, what are you doing?"

"I want to taste you," I rasped, adrenaline coursing through my veins. I hooked my fingers on the band of his sweatpants and pulled them down his thick, muscular legs.

"You should be resting." His protest was half-assed and weak. I smiled smugly, seeing his shaft already thickening.

"I'm feeling great," I whispered, leaning closer and rubbing my cheek against his length. "This will make me feel even better. So don't you dare say no."

"I wouldn't dream of denying you." His voice came out rough, sending anticipation down my spine. I could feel his burning gaze on me as I wrapped my hand around his shaft and licked him from base to tip.

He let out a strained groan, watching me with eyes that had grown dark and hazy. I laved at his tip, then took him deep into my throat. I heard him suck in a breath and I relished seeing his stomach—those mouthwatering abs—tighten.

His reaction sent a hum of approval traveling up my throat. Heat loomed in the pit of my stomach, moving lower and causing me to squeeze my thighs together to ease the ache.

I ran my tongue around his head again before sucking it into my mouth. Byron's head fell back with a, "Fuck, Madeline. That's it."

It was all I needed—the smallest amount of praise like that from my husband—to send sparks of pleasure fluttering through me. I sucked him again, taking him deep down my throat, gliding up and down.

His hand grabbed a fistful of my hair. "Look at me," he ordered in a rough, raspy tone.

My gaze flicked to him. "So fucking beautiful," he muttered. "And all mine."

I made a breathy noise of agreement around his cock. His hand tightened in my hair before he moved my head, controlling the rhythm. Up and down, deeper into my mouth with each thrust.

The tension in him built, matching the dark lust in his eyes. I ran my tongue across his crown and sucked his cock like it was my sole purpose in life. He slid in deeper. My eyes watered, but I remained still. I wanted to give him my everything. I wanted to show him how much I loved him. Trusted him. I let him fuck my mouth, dying to see him reach the crescendo and tumble over the edge. For me.

Because he was everything I needed. And I wanted to be everything he needed.

"Can I come in your mouth?" he asked, his lust-filled gaze focused on me.

I hummed my approval.

His groan rumbled in his throat, hoarse, and his breathing became labored.

He came in my mouth and I swallowed every drop of it. I licked my lips, holding his gaze as my skin burned under the heat of his stare. There were so many emotions lingering there and reflecting my own. That raw wave of devotion and love momentarily stilled me.

He released my strands and brought his hands to cup my cheeks, running his calloused thumb gently against my bottom lip.

"I love you, Madeline," he rasped, his dark eyes the shade of the deepest ocean.

"I love you too," I breathed.

He pulled his gray sweatpants up and then suddenly lifted me by the backs of my thighs and dropped me on the desk. A soft squeal escaped me when he spread my legs open, the evidence of my arousal staining my panties.

"My turn," he growled, taking my lips for a rough kiss.

Our tongues slid against one another. I moaned into his mouth while a deep, empty ache pulsed between my thighs. My fingers dug into his hair, turning our kiss deeper, as his hand slid between my legs.

He thrust two fingers inside me, and I groaned into his mouth. I was soaked, something about bringing him pleasure was so damn addictive.

Byron's lips trailed down my neck—nipping and marking me—and all the while, he slid his fingers in and out of me, spreading my arousal around.

Without warning, he ripped my panties, grasped the backs of my thighs, and hooked them up over his shoulders. He pressed his face between my legs, and my head fell back against the cold surface of his fancy desk.

Pleasure tore through me, my eyelids fluttering shut. I shuddered and writhed as he licked and sucked on my clit. My moans filled the air, my blood simmering like an inferno, and with one last nip of my clit, my orgasm tore through me. Light shot behind my eyes. My fingers dug in his hair as I rode the rest of the waves.

It would seem every time with Byron was better than the last, making me addicted to him. I never wanted to live without this—him—ever again.

He pulled back, wiping his mouth with the back of his hand.

"How much time do we have before our son wakes up?"

A small shudder ran through me as he fixed his darkened blue gaze on me. "About an hour."

"Then let's make the best of it."

God, did we ever.

It was a week since the fiasco with Marco. I was fully recovered and Byron had been there every second of the day, taking care of me. We talked. We kissed. We spent time with Ares. We were a family.

And as a family, we had every meal together. Byron had yet to leave to go to work, or anywhere else for that matter.

"Can I be excused?" Ares asked in a muffled tone, his mouth still full of the eggs he'd shoved into it.

I chuckled, seeing his chipmunk cheeks as he slowly chewed. "You can, but chew up your food first. And next time, smaller bites."

He nodded, then shot up to his feet the moment he swallowed his food. He left us without a backward glance as Byron and I chuckled behind him.

"Before you know it, he'll be leaving us without looking back to go to college," Byron mused.

"Oh God, don't go there. Not yet."

We were in the dining room, having breakfast. Just the three of us. People had come around to see us over the last three days—well, to see me. And to ensure I wasn't dying. I most assuredly wasn't. Billie almost flew back home, but thankfully, I convinced her it was unnecessary. It turned out my big sister was avoiding Winston.

Life certainly had a weird way of working out. It brought us all here. To this very moment. I had no doubt it would work itself out for my sister too. Whether that be with Winston or not.

"I have something for you."

I rolled my eyes. "Please, no more jewelry."

He chuckled as he reached for a folder and handed it to me. "No, not jewelry."

"Okay, I have to admit. I didn't expect papers," I muttered as I opened the folder. I started to read the words. English. French.

My mouth parted as I stared at the documents in my hand with disbelief.

Time simply suspended as letters and words danced in front of me. The deed to the Swan Hospital and license to resume operations of Dad's old business.

Raising my eyes, I met my husband's gaze. Shimmering with love and affection. It had been there all along, but people like his father and Marco got in the way. They'd robbed us of six years, but now, we were stronger. Nobody would dare get between us again.

Love, happiness, and so many other beautiful emotions twisted together, bouncing within my chest.

"I don't know what to say," I breathed, my voice trembling.

"Thank you and I love you?" His tone was playful, but the emotions on his face had my heart clenching. He was worried. "It was the reason I asked you not to take up the job at George Washington Hospital."

I blinked in confusion. "But how are we going to do this? You here and us over there?"

"Is that what you want?"

I shook my head. "No, I want us to be together, like a family should be. But I know your entire life is here. You have your empire and—" I was rambling, unsure of what he pictured for our future. Was he willing to have us all living separately? Did he want that?

"I can do my job from anywhere in the world," he stated. "I intend to spend every day with you for the rest of my life. I want to build a life where you and our children are happy."

"But I want you to be happy too."

"I will be," he stated with conviction. "As long as I'm with you. *You* are my home." God, it was terrifying to be so happy? To love so much? "I want to raise a family. My dream is to spend more time with my son." He paused for a moment, his gaze full of love and devotion. Byron—unlike his own—was an amazing father. A wonderful family man. "I hope we have more children. Heck, I'm all for being a stay-at-home dad to support your career."

I shot to my feet and made my way to him, sitting on his lap.

"Nothing would make me happier, husband," I rasped, my nose brushing against his. "Yes to more kids. Yes to you and me, together, every day. Yes to us moving to the French Riviera. But no to one thing."

His eyebrows shot up in surprise. "Can you elaborate on that?"

"I want to work at the hospital and manage that side of the affairs, but I don't want to run the hospital's finances and business dealings." I smiled sheepishly. "I'm bad at anything business-related." I skimmed my lips over my husband's neck. "And you're so good at it. I'd pay you. Every night, on my knees." I waggled my eyebrows.

Byron's body shook as he tried to hold back his laughter. "Then we've got ourselves a deal, baby. We're moving to the French Riviera."

Epilogue-One
Odette

Three Months Later

It was a month since we'd moved full-time to the French Riviera.

Byron insisted he could run his empire from anywhere in the world. And if there was a presence needed, he'd get his brothers to step in. I didn't argue. Washington was never my end goal nor my scene.

Slowly, with a lot of work and help, the Swan Hospital was back to its former glory. I passed the hallway leading toward exam room number five and my steps faltered. It happened every time I passed the painting. It brought bittersweet memories, but I'd never remove it.

The golden plate under the portrait called out, "In memory of the great work of Dr. Swan."

I brought my hands to my chest. It was the same image that my father had held in his hands when he died. The four of us in front of this hospital, happy and smiling for the camera.

It was a good memory. I chose to remember that, not the way he left us.

My gaze flicked to the painting next to it and my lips curved into a soft smile. It was our life today—a painting of Byron, Ares, and me on his yacht. We had to compromise. He'd move to the French Riviera, but he didn't want to live in our old two-bedroom stone home.

When I asked why not, his response was, "I plan on having many little Madelines and Byrons. We need at least five bedrooms."

I rubbed my flat belly. It turned out, Byron would get his wish. We lived on the yacht while searching for that perfect home. Ares was beside himself. Whenever we asked him, he insisted we could stay living on the yacht forever.

So much had changed in the last month. For the better. My dream came true, thanks to my wonderful husband. I practiced in my father's hospital and even had two other up-and-coming doctors on staff. We were able to track down some of the nurses who'd worked for Dad, and when they heard we were opening the hospital back up, they jumped at the opportunity to come back.

Life was good. And busy. Nights even more so, thanks to my insatiable husband.

"Dr. Swan to room five." The announcement came over the speakers again and I sighed, pausing my daydreaming for now.

My feet soft against the white hospital floor, I made my way toward the exam room where I first met Byron. I almost wished I could close that room up and make it only ours.

I shook my head at the sentimentality, then grabbed the handle, pushing the door open.

"Hel—"

My eyes widened and I stared at the transformed room. Dimmed lights—just like the ones from Le Bar Américain—hung around the room and flowers of all colors lay scattered. And in the middle of it all was my husband and our son.

"What—" My mind couldn't form a sentence. "How—" I shook my head. "What is all this?"

"Maman!" Ares ran over to me and took my hand, pulling me

forward toward Byron who lowered down to one knee. Both my husband and Ares were dressed in identical three-piece suits and looked devilishly handsome.

"What are you doing?" I choked out, my eyes darting between the two most important men in my life.

Byron pulled out a small, velvet box from his pocket and flipped it open. A beautiful diamond sparkled back at me, in a gorgeous vintage setting.

"Dr. Swan, would you make me the happiest man on this planet and give me the honor of having your hand in marriage?" Ares giggled, but I couldn't peel my eyes away from my husband. "Of your own free will."

My lip trembled while so many emotions rushed through me. Of course, my hormones enhanced it all. But to think six years brought us here. From an amazing night, to devastating heartbreak, only to make our way back to each other.

I blinked back tears and threw myself into my husband's arms, knocking both of us over.

"Yes, yes," I murmured, showering his face with kisses. "A thousand times, yes."

Ares joined in, rolling right with us and laughing happily. "Maman and Daddy sitting in a tree. K-I-S-S-I-N-G."

Byron chuckled against my mouth, but his eyes turned the deepest blue. "You want a big church wedding?"

I shook my head. "No, just your brothers, sisters, Billie, and us." I pressed my mouth against his ear and whispered, "Although be prepared for the priest to refuse us." He gave me a puzzled look. It was a funny thought, anyone refusing this man. I brought my lips to his ear. "Since we've sinned and are pregnant."

Surprise flashed in his eyes, immediately followed by such happiness that his eyes turned as light as the Mediterranean sky.

"The love of my life," he murmured against my lips. "You make me so happy." Our noses brushed together. "Are you happy, baby?"

I grinned at him, kissing the tip of his nose. "So happy. I love you so much that sometimes I fear I'll wake up and reality will slam into me."

"This is our reality," he rasped. "And I'll be convincing you for the rest of our lives."

Ten lifetimes wouldn't be enough with this man.

Epilogue - Two
Byron

Ten Years Later

"Daddy, Daddy."

Ares Etienne, Brielle Emmeline, and Achille Bastien held hands as they ran over to me. Ares, being the oldest, always held his little brother's and sister's hands, keeping them safe. He couldn't be more like me if he tried.

I grinned as they all jumped into my red Mercedes-Benz S65 AMG Cabriolet. Brielle and Achille didn't even bother with the door. Both climbing over it, their feet hanging in the air.

"Kids, how many times have I said, use the doors?" I groaned, but I couldn't keep the smile off my face. Ares was the only one who opened the door and slid into the passenger seat, securing his seat belt.

"How was school today?" I asked them all. Answers came in at the same time as I shifted the car into first gear.

"I got the best drawing—"

"Bad boy spilled my juice."

It took no time for Achille and Brielle to start shoving their shoulders into each other.

"What did you do in school today?" I asked Ares, keeping an eye on my two youngest in the back seat.

My eldest gave me a serious look. "It was good. I got my test results."

"And?"

He grinned. "I aced it."

"I knew you would." I flicked him a look. "You know, though, it's not all about those grades. Make sure you have fun too."

"I know, Dad. You're the only one who says that, by the way. All the other parents nag their kids to get all As."

I shrugged. "Not all parents are as great as your maman and me."

He rolled his eyes. At least he had that teenage quality.

"How about you, Brielle and Achille?"

They stopped shoving each other and grinned, like they were innocent little angels. My kids—all three of them—were so fucking adorable, I could barely take it.

"I played with my friends," Achille announced.

"And I caused... havoc." Brielle tested the word on her lips, then grinned. "Yes, havoc."

Achille shoved his shoulder into his baby sister. "You are a havoc."

"Achille, don't give your baby sister a hard time." He rolled his eyes. "You and Ares have to look after her, okay?"

"But not when she causes havoc," Achille muttered.

Ares burst out laughing. "Brielle will probably look after Achille and then beat him up."

I bit back a smile. Brielle, much like her mother, was a force to be reckoned with. She was only five, but she was fearless. She had the intelligence of a ten-year-old, and sometimes it took all of us to deal with her and outsmart her.

It was the highlight of our lives lately.

"Daddy, can we have ice cream?" My heart beamed every

single time I heard her call me that. I met her big blue eyes in the rearview mirror. "Pretty please."

"Maman won't be happy if she learns we had ice cream before we picked her up. You know she likes it as much as you do."

She blinked her eyes innocently. "We can go again after we pick her up."

Like I said, too smart for her own good. So fucking cute.

She wore a bright blue dress with pink bows, pink shoes, and a blue hairband. Her fashion drove Odette crazy. She definitely took after her Aunt Billie in that department.

The sun reflected off Brielle's necklace and I frowned. "Baby, what's that around your neck?"

If I thought the sun was bright, I was so wrong. Her smile practically blinded me. "Uncle Winston gave me a present for being so good," she announced. "It's a necklace with a real diamond."

No fucking shit. And by the looks of it, it was a big-ass diamond. Jesus fucking Christ. Was Winston trying to have my children beaten and robbed in school?

She jumped excitedly on the seat. "Oh, oh, oh, and Aunt Billie said she has a matching bracelet for me as soon as she comes to visit."

"My brother's going to drive me insane," I muttered. "And so is your Aunt Billie."

"Yeah, my siblings are going to drive me insane," Ares chimed in, his voice low.

We shared a look and then grinned. "But we love them anyhow," we said at the same time.

The saying started when Brielle was born because she cried—a lot. She was a fussy baby with acid reflux, allergies to milk, and everything else under the sun. But that wasn't the worst part. It was learning that Brielle had a heart condition. It had started with the hard pregnancy and then almost losing Odette and our baby girl. The first year was full of angst.

My heart twisted at the memories, but I decidedly pushed

445

them away. We were stronger because of her, and we'd come through it.

"We're here!" Brielle gasped loudly, ready to get out of the car while it was still running.

I parked and came around to open the door for my little princess. "Let's go get Mommy."

Ares and Achille ran inside, leaving us behind.

My daughter looked up at me with such reverence and smiled widely. "When I'm a big girl, I'm going to be just like Maman."

I smiled softly, my heart warming. There were days I still couldn't believe I was so lucky to have my family. My wife. My children.

"I know you will, princess. And I'll be here every step of the way."

Her face lit up. "Mommy said you saved the hospital for her. For all of us."

"I love your mommy, and I'd do anything for her. All of you."

Brielle's eyes glimmered, looking at me like I was the bravest hero in the world. "When I grow up, I'm going to marry someone just like you."

I winced. I'd rather beat any boy or man who dared approach my little girl.

"Mr. Ashford." Staff and patients greeted us, smiling at Brielle and me. They came to know our little princess really well during those first twelve months of her life.

"Maman!" Without a warning, Brielle let go of my hand and sprinted down the hallway. "Mommy!" she shouted, loud enough for the entire world to hear her.

Ares and Achille were already with her, bombarding her with the day's events. My wife's eyes found our daughter's, then mine, her face lighting up.

She opened her arms, and Brielle threw herself into them. With our baby girl in her arms, Odette straightened up, pressing a kiss to her chubby cheeks.

"I missed you," she murmured softly, her eyes on me.

"I missed you too, baby."

Brielle, of course, thought I was talking to her. "I was with you for the whole hour, Daddy."

My wife smiled up at me, her gaze soft. "Love you," she mouthed.

God, I'd never tire of hearing that. I'd never tire of watching her and our children. They were my whole world and nothing—fucking nothing—compared to this feeling.

I walked up to my family and leaned in to press a soft kiss to my wife's forehead.

"I love you too, baby," I whispered into her ear. "Date night. Tonight. You and me."

Her cheeks flushed. "I can't wait, husband."

My wife had turned the Swan Hospital into one of the most prestigious clinics in Europe. She was excellent at her job, and the care our patients got in this facility was unparalleled. But much like her father, she hated the business aspect of it. That was where I stepped in. I ensured nobody would ever take this hospital from her or our children for the next twenty generations.

I still ran my empire but had pulled away from some of it. We had enough wealth to last us several lifetimes, but we didn't have several lifetimes to enjoy our children. That was most important to me. To us. And I hadn't regretted the decision for a single moment.

I brushed the back of my hand over my wife's cheek, all my love overwhelming me like it did every single time. It felt like my heart would burst with emotions. I would love her in every lifetime. In every dimension. In every universe, until the very last star in the sky burned out.

Because I hadn't been living before laying eyes on her. She was what my life was about—love, family, and her. My wife. My home. My everything.

THE END

Acknowledgments

I want to thank my friends and family for their continued support.

To my alpha and beta readers - you are all amazing. You put up with my crazy deadlines and even crazier organization. I couldn't do this without you.

My books wouldn't be what they are without each one of you.

To the bloggers and reviewers who helped spread the word about every one of my books. I appreciate you so much and hearing you love my work, makes it that much more enjoyable!

And last but not least, **to all my readers**! This wouldn't be possible without you. Thank you for believing in me. Thank you for your amazing and supportive messages. Simply, THANK YOU.

I get to do this because all of you.

XOXO

Eva Winners

Made in United States
Orlando, FL
04 October 2024

52354418R00278